Fig

Fig

SARAH ELIZABETH SCHANTZ

MARGARET K. MCELDERRY BOOKS
NEW YORK LONDON TORONTO SYDNEY NEW DELHI

Dedicated to my mother; this book is for you.
Enid Schantz, 1938–2011

MARGARET K. McELDERRY BOOKS
An imprint of Simon & Schuster Children's Publishing Division
1230 Avenue of the Americas, New York, New York 10020

MARGARET K. McELDERRY BOOKS is a trademark of Simon & Schuster, Inc.
For information about special discounts for bulk purchases, please contact Simon & Schuster Special Sales at 1-866-506-1949 or business@simonandschuster.com.
The Simon & Schuster Speakers Bureau can bring authors to your live event. For more information or to book an event, contact the Simon & Schuster Speakers Bureau at 1-866-248-3049 or visit our website at www.simonspeakers.com.
Also available in a Margaret K. McElderry Books hardcover edition
The text for this book is set in Incognito.
Manufactured in the United States of America
First Margaret K. McElderry Books paperback edition March 2016
2 4 6 8 10 9 7 5 3
The Library of Congress has cataloged the hardcover edition as follows:
Schantz, Sarah Elizabeth.
Fig / Sarah Elizabeth Schantz.
p. cm.
Summary: In 1994, Fig looks back on her life and relates her experiences, from age six to nineteen, as she desperately tries to save her mother from schizophrenia while her own mental health and relationships deteriorate.
ISBN 978-1-4814-2358-8 (hardcover)
ISBN 978-1-4814-2359-5 (pbk)
ISBN 978-1-4814-2360-1 (eBook)
[1. Schizophrenia—Fiction. 2. Mental illness—Fiction. 3. Mothers and daughters—Fiction. 4. Self-destructive behavior—Fiction. 5. Schools—Fiction. 6. Family life—Kansas—Fiction. 7. Farm life—Kansas—Fiction. 8. Kansas—History—20th century—Fiction.] I. Title.
PZ7.1.S336Fig 2015
[Fic]—dc23   2014025394

I was never really insane except on occasions when my heart was touched.

—EDGAR ALLAN POE

A TIME FRAME

prologos: (Greek root for "prologue");
pro (before), logos (word); "before word"

Today is the twenty-first day of October. The year is 1994. Anno Domino. Common era. The Year of the Dog.

Today I turn nineteen. And today I will finish a story that must be told. The last thirteen years of my life. I hold my breath and I cross my fingers.

My story begins when I am six.

CHAPTER ONE

FAIRYLAND

1. "Clock" is derived from the word "bell." Wearing bells can
protect a person from fairies—and from falling into a fairyland
where time does not operate as it should.

June 11, 1982

Because I'm only six, I'm not allowed to go into the woods alone—
nowhere near the farmer's ditch, and most especially nowhere near
the Silver River. Daddy worries I will drown, and Mama worries
about everything.

I'm getting better at sneaking out. I crawl my way from the house
to the orchard, and then I run from tree to tree, hiding behind each
one until my arms become the branches. And I can be a rabbit too—
I can be the runaway bunny. The Johnsongrass is tall in the space
between the orchard and the ditch and hides me the rest of the way.
Once I'm by the water, the tall cottonwoods and thick raspberry
form walls to separate the worlds, and I can't be seen from the house
or the yard.

Mama is helping Daddy pack. I had tried to help but she got mad.

"Fig," she said. "Leave us alone!"

Then Daddy smiled at me and ruffled my hair with his big fingers.
He looked at me with eyes that said, *Sorry.*

"Go and play," he said, and his voice was soft, and the soft melted

Mama. The angry red drained from her face and she was almost normal again. Mama is always pretty, but without the red I could see the soft splatter of pale freckles around her nose. Daddy touched her arm and said her name in a quiet way. He said, "Annie," like he was reminding her of something she'd forgotten, and then she turned and smiled at me too. And with her voice, she said, "Sorry."

"I didn't mean to snap," she said. "I just need to talk to your father."

"Alone," she said.

Then she kissed me on my forehead—the special place between my eyes. The place Mama calls my third eye. "Everyone has them," she always says, "but not everyone knows how to use them. The third eye is a magic eye because it can see all the other worlds."

Mama is referring to fairyland.

She isn't talking about the world outside Kansas or even just beyond Douglas County, where we live on a farm. The closest town is Eudora, and Eudora, Kansas, is what it says on all our mail, and Eudora is where I go to school and will continue to go until I graduate from high school.

Eudora has a feed and seed, a hardware store, a pharmacy, a post office, a newspaper, a diner, a one-room library, a morgue, and a handful of churches scattered here and there, including the Sacred Heart of Mary, where my grandmother goes even though she lives in Lawrence now. Sacred Heart is more than a church; it's a private school as well. It covers all fourteen grades in one building, while the public school system has Douglas Elementary, Keller Junior, and Carter High. There is talk about closing down the high school and busing all the teenagers to another high school in another town in another county, but it hasn't happened yet.

———

Mama doesn't care for the Eudora Library. "All they stock is romance novels and car manuals," she says, and takes me to the public library in Lawrence instead. And sometimes we go to Topeka, but mostly we don't go anywhere. I stay within a triangle of highways and interstate. I stay inside the square acreage of the farm. I stay at home.

I visit the farmer's ditch when Mama takes her bath or does her yoga. This is where I bring all the meat I won't eat. This is my secret. I don't like the idea of eating something dead.

Stepping onto the bridge, I become a tightrope walker.

The farmer's ditch runs away from the Silver River, where my uncle likes to fish. And the Silver River marks the end of our land to the south. Everything on the other side of the river belongs to the McAlisters. While I dare the dangers of the ditch, I would never go to Silver by myself, and I am always careful about getting back to the house before the sun goes down—before anyone knows I am missing.

With arms outstretched like a tightrope walker, I walk across the board, but I only go far enough to toss the meat onto the other side before turning around. Returning to my side, I crouch behind the old log and wait for the dog to come and eat the scraps.

Mama hates dogs. "It's a phobia," she has said many times. Then she showed me the word in the dictionary, and I learned that *ph* makes the same sound as an *f*.

Mama was bit by her uncle's dog when she was little. The dog was named Sticker, and he bit her on Easter. Everyone was sitting at the table getting ready to eat, but first they had to close their eyes and pray. "I never did like to pray," Mama said, and this is when she slid out of her seat to sit under the table, where Sticker was curled into a ball of sleeping fur and hidden teeth.

———

My uncle Billy says, "Always let a sleeping dog lay." But Mama did not let Sticker lie. She scratched behind his ears, and Sticker whirled around and bit her on the face. "When I opened my eyes," she said, "I could see his throat." She was taken to the emergency room and stitched back together. This scar hides behind her eyebrow and is nothing compared with her other scar—the one that came later.

When the dog comes, I think about petting her, but I don't.

I stay behind the log, watching her watch me. We both practice being still. This makes her feel safe enough to come and sniff the pork chops or the drumsticks or whatever meat I've brought to her. Today, I brought a link of sausage. She never stops watching me, one eye dark and the other a cloudy blue. Because she watches me like this, I feel like I'm the one she's actually eating. And this is not the first time I've ever felt like a piece of meat. She never barks or howls or growls. She sniffs the air, and sometimes the sniffing makes her lips curl back into a smile that isn't really a smile. Her gums are a wet blue-black, and there are spots on her tongue.

I think she has a family, because she carries the bones away. At first, she is slow—she moves like she is only stretching—but then she runs. Once she is running, her feet don't even touch the ground. During the day, I try to run like this. I try to run away, but my knees get in the way because they don't bend right. And sometimes I catch Mama watching me. Her worry comes pouring out of her body like something spilling. It drips off her clothes, and her worry is the color of shadows, and it moves like water. From the porch, it seeps into the steps—pouring out into the grass where I am trying to run like a dog. Her worry comes for me.

* * * *

June 24, 1982

After a long day of working in the flower garden, Mama and I decide to have a picnic dinner instead of eating inside the house. The fireflies are coming out. Blinking yellow lights, on and off, here and there, they change everything about the orchard. And Mama and I go to another world—one like Wonderland, or Oz. We go to Never, Never Land.

When I asked if we could go to fairyland, Mama tried to scare me away. "Figaroo," she said. "You don't really want to go."

And then she said, "It can be very hard to come back from fairyland," and that was when she looked away and her face got all sad.

"Sometimes it's even impossible," she said.

Mama says if I do end up in fairyland, not to eat or drink anything while I'm there. "Those are the rules—otherwise, you can get stuck," she says. "It's like a spell."

When Mama talks about fairyland, she uses the word "lure."

Fairyland *is* a lure. I want to fly and make friends. Most of all, I want to be able to change the size of my body from big to small whenever I want.

I lie back on the picnic blanket, looking at the tangled branches above. In the changing light, I see the little green apples—still too hard and sour to eat. The black branches crisscross the sky. The sun is setting, and that side of the sky looks like melted orange and strawberry sorbet. On the other side, the moon is rising. And in the middle, the sky turns into violet—the color of my new favorite crayon. The darkness brings a chill, and the Kansas humidity turns into a cold damp. Mama wraps herself in a shawl to keep away the chill.

Mama packed a picnic dinner: cubes of cheese bought from the

Fergesons' dairy farm across the highway, and Stoned Wheat Thins, green grapes, new cherries, and little cucumber sandwiches cut into hearts using Gran's old cookie cutters. My belly is full like a pregnant woman. We're on an old quilt spread beneath the trees. Mama is wearing a white dress with crocheted edges—the one she calls a garden dress. "It's vintage," Mama says. "It is almost a hundred years old."

Mama collects old clothes, and this is what she wears when she isn't wearing paint-splattered blue jeans with peasant blouses or worn-out T-shirts.

She is beautiful in the delicate lacy gown, and I wish I was dressed up too, but Mama says, "You are already perfect, my dearest Fig."

She helps arrange all my stuffed animals so we are sitting in a circle while she reads out loud. When she's done with the Peter Rabbit books, we imagine the lives of all the rabbits on the farm—what their names are, who is related to who, what they do for a living, and where they live.

Daddy is away with Uncle Billy.

I think it's an emergency, but no one wants to talk to me about it because I'm only six years old. It doesn't matter that I was born from an emergency, or that I've been reading since I was four. It doesn't matter that I can read better than my entire class, and it doesn't matter that I know how to use a dictionary and an encyclopedia.

Looking things up is one of Mama's favorite things to do, and it is one of my favorite things to do with her. Mama keeps the encyclopedia in the living room. It belonged to her father once upon a time, but he gave it to her when she went to college.

"Not only do I want you to have knowledge at your fingertips," he said to her, "I want you to have a piece of home to forever keep."

Mama says she's lucky to have this encyclopedia. "Just like I'm lucky to have the few family photos I took with me to college," she will say, "and some of my mother's dresses, and the teddy bear that's now yours." But really she isn't lucky at all. She's only lucky to have these few things because everything else was lost in the fire that also took her parents away.

The encyclopedia has a black cloth cover with gold lettering. The cover looks dusty, but whenever I try to wipe it clean, I find there isn't any dust. Mama says it looks this way because it faded from the sun, but it must have faded from another sun, in another living room, because our living room is always dark—even when all the lamps are turned on.

I used to use the encyclopedia as a booster seat, and before that I used the same wooden high chair that Daddy and Uncle Billy used before they grew into boys who grew into men.

The encyclopedia is always open now, trying to catch new information.

It sits on a wooden stand, which makes it easier for a person to use because the encyclopedia really is that gigantic. It has to be. Daddy says most encyclopedias come in sets—sometimes an entire book for just one letter of the alphabet—but this one holds everything from A to Z. And this reminds me of Sacred Heart and how it covers everything from preschool to high school.

The dictionary is not as big or fancy. Mama keeps it on a shelf in the cabinet with the glass door. It has a wonky brown cover that is starting to fall off, and Mama showed me how it has a spine. "Books are bodies too," she said. "And the pages are the wings that make them fly."

Mama has another dictionary—a little paperback she carries in her pocket. She checks off all the words she looks up. She uses a pencil. Check. This is the dictionary I use to look up "lure."

lure: *something that tempts or attracts with the promise of pleasure or reward.*

The sky is now a darker violet, and the crickets are beginning to sing. Mama and I have been quiet for a long time. Once, I interrupted a quiet that was like this by saying, "It's too quiet," and Mama said there was no such thing. She said love is the ability to be comfortable with others in silence. She made it seem like I didn't love her, and that made me want to cry.

"Did you hear that?" Mama says, and I'm glad she's the one to interrupt the silence. She was sitting, but now she's standing—and that makes me dizzy. She's leaning toward the woods where the wild trees grow along the ditch. She cups her ear with her hand. I listen too, but I don't hear anything. Mama stands there, her face twisted with worry, and I know she's hearing something—something I can't hear.

I listen hard.

I listen until I can't help but hear all the rustlings in the parts of the world gone black. The deep whispers below the cricket song. And then I hear the sound of something coming. All the tiny apples in the trees above turn into human eyes. They look around. At the woods, and then they look at me. They look sideways and they keep blinking.

My stuffed animals huddle close together. They wrap their fuzzy arms around one another and don't reach for me. I pull myself up and go to Mama, but she only puts one arm around me even though I need both arms to feel safe.

———

She's using her other hand to listen, and her eyes dart back and forth like the eyes in the trees. I nose my way into Mama's shawl, trying to hide inside her, but she is too thin and there is no room for me. She tightens her grip on my shoulder, and I try to hide from how much this hurts.

"Run!" Mama screams. "Now, Fig! Run!"

And she takes my hand, and we are running. There is no time to grab my stuffed animals or even shout for them to run as well. Mama's bigger, and she can go much faster.

I make us trip and fall.

Mama has to stop again and again to pull me up. And then we're running again. And now we're coming into the front yard—through the cottonwoods and the long shadows of the cottonwoods—into the yard, where the grass is short and less wild because it is cut grass, but Mama doesn't stop. She lets go and I fall, and now she's on the porch, still screaming for me to run.

"Now, Fig, now!"

I am crying. I cry the way I cry when I cannot stop.

Why won't Mama come and get me? Where is Daddy? I want him to come home—to swoop down and pick me up with big strong arms and carry me inside, where the walls will make it safe again. But Daddy isn't here and Mama won't stop screaming. She keeps pointing at the shapes behind me where dark and light draw a line of safe and not safe. She screams and points at the world on the other side of the tall trees. At the shapes that stop moving whenever I turn to look.

"Are you any warmer?" the policeman asks. The one who wrapped me in a blanket.

———

The policeman sits in Daddy's armchair but doesn't lean back the way Daddy does. And he doesn't put his feet on the coffee table.

I'm sitting on the sofa, and Marmalade is next to me. She is next to me only because she was already there whenever it was that I sat down—I know this even if I don't remember sitting, or how I got inside. The cat is curled into herself, and every once in a while she twitches her tail. This is how Marmalade reminds me not to touch her. The cat doesn't like anyone but Mama.

The policeman sits on the edge of the chair like he's ready to pull his gun at any sign of danger. I try not to stare at the gun. It scares me. The policeman is younger than Daddy. His uniform is brown, and he keeps his hat in his lap. It's the same kind of hat worn by the bad man in *Curious George*, only brown instead of yellow. I hate the bad man with the yellow hat because he is always capturing George. Mama taught me how "capture" and "catch" have the same meaning. The bad man with the yellow hat captures George and takes him away from the jungle.

He takes George away from a world where he belongs.

I want to ask if the policeman saw my stuffed animals in the orchard, but I don't. We both pretend we aren't trying to listen to the conversation in the kitchen, where the other policeman is talking to Mama. They've been in there a long time. I can't tell what they are saying. They talk in hushed grown-up voices—interrupted only by the ticking of the grandfather clock.

"Don't be scared," my policeman says. Then he tries asking again. "Exactly what did you see?" he says, but I shrug. I have no idea what I saw. I'm not good at talking, especially not to strangers. Strangers and talking make my throat feel weird. I sit very still, and I don't say anything.

———

It sounds like Mama is crying, and this makes my policeman stand. He puts his hat on the coffee table before walking toward the kitchen without actually going in there. He checks on them from a distance, but he keeps looking back at me like he's worried I'll disappear if he doesn't keep looking. He turns, about to head back to Daddy's chair, when something in the dining room catches his eye. And now he's poking around in there instead. He circles the table where Mama works on her art—the same table where Daddy ate all his childhood meals. Except for Thanksgiving or Christmas, we never eat in the dining room. We always eat in the kitchen, even when we have company, which we almost never do.

There is a pile of broken china dolls on the table and a large coil of rusted barbed wire. The power drill is charging. The tiny red light blinks on and off in the semidarkness. There's a spool of copper wire and a wooden box full of pliers, wire cutters, hammers, and tin snips.

Mama has been making mobiles to hang around the farm, only she calls them dream catchers. She hangs them in the barn and from the trees—wherever she thinks they'll look pretty. They remind me of cobwebs. Caught inside the webs of copper wire are quartz crystals. They dangle amid the arms, legs, and faces of the broken dolls.

My policeman looks at the encyclopedia. It is still open from me looking up Newfoundland dogs, which is the kind of dog the Darlings had in *Peter Pan*. The nanny dog. The policeman picks up the magnifying glass—the one I left out. I broke the rule, and rules are important. I forgot to put the magnifying glass away. It is always supposed to go back inside the special black velvet bag to keep it from breaking into a million pieces or starting fires. Mama's parents died in a fire. This is just one reason my birth was bittersweet. Mama never got to show me off to her mother and father.

———

I want to take the magnifying glass away from him, but I don't. That would be rude. Instead, I hold my breath and cross my fingers to keep the magnifying glass safe. He brings the glass to his eye and then pulls it away. He does this again—back and forth—and as he does he never stops looking through the glass. And I have to keep holding my breath and crossing my fingers because he won't put it down. He brings the magnifying glass to his face and looks at me. The eye behind the glass is big and bulging and no longer matches his other eye.

I hold my breath in a way where he can't know. And my fingers are crossed inside the cave of the blanket he wrapped around my body. He looks at me through the magnifying glass, and I know he is only trying to be funny. I should laugh. I think about what it would be like to laugh right now. To be the little girl little girls are supposed to be. But he gives up just as I'm about to try.

Holding my breath and crossing my fingers works: He puts the magnifying glass on the encyclopedia, walks into the living room, and sits back down in my father's armchair. He doesn't pick up his hat. He leaves it on the coffee table between the two piles of Mama's art books. He leaves his hat on top of my three new library books.

His hat hides *The Headless Cupid*—the book Mama let me check out even though she said I was too young for it. "The book is supposed to be a little scary," Mama warned, but I promised not to be afraid. Mama looked at me and bit her lip. Then she said, "Okay, Fig, but only if we read it together." And this is what we were supposed to do tonight before I went to bed. We should be upstairs in my bedroom reading *The Headless Cupid* right now instead of talking to the police.

———

* * * *

I see the look Mama's policeman gives my policeman when he walks into the living room. Mama follows him—wringing her hands and biting her lip. She walks slow and looks confused. My policeman gets up, but then he stands the way I do when I'm waiting for a grown-up to tell me what to do. He starts for the door only after the other policeman does.

Before they leave, Mama's policeman stops and turns around. He pulls something from his shirt pocket and hands it to Mama. He calls her Mrs. Johnson, and I hold my breath and cross my fingers because Mama hates to be called Mrs. *Anything*. "My name is Annie" is what she usually says, but tonight she doesn't say anything at all. She just takes the piece of paper and looks at it.

She doesn't seem to understand.

"If anything else happens," Mama's policeman says, "call that number and they'll dispatch us straightaway."

My policeman puts his brown hat back on and winks at me, but he doesn't wink as well as Uncle Billy. Then he starts to turn the doorknob but changes his mind. Letting go, he squeezes his hand into a fist, and then he stretches all his fingers out again. He is watching me. Mama's policeman looks annoyed, like he just wants to go, but my policeman turns to Mama.

"Maybe there's someone you could call?" he asks. "Someone you two could stay with until your husband gets back?"

Mama shakes her head. "We'll be fine," she says, but her voice doesn't sound like Mama. It's too high. She apologizes for making them come all the way out here, and I'm relieved because she isn't going to call Gran, who is the only person we have to call. And I do not want to stay with her. I never have and I never will, but just in case, and because it's already worked twice in one night, I hold my breath and cross my fingers.

The policemen close the door behind them, and Mama wanders back into the kitchen. Marmalade stands, stretching. Then she jumps off the sofa and follows Mama.

I start to follow Mama too, but then I remember the magnifying glass and the important rule about putting it away. I head toward the dining room, and that's when I hear Mama's policeman laughing. Through the window in the door, I can see them on the porch. They are wavy through the old glass. They're getting ready to go down the steps, but Mama's policeman laughs so hard, he has to stop and grab the railing. His laughter seems to make my policeman nervous; my policeman turns to check the house, then he looks through the same window I am looking through, but I am quick—I duck behind the wall, and he doesn't see me.

Mama's policeman stops laughing long enough to call Mama crazy. "She said there were goddamn dingoes out there."

And I think of the program Mama watched last night. The one about the missing baby girl.

"On the eve of what would have been Azaria Chamberlain's second birthday," the newsman said, "we bring you the latest in the murder trial of the century."

First they showed a picture of the tiny baby in her mother's arms. Even though she was dressed in white, they made a big deal about a black and red baby dress.

"Not suitable," they said. "Not for a child." There was no baby in the dress they were discussing.

—

46

"The Chamberlains are Seventh-day Adventist," the man went on, "And according to an anonymous tip, the name 'Azaria' means 'sacrifice in the wilderness.'"

When they showed the baby's mother, Mama sucked in her breath and bit her lip. The other mother had a funny accent. Again and again, they showed her saying, "A dingo took my baby." But when I asked Mama what a dingo was, she looked at me like I had startled her, and then she said it was time for me to go to bed.

Their voices change, which means the police are walking away, so I unwrap myself from behind the wall and slide across the hardwood in my socks to crouch by the door. There is a slot in the door even though we have to get our mail from the box on the highway. I push the slot open to watch them walk toward their car, and now I can hear them better.

"Maybe it was coyotes," my policeman says, but he doesn't say "coyotes" the way Mama does. He makes the word rhyme with "boats" instead.

Mama's policeman laughs again. "'A dingo took my baby,'" he says, but then I can't hear them anymore—just the sound of car doors slamming, the engine turning over, and a car driving away, tires crunching gravel. I listen until all I hear are crickets. I close my eyes and watch them rub their legs together until their black bodies turn into tiny violins.

I put the magnifying glass away, but before I go into the kitchen I flip back to *d*.

dingo: a free-roaming wild dog unique to the continent of Australia, mainly found in the outback.

———

There's a picture of a mother dingo and her cubs. The mother's eyes and mouth are closed, and there's something about her face that makes her look like she is smiling. The same smile I've seen before; the one that is not a smile at all.

I think about the word "unique." Both Daddy and Mama use this word a lot. They are forever telling tell me how important it is to be unique. Daddy said everyone in the world is unique, but Mama shook her head and told him she strongly disagreed. "Unique" means "one of a kind." It means there are no dingoes in Kansas because there are no dingoes in America.

Mama sits in the kitchen at the table, and she still looks confused. The overhead light shines through her hair, turning the strawberry blond into white, and she's taken off the robe. Now it's draped over the back of the chair like a crumpled shadow. She's looking at her hands, rubbing them together. She rubs them in a way where it looks like she's trying to pull off her skin. It reminds me of when Uncle Billy skins a rabbit. After he makes all the different cuts, the way he pulls and pulls. And the fur slides off the body the way a sock comes off a foot.

I sit down at the table, across from my mother. I set *The Headless Cupid* on the table, hoping she'll remember the promise she made to me. But Mama doesn't look up. She doesn't look at me and she doesn't look at the book. She only looks at her hands, which she continues to rub away.

Marmalade brushes against Mama's leg and meows the way she does when she wants to be fed. But it's like Mama can't hear or even feel the cat, so I go to the pantry and grab the bag of Meow Mix. I fill the cat's bowl, spilling some, not that Mama notices. Marmalade makes awful noises like she is grinding bones with her sharp teeth.

———

With my hands, I sweep up the spilled cat food, and then I make a point to change the old water out for fresh water, but Mama still doesn't notice or say thank you like she normally would. She just sits there trying to rub herself away while the cat eats.

I sit at the table with Mama for a long time. Marmalade finished eating forever ago and left the kitchen for her spot in the living room.

I pick the book up and pretend to read, but I can't concentrate. I flip ahead, hoping Mama will tell me not to. Mama still doesn't look up. I begin to read chapter six because I am six years old, and almost right away there's a word I don't know: "initiation." I try sounding it out because I think doing this will make Mama be a mother—it will make her want to help me, only she still doesn't seem to hear me as I stutter through the vowels and trip over the *t*'s, and I'm forced to give up.

I close the book harder than I should and set it down with a thump. I am loud compared with the rest of the house, and I take a deep breath, trying to take the noisiness back into myself. Then I try counting to keep from holding my breath and crossing my fingers, which my body wants to do because that's what it's been doing all night. But I worry it won't work anymore if I do it too much. Besides, I'm not sure what it is I'd be trying to stop, so instead I count all the sounds the grandfather clock likes to make. I separate the sounds into categories of high and low.

The moths fly around the kitchen light and burn themselves on the hot yellow bulb. Caught inside the glass cover, they die. If Daddy was here, he'd use the step stool to climb up and take the cover down. He'd dump the dead bugs in the trash and wash the cover like he'd wash a plate; he'd dry it with a dishcloth and screw the fixture back into the ceiling. The moth wings sizzle.

Mama finally stops rubbing her hands, and she looks at me. She looks right into my eyes, and I see how her eyelashes look like spun gold. She blinks her tears away and her whole face changes: My mother returns.

"Oh, Fig," she says, "you must be so scared."

She gets up and comes to me, covering my body with her body. She is a mother spider with a million arms to wrap around me. I can't see anything because my face is buried in her belly, but I wonder if she can see the book—if she is remembering. Still holding me, Mama whispers in my ear, "It's time for bed," and when she pulls away I make sure her eyes follow mine, and now we are both looking at *The Headless Cupid*.

"Maybe tomorrow," Mama says, and I feel bad because when I look at her again the tears are back. They are rolling down her cheeks. "Maybe tomorrow," she says, and then she offers me her hands to pull me up, and I let her. We leave the book behind, and Mama forgets to turn off the kitchen light. On the stairs, she walks behind me like she's afraid I might fall. But then she walks like this even after we've reached the top and we are walking down the hall to my bedroom.

Mama gets my nightgown from the top dresser drawer. "Put this on," she says. "I'll be back to tuck you in." As I pull the nightgown over my head I hear Mama in the bathroom—the sound of the medicine cabinet being opened and then the clatter of bottles being moved around. She is looking for something she can't seem to find.

With my nightgown on and my short hair full of static, I go to the bathroom. Mama looks at me in a way that makes me feel like she doesn't want me here. That she doesn't want me to see what she is doing.

"I need to brush my teeth," I say.

Mama smiles. "Of course you do," she says, but doesn't move out of the way. I have to stand in the doorway while she continues to look through the cabinet.

After she pulls everything out, she finds what she's been looking for—a small brown plastic bottle that looks like all the other small brown plastic bottles that are kept in the cabinet. She puts everything back but this one—this one she holds on to. With her fingers wrapped around the bottle, she steps back to make room for me to brush my teeth, and when she steps back the bottle rattles.

Mama stands in the doorway, watching me. Her face above my face in the mirror. We look alike and we don't look alike.

There is no red in my blond and I have no freckles. I am the same kind of thin as Mama, only my face is round while her features are more severe. Mama has hazel eyes, streaked with green and gold. My eyes are brown and boring. Mama is beautiful and I am something else. But Mama doesn't make me feel ugly the way Gran does; Mama makes me feel like I'm the prettiest girl in the entire world.

When Mama goes into her room, I listen to all the familiar sounds. The way the rag rug muffles her steps, and the sliding of a dresser drawer as it opens and closes. I hear the soundlessness of Mama as she pauses to look in the mirror—the one from Daddy with the two brass birds cast to look like they are ready to fly away. When Mama comes back, her hair is down and she's wearing a long white nightgown like the one I am wearing. Soft cotton and eyelet flowers. She leads me to my room, and when I get into bed she sits down next to me.

———

"Do you think you can sleep?" she asks.

I don't want to be brave anymore. I hear something in the yard, and I'm worried about my stuffed animals. I don't want them to be cold or to get hurt. I worry about rain.

Mama brings the quilt to my chin and tells me to breathe. I breathe the special way she taught me—where I fill my belly with air and make it as round as a balloon. While I breathe, Mama starts to build the protective dome she builds around my bed whenever I am scared. She stands to shape the air with her hands. They move like she is working with clay.

"I make it from love," she says. "And nothing bad can get through."

Mama calls the construction of the dome a ritual. "Rituals are important," Mama says, and I realize this is what I've been doing. Holding my breath and crossing my fingers is a kind of ritual to make something stop or not happen. When Mama's done building the invisible dome, she rubs her hands together. She's thorough, and I can almost see it—the way light hits glass and makes it not so see-through anymore. I see the scratch marks on the other side where something tried to claw its way in but couldn't get through.

Mama is still asleep when I wake up. With the sun in the sky, the world is safe and warm again. I look at the orchard from my window. I can see the quilt, and some of my stuffed animals—the trees, and the slope of the land, hide the others.

I get dressed and go to the orchard to gather everything and take it back home with me. I walk the path that last night had to be run. What I am doing is called tracking. Uncle Billy taught me.

I track Mama. And I track myself.

———

The birds are singing and the sky is blue. The southern pasture is sun kissed with dandelions and buttercups, and the bright sprinkle of yellow makes me smile. A group of rabbits scatter when I come upon the remains of the picnic, but everything else is as it was.

My stuffed animals sit in their circle, and my teddy bear is still leaning against the picnic basket, the cloth napkin in his lap damp from the morning dew.

I breathe in, and the air makes me stand up straight and tall. I hold the air inside my body and I cross my fingers until I'm no longer scared, and then I head toward the woods and the farmer's ditch. I don't try to hide what I am doing. Today is one of those days when Mama will sleep in late.

This is where the animals come to drink. Wild and not wild. And this is where I feed the dog, but she is nowhere to be seen.

Instead, I find an owl pellet—matted and gray. Using my fingernails as tweezers, I pick out the tiny white jawbone of a field mouse. The sun shines through the trees, turning parts of the water into gold. Where the light doesn't reach, the water stays dark: black like the reverse side of a mirror.

It takes three trips to carry everything back to the house, and when I'm done I fall asleep on the couch. When I wake up later, I peer into Mama's room. She's sleeping on her side, facing the other way. She still hasn't moved, and Marmalade is curled up by her feet. The sun shines through the curtains and turns Mama's skin into lace.

My stomach growls and I realize I'm hungry, but I don't want to bother Mama. In the kitchen, while I'm waiting for my toast to toast, I try reading *The Headless Cupid*. The book opens to chapter six again, and I find that "initiation" isn't the only word I don't know.

———

But at least I can pronounce the other ones—words like "occult" and "ordeal." I'm more than happy to abandon the book when it's time to spread my toast with butter and homemade strawberry-rhubarb jam. I wonder if there's a difference between "cult" and "occult." The word "cult" had something to do with the picture of baby Azaria's black and red dress. The picture of the dress without a baby actually wearing it.

The apple juice hasn't been opened, and my fingers fumble to break the seal on the plastic jug. It's hard to pour because it's so full. I put my glass on the floor to try—something Uncle Billy taught me to do—but instead of coming slowly, the juice rushes out, spilling everywhere. It spills across the black and white tiles, square after square like a game of checkers. And this is when Daddy comes home. He is alone. I don't know where my uncle is.

"Have an accident?" my father asks, smiling.

Daddy puts his backpack down and gets on his hands and knees to help me clean. When we're done, we stay on the floor. The floor glistens, and the house takes a deep sigh. Daddy calls this settling. He tosses the used rags into the sink and wipes his fingers dry on his blue jeans. He kisses me on the very tip top of my head: According to Mama, this is my crown chakra.

"So where is my beautiful wife?" Daddy asks, and when I tell him she's still asleep I see the way his face changes. How he checks the clock on the stove.

I might read better than any kid my age, but I can't tell time.

Daddy is heading up the stairs fast, and I hold my breath and cross my fingers to make the bad feeling go away, but it doesn't go away, so I quietly follow my father. I stand in the hallway. And Daddy is saying Mama's name. He says it softly like he does when he's saying my name to wake me up for school. Each time, a whisper.

"Annie. I'm home."

But he's too quiet, and she isn't waking up. And so he says her name a little louder: "Annie," he says. Louder and louder, he says her name. Again and again. He says "Annie?" like it's a question, and then it's not a question anymore, and he is shouting, and her name is no longer a name.

I come to stand in the doorway, where I can see what I don't want to see. Daddy sits on the edge of the bed, and Mama is still on her side like before, but she is no longer made from lace. She is made from shadows now. When Daddy tries rolling Mama over, Marmalade hisses at him, and her teeth are sharp and blue-white. Daddy moves Mama, and Mama's arm rolls off her hip, falling in a twisted way. Daddy rolls Mama onto her back, and her body buries her arm, where it gets folded even more wrong than before.

Screaming is different from shouting.

I've never heard my father scream before. He sounds like a little girl. As he screams, my body fills with silence. And I am choking on the quiet lodged inside my throat.

Daddy is shaking Mama. Her face jiggles from side to side, and I wish he'd stop. I am worried he will hurt her. Mama is Sleeping Beauty.

Daddy grabs the phone from the bed stand and holds it between his face and his shoulder. He does this so he can still hold Mama with his other arm. One spin on the rotary, and I remember this sound from somewhere as I listen to the ringing. A woman's voice comes on the line; she is loud. "Operator. How may I help you?"

Daddy is looking at me now, and because he is, it feels like

—

I'm the one he's talking to. There is spit on his lips, and his jaw is clenched. He asks to be connected to emergency services.

"Right away," he says. "I need an ambulance."

At the hospital in Lawrence, I'm not allowed to move.

"Don't go anywhere," Daddy says.

There's a television fixed to the corner of the ceiling. I sit on a love seat, watching the soap opera, only there is no volume. A woman sits before a mirror, talking to herself as she brushes her long red hair. Then it's a different room, and a different woman. This woman has long black hair and has fallen asleep on a couch. A tall man is watching her. I stare until the characters turn into fuzzy little dots, and when I close my eyes my brain is filled with the same black-and-white static.

Daddy kisses me on the forehead, and his breath smells like coffee. He paces back and forth from the waiting room to the hallway with the big double doors at the end.

The doors that swallowed Mama.

On the coffee table is a stack of magazines and a blue vase full of fake flowers. Mama hates fake flowers. "They're unnatural," she says. "Because they don't die."

Under the television in the waiting room is a painting of a snow-covered meadow with a small house and dark woods in the background. Looking at the white snow makes me feel cold. Daddy comes back and he, too, is shivering.

"Come on," he says. "Follow me."

I stand and I begin to walk. But I'm not the one making my body do what it is doing. I follow my father. I follow him all the way into the painting—into the snow-covered pasture behind our house. The snow is deep—deeper than any snow I have ever seen. *Walk behind me,* Daddy says. *Use my footprints as places to step.*

I step into the holes he leaves behind, but sometimes I miss.

His legs are longer than mine, and I can't always make it from one footprint to the next. I step on the snow by mistake and it holds me. It is strong and I am small. But when I try to walk on the snow, it collapses and I'm swallowed by the cold white.

Inside the hole, Mama is Snow White, and the seven dwarves have come to get her. They carry her down the stairs, through the living room, and out to the driveway. They slide her glass coffin into the back of the ambulance. "Sir," one of the dwarves says as he takes a pen from the breast pocket of his white jacket, getting ready to write, "do you think your wife had reason to attempt suicide?"

Daddy looks at me. He says no but nods yes. And then he hands over the little brown bottle from the night before, only there is no rattle.

This bottle is quiet.

CHAPTER TWO
THE CRUCIFIXION

hang: v. 1. *To fasten from above with no support from below;
suspend* 2. *To attach at an appropriate angle* 3. *To hold or incline
downward; droop* 4. *To attach oneself as a dependent; cling*
5. *To depend:* It all hangs on one vote.

June 23, 1982

Gran doesn't have a guest bedroom, so she unfolds the sofa and
turns it into a bed, but she doesn't call it a sofa. She calls it a davenport. I stand there feeling stupid as she puts the sheets on the mattress and fluffs the pillows. I should offer to help, but I don't know
what to offer. I've never slept anywhere other than home—except for
once upon a time, when I was born—when I must have slept in the
same hospital where Mama is now resting.

When Gran is finished, she straightens herself out, only she can't
stand straight—not the way other people can. Daddy says this is why
I need to drink more milk. I might get Gran's back, the kind that
goes crooked with age, and the reason my grandmother is shrinking.
But I don't look like Gran. She has the same black hair as Daddy and
Uncle Billy, only now she has to have it dyed.

I think it's strange how you can inherit one thing from a relative
and not the other.

Not only does Gran get her hair dyed, she gets a permanent every

---

month. I don't understand why it's called a permanent since she has to get it redone all the time, but when I asked, Gran said what she always says: "Fig, you are too smart for your own good." I don't say anything to Gran about her osteoporosis or my risk of getting it. I am learning what not to say when I'm around her. I am learning how not to talk at all.

"You'll have to sleep in your underwear," Gran says. "Tomorrow, we'll go to the farm and pack a suitcase."

I hadn't thought of that. I want to ask how long I'll have to stay with her in Lawrence, but I'm afraid the question will upset her. I'm too scared to even tell her I don't own a suitcase. So I keep practicing silence.

"Well," she says, "undress."

I fold my jeans and put them on the floor. I roll my socks into a ball the way Mama showed me, and I leave my T-shirt and panties on. I get into bed, and the sheets are scratchy next to my bare skin—they are not soft like the sheets at home. Gran doesn't say, "Don't let the bed bugs bite," and she doesn't kiss me good night the way Mama and Daddy always do. And my grandmother does not build an invisible dome around the davenport to protect me from the night.

She turns off the lamp and sits in the little chair on the other side of the end table. And I can see her. The living room doesn't go black the way my room does back at the farm if there is no moon. This is a neighborhood in a city. There are porch lights and streetlights; they shine into the house even though the curtains have all been drawn.

"Fiona," Gran says, "I spoke with your father. Your mother will be just fine." My grandmother pauses. Then she says, "He told me to be sure to tell you that none of this is your fault. He says he'll come to see you just as soon as he can." Gran's words come slow and sharp,

—

as if she can see each one before she chooses what to say. But when she speaks again, her words come faster because these are words she knows by heart: "If I should die before I wake, I pray the Lord my soul to take. May He guard me through the night and wake me with the morning light."

I wish she would leave, but when she does I wish she had stayed.

I listen to the cars driving by and watch the shadows they cast across the walls. The passing shadows are bigger than the actual cars, and the refrigerator hums, and there is a ticking that doesn't come from a clock, at least not any clock I know about. I don't know where it's coming from, and after that prayer I'm too scared to fall asleep. My parents don't believe in God, and because they don't, neither do I, and I wonder if not believing will make me die while I am dreaming.

And the ticking does not go away. *Hickory, dickory, dock, the mouse ran up the clock. The clock struck one, the mouse ran down, hickory, dickory, dock.* Tick, tock.

I get out of bed and tiptoe across the living room, toward Gran's bedroom. I hold my breath and cross my fingers. She left her door cracked open, and when I push on it the thick carpet makes a shushing sound. *Shh!* it says as I climb into bed with my grandmother. The sheets are slippery and cold, and I am careful not to actually touch her body. I practice not really being here.

I have trespassed enough for one night.

Trapped by the covers, I do not move again. Her room is darker than the living room, but some light does creep in around the edges of her curtains. It reflects along the rectangular mirror above her dresser, where it grows and shimmers the way light does on water. The light moves across Gran's perfume bottles, and in the glass behind the bottles I see the reflections of the perfume bottles. I see the shadows of the bottles and the shadows reflected in the mirror as I focus on being still, on not moving. I hold my breath and cross my fingers. I focus on not being here at all.

In the morning, I wake to find Gran gone—her side of the bed already made. When I walk by the long mirror that's on the wall above Gran's dresser, I don't see myself in the glass.

I backtrack until I find a girl in the mirror. She turns when I turn. And when I stare at her, she stares back. Her eyes are round, a deep brown so dark, they are almost black.

She looks like me, but when I smile she frowns.

Gran is in the kitchen, already dressed, standing in front of the stove, waiting for the kettle to boil, and she is not alone.

A woman I've never seen before is sitting with her chair turned away from the table because she has a briefcase in her lap. The open case works to hide most of the woman as she bends forward, shuffling through papers. I can see the top of her head—brown hair, dull and business-like, and I can see her legs. She is wearing panty hose and beige pumps. There is a run in her stocking.

Mama always says, "Never trust a woman who wears nylons." Mama doesn't approve of a lot things the women in Kansas do or wear. She doesn't approve of high heels, perfume, or makeup. "They test cosmetics on poor little creatures like bunny rabbits and monkeys," she has explained. And Mama doesn't approve of shaving your legs, or even your armpits—she prefers to go "all natural," as she likes to say.

The woman with the pantyhose pulls out a manila folder, which she sets on the table before closing the briefcase with a click. As she bends over to put the case on the floor, her glasses slip off her nose, but a special string keeps them from falling to the floor. The glasses swing in the air for a second before she grabs hold of them with long fingers and repositions them on her face. The glasses perch at the very end of her nose, and there is something birdlike about this.

Gran sets two coffee cups on the table, and even though I know she saw me she is waiting to acknowledge me. First, she spoons instant coffee crystals into both cups, and I think about Daddy, who hates instant coffee. He even calls it "absolute blasphemy," and yet he keeps a container at the farm for Gran. That and a tall bottle of Beefeater gin.

Gran pours the hot water into the cups, and I watch the steam rising into the air. I can't feel the thick June humidity inside the house like I can at the farm. The air-conditioning cuts it. The bird-woman begins to stir her coffee as Gran turns and looks at me. Still holding the kettle, Gran says, "Good. You're up."

And now the other woman is looking at me too. I stand in the living room, awkward. I haven't gotten the chance to get dressed, and I feel naked in my T-shirt and underwear. My skin goose bumps as I look at the floor. And I can feel the bird-woman looking at me. Up and down—her eyes miss nothing. I tug at the bottom of my shirt, trying to make it longer.

"Hello, Fiona," the woman says, taking a sip of her coffee. "I'm Alicia Bernstein. I'm from Social Services. I'm here to talk to you."

From the corner of my eye, I see Gran go rigid. Her hands become tight fists, one still wrapped around the kettle handle. Then she returns the kettle to the stove, and without turning to look at us again Gran says, "I'll be outside if you need me."

Grabbing the newspaper, my grandmother quickly exits to keep the cold air from escaping. At home, we leave all the doors and windows wide open to encourage the breezes to sweep through the old house, but here all the windows and doors are shut so tight, I can't breathe.

The davenport has been folded back into a sofa, and I find my clothes waiting for me on the center cushion. Alicia Bernstein from Social Services watches. She watches me pull my jeans on, and then she watches me come into the kitchen. Even though I'm dressed now, I still feel naked.

I look out the window before I sit down. Gran is sitting in a lawn chair working a crossword puzzle, and I can feel Alicia Bernstein's eyes watching me. A squirrel drops out of the oak tree and darts across the small square of lawn, but my grandmother doesn't look up. As she ponders a clue she fiddles with her mechanical pencil. She waves it back and forth the way she wags her finger at me when I've done something wrong. And now she is bending over to fill in another blank space.

Alicia Bernstein from Social Services asks the same questions the police kept asking the other night. She, too, wants to know what happened in the orchard.

I hold my breath and cross my fingers before I tell her I think I saw coyotes. This time I perform the ritual to make her believe me. I pronounce "coyote" the way Mama does, and Alicia Bernstein looks surprised. Then she scribbles something on a pad of yellow paper with green lines.

"I met your father last night," she says, finally looking up again. "We talked for a long time. He told me all about how smart you are." And this is when she pauses. She sits there with her mouth slightly open, looking at me like I'm supposed to agree with her about me

---

being smart. But I don't say anything. I stare at my hands. My fingernails are dirty and need to be trimmed.

Alicia Bernstein makes a clicking noise with her tongue and I know she is still watching me, even though I refuse to look at her. She puts the manila folder and pad of paper back into her briefcase and focuses on drinking her coffee. She acts like this is the only reason she is here. She takes her time and she never stops watching me. She slurps every time she takes a sip and the slurping makes me thirsty. The cup she is using is from Gran's china set—the set that inspired the entire kitchen decor.

Every piece of china is so white, it is almost see-through. And so thin I can't help but break Gran's dishes all the time. The china is decorated with a simple splash of silver and aqua stars that remind me of the cartoon *The Jetsons*. The stars match the speckled Formica table and countertops. Uncle Billy tiled the wall above the stove to match the pattern on the china, and the tiles create their own repeating pattern: three white squares, two aqua, followed by one silver—again and again.

"Well," Alicia Bernstein finally says, "because you are so smart, we'd really like to study your brain to see exactly how it works."

I use one fingernail to scrape dirt from another, and I wonder who she means when she says "we." I also think about Gran. Maybe she's right. Maybe being smart is a bad thing.

The bird-woman leans forward and says, "We asked your dad, and he gave us his blessing." Alicia Bernstein continues to talk. "You will come in every day for a week," she says, and now she is standing. "See," she says, and I can't help but look.

I look even though I don't want to.

She is pointing at the pantry door like a teacher pointing at the

—

34

chalkboard. She is pointing at the calendar hanging from a nail on the white door. It's just like Gran to own a calendar without any pictures. June is nothing more than a series of squares with numbers typed into the bottom right-hand corners. Alicia Bernstein sweeps her bony pointer finger over the squares for next week—Monday through Friday. In shaky cursive, Gran has written the word TEST inside every block.

"See," Alicia Bernstein says again, and her smiling is no longer forced, it is real this time. "Everything is all set in stone." And I have no choice in the matter.

The following week is a blur of buzzing fluorescent lights, strangers, and weird pictures. Every morning, Gran wakes me up early and feeds me breakfast. I drink Tang and eat sugar cereal—both of which I'm not allowed to eat at home—and my stomach hurts. Then we get into her Buick and drive to the ugly brick building where the doors are guarded by two flags: America and Kansas.

While Gran sits in the waiting room working her crossword puzzles, I'm taken into different rooms by different people who play relay with the manila folder Alicia Bernstein had. On the third day, a woman named Wendy places a stack of black-and-white pictures on the table. They are large and square. And they are upsetting. I'm supposed to tell a story about what I see. "I see a little girl sitting on the steps," I say, and Wendy smiles a disappointed smile.

She holds the picture higher, and she says, "Tell me everything you can about the little girl. What's her name? Why is she alone? Is this where she lives? Are there people we can't see?"

And I try. I try to tell the stories in the black-and-white pictures, but I get distracted. The kids on the posters and in the pamphlets all around are also telling stories, and I want to help them run away from the stories they are trying to tell. "A story is made from three parts," Wendy explains. "It has a beginning, a middle, and an end. You need to include all three, okay, Fig?"

Wendy says, "No more happily ever after, okay?" but the ending is the hardest part to tell.

On Friday, when I finish, Alicia Bernstein steers me back to the waiting room, where Gran is sitting surrounded by more brochures: *Overcoming Depression. Teen Pregnancy. Anxiety Disorder.*

"It was so nice to meet you," Alicia Bernstein says, and reaches out to shake my hand while her other arm clutches the manila folder. The children in the posters all warned me about Alicia Bernstein. "She's a social worker," they explained. "Her job is to take kids away from their parents."

I let the social worker shake my hand, but I'm careful to also hold my breath and cross my fingers; I cross the fingers on both my hands, the ones behind my back and the ones inside her fist. I hold my breath and cross my fingers because I never want to see Alicia Bernstein ever again.

September 1982
Summer ends and the new school year begins, second grade with Mrs. Olson. Most school nights, I stay at home, and just being in my house makes me less worried about Alicia Bernstein coming to take me away. Mama is still in the hospital. Daddy says she needs a place to rest. "A little break," he says. "A time out."

I ride the bus back and forth—home to school, school to home, and on the weekends I go stay with Gran. She stops at a gas station along the way and buys me a *Wizard of Oz* suitcase because it's the only kind they carry. "I don't have time to go anywhere else," she says. Daddy calls the suitcase "tourist paraphernalia." It is blue and there's a picture of Dorothy standing on the yellow brick road, holding Toto. I can't tell if she's at the beginning or the end of her journey. Underneath, written in white cursive, the suitcases reads: *There's No Place Like Grandma's*.

I never get into Gran's bed again.

I sleep in her living room. Wrapped in scratchy sheets, I watch all the shadows, and I listen to the ticking that never seems to stop. And I suck my thumb. But when Gran sees, she yanks it from my mouth. She doesn't care if my teeth scrape against my skin, and she doesn't care when I get cut. I learn how to fall asleep without my thumb, but once I'm dreaming it sneaks back into my mouth. Gran buys a product from the drugstore called Hoof. It's applied like fingernail polish. I try to remind Gran of Mama's disapproval regarding makeup, but Gran says this isn't cosmetic.

"Fiona," she says, "this is about good hygiene and conquering bad habits."

Gran paints my thumbnail before I go to bed. Hoof tastes bitter—like burnt coffee, horseradish, and licking batteries all at once. But it doesn't take long to chew it off. After Gran goes into her room, I chew and spit the bad taste into the thick carpet. While the taste never goes all the way away, it does get better, and the comfort of my thumb makes up for it.

Gran replaces Hoof with a splint.

It goes around my elbow to keep my arm from bending. This way, I can't get my thumb into my mouth. The splint makes sleep impossible. I lie for hours watching the shadows of the passing cars drift across the ceiling and then across the floor, where they stretch—growing even longer, and longer still. I cannot sleep, and not sleeping makes me scared of everything. And the ticking continues. My arm throbs, and I'm still awake by the time morning is announced by the boy on the red bicycle as he hurls the daily newspaper at Gran's front door.

Gran surrounds herself with other old ladies, and they all look at me like I've done something wrong. They look at me, and I know they know.

They know all about my mother.

They play hearts and talk about their dead husbands. My grandfather died from heart failure, but Gran makes it sound like he was the one who failed and not his heart. Mrs. Nelson is the only one with a husband who is still alive, and sometimes the card games are at her house. Mr. Nelson has emphysema from smoking cigarettes since he was eight years old. He is plugged in to a big tank that helps him breathe and makes the living room sound like the inside of an aquarium.

Mrs. Nelson has several large paintings of Jesus Christ. Gran points to them with her bony, crooked fingers and tells me all the titles: *The Immaculate Conception. The Birth of Baby Jesus. The Crucifixion. The Resurrection.* When she says "conception" and "crucifixion," she whispers like she does when she says "cancer," "lesbian," or "university."

Jesus is always surrounded by rays of light.

In *The Crucifixion*, someone has hammered gigantic nails into his wrists, and there is a lot of shiny blood. Gran makes me look at this, but she won't let me watch *St. Elsewhere* even though I'm allowed to watch it at home.

—

Gran is worried that I will go to hell. She wants me baptized. She wants me to take my first communion. When I ask Uncle Billy what communion is, my question makes him laugh.

"That's when we eat the flesh of Christ," he says. "And then we drink his blood."

Gran still goes to church in Eudora because that is where she got married.

The Sacred Heart of Mary, only I read it as "scared" instead of "sacred" every time I see the sign.

Gran introduces me to the priest, and when she does she calls him father even though he's young enough to be her son. He, too, knows about Mama—I can tell by the way he looks at me. And even though he's taller than Daddy, he is nowhere near as strong, and his skin is see-through like he never goes outside.

Gran makes me go to Sunday school.

Candace Sherman's teenage sister is our teacher. We're supposed to call her Miss Sherman, but Candace messes up all the time and calls her Buffy. Candace Sherman is in the same grade as me, and so are her two best friends, Sissy Baxter and Tanya Jenkins.

Sissy's family owns and operates Baxter Lumber, and Tanya's mother works part-time at the salon Curl Up & Dye, which is in Lawrence and happens to be where my grandmother goes to get her hair done. According to Gran, Tanya's mother is going to night school to be a nurse.

Candace Sherman lives in a ranch house made from bloodred brick, and her daddy grows corn and alfalfa. Once upon a time, back in high school, Daddy dated Mrs. Sherman. I've seen the pictures in his yearbook. Mrs. Sherman was the homecoming queen, and after

—

graduation she was a beauty queen. Gran still has all the newspaper clippings in her scrapbook. The year Daddy finally made his way to Cornell was the same year Mrs. Sherman was crowned Sweetheart of Mid-America. Now she works the beauty counter at Eudora Drug on Tuesdays and Thursdays, and Gran often goes to her for advice on how to erase her wrinkles.

In Sunday school, we color bubbly cartoon pictures of Jesus and his herd of baby sheep, and everyone there knows I'm going straight to hell.

I can't help but fall asleep when Buffy reads out loud.

To wake me, Buffy hits me on the back with a wooden yardstick. It's exactly like the Little House books before Laura got to be the teacher and was nice instead of mean like Buffy. There's a little playground in the churchyard where statues of angels watch over the children as they play, but I never get to go outside.

I have to stand in the corner of the classroom with my arms stretched out.

I turn my palms toward the ceiling so Buffy can place a bible on each hand. I have to stand like this and hold the bibles without bending at the elbows or lowering my arms. I get in trouble for being double jointed until one of the nuns tells Buffy I can't help it. The burning begins in the armpits, and from there it spreads.

For every time I fall asleep in class, I'm to stand like this for five minutes. If an arm wavers or a bible falls, Buffy doubles and sometimes even triples the amount of time I am to be disciplined. The burning moves toward my back, into my shoulder blades. And this is where my wings would attach if only I could fly away. Five minutes turn into ten, and ten minutes turn into fifteen.

And this is how I learn to tell time.

———

*　*　*　*

Adam and Eve get stuck in my head.

Like Eve, I was cut out—emergency Cesarean, seven years ago come next week. Daddy says it's just another creation myth. "Don't believe everything you hear," he says. "Your birth has a story too."

And this is what I've been told.

Mama and Daddy meet in college, fall in love, and are married—just the two of them, at the courthouse, both in blue jeans. They decide to leave the rat race behind and come to Kansas, to the family farm where Daddy grew up. They begin the long process of converting the farm to all organic, and I'm conceived.

Daddy tells Mama that she glows.

Mama joins a home-birth group because she wants to have me all natural. She picks out a midwife and begins to grow me while Daddy plants corn and sweet potatoes. Mama starts a sunflower patch, tall and yellow. She plants herbs in one garden and flowers in yet another.

I grow bigger and bigger and take up all of Mama. When I'm supposed to turn like all babies do, there isn't any room. And Mama has no doubt I'll either turn when the time comes or she'll just have to push me into life backward.

Mama nests. The other women in her group have babies one by one—all at home. One woman gives birth outside at sunrise, and another delivers the baby right into her husband's hands. They all describe childbirth as empowering.

Empowering.

Mama's contractions come fast and hard. She always says, "It felt like I was being split in half." The midwife comes but refuses to do the home birth.

Mama must be taken to the hospital, and this is called transport. Mama agrees to go but she can't stop crying. She tells them she can do it—deliver me breech—but the nurses and doctors all ignore her, prepping for surgery instead.

Just as God put Adam to sleep, the anesthesiologist does the same to Mama, and I am born from a dream like I'm not real.

Uncle Billy wants to take me for a walk before he drives me back to Gran's. The morning frost has turned the clover into clumps of silver. The sky is not blue, and the sun looks far away. Dolly, the llama, stands guard chewing her cud. She watches as we pass through the paddock of black and white sheep.

I have a loose tooth. I've already lost two of them and the tooth fairy brought me a shiny silver dollar each time. With my tongue, I push this loose tooth forward until I taste the blood, and then I spit just to see the red.

Uncle Billy answers all the questions I don't actually ask out loud.

"Fig," he says, "your mother has a disease called schizophrenia."

And then he tells me that Mama was nineteen when she first struggled with the disease. The number nineteen feels important, and I say it to myself quietly. "Nineteen," I whisper, and I can still taste the saltiness of my blood. "It can be hereditary," he is saying, and I am still whispering the word: "nineteen."

But then I stop, because now I'm wondering if I, too, will inherit the disease when I turn nineteen. Gran is always going on and on about how Mama and I are like paper dolls. "Cut from the same paper," she always says, and when she does she shakes her head and makes a clicking noise of disapproval with her tongue. And now I'm

———

scared. I'm scared to even think about the number nineteen. Let alone say it out loud, even if I only whispered it.

Uncle Billy tells me Mama's aunt has the disease as well. "The one who lives in Connecticut," he says, as if I know all about her, when I know nothing. I've only been told that everyone on Mama's side of the family is dead.

"With your mother, the disease manifested itself a few weeks after your grandparents died in the fire," Uncle Billy says. "Annie used to talk about how scary it was. She saw and heard and even felt things that weren't really there. But she found a special doctor and started taking medicine and all the symptoms went away. She met your dad, fell in love, finished college, and moved out here."

He explains how she had no choice but to go off her medication once she was pregnant.

"It can harm the fetus," Uncle Billy says. "After Annie had you, she really wanted to breast-feed, which meant not going back on the medicine right away. She'd had no problems during the pregnancy, and she ended up nursing longer than she ever expected. Three years passed and still no meds, and still no symptoms. That was when she began to wonder if she'd been misdiagnosed."

Uncle Billy pauses, looking at me the way people do when they need me to understand.

"It made so much sense when we thought about it," he says. "We all ended up coming to the same conclusion. We decided the first doctor paid too much attention to her family history and not enough to the fact her nervous breakdown likely resulted from having just lost her parents to a fire."

Uncle Billy doesn't actually explain how Mama was mistaken, how they all were. He said enough when he said, "Your mother has a disease called schizophrenia." He assumes I understand. "Sometimes the disease goes dormant," he says. "It hides for a while before it resurfaces." My uncle makes the sickness sound like a monster—and I can see it. Lurking in the shadows, hidden somewhere in my nineteenth year, ready to jump out and get me. Was this what was chasing me and Mama? Does this disease have yellow eyes and sharp claws and hungry teeth? Is it going to try and scare me to death?

Uncle Billy tells me how my parents asked him to talk to me about the disease. He explains how hard it is for them. "Your mother wanted me to tell you how sorry she is," Uncle Billy says. "She didn't mean to scare you like she did. She wanted me to make sure you knew there was nothing chasing you that night."

We're standing where I stopped to spit, and I can still see the red. I know my uncle wants to walk all the way out to the river, because the Silver River is his favorite place in the world. My favorite place was being inside my mother, where I felt safe because I didn't feel anything. Where I was safe before the scalpels cut me out like I was a piece of meat and not a baby. Sometimes Mama takes me to the Silver River too, and we play in the wading pool. When we go, she almost always sings, *"Take me down in the river to pray,"* which is weird because she doesn't believe in God.

I look at Uncle Billy. His eyes are a lighter shade of brown than mine, and as I study them his pupils turn into pinpoints because the sun is coming out. I push again at my loose tooth. I use my tongue like I did before, but this time I do not spit. This time, I swallow the blood.

Uncle Billy starts to walk again, and I follow, half running just to catch up with his long strides. We cross the ditch using a different bridge than the one by the orchard. This one is wider, not just a plank of wood thrown across the water. And now we are walking without talking. We walk until we reach the Silver River.

This is where the water is still calm and shallow, but if I followed it downstream, I would arrive at the place where it begins to rage. At this place, the water rushes forth so fast, it runs white. There, the white water crashes over the big rocks into a waterfall, and the waterfall fills the pool below with deep underwater chambers.

From the waterfall, the river splits: On the McAlister side, the river remains a river—wide and rushing onward, but our side is different. On our side, when the river resurfaces, it is channeled by curving walls of rock. Here the water calms and forms the shallow pool where Mama takes me to play. This is where Uncle Billy finally pauses. Here where the water turns white before it leaps over the rocks. The waterfall is loud, and when my uncle speaks, he almost shouts.

"Your grandfather made that pool," he says, pointing at the wading pool below, farther down from the falls. "He hauled all those rocks and piled them into dams and walls to tame this river. He turned chaos into a place of peace." My uncle stands there looking at the quiet pool, so I do the same. The stone wall circles out from a weeping willow that slants across the water. Uncle Billy shakes his head and sighs, and then he gestures for me to follow him down the stone steps embedded in the side of the steep hill.

When I reach the bottom, my uncle is already sitting on a rock by the pool, skipping stones. I stand on the last step to listen to the waterfall, which now sounds different from how it did when I was above it. Mama's shown me pictures of the gorges in Ithaca, where she used to live. She's in the photographs too, tiny compared with

———

45

the gigantic waterfalls behind her. This is how I know how small our waterfall really is. I try to see through the white curtain of water, but the falling motion makes me look down. The water here is so deep, it turns to black.

I ask Daddy how to spell "schizophrenia," and he tells me Mama has started taking her medicine again.

"Once the doctors get it all figured out," he says, "she can come home." Just when I think he's never going to spell "schizophrenia," he grabs a piece of junk mail from the foyer and writes the word on the back of an envelope. It has the same *f*-sounding *ph* as "phobia," and I wonder if *ph* is only used in words about the brain and how it works.

I try to pronounce "schizophrenia" and get it wrong every single time.

The loose tooth doesn't help. It turns the *s* and *z* into a waterfall of spit. Daddy tries to help. He breaks the word apart, syllable by syllable, and I repeat each one like an echo: "Skits." "O." "Fren." "Eee." "Uh." Broken into five different parts, I say it perfectly, and now I know I could pronounce the word if I wanted to.

But I don't.

I'm too scared to say it out loud now that I know I could. Just like I'm too scared to say "nineteen," I worry that saying "schizophrenia" will act like a spell and either make Mama worse or make me get sick too, or both. Because Daddy keeps trying to help me pronounce "schizophrenia," I find a way to change the subject. I tell him there was another word I couldn't pronounce—the one I tried to read in *The Headless Cupid*.

Even though I can see the word clear as day inside my head, I pretend I can't. Even though I can actually see the word on the page, I pretend I can't. I pretend I can't remember how it was spelled, so I ask where the book is and Daddy shakes his head. "I'm sorry, Fig," he says. "It was overdue. I returned those books a week ago." I make a sad face, and he apologizes again and forgets all about helping me pronounce "schizophrenia."

That night, I go to Gran's and my tooth falls out.

I'm in bed, and she's already asleep in the other room—I can hear her snoring. I hold the tooth between my fingers and use a slant of yellow light from a streetlamp outside to examine it.

It looks like the other teeth I've lost. The root is sharp and jagged and painful looking.

I put it under my pillow like I did before with Mama. I climb out of bed and find the envelope I shoved into the back pocket of my jeans, the one Daddy wrote SCHIZOPHRENIA on in careful lettering, and I put the tiny tooth inside. And then I put everything beneath my pillow.

I don't have to wear the splint at night anymore. Gran says I broke the habit. And sleep comes so much easier than it did before, especially tonight. The house is quiet. There is no ticking. And without my tooth, I feel lighter. I fall asleep thinking about the tooth fairy and what she will bring, but in the morning when I awake I find no silver dollar waiting for me. There is nothing under my pillow but an envelope addressed to schizophrenia.

CHAPTER THREE

HAPPILY EVER AFTER

wait v. 1. To remain in expectation

October 21, 1982

I am seven years old today.

Gran is driving me home from her house, where she threw me a party. I've never had a party before, and I don't ever want one again.

All my other birthdays were special without a big party. And we always celebrate it on the actual day. Not the weekend right before like Gran insisted on doing. "You want your friends to actually come," she said. As if I had friends in the first place. Usually Mama bakes a carrot cake with cream cheese frosting, and the only people who come over are Uncle Billy and Gran. They sing "Happy Birthday" and I open presents and we eat cake—simple, but perfect.

This year, Gran decorated her living room with pink and white streamers and bought a cake from the grocery store that read *Fiona* in pink frosted cursive, and made me wear a cone-shaped hat that said *Birthday Girl!* And all the girls she invited stared at me and whispered into one another's ears whenever there were no adults in the room. I didn't know any of them—they were all the granddaughters of Gran's old-lady friends.

One girl gave me a bendable fake Barbie doll, which I'll have to hide from Mama because Mama hates Barbie. I don't know why. Mama hates a lot of things that other mothers like.

I stuffed the doll way down at the bottom of my backpack, under all my school supplies. I can't put her in the Dorothy suitcase, because one of my parents is bound to unpack all my clothes when I get back to the farm. I miss my normal birthdays, but everything is about to go back to how it used to be before Mama got sick. I hold my breath and cross my fingers.

On the phone today, Daddy said, "Mama coming home is your biggest present of all."

And he is right. I can't wait to see her, and I'm not worried about Alicia Bernstein from Social Services anymore. It's been four months, but Mama is back on her medication, which means she is all better. Because Mama is better now, I too, get to move back to the farm for good.

Daddy keeps saying, "Everything is going to be okay." And I believe him. I'm not even worried about turning nineteen. Inheriting the disease wouldn't be so bad. All I'd have to do is take the medicine and I'd be just fine.

Gran takes the interstate, and I ride in the back. When we left her house, it was raining, but now it's not. The sky is a wash of gray, and Gran's car glides along and you can barely hear the outside world the way you can in Daddy's truck or Mama's rusty Volvo. Part of the sky is as green as a bruise, and there are black things coming down that look like lassos, and Gran says, "Those are tornados."

I look at the plains, where gigantic shadows sweep across the land as Gran watches me from the rearview mirror with sharp eyes. She tells me how safe we are.

———

"Perfectly fine," she says.

She guides the long car off the interstate and into a gas station. From the backseat I watch her struggle with the pump—her hair and jacket ready to blow away. She knocks on my window even though I'm looking right at her. Muffled by wind and glass, Gran says, "Don't get out of the car." She looks at me funny, tilting her head and squinting, and she says, "Promise me, Fig."

And I nod my head. With my fingers, I make an X to cross my heart.

Gran never talks like this, and she never calls me Fig—just Fiona, which Mama says is only my name on paper. Daddy wanted to name me after his mother, because she'd been named after her mother, who had been named after hers, and that list goes on: forever backward. Somehow this list is more important than naming me after the grandmother I never got to know.

The name *Fiona* is the only thing Gran and I have in common.

I watch my grandmother make her way through the pumps and across the lot, toward the station to pay. A piece of tumbleweed rolls past before getting sucked into the sky like there is a God and he's drinking the world up through a straw. For a moment, I think Gran might blow away, but then she's inside.

That's when I break my promise. I get out of the car. I have to see how it feels.

The wind picks me up and throws me. The next pump over stops my body. My hair and yellow sundress are blowing away, and I've scraped both knees. The blood rises up in little dots.

I see Gran coming for me—steps like slow motion. Trash flaps through the air, and when she calls to me her voice is stolen by the wind. She reaches with one arm and I grab hold of it with both of mine. She pulls me up and drags me through the wind, shoving me into the car as if I'm trying to resist when I'm not. As we drive away her angry eyes glare at me from the rearview mirror.

Daddy is always talking about how strong nature is, and I finally understand. I want to tell Gran, but every time I try she puts her hand up to stop me from talking. And then she's just struggling to drive against the wind, and I know better than to talk. I practice silence as I watch her fingers clutch the steering wheel so hard, her age spots disappear by turning back to white. And wrapped around her right hand I see her beloved pearl rosary.

This rosary has been in Gran's family forever—passed along from mother to daughter, from one Fiona to the next, a procession that had to stop when Gran only gave birth to sons.

This rosary does not bear the Passion of Christ but Mother Mary instead. Like the chain connecting all the shiny pearls, Mary is made from silver, and her image dangles in the air right now. She bears her heart for all to see, and she stares at me. Exposed and wide open, her heart is trying to tell me a story. Swords and wounds and blooming roses, her heart is like a shooting star.

When we get home, Mama doesn't come downstairs to greet us, and Daddy acts like she isn't even here, even though we all know what a big deal it is that she's come home. Instead, he mixes his mother a tall gin and tonic, and when she takes it the pearl rosary is still wrapped around her wrist.

Daddy says he's been watching the news. "No need to go into the cellar," he says. "But I do think you should stay the night." And he hands Gran one of Mama's nightgowns and leads her to the guest bedroom. I can tell it's weird since this used to be Gran's house where she raised two boys and lived until Mama and Daddy moved in to have me and live together happily ever after.

Mama says Gran always wanted to stay in Lawrence, where she'd been born and raised. She called Gran a city girl who married a farm. "It was the patriotic thing to do," Mama said. "It was World War II, and lots of sweethearts tied the knot before they should have. All the guys were enlisting, and no one knew who would come back and who wouldn't."

Gran goes straight to bed, but I don't. I know that Mama is upstairs waiting for me. I go to her room, and Mama opens the door before I have a chance to knock.

She seems like herself again—before the medicine, and the too-much-medicine.

I milk her for all the love I can get. She tends to my knees with careful tissue and stinging peroxide and helps me get ready for bed. With my flannel nightie on and Band-Aids plastered across my knees, the whole big lesson about nature seems silly, so I don't talk about it. And even if I tried, the words to explain my experience have all blown away.

But Mama's crying anyway and telling me how much she's missed me. "I'm so sorry," she says, wiping tears away.

We're back in her room again, sitting cross-legged on the brass bed, when she pulls my present out from where she had it hidden under the pillow. And she tells me to open it. She's watching to make sure I'm happy, and it's not just about my birthday.

I try to make the moment last forever. I'm careful as I peel off the tissue paper, trying not to tear it, but I can't help it; the rip runs away from me to reveal the gift: a glossy wall calendar with picture after picture from *Alice in Wonderland*. Mama says the illustrations

———

are from the original book. They are not from the Disney movie. Disney is yet another thing my mother hates. "It's sexist," she has explained a million times, "the way the women are portrayed as villain or maiden in distress."

Mama looks at me and says, "Happy birthday, my precious Fig," and then she brushes my bangs away so she can kiss my third eye.

Mama lets me crawl under the covers, and I know she'll let me stay the night. Daddy has to sleep downstairs on the sofa with the television turned on anyway. Just in case the tornados do turn around and make the screen go all red with a million warnings. In case the newscasters say, "No school tomorrow."

I wrap my arms around Mama, and I hold her like I'm the mother and she's the daughter.

I like the way it feels, but it makes me worry, too. What would Gran say if she saw? But then I breathe in Mama, and she is warm, and my eyes can't help but close. It is so still right here, while outside the anxious wind rifles through the farm, looking to take something away.

Daddy says Mama needs to rest again.

She's trying out a new medicine to see if it will make her feel better—but I already know what these pills do. They don't make her better. They just make her tired.

"Do you want to go for a walk?" he asks, "Maybe check for eggs?"

But I'm mad at him. I wouldn't bother her. I'd only give her a kiss, and then I'd leave—maybe I'd offer to get her a glass of water, or ask if I could curl up beside her and take a nap too. If she said no, I'd understand. And I'd go away.

I glare at Daddy, which is hard to do because he's so much taller.

—

53

I give up, turning around and running down the hall like I've been told not to do because the sound startles Mama.

There are new rules, and they make everything different from before. Daddy says, "Rules are important," but Uncle Billy says, "It's important to learn the rules so you can learn when and how to break them." I run into the bathroom and slam the door behind me. Then I lean against it, listening. I don't hear anything, which means Daddy is still standing guard. He is protecting Mama.

I slide the lock over so no one can get in, and then I climb into the bathtub.

I don't take off my clothes. I'm not planning on taking a bath. I like the old claw-foot. The way it slopes and the plug with the chain to keep it from ever getting lost. I like touching the places where the enamel chipped and watching the daddy longlegs who lives in the drain—the one who only has seven legs now because of me.

Alex Turner says daddy longlegs are the most poisonous spiders in the world. Alex talks about spiders all the time. Last year, he told the class everything he knew about daddy longlegs. "Even though they are superpoisonous," he said, "they are completely harmless because they have no fangs." When I told Mama, she said Alex was wrong. "That's just an urban legend," she explained. But I still like the idea: I could be poisonous like that.

I hear Daddy walk toward the bathroom. I can tell when he pauses, listening through the door. He says, "Fig?" but I don't say anything, so he says, "Fig, leave your Mama be. Do you hear me?" He stands there as if I'll answer, but finally I hear him sigh. And he walks away. I listen to his steps as he goes down the stairs.

I listen until I can't hear him anymore.

I'm still in my nightgown. When I tuck my knees under my

—

chin, the skirt part slips down and I can see my knees. I have scabs from the tornado knocking me over—the tornado that Gran insists wasn't a tornado. "The real tornados were very far away," she told my father. She looked at him long and hard with her dark eyes and said, "I thought they said her IQ was exceptionally high?"

The scabs are scattered across my knees the way stars make constellations in the sky.

I trace them as if to play connect the dots. On my left knee, I trace a sun. The kind of sun I like to draw—a circle with little triangles all around for the rays. When I trace the scabs on my right knee, I discover a volcano.

The kids at school don't call them scabs. They call them owies—and so do some of the grown-ups, like Mrs. Olson. "Owies." I don't think this is a very grown-up word to use. Unlike owies, scabs aren't about being hurt. They are proof I am healing.

I've had enough scabs to know that in a day or two these ones will disappear. They will leave behind brand-new skin like nothing ever happened.

I pick one to see what is underneath. There's no blood, just pinkness. Pink like Wilbur the pig in *Charlotte's Web*. Not the color of our pigs, which are black and white and gristly. I choose another scab because it looks like a bleeder, and it is. It turns into a little bead of blood and looks like it did when I first got hurt.

Then I pick them all, one by one, and my body is an Advent calendar. Sometimes I have to pinch the skin to coax the blood. And sometimes I mess up and the skin peels too far. The skin runs away like the tissue paper did when I was opening my birthday present.

The sores spread like watercolors on wet paper, and the bleeding makes me feel the way I did when I still sucked my thumb. It makes everything stop.

I pull myself out of the tub and go to the door. I unlock the latch and I get back into the claw-foot. I check my knees and find I have to pick more.

Pick, pick, pick.

Once the blood is good again, I start to cry. I'm careful not to actually call out for Mama. I cry like I can't help but cry—the way a person really cries when they are very hurt. But she doesn't come. No one does. Even when I am really crying, even when I cry for Mama. No one comes.

"That's not a real Barbie," Candace Sherman says. And she keeps her arm up like she's still waiting for Mrs. Olson to call on her. She does this so no one else can get a turn till she's said what she wants to say. "*That* is the fake kind they sell at Kmart. That's why she's so bendy, Fig. Not because she's a special edition."

And the whole second-grade class giggles.

The way show-and-tell works in Mrs. Olson's second-grade classroom is each student only gets to do it once a year on his or her birthday. If your birthday is in the summer, your birthday show-and-tell is on your half birthday, or whatever closest day is available. The only other show-and-tell you get is if you travel outside Kansas.

I'm lucky because we never go anywhere.

I'd been hoping Mrs. Olson would forget my birthday because I was careful not to remind her like the other kids always do, but she remembered. Even if it took her a few days, she remembered.

After morning recess, she pulled me aside to tell me I was up first thing after lunch before language arts. I was about to beg her not to make me, when I remembered I still had the bendable Barbie doll in my backpack. I imagined the other girls coming up afterward, asking to play with her during recess. Asking to play with *me*. And this was the stupid reason I agreed to do show-and-tell.

I watch the school bus drive away, and then I stand in the road watching the dust settle. I'm the first kid picked up in the morning and the last one dropped off.

The days are getting shorter, and the moon is coming up—the kind that Daddy calls a harvest moon. It's as orange as a pumpkin, and it looks too heavy to go any higher.

I open my backpack to get my sweater.

There's the fake Barbie.

Her legs stick out and make the letter V. I take her out. And I bend her into impossible positions, positions that don't make sense. Positions that scare me because the expression on her face never changes. Sometimes this happens to Mama, but when it does she is never smiling.

I bend her until her back should break.

I force her head into her crotch and jam her legs and arms until all her joints bend the wrong way. I straighten her out and strip off her clothes. I pop off the rubber high heels, letting them fly one at a time like champagne corks. I undo the Velcro on her blouse and slide off her jeans, and I'm surprised to find she isn't wearing any underwear. She doesn't have nipples or a belly button or a vagina, but she does have something resembling a butt crack.

I stuff all her clothes into the culvert. And then I put the naked fake Barbie back into my pack, buried under my Trapper Keeper—just in case.

—

Just in case I get home and find Mama feeling better. Good enough to leave her room, have dinner with us, and maybe even help me with my homework. I was wrong to think that everything would go back to how it was. Sometimes holding my breath and crossing my fingers doesn't work.

"Fig, we have to be patient," Daddy keeps telling me. "The medicine doesn't just start working overnight. It takes a while for the doctors to find the right dose, to see what combination of drugs brings the most relief." And this is when he always pauses. He pauses and looks at me for a long time. He looks tired every day. And finally, after forever, Daddy will finish the speech. "It will take some time," he says.

But he is never specific; he does not elaborate. He does not show me on the calendar how long it will take. This is because he doesn't know. And if Daddy doesn't know, that means no one does. "We just have to wait and see," my father says, and I swear he tells me this every single day.

Mama does come downstairs while Daddy and I are eating. We're sitting at the old oak table in the kitchen. Through the French doors, I can see the table in the dining room. The pile of broken china dolls is still there next to the coil of barbed wire, but Daddy must have used the power drill, because it's no longer there.

No more blinking red light.

Gran gets after Daddy about how Mama shouldn't use that space to work.

"If Annie is going to insist on being an artist," Gran says, "then she should act like one and turn the attic into a studio." But Daddy always tells Gran he doesn't mind.

He likes Mama out in the open—where he can see her.

Daddy slides his chair back, like he's going to get up. The way that men do on TV whenever a woman comes into the room. But he doesn't get up—he watches Mama, who is standing in the doorway, her hair tangled and face as pale as a ghost. She's wearing Daddy's terry-cloth bathrobe, and in reaction to us staring she tightens the belt. I've seen Mama tired before, but not like this.

Maybe Mama has cancer like Sissy Baxter's mother does. Maybe she has cancer instead of schizophrenia? I was hiding in the coat closet when I heard Sissy Baxter tell Mrs. Olson.

"How is your mother?" Mrs. Olson asked, and that's when Sissy Baxter started crying. Mrs. Olson let her cry. But then Sissy Baxter stopped crying like it was something you can just turn off. That's when she said, "Daddy says Mom's going to be okay after she gets the mastectomy." Sissy Baxter didn't trip up when she said "mastectomy." Sissy Baxter said "mastectomy" out loud the way I wish I could say the word "schizophrenia."

"Are you hungry?" Daddy asks, and I remember where I am. Mama looks at him like she doesn't understand what he is asking.

"It's ham," Daddy says. "The end of what Billy cured last year."

I cringe.

I still can't stand the idea of eating meat, but I've stopped feeding it to the dog. No matter how many times Mama insists nothing was actually chasing us that night, I remember all those yellow eyes. What if they really were coyotes? What if I was the one who lured them to the farm by leaving all my scraps by the ditch? Now when I pocket the meat from my plate, I bury it deep in the kitchen trash instead.

Daddy is always going on about how important it is to know

—

where your food comes from. But the slaughter is hard on me—it's always come after my birthday, once it's cold enough that all the flies have died. This year, I hid inside my bedroom to avoid it but I forgot about the curing, which is still to come, and soon.

Daddy also says, "There is no cure for schizophrenia."

Mama is staring at the oven like she can see the ham inside, even though there is no window. Just white enamel and an oven mitt hanging from the handle. Maybe Mama has been hiding in her room for the same reasons that I hide in mine.

Maybe we can hide together.

"Tobias," Mama says, "don't get up. I'm fine."

Her words are heavy and slow, and she doesn't once look at me, not even when she gets a glass from the cabinet and her robe brushes against the back of my chair. She fills the glass with water from the tap. Looking out the window, she drinks the water and fills the glass again before she shuffles out of the kitchen, up the stairs, and back to her bedroom.

After dinner, I go to get my homework, but my backpack isn't where I thought I'd left it.

I start upstairs to see if it's in my room, but when I reach the top of the stairs I notice the door to Mama and Daddy's room is open, when it's been closed for days. Mama is sitting on the bed, leaning over, and she appears to be looking at something I can't see.

Her long blond hair is a curtain to hide behind.

She has brushed it since she came downstairs, but it still needs to be washed. Daddy calls her hair strawberry blond, but Mama says it is dishwater blond. "Fig," she says, "you're the true blond, the one with the golden locks." Only I have no locks, because Mama insists on keeping my hair cut short. I don't really care—even if the girls at school make fun of me. And call me a boy.

Short hair is much easier to manage, and Mama needs life to be a little bit easier than it is. If I can help make life easier, then it won't take as much time for the medicine to start working.

The floorboards squeak and Mama looks up. Her hair falls away and I see her face. Downstairs, the front door closes, and I know Daddy's gone out for his evening walk. He says it's to check on the animals, but Uncle Billy says it's his time to get away—that Daddy's done this ever since he was a boy. "We all have our rituals," my uncle said, winking at me the way he always does.

"Fig," Mama says. And she says my name like it's the first time she's ever said it out loud. Like she's trying it out, and now she is smiling and her whole face brightens. Her bedside lamp is turned on, casting an amber glow on the room, and making her not look so pale.

"Darling," Mama says, patting the bed. "Come sit a minute." While her words are still heavy, they are beginning to come faster.

I do as she says.

I try not to look at the naked fake Barbie in her lap, or my opened backpack, which I couldn't see before. The entire room looks different from how it looked when I was in the hall. There are deep shadows in the corners, and the white bedspread is more worn than I remember. I run my fingers across the white, feeling the tiny bumps in the weave.

Mama holds up the doll, and now I have to look. She turns it around, looking at the fake Barbie in a way that makes me feel like there's something I can't see that she can see clearly. "Did you get this for your birthday?" she asks, and her words are coming even faster.

—

64

I nod, looking down. My knees poke out from under my skirt. My socks are bunched around my ankles because the elastic is worn. The scabs are almost healed, but I want to rip them off again. I can remember the way the blood felt. It was hot, and everything stopped long enough for me to really catch my breath and breathe again. I think about my fingernails, and then I think about using something else to do the picking—maybe something made from metal.

Mama pulls a permanent marker out of her bedside drawer and starts drawing on the fake Barbie. She draws little black arrows all around the doll's breasts, stomach, thighs, and buttocks. The marks remind me of sewing stitches. Mama must assume all Barbies, fake or not, come naked, because she never once asks where her clothes have gone. Instead, she makes her perfect arrows, and I can tell she's really concentrating by the way she works her tongue back and forth. This is what she does when she works on her art.

"There!" she says, her tongue normal again. "Do you know what I did?"

Mama tells me she did exactly what a plastic surgeon does to a woman's body before she goes in for surgery. She explains how all the areas marked are the parts of the body women are made to feel most ashamed of, and she points at the arrows on the fake Barbie's tummy and says, "Nip and tuck!" She says it so the *p* in "nip" pops and the *k* in "tuck" clicks.

I think about the long, purple scar on Mama's tummy from when I was born. Sometimes I wish I could unzip that scar and crawl back inside. I'd find a new way out, and this time she wouldn't have to get cut open. "Butchered," Mama sometimes says to describe the operation.

Mama holds the doll and points at her feet. I think about the tiny rubber heels I took off. I worry a rabbit will try to eat one and choke to death. Mama is not just a feminist but an environmentalist as well. I see how the doll's feet were made to only wear high heels. Mama touches the pointy toes on each foot and asks me if I've ever heard of Chinese foot binding.

Her words are no longer flat. Now they come fast, and over-pronounced.

"The term 'binding' is very misleading," Mama says. "Binding implies the cloth kept the girl's feet from growing, but there is much more involved. The ideal age to begin was when a girl was three. You're much too old," she says, smiling as if to comfort me.

"First, the girl's feet were broken. They tried to do this during the winter so the cold would help to numb the pain." Mama pauses to take a drink of her water. "The cold also helped to stop infection," she says. And then she hands me the naked fake Barbie doll.

I know she wants me to examine it, so I do, and I find her feet are nothing like my own.

"It was the mother's job to break her daughter's feet and do the binding," Mama says. "She'd fold the broken toes under and wrap the binding cloth around the foot as tight as she could. At night, she slept on top of her daughter's feet to cut off the circulation and thus ease the pain."

Mama is talking way too fast. I try to keep up.

Mama explains how the mothers had no other choice. In their own way, they were being very kind. She uses the word "compassion." Mama tells me the practice of foot binding has lasted about one thousand years. "There is no way to unbind a bound foot," she says. "Trust me, the communists tried." The most desirable size was no longer than three inches. "These feet were called golden lotuses," Mama says. "Anything bigger was ridiculed."

Mama says large feet were called lotus boats, but then she stops talking. She stops in the middle of a sentence, and her hazel eyes have caught on fire. And I realize that Daddy has returned.

He must be standing in the doorway. I can smell the cold air and the manure. He steps into the room and ruffles my hair. He is looking at the doll I am holding. There are bubbles of spit on Mama's bottom lip.

"Good night, Fig," he says. And I say good night too. I say good night as I grab my backpack, and I leave as fast as I can.

I leave so fast, I don't realize I still have the naked fake Barbie until I'm in my room with the door shut behind me. And this is where I drop her. I let go like she's about to burn me.

In the morning, when I wake up, I go to the bathroom and the door to Mama's room is closed again. And I can hear her snoring, which she never used to do. I go back to my room to get dressed.

Before I put my socks on, I inspect my feet. They've always been big, but they've grown even larger; overnight, they are absolutely gigantic.

I pick up the naked fake Barbie and hold her so she can also see my feet.

"What do you think?" I ask. I talk in whispers, afraid of my own voice.

She zooms in, taking a closer look at my lotus boats. My toes are hairy and my nails are dirty and need to be trimmed. Mama is the one who cuts my nails. I pull the Barbie back really fast. She is disgusted. She stands in front of me, tilting her head to study my face. She puts her hands on her hips and shakes her head.

"*Something* must be done," she says, and then she blows out her breath the way I do after I've been holding it in and crossing my fingers to make a wish.

When the morning bell rings, I hide behind the shed and wait until everyone's inside.

And then I unzip my backpack and start pulling out the supplies—first the scissors, then the hammer. The roofing nails are still attached to one another by wire. The Ziploc baggie opened by accident inside my pack, and the little tubes of lipstick all spilled out. Gran gets these from the woman who goes door to door, from one old lady to the next, and always says, "Avon calling." These are samples and look exactly like regular lipsticks, only smaller. Gran has hundreds, but I've only stolen thirteen.

The last thing I take out is the naked fake Barbie doll.

I wrapped her up with rubber bands so she can't move anymore. I cut off the end of my shoelace and used it as a gag to silence her.

I didn't much like what she had to say.

Despite the rubber bands, she squirms around in my fist. The little arrows Mama made don't come off. They won't smear even if I spit on them and try to rub them away with my thumb. I cut off her hair and I can see the hundreds of tiny holes where her hair was fed through like one of the Chia Pets I've seen on the television. She is crying and looking at the ground where her hair landed in plastic clumps of platinum blond.

Next, I break off two of the roofing nails.

I put one nail between my lips as I hammer the other through her left hand. She is screaming as I attach her to the back of the shed, where the other kids carve their initials into the wood. The gag turns her screaming into a squeaking, and she is a mouse. The second nail bends and I have to get another, but it goes right in and the naked fake Barbie sticks to the shed like the letter *T*, only with a head. She passes out from the pain, and her head droops like a wilted flower.

I twist open a sample lipstick and smear it on her wrists. She opens her eyes, coming in and out of consciousness. She blinks her blue eyes as I hold her head up. I smear her eyes with lipstick, and she can't see me anymore. Her head just rolls when I let go.

The lipstick goes farther than I expected and I don't need another, except this one is too orange so I use a different one. It's bright red, and once I'm satisfied with its likeness to blood, I pack up.

I peek around the corner of the shed and make sure no one is around. I go straight to the nurse's office. I don't run, but I do walk fast.

I tell the nurse I've been in the bathroom with diarrhea. I act like I'm embarrassed to say that word: "diarrhea." She touches my forehead with the back of her hand and takes my temperature. The mercury climbs up to normal, and this is the only normalcy in my life. The nurse hands me some water and I gulp it down. When I'm done, she uses her hand to crumple the cone-shaped paper cup, which she tosses into the trash can.

I tell her I'm feeling much better. That I have an important test to take. I hold my breath and cross my fingers to make it work, and it does. The nurse writes a note for me to give to Mrs. Olson, which will excuse me from being marked down as tardy.

The dandelions are dying, but they're all I have. When I picked them, they bled white milk, and I had to wipe it off my fingers. These three flowers were the only ones left in our yard that hadn't yet gone to seed. When I cut my shoelace this morning, I messed up and cut off way too much, but using what's left I tie the dandelions into a bouquet. I wish I could do better. I wish I had some ribbon instead, and all I have for a card is a piece of pink construction paper I stole from the art room and a stubby pencil I can't go sharpen. Mrs. Olson continues to sit at her desk instead of going to eat lunch with the other teachers in the lounge.

I use the thin line of light shining into the coat closet to carefully write the note I wish someone would write to me:

Dear Sissy Baxter,

I'm sorry about your mother. I hope she gets better real soon.

Sincerely,
Fig Johnson

I fold the fibrous pink paper into an envelope to hold the wilted dandelions, and then I slip the package into the side pocket of Sissy Baxter's brand-new Strawberry Shortcake backpack. I sit down and I hold my breath and cross my fingers—please, please, please, let Sissy Baxter understand; please don't let her make fun of me instead.

Principal White looks uncomfortable in his clothes. Tight necktie, and the way his shirt seems to tug at his elbows. He sits on the other side of his gigantic desk—an island to separate his world from mine. He has a large calendar on his desk. When one month is over, you just tear away the sheet and the next month is there, waiting.

—
67

I look at the cardboard backs of all his framed photographs, and then I look at his nameplate, which reads PRINCIPAL WHITE.

In his back-to-school speech, Principal White said, "The difference between 'principle' and 'principal' is the word 'pal' that's in my title," and then he did that thing grown-ups do with their fingers that's supposed to look like quotation marks. "That's right," he said, "I am your *pal*." And when he laughed, I saw his big yellow teeth.

On the wall there is a framed photograph of Principal White holding a large fish. The fish is still alive, wet, and squirming; the fish is trying to escape the paper, ink, and glass. I recognize the river. This is the Silver River, but not the section that runs next to our farm and works as a property line. This section runs through Silver River Park on the other side of town.

In the photograph, Principal White is smiling. He wears a khaki hat with hooks and flies attached to the brim. Uncle Billy is a fly fisherman too.

This is why I know that these flies are also called lures.

The Principal White in the picture looks relaxed and comfortable in his clothes, unlike the man in front of me. He appears to be waiting but doesn't tell me why I'm here.

It's dark inside his office. The venetian blinds are slanted, and the sunlight stripes the air, highlighting all the dust. Gran says ninety percent of all household dust is dead skin. If this is true, just by breathing, the principal and I are eating each other. The word for this is "cannibalism." I can see the page in the dictionary from when I looked it up months ago. I used the wonky dictionary in the cabinet. There was a crease in the page and not a single one of Mama's check marks.

—

This is called a photographic memory.

I've been reading all the results from the tests I took at Social Services. I found the manila folder in Daddy's desk—in the drawer that is like a small filing cabinet. Inside the folder, I found the report on me, and next to mine was the one on Mama. The release papers from the hospital. Daddy put me and Mama next to the farm records and the bank statements.

There's a light knock on the door, and Principal White looks up from his paperwork. His glasses have thick, yellow lenses, which magnify his eyes. I look at my hands. I fold them in my lap the way some people do when they are praying. This is not the way Gran prays. She turns her fingers into a steeple—she is never soft, always stiff.

"Mrs. Olson," Principal White says. "Do come in—please, have a seat." And he gestures with his arm, showing her where to sit, the way a magician does before he makes something disappear or reappear. And for the millionth time, I wonder what happened to my tooth, the one I lost at Gran's.

My teacher sits on one of the chairs against the wall.

She sits on the edge of her seat, holding a bag I've never seen before. It looks like it was made from a blue plastic tarp, and there is a red zipper along the top. She sets it down, and her hands flutter to her lap as the slanted light from the blinds dissects her fat knees by turning them into stripes. I pick at the lint stuck to both of my knees because I am wearing cable-knit navy blue tights. I rub the scratchy material against my scabs, and once again I really want to pick, but there is no way to get my fingers inside my tights, not right now, so I press on the scabs instead.

I press until the soreness presses back.

A button on Principal White's telephone lights up red, and then it makes a buzzing sound. Principal White smiles at Mrs. Olson and pushes a different button, "Yes?" he says.

"Mrs. Johnson is here," a woman says, her voice garbled by the intercom at the same time that I can hear the real voice coming in from the slightly open door behind me.

I turn to watch Mama come in. Her long hair is loose around her shoulders, and her cheeks are flushed. She's wearing her favorite wool shawl and a pair of paint-splattered blue jeans. She has thick wool socks on, which she wears with her black cloth Mary Janes—the kind her friend sends to her from Chinatown in New York City.

I used to have a pair. Mine had a splash of embroidered red roses across the toes. I'm pretty sure I'm in trouble, and I wonder if this is making Mama snap back into reality. I hold my breath and cross my fingers.

Principal White waves his arm again, gesturing for my mother to take a seat. And it's just before she does that I see the rip in her jeans. I can see the curve from thigh to buttock, a flash of white skin and black cotton, and I press even harder on the scabs. Once Mama is settled in the chair next to me, the principal nods at Mrs. Olson to begin.

"The doll was first discovered this morning," Mrs. Olson says, and she can't seem to bring herself to look at Mama. "This morning, the recess monitor spotted a crowd of kids behind the shed and went to investigate." Mrs. Olson pauses, as if she's out of breath. Mama is staring at her, and I can tell this bothers Mrs. Olson.

"The children were all gathered round, and that's when the monitor sent for Mr. White. Mr. White asked all us teachers to come and have a look—in case one of us could recognize it," and when Mrs. Olson says the word "it," she whispers the way Gran does with certain words.

Principal White leans forward, resting his elbows on his desk. "Mrs. Olson thought she recognized the doll," he explains.

"Well," Mama says, smiling cheerfully, "you either did or you didn't." And from the corner of my eye, I watch Mama turn into the Queen of Hearts.

Mrs. Olson nods, looking at the bag. She tries to begin once again. "It's just—it had been so mutilated," she says. "But after close inspection, I decided it had to be the doll belonging to your daughter. I remembered one of the observations made during Fig's show-and-tell in regard to the doll's extreme flexibility. It was this very characteristic that helped me identify it as Fig's Barbie."

Mama uncrosses her legs and does not cross them again, no matter how hard I hold my breath and cross my fingers. Principal White blushes and has to look away. Mama is now smiling her polite but angry smile. She says, "I have no idea what you're talking about."

Principal White nods to Mrs. Olson, who nods back.

Mrs. Olson grabs a Kleenex from the box on the principal's desk. And another tissue pops up to replace it. Mrs. Olson opens her blue bag and uses the white tissue as protection as she pulls out the fake naked Barbie. She holds the doll at a distance like she's afraid it might be contagious.

One of Barbie's hands is torn off, and I can see the wire inside that makes her so bendy. Someone tried to remove the red and orange lipstick, and I can see the black marks my mother made when she was pretending to be a plastic surgeon.

Mama takes my hand, cupping it with both of hers. Her palms are sweaty, but she keeps smiling at Principal White. "Fig isn't allowed to play with Barbie," she says, and she says it like Barbie is another girl my age. Then she squeezes my hand, and my heart starts racing inside my chest.

"Barbie is the ultimate icon of a male-chauvinistic society," Mama says, and now she is an actress playing herself. A star in her own movie—everything practiced, and I'm just a prop. Mama stands. "Come along, darling," she says. "I simply don't have the time for such puritanical nonsense."

Principal White also stands. He has no idea what's happening, and I almost feel sorry for him. He is trying to show her my backpack. Full of evidence, it would prove what they are trying to tell her. But my mother ignores them. And when she turns around, they both can see the hole in her jeans.

Mama drags me out of the office and through the maze of secretaries, who all look up from their typewriters and telephones, covering their O-shaped mouths with their perfectly manicured hands. My mother swings the glass door open and pushes me into the hall, where our footsteps echo. I hold my breath and cross my fingers.

Outside, Mama opens the car door and I climb in. She starts to come around to her side, but then she stops. Standing in the road, she looks at Principal White's window, and I wonder if he's in there watching her as well. Then Mama does something I have never seen her do before.

She reaches into her pocket and pulls out a pack of cigarettes. She puts a long white cigarette between her lips and dramatically lights it with a strike-anywhere match. She takes a long drag and extinguishes the flame on the match with her exhale.

My mother comes around to her side of the car, opening the door and sliding into her seat. She rolls her window down and starts the car—smoking the entire time. Before she drives away, Mama turns to look at me. She smiles, but her lips are shut tight. And as she smiles two thin clouds of gray come twisting out of each nostril, and my mother is a fire-breathing dragon.

October 29, 1982
According to the man on the evening news, baby Azaria Chamberlain was not taken and killed by a dingo. Her mother is convicted for her murder and sentenced to life in prison. This time they do not show the photograph of the mother holding her baby. They just show the picture of the black dress, trimmed in red. And then a picture of the campsite where Azaria died. Ayers Rock glows red against the blue Australian sky. I watch the program all by myself.

Principal White and Daddy came to a compromise and created a suitable punishment for my vandalism. According to the dictionary, vandalism is the willful or malicious destruction or defacement of public or private property. I had to look up "malicious," too. It comes from the word "malice"—a desire to harm others or to see them suffer. This word made me think of Barbie.

I could see her in my head all over again. The way she squirmed inside those rubber bands and how her face responded to the nails and the hammer—how her eyes squeezed shut and her face scrunched up and she didn't look like a doll anymore because she was in so much pain.

She looked like the smallest woman in the world.

And for a split second, she looked like Mama.

The incident will not go down on my permanent record—Principal White made this promise to my father—and unlike my grandmother's hair, these records really are permanent. "Had the circumstances not been what they were," Daddy said, "you would have been suspended." My father doesn't bother to define the circumstance. I know exactly what he means. He means Mama.

Instead of suspension, I am benched. For two weeks straight, I have to sit on the bench during lunch and recess, where all the other kids can see me.

And this is how everyone comes to know that I'm the girl who crucified Barbie.

Halloween is always difficult for farm kids to celebrate because we can't trick-or-treat unless we have our parents take us into town. So Douglas Elementary throws a big party every year and everyone, including the teachers, comes to school dressed in costume.

Principal White is a fisherman and Mrs. Olson is a witch.

The party is in the gymnasium. Set up along the walls are long tables are covered with paper tablecloths, dishes full of candy, and punch bowls with dry-ice and Hawaiian Punch. A disco ball turns, throwing fragmented light around the room. They always play the same songs: the theme from *The Addams Family*, the song about the "one-eyed, one-horned, flyin' purple people eater," and, for the grand finale, "The Monster Mash."

I've never had a store-bought costume before, but Mama was too tired to make one this year. Daddy says the doctors are trying to regulate her medication. "For now," he says, "we need to let her rest." So Gran went to Kmart. One size fits all, the dress is made from tulle and silver sequins, and the costume name, *Princess Cinderella*, is written across the package in sparkly blue cursive. There's a plastic tiara that's supposed to look like silver, embellished with the same fake diamonds that adorn the matching wand—not that Cinderella had a wand. The wand belonged to Cinderella's fairy godmother, and the fairy godmother used it to make everything better. I wish I had a fairy godmother. If Mama and Daddy both died, I'd have to go live with Gran.

Princess Cinderella also comes with glass slippers. A pair of high heels made from clear plastic that are way too big for me. Gran wadded up toilet paper and stuffed the toes to match my white tights but it's still impossible to walk in them.

Halloween 1982

Daddy and Gran must have forgotten about my punishment, but Mrs. Olson does not.

"There are absolutely no exceptions," she says. And then she tells me to sit on the bench in the hall by the party. I watch the kids walk back and forth between the gym and the bathrooms.

I am not allowed in the gymnasium.

Candace Sherman is also Princess Cinderella. Her blond hair falls in perfect ringlets around her tiara. She clicks across the linoleum in a pair of glass slippers that look like they were made just for her, even though our feet can't be that much different in size.

Candace Sherman makes it a point to go to the bathroom a lot. Each time, she brings along another girl. She brings Sissy Baxter first. Sissy is the only one who doesn't laugh. She looks at me and bites her lip while Candace whispers in her ear, and when Sissy looks at the floor Candace pushes her so hard, she almost falls down. And I wonder if this is because of the stupid dandelions.

When it's Tanya Jenkins's turn, Tanya turns hysterical. She can't stop laughing at me; she sounds like a hyena. But Candace Sherman doesn't just bring Sissy Baxter or Tanya Jenkins. She brings along all the girls she normally would never talk to: girls like me. She puts her arms around them—these girls who are targets of her teasing too, and parades them past. Candace points at me and whispers. She makes each girl look, and then she says something that makes them laugh.

As soon as they have their backs turned to me, I wave my stupid wand. I turn them into toads and worms. I turn Candace Sherman into a schizophrenic, but it's not awful enough. So I try again. This time, I turn her into me.

CHAPTER FOUR

PALINDROMES

doll: n. 1. *A child's toy representing a human being.*
2. Slang. *a. An attractive person b. A woman c. A sweetheart*
3. Doll, *nickname for* Dorothy.

doll: v. 1. *To pet, indulge* 2. *To dress up; to dress smartly:*
She got dolled up for the party.

July 10, 1983

Mama gets third-degree sunburns from working in the flower garden. And it isn't because she didn't wear her straw hat, or a pound of sunscreen like me, as we pulled the weeds and thinned the zinnias. But her new medication makes her burn no matter what: face, neck, shoulders, back.

I stand in the doorway wearing my suit of flesh unharmed by the same sun, and I watch Daddy apply aloe to Mama's burns. He uses a leaf from the plant in the living room to soothe her angry skin as she sits on the edge of her bed with her fingers curled into tight white fists. She is burned even where her shirt covered her, and she flinches despite Daddy's gentle touch. And then she begins to cry. Large white blisters burst from Mama's freckled shoulders; full of water, they, too, want to weep. Mama cries, and she doesn't wipe her tears away.

—

"I'm screwed either way," she says. "If I take the medicine, I can't go outside. But if I don't—" And this is when her voice trails away. Mama looks out the window at the setting sun, and she repeats herself: "If I don't take it," she says, "then I can't do anything."

I sit inside the potting shed.

It is cold in here with the walls made from stone. The one window looks at the garden, and standing in the distance is the orchard. Mama's straw hat hangs from a hook, and on the worktable amid the stacks of terra-cotta pots her work gloves remain as she left them; the stiff leather fingers continue to curl as if her hands are still inside. Ready to dig more holes and plant more flowers.

Last summer, I was helping Mama plant herbs when she suddenly sighed and smiled at me. "This is my sanctuary," she said, and then she turned her attention back to the starts in their trays. I watched as she carefully jiggled the baby thyme from its cradle of black plastic, roots and all. I think about the other kind of time, as in clocks and calendars. And when I wonder if yesterday was the last time Mama will get to work in the garden, I hold my breath and cross my fingers that I am very wrong.

Christmas 1982
Daddy's sitting in his chair, and Mama's on the rug with me. We're in our nightgowns—long, white, and soft. Marmalade watches from her spot by the fire. Mama's long hair is trying to stand up, and Mama says my hair is doing the same thing.

"It's static electricity," she says, "because we're crawling around the way we are."

And I think about the static on the television—all the fuzzy black and white dots, and the way it sounds like silence even though I know silence doesn't have a sound.

Daddy ruffles my hair and laughs.

I feel my hair moving; it stands up and dances, and I am Medusa. My hair is full of snakes. I don't want electricity inside my body. I hold my breath and cross my fingers to try to make it go away. Mama says I am mostly made from water. And I'm scared I'll be electrocuted.

While the presents from my parents are always wrapped, the ones from Santa never are. Wrapped in blue snowflakes, the new calendar full of unicorns is from Mama. Daddy gives me every single book in the series called The Littles. Mama jokes about his masculine choice of wrapping paper: Christmas-colored plaid.

A baby doll is waiting for me underneath the tree as if she just arrived from nowhere—delivered by the stork, she is nothing but a magic trick. I don't believe in Santa Claus—not anymore. Not after all the teeth I've lost—the one that disappeared, and the ones I've been collecting, keeping for myself. I keep them in the enveloped marked SCHIZOPHRENIA. I keep this envelope and my teeth in the space between my mattress and my box spring. And I don't believe in Santa or the tooth fairy or the Easter Bunny.

I don't believe in anything.

The baby doll is under the tree like she's asleep inside her beautiful cradle made from wood the color of black cherries. A heart has been carved away at each end like the space the cookie cutters left in the dough for Valentine's Day last year. Tucked around the doll is a tiny patchwork quilt. And I recognize the fabric. There are squares cut from all my old dresses and bits of faded denim from worn-out blue jeans. Interrupting the pattern of squares and triangles are embroidered swirling flowers and looping spirals. Drawn in bright thread, they zigzag and meander. And they trespass.

Daddy calls it a crazy quilt. And I whisper the word "crazy," but no one hears me.

"Do you like her?" Mama asks. "You can hold her if you'd like."

The doll looks like she is sleeping, and Mama is staring at me—eyes on fire, but she is talking normal. Her words come out at the right speed, right volume. No spit. "You should call her Turtle," Mama says, "Because her face is all scrunched up." And Mama scrunches her face too.

Even though I didn't want a doll, she still had a name: Elizabeth Rose—a beautiful name with an even prettier one in the middle. I didn't get a middle name.

Just Fig or Fiona, just weird or old fashioned.

Mama picks Turtle up and holds her for me to see. She shows me her dress—periwinkle blue, the color of my new favorite crayon, and then she lifts the dress so I can see her diaper. Turtle is the kind of doll that pees.

Mama shows me all the ways to hold a baby.

Then she settles with Turtle in her arms the way Sissy Baxter's mother held Sissy's brand-new little brother back in kindergarten.

Mrs. Baxter came to show the baby to the class. She sat in the rocking chair Miss Ada always used for story time. Mrs. Baxter sat in the rocking chair but she didn't read out loud from any of Miss Ada's beautiful picture books. Instead, Miss Ada helped us gather around Mrs. Baxter in what she called a semicircle, which is the same shape as a crescent moon. And we were allowed to look but not to touch. And this is how I sit with Mama. She shows me all the different ways a person can hold a doll. I look, but I don't dare touch.

*　*　*　*

I keep Turtle on my window seat, tucked into her wooden cradle, wrapped in the crazy quilt. I keep her there and I never play with her.

Mama comes into my room, again and again, always asking if I just adore my new doll. And I cross my fingers to lie. I don't have to hold my breath. I cross my fingers, and I say, "Yes," and Mama is already sitting in the window seat, running her finger down Turtle's plastic nose, which I've been told is how she used to help me fall asleep when I was still a baby.

I see the way Mama is eyeing the plastic baby bottles, still imprisoned in their package on the floor beneath my desk. This is where I keep them. These bottles are special bottles. They make Turtle pee. Filled with water, you stick the hard nipple into the hole in Turtle's hard mouth and let the water run through her body until she wets her diaper.

Turtle came with doll-size disposable diapers, but Mama made more by cutting up all my old cloth ones—that is, the cloth diapers Daddy didn't already ruin. He uses them as rags to apply linseed oil and beeswax to the wood he works in his shed. My father has a way with wood.

Mama is looking at the bottles still captured between the clear plastic and glossy cardboard, when I tell her I prefer to breast-feed instead. Only I say "nurse." And this is when she tilts her head and looks at me. I hold my breath and cross my fingers to make her smile, and she does.

She smiles at me, and she says, "Good for you, Fig."

Mama's features are no longer sharp—not the way they used to be. Her face is getting puffy, and her body is becoming softer and softer. She blames it on water retention. Whenever I can, I cuddle up next to her and we spend the winter as one. Hibernating together, we read away the cold evenings and the weekends between the days when I have to go to school. We sit in the living room on the red velvet sofa by the fire or under the heavy quilts in Mama and Daddy's big brass bed.

Last week when we went to the library, I tried to check out *The Headless Cupid* again, but this time Mama wouldn't let me. This time she flipped through it, reading different sections to herself. Then she closed the book and put it back on the shelf, looked at me, and said, "No. You just aren't ready yet. But, Fig," she said, "I swear I will let you read it when the right time comes—and I promise you, it will only make it that much better. I swear it will be worth the wait. You just wait and see," she said, and then she kissed me on my third eye.

So I am reading *The Littles* instead while Mama devours Virginia Woolf; she is trying to read every book she ever wrote—and her essays, too. Mama either borrows the books from the library or buys them from the bookstore in Lawrence. She brings them home and stacks the books on the floor by her bed. Marmalade loves to rub against this tower and often knocks it over in the middle of the night.

Mama reads certain passages out loud and explains how Virginia was known for writing stream of consciousness.

"This style of writing," Mama says, "attempts to mimic the way the human brain actually works—the way we think, or rather the way we dream while we are still awake. The thought process is a constant blending of perceptions, memories, and epiphanies. The word stream implies the flow of thoughts or words, uninterrupted or censored, and not always punctuated, because ideas are never neat or tidy, nor are they linear. Our thoughts circulate, Fig. Our ideas move like water."

Mama used to read for hours at a time, but now she falls asleep between the pages. I think she stops and talks to me as much as she does just to try to stay awake.

"I hate this medication," she often mutters, and even though she's talking more to herself than to me, I have to hold my breath and cross my fingers because it's my job to make sure she doesn't stop taking it. Even if it means she can't work in the flower garden like she used to. Even if it causes her to fall asleep whenever she tries to read.

Tonight, she drifts away, and her hands are a cradle to hold her book. Tonight, she's reading *To the Lighthouse*, and yesterday she finally finished *The Waves*, which Mama said "was like drowning, only I was drowning inside the dreams of all the different characters in the book."

And I wonder if it helps to write about water when one is writing stream of consciousness.

I take the book, careful to keep her place with my fingers as I locate Mama's bookmark; it got buried by the quilt when Mama folded it over—lately, Mama has been getting really hot. "I'm burning up," she will say as she peels off her sweater or kicks away the covers. I find the bookmark, only it's not a real bookmark, and I wonder what happened to the one I gave her—the one with the water-color butterfly and the long blue silk ribbon.

Instead, she's using one of the printouts from Eudora Drug—the ones from the pharmacist that come stapled to the white paper bags full of Mama's endless medication. This one is for Valium.

VALIUM is typed in boldface at the top of the printout and

highlighted by a thin strip of bright yellow. This bright yellow is fluorescent like the colors all the popular girls at school wear these days. Only they call it "Day-Glo"—these girls who wear pants with stirrups, and a hundred rubber bracelets to swallow their perfect arms, while I just wear what I find inside my closet or dresser drawers. Clothing picked out by someone else. Clothing mostly picked out by Gran.

Mama has three available refills of Valium remaining.

I scan the possible side effects—dizziness, a spinning sensation, blurred vision, dry mouth.

I tuck the printout for Valium into the book and put Virginia away for the night. Virginia and her stream will rest between Mama's water glass and the telephone, and when I pull the chain on the lamp the light turns off and the night comes flooding in to my mother's bedroom like a jar of black ink spilling—and I think, *Everything moves like water.*

Kansas is still covered in a crust of yellow-white snow and contained by a sky dome of dull gray—but the weather is growing warmer, and Daddy is racing against the fast-approaching spring to put his father's red-belly tractor back together again. With or without Uncle Billy, Daddy spends every day in the barn working on what he calls "the beast."

He torches iron rods until the metal is angry hot, and he fills the air with blue-white sparks and the hot smell of melted metal. The black lenses of his protective eyewear reflect the display of shooting stars, but despite his determination, Daddy comes home every day cursing yet another failed attempt to resurrect this machine.

Sometimes I watch my father work, and other times I lie on the floor outside my mother's bedroom, surrounded by the portraits of my father's family. They stare down at me from their oval frames, where they float amid a garden of wallpaper roses. I lie here listening to the softness of my mother resting, and I let my fingers wander. They search for scabs to worry, but I haven't any, so they worry the edge of the old Oriental runner instead. When Mama does reemerge, she always appears refreshed. She never asks why I'm on the floor—she just smiles at me and pulls me up. And together we go downstairs to fix some tea, eat cookies, and read some more.

March 21, 1983
I try to blink away the sleep.

Mama is wrapping me in her wool shawl and telling me to sit, and then she's helping me step into my galoshes. She holds my hand and guides me down the stairs. I am a baby bird under a Mama-bird wing. Daddy's outside in the truck, and the engine is running.

It still looks like night, but Mama says, "It's almost morning."

We get in the truck and drive in silence. It's a Monday, the first day of spring break, and for a second I wonder if we're going on a trip, but we don't go far. Daddy pulls over and parks next to the pasture where the pigs have been. I look at Mama, and she smiles, nodding her head. She says yes without saying anything at all. She brushes away my bangs and kisses me on my third eye the way she always does.

I'm careful to be quiet the way they are.

Daddy pushes the top wire down and steps over the short fence with his long legs. Mama lifts me over, and when Daddy takes me he holds me long enough that it's a hug. And when he sets me down, I grow tiny again in the tall Johnsongrass.

———

We walk across the pasture, past the stable, and still we continue walking. We stop once the pasture meets the woods. This is where the tallest cottonwoods on the farm stand guard. They dip their roots into the deep farmer's ditch and drink forever from the lazy water.

The sun is rising, and the horizon turns watercolor pink. Mama sits and invites me onto her lap, taking her shawl and wrapping the soft wool around the two of us. And I think this is how it's supposed to be. Everything is working out—Daddy was right after all.

It was just a matter of time.

My father squats down beside us, chewing on a blade of grass. He uses a flashlight to show me where Matilda is, but as soon as the first piglet begins to come, we don't need the light anymore.

The gilt lies on her side like nothing is happening. Like she's still asleep. But then the piglet slides out, feet first. The head gets stuck inside the mother, and just when I think he'll never come he does. He sniffs his mother's tail, and then he tries to stand. He falls, but on his second try he makes it to all fours. He tries to walk away, into the woods, but he can't. He is still attached to his mother by the spiral of blue umbilical cord—a leash to keep him near. The cord stretches, and as the firstborn strains toward the woods, another is born.

This one also tries to run away.

Matilda has delivered six baby pigs by the time the roosters have stopped calling in the new day. The babies come covered in wet cobwebs that Mama calls the afterbirth. The black-and-white newborns wobble, and soon are sticky with mud and dead grass.

"It's good for them to eat the dirt," Mama says. "It's full of iron."

They root around, clumsy and unstable, except for the one who never moves at all—the only baby who doesn't try to run away.

Daddy starts to build a temporary fence to keep the other pigs away from Matilda. Mama rearranges her body and my body—she is growing restless. She wraps the shawl around my shoulders before she stands, and she tells me she's going to walk back to the house to make breakfast. She takes long strides across the pasture, her white nightgown parting the Johnsongrass, and it isn't long before I can't see her anymore.

I stay to watch Matilda and her babies.

It gets hot and I let the shawl slip off my shoulders. Kicking off my galoshes, I wiggle my toes, which are tiny and white compared with the dark bristle of the gilt and the deep black of the torn-up pasture. All the living piglets have nursed, and Matilda has licked them clean, cut them loose, and consumed their placentas by the time Mama returns with a small bucket of boiled potatoes and the picnic basket. She dumps the potatoes on the ground, and the mother pig eats without getting up.

Mama has a thermos of milky sweet coffee and, wrapped inside paper towels, toasted English muffins with butter and chokecherry jam. She has two red-and-white sticks of peppermint candy that we use as straws to suck the juice from swollen oranges.

And this is when I make my decision: Today, when I go back into the house, I am going to march up the stairs and go straight to my bedroom. I'm going to mark the square for today on my unicorn calendar. I will make a big black X and this X will mark the day Mama got all the way better. But for now I sit with Mama in the shade, and we don't talk. We sit and eat and watch instead.

I'm ready not to understand everything I see.

When Matilda has finished eating her potatoes, she shakes the nursing piglets off her body by standing for the first time since she gave birth. Her babies try to latch on again, but she pushes them away with her snout. Then Matilda approaches the dead piglet, and the others fall back. Matilda sniffs the small, still body before she picks it up with her mouth. And this is when Mama catches her breath. She clenches her pale hands into fists that turn whiter because she's squeezing herself way too hard, and I know what she is thinking: Mama thinks Matilda is going to eat her baby.

The mother pig carries the stillborn to the edge of the woods where the wild raspberries grow thick. Matilda places the baby on the ground. Using her front hooves and snout, she begins to tear at the earth while the stillborn waits. Matilda finishes, and returns to her dead baby to nuzzle it toward the hole. And then I can't see the baby anymore, cradled now by a shallow grave. As Matilda covers her stillborn with a blanket of brown-black soil, Mama begins to cry, but that doesn't mean she's acting crazy. She is having a normal reaction to something sad.

Mama leans forward, uncurls her hands, and presses them against the earth, palms down. So I do the same.

It feels like how praying looks.

I stretch my fingers as far as they will go and push my palms against the cold dirt. I am trying to feel all the bodies buried below, but Mama gives up almost right away. She leans back, and then she's standing, shielding her eyes with dirty hands. She watches Daddy work.

I remain very still and will stay like this even after Mama drifts away and Daddy has finished building the fence. I will stay, bent forward, palms down.

I am trying to feel my dead relatives. Daddy's father is buried in the cemetery behind the Sacred Heart of Mary, and even though his body is far away, this earth is connected to his earth. Mama's parents turned to ash, but with my hands pressed against the ground, I still feel connected to them somehow. Connected to all the people I never got to know.

And I will stay like this until I feel their bodies pushing back.

Back in my bedroom, I select the black Magic Marker from the pile of markers in my desk drawer. The one that smells like licorice.

The unicorn calendar is on the wall in front of me, and I take the marker and I draw an X.

The X is big and black—a railroad crossing, it marks the spot. Like a cobweb, the X reaches into each corner of the white square for March 24, 1983, and I stand here admiring the geometry. I don't leave until the scent of licorice finally disappears. Then I follow the scent of spring—the hint of lilac, overpowered by the deep musk of freshly turned fields, and the smell of animals being born everywhere in Douglas County. Their numbers cancel out the one who didn't make it.

I wander past Mama's herb and flower gardens, untended now, and yet I find the unruliness beautiful—the wild nature of the flowers and the weeds in the otherwise domesticated space. I pass these gardens where the dandelions are just poking through and the bindweed is beginning to spiral away, out of control. And I walk through the orchard, where the apple blossoms, two weeks early, are white and delicate, their centers dotted with sticky yellow stamen hearts.

I pass through the bramble of wild raspberry where the buds are still tight and green and the new thorns haven't yet formed, still harmless. And here I stand, in the cold shade of tall trees, watching the farmer's ditch rush forth. Barely contained by the bosom of the mossy banks, this water washes everything away. I watch this rushing water, and I can only imagine the rising levels of the Silver River. But as much as I'd like to go see, there are still rules—said and not said—about where I'm allowed and not allowed to go.

Uncle Billy was the one who answered the ad for a used tractor in Missouri, and today he and Daddy are driving down there to buy it. "We'll be gone for one night and two days," my father says.

My uncle arrives at eight thirty in the morning with a box of doughnuts, and Mama smiles at me. "Just this once," she says.

I choose a glazed doughnut, but Mama surprises me by picking one with chocolate frosting and cream filling. She keeps smiling at me as she licks her fingers between sticky bites, and when she's done the chocolate on her teeth turns her into a fairy-tale witch. Uncle Billy eats three doughnuts in a row without looking at what they are and washes them down with two tall glasses of cold milk. Daddy dunks his powdered doughnut into a cup of coffee as he studies the road map on the table, and when he's done there are still half a dozen left.

Grabbing the box of doughnuts, Uncle Billy says, "These are for the new mother." And he winks at me. "Not only does Matilda deserve a treat, they'll sweeten up her meat. Ancient family secret—so, Fig, don't forget."

"You're so full of crap," Daddy says, standing up and folding the map into a neat rectangle. "Our family never raised pigs till now." No one mentions that I never eat the meat I am served.

When Uncle Billy comes back from the pigsty, he and Daddy climb into my father's Dodge Ram and drive away, with Mama and me waving good-bye from the front porch. The redbud is in blossom, as is the bush honeysuckle trying to strangle the ditch along

---

the driveway. We watch the dust settle, and we still have most of the day before Gran comes to stay with us. I'm hoping Mama will want to take a walk with me to pick the early spring wildflowers, the yellow fawn lilies, the violets, and the spiderwort, and maybe even press them between sheets of wax paper using the encyclopedia, but when I ask her she says she needs to get the house ready for my grandmother.

For dinner, Gran brings Chinese takeout from Lawrence in paper cartons, with plasticware, fortune cookies, and those paper placemats with the red-and-white illustrations of the Chinese zodiac. Mama tells me what sign I am.

I am a tiger.

The picture shows the profile of a tiger walking. Instead of black and orange, the stripes are red and white. Mama says she's a tiger too.

Gran stands before the kitchen sink, waiting for the dishwater to fill. With her back to us, she says, "That figures. Two peas in a pod, and no room for anyone else."

I read the description for tiger: *You are sensitive, emotional, and capable of great love. However, you have a tendency to get carried away and be stubborn about what you think is right; often seen as a "hothead" or rebel. Your sign shows you would be excellent as a boss, an explorer, a racecar driver, or a matador.*

Mama reads the description over my shoulder. "Racecar," she says. "That's a palindrome, but it's not as good as 'Madam I am Adam.' I do love a good palindrome."

"What in the world is a palindrome?" Gran asks, but doesn't turn to look at us.

—

"It's a word or phrase spelled the same backward as it is forward," Mama says.

"In other words, nonsense," Gran says, and ties an apron around her waist. She stuffs her hands into the pink rubber gloves she brought to the farm along with her leather suitcase and her leather bible.

"No," Mama says, winking at me. "'Nonsense' is *not* a palindrome."

Last night, I heard Mama talking to Daddy in their bedroom. I crouched outside their door and watched through the keyhole. Mama was crying. "I don't need a babysitter," she kept saying, and the more she said it, the more the *s* in "babysitter" hissed. She told Daddy we'd be fine without my grandmother watching over, but Daddy didn't say anything. He just stood at the window staring at the open Kansas sky through the old wavy glass.

"Mom," I say.

I blurt it out the way people do when they are interrupting. Mom is easy, but it takes Mama a second to understand. I think she thought I was suddenly calling her something new, which makes sense, because everyone treats her different now.

"That's right," Mama says. "Both 'mom' *and* 'dad' are palindromes."

I think about this, and it makes perfect sense; there's something reliable about the backward being the same as the forward.

Gran shakes her head, setting a plate to dry in the dish rack. It's upside down, and I can't see the two lovebirds in the sky. Whenever I help Mama wash the dishes, she tells me the story behind the Blue Willow—how the birds are the souls of two lovers who committed suicide because they were forbidden in life to be together. I didn't know what suicide was until Mama tried to kill herself.

—

At first, I think Mama is looking at the plate too—thinking what I'm thinking, but then I see she's not. She's studying Gran instead. She watches Gran wash another plate, and as she does, Mama's face softens. Grabbing a dish towel, Mama goes to stand beside her mother-in-law and begins to dry the dishes by hand, which is something Mama never does. She always leaves them to drip-dry on the rack.

I take my Chinese zodiac placemat upstairs to my room. In the window seat, I do the math. I figure out what sign Daddy is. A dog: *A dog will never let you down. Honest and faithful to those they love, dogs are plagued by constant worry.* But then I realize Mama is wrong. She's right about us being the same sign, only we're not tigers. We are rabbits.

We are shy. We avoid adventure. We prefer to stay at home.

I decide Mama must be right. She said something about the years being different in China than they are here. I try not to get too confused. I ignore the tiny caption under every sign where the years are written.

If it's 1983 in China like it is here, then right now it's the Year of the Pig.

I fold the placemat and stick it under my mattress with my baby teeth and the *Alice in Wonderland* calendar that Mama gave me on my seventh birthday. I'm collecting things that are important, and this is where I can keep them safe—these souvenirs, these things to keep me from forgetting. Someday, they will help me tell the story of my life.

It's dusk when Daddy and Uncle Billy pull into the driveway. The trailer is hitched to the back of the truck with the green tractor secured to it by way of rope and sturdy metal clips. Mama is right

—

there by the passenger-side door where Daddy's sitting, and through the open window he looks at her like he can't breathe.

The second he steps out, she throws her arms around his neck.

Over Daddy's shoulder, I see the way Mama looks to make sure my grandmother is watching. Mama leans back, away from Daddy, but she's still clutching his arms, and this keeps her from falling. She looks at Daddy like he's been gone forever, like the lovers in the movies Mama always says are terrible but watches anyway. Then she straightens herself out and frames his face with her hands and kisses him in a way that makes me uncomfortable. Her kissing sounds wet, and it looks like she is trying to eat my father's face.

Maybe I should have waited a little longer to mark the calendar, to X the spot for the day my mother got better.

Uncle Billy clears his throat, and I realize he's standing behind Gran and me. He puts his arms around us, cupping our shoulders with his hands. The light from the barn turns on like it does every evening at dusk, and in the dirt, our shadow turns the three of us into one—a lumpy person with two arms and six legs. We are almost a spider or an octopus and I am almost eight and nineteen minus eight is eleven, as in eleven more years to go.

"What do you think of the John Deere?" Uncle Billy asks.

He looks at the tractor the way Mama looks at art. The tractor reminds me of a grasshopper, and even though it's nowhere near as pretty as the old red one, I'm happy to have something else to look at while Mama eats Daddy. Gran and I nod our heads, and we tell him we like the tractor.

CHAPTER FIVE

TRESPASSING

dis·in·te·grate: v. 1. *To separate into pieces; fragment.*
2. *To decay or undergo a transformation.*

November 6, 1983

I'm in the third grade, and we're supposed to choose a fairy tale and make our own book at home. Mama is excited. I don't tell her I want to do *Rapunzel*, because she's already decided on *Little Red Riding Hood*.

My mother took a multimedia-art class when she was an under-graduate at Cornell, before she met Daddy, and this is where she learned to make pop-up books. She thinks it'll be fun to make one for the assignment, and laughs.

"You'll be the only kid who does," she says, as if this was a good thing.

Mama buys tubes of paint, an X-acto knife, and two variety packs of Sharpies from the Hobby Lobby in Topeka. Not just black, but all the colors of the rainbow—one set of regular markers, and one set of fine-tip. And she buys two new scissors, a pair for me and a pair for her.

Back home, before we begin, she takes all the cereal outside. She dumps each box—opened or unopened—into the yard and laughs.

—

The crows Daddy tries to keep away with faceless straw men come, and for days will peck the dead grass for cornflakes and Cheerios.

My scissors are meant for paper, but Mama's are for cloth—they're expensive, stainless steel. The shine is dangerous.

She does most of the cutting because my scissors don't make it through the thin cereal-box cardboard. I make the axe for the wood-cutter. I use a toothpick for the handle and a scrap of cardboard for the blade. It starts out silver, but Mama says, "Add more red."

I use a red paint pen, and it's leaky—hard to control.

Mama forgets to have us write anything, but the pictures say enough. There is red paint all over the kitchen table, all over me, and on Mama, too. Daddy comes in for dinner and studies Mama's face. She talks to him in a shrill voice that doesn't sound like Mama. Daddy takes Mama into the guest bedroom that is also Daddy's office, and where he sleeps these days. And I am left alone with my dinner. The spaghetti is from the night before, still cold.

Instead of eating, I carefully separate the red-soaked pages and don't tear a single one. The woods pop up, then the wolf, the house, the grandmother herself, and finally the woodcutter, his axe spring-ing upward. I look at the wolf's belly, the damage already done, and little Red's head poking out from the slit that Mama made.

I can hear them through the heating vent in the floor—their voices tinny. Daddy says, "You have to try to let go." A pause. "Are you having any of those *other* thoughts?"

Mama yells at him. She says she's perfectly fine. Then she says she's stifled. She says it like it's Daddy's fault. And then I hear the sound of Mama leaving. The front door slams, and then her Volvo spits out gravel because she's driving too fast on the driveway.

Little Red Riding Hood looks at me. Because she's made from

cardboard, her neck is stiff. *Why did you cut me out?* she says. *I didn't want to be saved.*

I study Little Red Riding Hood. I think about telling her, *I didn't ask to be born*, but I don't. I don't say anything.

The next morning, the pop-up book is gone and Mama hasn't yet returned. I wonder where she is. Daddy keeps me out of school for the day. He needs my help on the farm. They are weaning all the baby lambs by taking them away from their mothers. And the world is loud with the sound of crying sheep.

The following day, I go back to school and Mrs. Jefferson takes me aside during free time. She says not to worry, that she's talked to my Daddy and she understands.

She says, "Don't worry about turning the assignment in," and then she pats me on the head.

When school is over, I don't get on the school bus like I normally do. I've been told to wait outside for Gran to pick me up. Before I left the farm, Daddy said, "Your mama needs some time to rest." In the back of my grandmother's Buick, I find my suitcase. Gran packed it for me. She packed it with everything she thinks I need. This includes Turtle and the unopened package of baby bottles.

Every house on Gran's block looks the same only painted three different colors. Gran has one of the baby blues, but there is also beige and red. And everyone has a paper accordion turkey in their picture window, and some people have dried corn hanging on their front doors.

Come Christmas, the turkeys will be replaced by Christmas trees, and plastic Santas will drive sleighs across the tidy yards, but it still hasn't snowed and that's all anyone ever wants to talk about.

Uncle Billy comes over every night after Gran and I have finished eating dinner—only Gran calls dinner "supper." He brings chocolate malts in tall foam cups from the ice cream parlor in downtown Lawrence, where he's been working a construction job. My uncle can do almost anything, and even Daddy refers to him as a "jack of all trades."

For three nights in a row, the three of us watch television, but on the fourth night Uncle Billy persuades Gran to play cards instead. Even though the dining room table has already been cleared, my grandmother insists on using the card table. "That's what it's for," she says.

Uncle Billy slides it out from where it's kept behind the sideboard. As he unfolds each leg he says, "Ma is a stickler for tradition and the simple comforts that come from the basic security of a good, solid routine." And he doesn't wink until after she's turned away to collect the deck of playing cards from the junk drawer in the kitchen.

Jesus Christ hangs on the wall as we play Kings on the Corners. Daddy carved it from a block of blond linden, before I was born. He made it for Gran after my grandfather died so she wouldn't get lonely. Once upon a time, this Jesus hung from the wall above the fireplace. He hung in the same spot where *Christina's World* now hangs. This is Mama's favorite painting, but it makes me feel sad. It makes me feel stuck, like I need to climb out of my body.

Daddy is not just a farmer. He made my old rocking horse and all the new cabinets in the kitchen. He made Mama's rocking chair and her easel, and I'm pretty sure he's responsible for Turtle's cradle, too. But I haven't seen him making anything new for a long time.

—

I look at Jesus, who cannot return my gaze because his head lulls forward.

This Christ is only eight inches tall, and yet my father mastered every single detail: each tiny thorn along his ragged crown, the nails piercing through his palms, the trickle of blood, his nostrils flared in pain, and even the wrinkles of his loincloth. But the perfection of these details is nothing compared with the sense of suffering my father managed to express with nothing more than his hands, a chisel, a set of carving knives, a piece of wood, a chunk of beeswax, and his imagination.

It's like Daddy was suffering too and found a way to use his pain to form the figure of this man—this holy son.

I ponder Jesus, and I wonder what my father could have suffered. And then I do the math. Daddy was nineteen years old the day his father died.

Nineteen.

I will be nineteen in eleven years.

When I first met Mrs. Jefferson, she was greeting the class. Wearing a neck brace, she stood at the door, ushering us into the classroom. We went single file, and she took the time to introduce herself to us individually. One by one, she even shook our hands and said, "Pleased to meet you."

After we were seated, she stood at the front of the class and explained the brace around her neck—only she called it a soft cervical collar. "Whiplash," she said, and this was the first time I saw her perform the ritual of sighing and then biting her lower lip.

I felt sorry for her. Her head seemed stuck, and she looked miserable. Whenever she sat down or leaned over to pick something up, she clenched her jaw and grunted like a pig. Two weeks later, she came to school without her brace. I could see her neck and the necklace she was wearing—a simple gold chain. While the class was getting settled, I approached her desk and asked if she was feeling better.

"Will you still have to wear your soft cervical collar?" I asked, and when I did, Mrs. Jefferson looked like she was going to cry. And she never did answer my question. Instead, she sighed and bit her lip and twisted her wedding ring around and around her finger. Then she looked me in the eye and said, "I can't believe you remember what it's called."

Third grade is about becoming more self-sufficient. We are supposed to get used to doing homework, only Mrs. Jefferson takes me aside and says I'm to do mine at school from here on out. While everyone else is reading, I work the assignments at my desk and hand them in at the end of the day. Phillip Booth, who has carrot-red hair, buck teeth, and bad breath, never reads. He sits behind me, but even if he didn't, I'd still be the target for all his spitballs. His aim is impeccable. It always draws attention to what I am doing.

Candace Sherman sits to my right, across the narrow aisle. Spitball number three bounces off my shoulder and hits her foot. She's wearing a pair of purple Jellies, and when she kicks the spitball away, her eyes land on me. She watches me forever before she raises her hand. Candace raises her hand even higher, but Mrs. Jefferson is lost in her own novel. To break the spell of *Sense and Sensibility*, Candace clears her throat.

"I think it's totally unfair," Candace Sherman says now that she has the teacher's undivided attention. "Why does everyone treat Fig like she's a princess?" Candace asks. And once again, Mrs. Jefferson sighs and bites her lip.

"Fig is very gifted," my teacher says, and I wish she wouldn't.

Candace Sherman glares at me while Mrs. Jefferson tells everyone how incredibly high my IQ is. She takes one of my truest secrets and shares it with the entire world. While Mama appreciates my IQ, Daddy says, "Intelligence can't be measured." And every time the school tries to get me to skip a grade, he refuses. My father says I need to be a little girl. "Childhood is more important."

Mrs. Jefferson stands next to my desk while she defends the reason I'm doing my homework at school. She rests her hand on my shoulder and lies to the entire class, and I have to cross my fingers for her. And because I'm already crossing them, I decide to hold my breath as well, because maybe I can make her stop. Mrs. Jefferson uses my IQ as an excuse even though everyone knows the real reason. They might not know all the details, but they do know about Mama—sometimes I think they know more than I do.

Daddy says Mama isn't crazy.

"She's sick," he says. "It's a disease."

But Candace Sherman seems to disagree. Later, during recess, Candace uses all the words Daddy says are cruel or wrong or outdated, and because she does I decide not to tell him or anyone else—especially not Mrs. Jefferson. Gran talks about how everyone in Douglas County thought my father was going to marry Candace Sherman's mother. Had this happened, neither Candace nor I would exist today. I think about this a lot, and I wonder if Candace ever does.

I want Candace Sherman to forget I exist right now, so I continue holding my breath and crossing my fingers. I hold my breath and cross my fingers to make Mrs. Jefferson go back to treating me like she did before the stupid pop-up book that never even got turned in or graded.

———

Gran is not the only one who desires the security that tradition and routine bring. I, too, wish everything could be the way it was before Mama went to the hospital: simple, uncomplicated, and a little bit boring. This is what I want. I hold my breath and cross my fingers.

While I was staying with Gran, wild dogs got into the chicken coop and killed two hens; they injured the rooster, and Daddy had to put Mr. Cocky down with his twenty-two.

Uncle Billy looks at me and says, "That is called mercy."

And there is still chicken-noodle soup when I come home, and when I look at it, Daddy says, "Waste not, want not." But I know he knows I won't be eating it.

Our neighbor Frank McAlister trapped one of the wild dogs and called Animal Control to come and pick him up. They put the dog to sleep, and then they studied his body and reported back. The dog had hundreds of lead pellets imbedded in his skin from years of trespassing. I want to ask what color eyes he had. To see if he is related to the other dog, the mama dog I used to feed. I want to ask, "Was one eye dark and the other a cloudy blue? And did they glow yellow in the dark?" But I don't. I don't say anything at all.

Mama was the one to come and get me from my grandmother's house, and this time she only apologized once. And this made her seem way better than when she kept saying sorry over and over again after she came home from the hospital. But she's still afraid of the wild dogs. Daddy says this fear is different from the other kind. This fear is different from the kind that's caused by her disease. He tries to explain: "Those dogs are very real," he says. "They're not just in her head."

—

The first snow of the year finally falls, leaving a thin layer of white on the land. Daddy finds tracks going from the farmer's ditch to the paddock where the sheep are kept. And even though the tracks trespass through the orchard, he doesn't make the connection. He doesn't once stop to consider the possibility that Mama and I were actually chased that night.

I spot three German shepherds on my way to meet the school bus; they look nothing like the dog I used to feed. They stand in the pasture—dark compared with the snow. The cottonwoods are bare, the branches a tangle of black against the gray expanse of morning sky. From the nests secured to the treetops, hundreds of meadowlarks lift only to settle back into the branches seconds later, but the dogs don't look up. They stare at me, and I stare back—and I almost miss the bus.

Later, when I tell Daddy, he says the wild dogs around here are full of German shepherd, and starts walking with me in the morning. He does not need to walk with me in the afternoon.

"Those dogs are nocturnal," he explains. And he doesn't have to tell me what this word means. I already know. Mama is nocturnal too.

There are rumors about the feral dogs. Mostly people say they're part coyote, but on the bus Trent Wallace tells Candace Sherman and Sissy Baxter they're part wolf.

He says, "That's what my pops told me," but when I tell Daddy, he laughs. He doesn't like Trent's father, who owns and operates Wallace Dairy and lives in the biggest house in Douglas County—the one Mama always likens to the plantation from the movie *Gone with the Wind*.

"I saw the Wallace calf that got killed," Daddy says. "That carcass was riddled with bite marks and scratches—wolves don't do that.

—

Wolves know how to kill. They don't play with their food. They go straight for the throat."

Mama spends her days standing in the day porch, where three walls are all windows. She uses Daddy's binoculars to search the world on the other side of the cold glass. But then the first blizzard of the year comes and buries the threat with the deepest white snow I have ever seen.

"Any wild dog left alive," Daddy says, "is denned up for now."

Still Mama smokes a lot. She thinks that no one knows. She hides behind the catalpa tree, where she can't be seen from the house. I find her cigarette butts stuck into the snow, and when she comes inside she always smells like breath mints and the oil she wears made from amber and myrrh. But she can't hide that the artist callus on her middle finger is now stained an ugly yellow.

The blizzard knocks the power out, and Mama has to get the emergency candles. Daddy lights a fire, and after we eat dinner in the kitchen Mama and I curl up on the sofa and she reads *The Snow Queen* out loud as the wind shakes the house, turning the outside world into a whirl of white.

Daddy makes hot cocoa with miniature marshmallows for all of us, and after he has passed us our mugs he sits on the floor to listen to the story. He rests his head on Mama's lap, and she strokes his thick black hair with her fingers between turning pages.

Later, in my bedroom when everyone is asleep, I sit in my window seat and watch the snow. I watch the farm as it circles around in a snow globe of its own making. In the howl of the wind, I can hear the howling of the wild dogs, and I wonder if everyone got it wrong. Maybe Mama was right after all. Maybe she really isn't

—

a schizophrenic. I think about the dog I kept feeding. She didn't look like a German shepherd, but with her different-colored eyes and mangy blue-black fur she also didn't look like someone's pet.

But then I start thinking about what it'd feel like to have everyone think you're crazy when you're not. It might even be enough to drive you crazy for real. Then again, the crazy you might become might be the kind of crazy that can go away if you find out you actually weren't crazy to begin with. And maybe it's the kind of crazy that really does get better from resting all the time and taking a lot of long, hot baths. Outside, the world howls, and I hold my breath and cross my fingers.

March 30, 1984
Just as the weather turns from cold to warm I get the chicken pox and Gran becomes overly concerned about me scarring. "She already has that nasty habit," she says, only she's whispering as if this is enough to keep me from hearing her.

Mama and Daddy have to shear the sheep, so Gran comes to stay with us and care for me. She coats my body with calamine lotion, and I turn to clay. When I move my arm, the pink crust cracks as if my elbows were made from plaster and I could break into a million pieces.

Gran puts mittens on my hands and socks on my feet even though the days now are quite warm. She wraps Ace bandages around my wrists and my ankles to keep me from taking them off. This is worse than when she made me wear the splint. The only time I see my hands or feet is when she soaks me in an oatmeal bath. I feel like Gretel from the fairy tale. The bathtub is the cauldron and Gran is the hungry witch. Sitting on the toilet, she leans over to squeeze the sock filled with oatmeal and to stir the milky water. She is cooking me.

My fever remains high, and the mercury climbs to a hundred every time. I am burning up. I can't read because of my mittened hands and my foggy brain. I try to watch TV, but all I want to do is scratch myself. I am trapped inside my skin.

I lie on the couch, and Gran works her crossword puzzles. Her pencil scratches the paper every time she writes an answer. When she goes to use the bathroom, I rub my face against the red velvet sofa, or scratch myself through my clothes using my teeth. Gran always returns, and this is when she helps me drink water through the bendable straws she bought for me.

When Mama comes to check on me, she is always red and sweaty with bits of raw wool stuck in her hair and on her clothes. I can smell the greasy smell of lanolin, and some of the fibers remain after she leaves. They float around like dandelion seeds. And I try to blow them away, but I always run out of breath and they land on me and make me itch even more.

My fever breaks, and the chicken pox have all scabbed over. I feel much better and I only itch for Gran to leave. Finally, she drives away in her long blue Buick followed by a cloud of dust. From the porch, I wave good-bye—no more mittens, no more socks, and no more yards of bandaging.

No longer bound, I stand amid piles of wet fleece that Mama's been washing since dawn. "You're free," she says, and she's smiling but exhausted. I can tell she wants to be alone.

I walk to where the sheep are being pastured.

They are different animals than before I got sick. Now they

are naked, pink albinos. Freshly sheared, the ewes stand under the late-morning sun, exposed. I'm barefoot, and the tall Johnsongrass tickles one of the pox scabs on my ankle. I reach down, and my body responds to my fingernail. The blood comes easily. This time, I pick the scab for a different reason than when I picked the scabs on my knees. I am not doing it to get attention. I am doing it because there is no one here to tell me not to do it.

The scab was a miniature volcano, and now it's erupted.

This time, I am more aware of the warmth that comes from bleeding than I am aware of the pain. I use my finger to wipe the blood away, and then I watch more blood bursting to the surface—bright and red. This blood was blue only seconds ago, and from red I watch the blood turn brown as it dries on my finger. The brown highlights the wavy pattern of my fingerprint, and like a snowflake I am the only person in this world who comes with this particular design.

Only two and a half weeks before the school year is over and summer becomes official. Mama buys green grapes from the grocery store, and the three of us sit on the porch and watch the sun set. The apple blossoms have fallen, and in their place new fruit grows—tiny, green, and hard.

Daddy tries to peel a grape for Mama.

My fingers feel anxious as I watch my father try. His fingers are large and clumsy and I wonder how he ever managed to carve the intricacies of my grandmother's wooden Christ. I realize his nails are too short as he scrapes away more fruit than skin. When he's done, he hands Mama a tiny moon—it is green and pocked deep with craters.

Mama takes it anyway, popping it in her mouth, and as she

chews never once does she stop smiling. The sunset paints her skin pink and orange—and even now that she is puffier, she is still the most beautiful woman I've ever seen.

And this is why I must give her something perfect.

I use my fingernail to peel off the thin grape skin, strip by careful strip. Skinned, the fruit is smooth and wet; it glistens. Mama smiles as I hand it over. She studies the perfection and is gentle with my gift. She nods her head in gratitude, and then she eats it. After she has swallowed it, Mama stretches her arms into the air. She folds her hands behind her head, and then she says, "This is the life for me!" And later, by the light of the moon, she will pull all the weeds from the flower garden for the first time in almost forever.

Every time the sore on my ankle scabs over, I have to peel it off again. I am chasing after the warmth—the kind of warmth that connects back to my heart and relaxes me. Only it doesn't happen every time, so I'm forced to keep trying.

The sore has gotten red and hot, circled by rings of swollen white. I repeat everything Mama did the night of my seventh birthday— the night we both came home again.

I clean the wound with Q-tips and hydrogen peroxide. I begin to like the sting of the cleansing white foam, so I add more. Then I care for the wound the way Daddy would. I smear it with Neosporin the way he always does when he nicks himself while working wood. I do this once a day, but nothing changes. Then I do it twice a day. And finally three times. Next, I sneak droppers full of Mama's tinctures—Echinacea and goldenseal, everything I've ever heard her use to fight infection. And I shudder from the bitterness and the alcohol.

—

I cut my fingernails as short as I can even though I don't want to pick anymore because picking hurts too much. The pain is not worth the warmth, which is now too hot. The redness and the hotness do not go away; they outdo any temporary pleasure as the infection spreads. My ankle swells, and a purple streak begins to climb my leg like the mercury in the glass thermometer which indicates the return of my fever.

It takes Mama forever to even notice, but when she does she gives me Tylenol and puts me in a hot bath with Epsom salts, and then she squeezes the sore until it shoots green-yellow pus. When she squeezes, I swallow the need to scream. The screams turn into heavy rocks inside my stomach.

The infection gets better for a day, and then it gets worse than ever. The wound grows bigger and rounder; pregnant with pus, the pus threatens to explode as the purple streak inches past my knee. Headed for my heart. Mama drives me to the emergency room in Lawrence.

I miss the last two days of school because I have to stay in the hospital instead. The doctor explains how it began as staph but turned into cellulitis. His teeth are too small for his face, and his lips are very chapped. I'm tempted to peel away all of his dead skin and the patch of dried shaving cream by his ear.

"Fiona," he says, "you almost lost your foot."

My foot is suspended in the air, hanging from the ceiling in a sling. "It's important to keep it elevated," the nurses like to say. "To keep it above your heart."

There is an IV in my wrist. The needle is taped into place and attached to a long, clear tube attached to plastic bags of saline, antibiotics, and pain medicine. This all hangs from something that reminds me of a coatrack, only there's an electrical-looking box attached and used to monitor my vitals. The screen has green lines and a picture of a heart. The heart is not the anatomical kind but the shape of a Valentine—an outline of red light.

At night, Mama sleeps on the plastic armchair by the window, folded into her body. And the moonlight makes her glow. Daddy has to get back to the farm before the sun goes down, to water and feed the animals. When Uncle Billy comes to visit, he gives me his lucky rabbit foot. I wrap my fingers around the softness.

Uncle Billy looks very worried.

"Fig," he says, and I look up at him. "Will you promise to always take care of yourself?" he asks, and I think I manage to nod.

I am squeezing the furry charm. I squeeze as hard as I can, and I think I can feel the bone inside, even though I know the rabbit foot is a fake. Uncle Billy kisses me on both cheeks, and despite the lingering scent of peppermint soap I can still smell the fish. He spends this time of year wading through the Silver River, casting lures.

After he leaves, I dangle the rabbit foot in the air from the chain of tiny steel beads. The fur is dyed the most unlikely shade of blue—the Crayola color called Indigo. The color of the summer sky right before night falls. When I go home, I will keep this charm between my mattress and my box spring because it is beloved.

In the morning, the nurse comes to drain my ankle because the superantibiotics are not enough.

First, she numbs the area with a shot. With gloved fingers, she opens a plastic package containing the largest syringe I have ever seen except for the oral ones Daddy uses to deworm the sheep. But this one has a needle, which she sticks into my ankle before slowly pulling back on the plunger. This is the opposite of getting a shot, and all I can feel is the pressure of my ankle releasing as the clean tube fills with pus. The tube is marked with black lines and red numbers and reminds me of Gran's favorite measuring glass.

Mama holds my hand, but Daddy cannot bear to look. He stands by the window, and because we're on the third floor his head is surrounded by rain clouds. I fill two large syringes, and when no pus comes out anymore, they tell me I'm ready to be released. "Sometime this evening," the nurse says before she shows Mama how to properly clean and bandage my wound.

The doctor writes a prescription for oral antibiotics. I hate swallowing pills, but he doesn't care. "You will take three a day for the next two weeks before I reevaluate the situation."

He repeats himself. The doctor says "This was a very serious infection" again and again while we all nod our heads and stare at him dumbly. Then he asks if he can talk to me alone, and Mama and Daddy go stand in the hallway, where I can't see them anymore. Dr. Serious stands at the end of my bed, and because my foot is hanging in the air my leg cuts my vision of him in half.

"I'm just trying to understand," he says. "It's been months since you had the chicken pox."

Dr. Serious squints at me like I am hard to see.

"If properly left alone," he says, "all the pox should have healed just fine."

The phrase "left alone" echoes in my head. Mama and Daddy come back in when the doctor leaves with my chart. Mama asks, "Won't it be nice to go home?" and Daddy answers for me. "Yes," he says, but all I hear is "left alone."

———

I have to be taken out in a wheelchair.

"Hospital policy," the nurse explains, but won't let Daddy push me. Daddy and Mama walk on either side of the wheelchair until Mama suddenly stops. We are passing by a long window, only it doesn't offer a view of the outside world. It looks into another room. From the wheelchair, all I can see are balloons drifting on the other side of the glass. They are the kind of balloons that look like inflated tinfoil. This must be the nursery. Once upon a time, I was kept in there.

The nurse stops pushing only after Daddy stops too. I turn to look at Mama. And she is looking through the window with her forehead pressed against the glass.

"Annie?" Daddy says. And he turns her name into a question, which is never good.

I hold my breath and cross my fingers. With her head still against the thick soundproof glass, Mama turns to look at Daddy. My fingers are cramping, and I'm about to turn blue when she finally steps back, pulling my prescription from her purse.

"I need to get this filled," she says, and I can tell Daddy doesn't know what to think.

"Makes sense to me," the nurse says, her voice disembodied.

Daddy nods and starts walking, but I see the way he continues to look back at Mama, who I can't see anymore because the nurse is pushing me again, trying to keep up with my father's long strides. Both Daddy and Uncle Billy are very tall, Paul Bunyan–size.

The lights in the elevator flicker as we ride down. Daddy smiles at the nurse the way he does when he's uncomfortable.

—

"Them babies sure do tug the heartstrings," the nurse says. She says this as if she understands everything there is to understand about my family.

I want to tell her the truth.

My mother is crazy, I would say. *A real nut job.* Which is what Phillip Booth likes to say, but I don't. I don't say anything at all.

Daddy goes to get the car, and I wait in the wheelchair. I can feel the nurse's breath on my neck despite the already thick humidity of this after-rain world. The cinnamon gum is not strong enough to mask her sour breath. When Daddy pulls around, she helps me get into the back of Mama's Volvo. Through the window, I watch her push the empty chair back into the hospital, where she leaves it in the crescent-shaped vestibule.

I fall asleep waiting for Mama. When I wake again, the sky is dark and the streetlights are now burning—the air still thick with humidity, there are now thousands of moths dancing around the yellow globes. Mama is getting into the car. She puts the medicine on the dashboard. It's in a white paper bag, stapled shut with the instructions attached.

When she tries to put on her safety belt, it gets stuck and won't come out.

She turns around and pulls, but it still won't budge. She yanks and yanks, and then she screams, "I hate this place!" Her face is red, and I can tell she was crying long before she got into the car. And Daddy is climbing out of his seat and rushing around to help her.

"Annie," he says, "let me try."

Mama is taking deep breaths, and Daddy says, "I can fix it." He says this again and again, and finally the strap slides out from where it was stuck inside the wall. He clips the buckle shut, and now Mama is rummaging through her purse. I hear the rattle of her pills, and she is checking each bottle—searching for the right fix. And in the side mirror, I watch as she swallows a blue circle with a heart carved out of the inside. At least that's what it looks like to me.

Daddy is in the driver's seat again, and when he turns the key Mama catches my eye in the passenger-side mirror, but she doesn't smile or look away. She stares at me instead. Daddy pulls away from the curb and the tires make a noise like rain as they roll over the wet street, and Mama still doesn't look away.

Lawrence falls behind and she continues to stare. And even though I often can't see her in the long gaps of country darkness, I know she is still there—in the mirror, watching me. And when we pass a lonely streetlight or a house lit up, she is illuminated by the temporary brightness, and she is there. She is there when a car comes from the other directions, and as the headlights turn to tail-lights, she is glowing red and she is still staring.

Her stare is empty but sometimes angry. Mama stares at me like she doesn't know who I am or why I'm in her mirror. Like a caption to explain an image in a book, there is a warning below her stare. It reads, *Objects in mirror are closer than they appear.*

CHAPTER SIX

NESTING DOLLS

wormhole: a "shortcut" through space-time.

September 1984

When I enter the fourth grade, Mama starts seeing a new therapist and she seems to get better every day, and it matters less that I will be nineteen in ten years.

On Saturdays, she takes me to the Dairy Queen and we order strawberry milkshakes, which we suck through straws as she drives back home. I wonder if these milkshakes are the reason she is getting fat, but as long as Mama is happy I couldn't care less about her weight.

Now I just have more of her.

The whine of the tornado alarm loops and the television screen goes red.

And the warning repeats itself: TAKE IMMEDIATE SHELTER.

Mama fills a plastic jug with water, and Daddy grabs a box of crackers and salami from the pantry. They usher me out the back door and toward the cellar. The wind slaps against my face and stings my cheeks. I pull on the double doors because both Mama and Daddy's arms are full. The doors fly open. Once we're all under the house, Daddy pulls the doors shut again and he secures them

—

with a two-by-four, and I expect silence to follow but there isn't any. The sounds aren't even muffled. The siren nags and the wind is just as angry as it was before.

Mama pulls on the string to turn on the light, and all I see are amoebas swimming in the dank air—blue-black, they are like the rainbows motor oil makes on water. Daddy sits on the bench across from us. The lightbulb swings back and forth, and his face goes from dark to light, again and again.

Outside, the world is blowing away.

And I think about what it'd be like to lose everything. Would we start over somewhere else? Somewhere far away from here. Is the fourth grade different in a different place?

The barn is picked up in one piece and hurled to Missouri the way they throw discs in the Olympics. The trees are next—the ring of cottonwoods that protect the house. The massive trees make a popping noise as they are ripped from the ground. And it sounds like rain when God shakes the earth from their tangled roots. Next, the tornado plays with the house the way a cat plays with a mouse—it paws at all the windows before it smashes all the glass.

It takes the house apart, board by board. The nails scream as they come undone after a century worth of holding.

Mama reaches into her jeans and pulls out her medicine. She shakes a pill from the bottle and swallows it without any water. Another blue circle with a heart carved out. Then she sits with her elbows on her thighs and her head in her hands. I see her knuckles poking out of her hair. Daddy leans back, watching the ground. Neither of my parents looks up. There is a dead centipede on the dirt floor.

Gran once told me about a tornado that came through here when my father was a little boy. It took the Fergesons' original two-story farmhouse. Tossed it to the sky and heaven kept it.

Bits and pieces of their farm were found scattered across the county for weeks after. We still have their white enamel kitchen sink out by the train tracks, half-buried. In the summer, the chicory grows a blue fairy ring around it.

When the Fergesons crawled out of their root cellar, the only thing left was their front door. It stood there in its frame, the three steps leading up still intact. And sticking out of the keyhole was the key where they'd always kept it to keep it from getting lost. When Gran sent Daddy across the road with a casserole, Mr. Fergeson opened this door for him like their house was still there.

When Daddy tells the story, he always says, "That was the day I stopped believing in God."

Before Daddy's grandfather bought the farm, there used to be a cider house, but it, too, blew away. Ever since we Johnsons moved in, nothing on the farm's been touched by the tornados that sweep through Douglas County as routine as a housekeeper and her broom.

I lay my head in Mama's lap. Through the crack between the cellar doors, the world is a filthy color green. As Mama strokes my head I pray. I pray for my family to begin anew. I hold my breath and cross my fingers. And the repetition of my praying puts me to sleep—but when I wake up, I find myself in my bed, and it's a new day just like every other one that came before, and our house is where it's always been. We will not be moving away to start over somewhere better; somewhere over the rainbow is not a place we get to go, or have. The only difference is I don't have to go to school today.

The storm broke the kitchen window and the yard's littered with

—

mangled tree branches and the gardens are all a mess. The hens did not survive, and I help Daddy clean the coop. The straw floor is plastered with egg yolk and broken shell. The black and white feathers are everywhere—woven into the chicken wire, caught in the splintered wood. The bodies of the flightless birds themselves lay where they were dropped, and when I pick them up they are limp and cold.

Uncle Billy has work in Colorado and is leaving town for a spell. In the winter, he often goes to work at the ski resorts in Aspen or Steamboat Springs.

"It's the only way I can afford to have any fun," he says. And then he winks at me and says, "Someday you will come along and I will teach you how to fly."

He wants to give me my birthday present even though my birthday isn't for another twenty-one days. He insists I open it in front of him. The box is wrapped in silver paper with a long ribbon tied all the way around. The ribbon ends in a fancy black velvet bow at the top.

The box is gigantic, almost as tall as my chest when I am standing.

Uncle Billy grins. "Go on," he says. "Open your present."

I fill the living room with the sound of tearing paper. What I peel off, Uncle Billy gathers and tosses to the side. He lets me use his pocketknife to cut where the cardboard flaps have been taped shut. Inside the box is another box wrapped in red with yellow ribbon. And because of how big it is, Uncle Billy lifts it out for me, and I use his knife again to cut the ribbon.

In this box I find another box.

I unwrap paper, undo ribbons, and cut open boxes. The living room fills with wadded-up wrapping paper, ribbon, bows, and empty cardboard boxes. Marmalade busies herself by chasing after all the paper and attacking it. Uncle Billy acts as if everything is normal.

"Open your present," he keeps saying every time I find another box.

I'm left with a small box that fits in my lap. It looks like the first present, only smaller. The same silver paper, but instead of ribbon Uncle Billy has written, *I love you.*

Inside I find a wooden doll.

She is not shaped like any doll I have ever seen. Her hair, face, and clothes have all been painted on. She smiles at me with her rose-bud lips, and she wears a head scarf, a cloak, a long skirt, and an apron. Every garment is decorated with flowers—bright reds and pinks and oranges contrasted sharply by the application of black.

"Open your present," Uncle Billy says again.

And he shows me how her body unscrews. How she comes apart at the middle. I pull one doll from another.

"They are nesting dolls," he says. "Matryoshka." And this is a doll I can actually love.

"They come from Russia," Uncle Billy says. And there are five altogether, but I like the smallest one the best. She looks exactly like all the other ones, only smaller—and she is solid.

She cannot be opened.

Today is the first day of 1985.

Uncle Billy comes back for Christmas and stays long enough to celebrate New Year's Eve.

And it is bitter cold outside, but Uncle Billy doesn't care. He wants to take a walk before he drives back to Colorado in his little pickup truck. He wants to walk with me.

———

We walk out to the old railroad spur where the busted-up tracks are buried by the perfect snow. From here, I can see the cut of the Silver River, and the dome of Kansas sky is blue today like a robin's egg. There are roses in my uncle's cheeks from the cold, and as we walk we are surrounded by the clouds we make just by breathing. I feel like I am floating. And this is why I can't be sure of what I see. I see the silhouette of a dog in the distance across the water. As she trots she continues to stop and turn around, and when she looks so do I. There are three of them, impossibly small. They chase their mother, and the pups are nothing more than black dots on the white snow.

March 3, 1985
Mama begins her annual spring cleaning.

And her first focus is my bedroom.

I sit in the window seat and watch her make decisions about what I get to keep. She rounds up all my stuffed animals, both ratty and not ratty, and tosses them into the cardboard box while I pretend not to care. I pretend I'm not a little girl anymore.

The box is the same big box from Uncle Billy, only now it takes instead of gives. It swallows my entire childhood, which will all be donated to the Goodwill in Lawrence. Mama doesn't look underneath my mattress, and she leaves my nesting dolls alone. They stand on the top of my dresser, where I lined them up in a row. Large to small, they watch Mama sort through my belongings, and they can't help but smile because that is how they were painted.

Inside my palm, I am holding my uncle's lucky blue rabbit foot. I hold it the way Gran sometimes holds the silver Virgin at the end of her rosary. I squeeze it as Mama boxes up the Lincoln Logs, the Legos, and all my tiny Fisher-Price people—but she leaves my teddy bear alone. The one her mother made for her once upon another time. Her mother made this bear for Mama. The fingers of this grandmother cut the pattern and stitched the stitching and stuffed the stuffing. I love this teddy bear, but he also scares me. He is like a stranger, someone I don't yet know. Someone I'll never truly understand.

Mama keeps a framed photograph of her parents by her bed. One of the few pictures she packed and brought along to college. The picture was taken before there was color film, yet this black-and-white photograph is in color. My grandmother wears a violet dress and my grandfather has a red carnation in his breast pocket. Mama explained how her mother painted the picture. And now I wonder if the dress was really violet and the carnation red, or did she add the colors she desired?

The teddy bear, the encyclopedia, some old dresses, and the photograph are the only things Mama has left of her childhood. And the story of the fire is enough to make me want to stay on the farm forever. I'd rather die than live a life without my mother or my father. I would hate to have to survive the way that Mama did, all alone. But now she has Daddy and me, and Uncle Billy. Now she even has Gran.

Mama wraps Turtle in the same flannel receiving blanket the hospital wrapped me in when I was born and lays the doll down in her cradle. Turtle pretends to be asleep. Her eyes are closed and Mama takes the tiny crazy quilt—the one I know she pieced together using my old clothes—and she tucks it around the doll carefully. If it was up to me, Turtle would be the first toy to go.

Mama is on her knees, wearing one of her many pairs of faded corduroys and a peasant blouse with bold Mexican embroidery in bright colors around the neckline. She doesn't wear her vintage dresses anymore. "They no longer fit," she says, looking sad. I know she misses wearing the one dress that used to be her mother's. As Mama leans forward to snag a runaway Lego from beneath my bed, her hair comes loose and falls down her back like water.

As she stands she's caught by a thick ribbon of sunshine coming in and her eyelashes are so blond, they vanish in the light. She complains a lot about the weight she's gained, and I feel sorry for her. She used to be the same kind of thin as me. The kind of thin that can't get fat even if you try. Daddy used to joke how the two of us would never last through hibernation if we were bears. And now he doesn't talk about weight at all.

Mama closes the box by folding the flaps into one another. And as she does she leans over and I can see the top of the scar—the place from where I came. But then she is trying to lift the box. It proves too heavy for her to lift alone, so she calls for my father, and together they carry my childhood down the stairs and out to the truck like this is no big deal.

I dream someone's in my room, and this dream wakes me up. But when I sit up, I find I'm all alone. With my door half-open, I can hear Marmalade prowling the house.

Mama says cats can see ghosts and fairies, and Uncle Billy says, "They also like to eat mice."

I feel the emptiness of my room in the pit of my stomach as if I'm hungry. The moon is almost full. With my curtains drawn, everything in my room is cast in silver light. The row of nesting dolls are no longer five, but one. Mama must have put them back together, and this makes me mad. She is *my* doll.

Pregnant with quadruplets, the mother nesting doll smiles at me.

—

She lifts her painted hands from her curvy hips and rests them on her big belly the way pregnant women always do. "I'm about to pop," she says cheerfully, but when I blink she turns back to wood and paint.

I look to the window seat, needing something familiar. Something I know well to ground me in this world. My teddy bear leans against the glass the way he always does—brown and soft, he looks back at me with button eyes. The cradle is on the other side of the window seat, just as Mama left it, but both the quilt and the doll are gone.

I get out of bed for a closer look. And I find the cradle really *is* empty. The moon pokes through one carved-away heart before the light is devoured by the shadows.

The girls at school tell stories on the bus, and there is one they like the best, about a china doll that comes alive at night. With her porcelain fingers, she gouges out your eyes while you are sleeping. And when I look out the window, I swear I see Turtle walking through the orchard, toward the river. Unsteady on her fat plastic baby legs, she does not look back at the house.

She is running away.

I watch until I cannot see her anymore. Then I climb back into my bed. And I can't tell if I'm awake or dreaming. As I fall back to sleep, I startle from a dream in which I'm falling, and this is how I know I am awake even though I've had dreams inside other dreams before. Someone is moving around downstairs. I can hear the sound of walking—back and forth, back and forth, and the rhythm is familiar; it lulls me back to sleep, and this time I sleep till morning.

I wake to the sound of Mama coming into my room. I rub away the sleep in my eyes, and when I can see again I see Turtle in her cradle in the window seat tucked under the crazy quilt. Like she always is.

———

Mama looks at me, and her mouth is open as if she's about to say "Oh." And then she does say "Oh." She says, "Oh." And then she says my name. She says, "Good morning" and "Rise and shine!" She continues to greet the new day in every possible way a person could. "Up and Adam!" And then Mama looks around like she has no idea what she is doing, so I jump out of bed and give her a hug.

May 12, 1985
For Mother's Day, I get Daddy to drive me to the new flower shop in Eudora. We leave the farm before Mama wakes up so it will be a surprise. The Flower Lady is on Main Street, and Daddy parks in front of the shop and hands me a twenty-dollar bill to go buy something for my mother. Then he runs into Baxter Lumber to get supplies; it's time to begin the annual repair of all the fences on the farm.

I've never been in a flower shop before. A brass bell is fixed to the door, and it rings when I open it. I step inside, and the smell of flowers is intoxicating. The Flower Lady reminds me of the potting shed, only better. It is the most beautiful place I've ever seen.

Large tin pails boast freshly cut tulips, irises, and daffodils. Wooden crates stuffed with green moss serve as drawers offering tiny wire chairs and tables, fairy-size, for decorating your flower garden. These bins also offer stakes made from old forks and butter knives; the names of herbs, like rosemary and oregano, have been stamped into the handles, and I almost decide on these for Mama, but I don't have enough money. A variety of vases sit atop a small antique table, waiting to be bought, and toward the back there is a refrigerated room; through the glass, I see orchids and anemones. I see roses of every color, big and small. I also see sprigs of purple lilac.

Amid a burst of baby's breath, an array of greenery sticks out of a white plastic bucket like a plume of emerald feathers, and behind the counter, almost hidden by the large, black old-fashioned cash register, I see Sissy Baxter perched on a stool, reading a book. She is too young to have a job, and I realize she is here by choice. Her parents own the hardware store next door, and if my parents owned Baxter Lumber, this is where I'd choose to be as well. That is, if the owner would allow it.

Sissy Baxter does not look up—not until a young woman comes through the swinging Dutch doors behind the counter that divide the back of the store from the front. "Hello," the woman says, her hair a nest of short black curls. "Welcome to The Flower Lady." And this is when Sissy looks at me. Our eyes meet, and she blushes; quickly returning to her book, Sissy turns the page, bends farther forward, and squints at what appears to be an illustration of a poppy.

The Flower Lady smiles at me. Wiping her hands on her floral-print apron, she steps closer and asks, "Are you here to get something for your mother?" I look at my feet and shrug. I consider fleeing, but then the Flower Lady is hooking her arm into mine and leading me toward the whitewashed worktable pushed up against the wallpapered wall. The surface of the table is littered with scraps of colorful paper, rolls of green tape, spools of green wire, scissors of every shape and size, pruners, pins, a stack of crisp white paper doilies, and loose bits of flower material and greenery. Bolted to the wall above are a roll of brown paper and a roll of cellophane.

I see the small bouquet before the Flower Lady even picks it up to show it to me.

"It's called a tussie-mussie or a nosegay," she says as she hands me the cone-shaped flower arrangement. The small bouquet is wrapped in one of the white paper doilies, and as I study it the Flower Lady explains the Victorian tradition of using flowers to communicate. "It was a secret language for a time when people had difficulty expressing themselves otherwise," she says, and it's my turn to blush now because I know Sissy Baxter is listening to everything we say.

I let the Flower Lady help me make my own personal arrangement for Mama. The focus is red geranium for comfort and good health, but we add basil for best wishes and honeysuckle to represent the bonds of love. To reinforce the meaning of the geranium, the Flower Lady bundles the tussie-mussie with a length of red silk ribbon and ties it into a heart-shaped bow. This is the kind of bouquet I wanted to give to Sissy Baxter back in second grade.

When it's time to pay, the Flower Lady steps behind the desk and traps Sissy Baxter in the corner. I hold my breath and cross my fingers to keep the shopkeeper from asking questions about whether or not we know each other, and it works—she continues to ignore that we are the same age, that we live in the same town, and that we must know each other. Instead, the shopkeeper leaves us to talk only through flowers.

When the Flower Lady punches the mechanical buttons on the register, the cash drawer opens and Sissy Baxter has to pull her book away from the counter. Using her finger to keep her place, Sissy holds the book against her chest and I get to see the title: *Floriography: The Language of Flowers*. I take a picture of the cover with my eyes. To do this, I have to blink; if I continue to see the image in my brain, then it is there forever.

When I open my eyes, I catch Sissy Baxter looking at my hands—at the tussie-mussie I am holding. And I recognize the task her eyes are performing because it is something I do all the time: Sissy Baxter is taking inventory of the flowers. She is decoding the message I've

——

written to my mother, and I realize I don't care. I even reposition the flowers so she can see them better.

The Flower Lady hands me my change and says "Have a good day," but Sissy Baxter is the one who smiles the biggest smile, and then she says, "Please be sure to come again!"

When Daddy and I get home, Mama has woken up. She's in the living room, sitting in her rocking chair. And I see what she is holding. How could she be so careless as to come downstairs? My heart is beating too fast for me to even attempt holding my breath, and if I can't hold my breath, I can't cross my fingers. This ritual only works if I can do both actions at the same time. Instead, I try to get Daddy to turn around before he sees, but Daddy looks at me and his eyes are wet. He pushes past my little-girl body, into the house.

Mama doesn't even notice. Somehow she didn't hear us pull into the driveway or come into the house, and somehow she doesn't sense us standing here and watching her.

She is trying to nurse Turtle.

Mama uses one hand to support the doll's head, to keep her close, and the other to hold her breast in offering. She presses her nipple into Turtle's plastic mouth, which was designed to take the special bottles full of water that make the doll go pee. She is wrapped in my old receiving blanket, and the crazy quilt has fallen to the floor, beyond my mother's reach. I let go of the bouquet; I drop my ability to comfort my mother and her good health as the red geranium comes undone from its bed of best wishes and the bonds of love.

Mama adjusts her position, and as she does Turtle's foot comes loose from all that swaddling. Mama goes to cover her up again but stops first to study the tiny foot. She touches it with gentle fingers, soft. She looks at this tiny foot as if it's the most beautiful thing she has ever seen. Then she covers it again and she never once stops singing: *"Hush little baby, don't say a word. Mama's gonna buy you a mockingbird. And if that bird don't sing, Mama's gonna buy you a diamond ring."*

Another word for forever is "infinity." Infinity has a symbol: It looks like the number eight, only one that's fallen on its side—exhausted from too much time. And it takes forever before Mama looks up—even after Daddy says her name. He says it several times, and then he just says, "My poor, sweet Annie." And this, too, takes forever. Infinity. And when Mama finally does look up, she doesn't seem to see my father. She only looks at me, and then she looks at Turtle. Like the symbol for infinity, Mama loops between the two of us, and I know what she is trying to do.

She is trying to figure out which one of us is real.

Before I go to bed, I go into the bathroom and lock the door. There is a scab on my elbow from when I fell in PE and scraped it on the asphalt. I haven't picked since I came home from the hospital with cellulitis, but I can't breathe.

I must pick again.

I wash my hands with scalding hot water and oatmeal soap. I rinse, and then I check my nails for dirt, and find I have to wash again. My fingers turn red from the heat and they are slippery and white with the second lathering of sweet soap. Once my hands are spotless, I sit on the floor.

This time I notice something different. It's not just about the wound. I become two different girls. There is the girl with the sore on her elbow, and there is the girl with the sharp, clean fingernail.

This time I focus on being the second girl.

I focus on the way her finger bends, and then I test out all her fingers. Her pinky works far better than I expected. And her pinky is my pinky. I am cross-legged inside the tub when I scrape off the scab and expose the meat inside my body.

With the scab pinched between my thumb and forefinger, I twist my arm until I can see the bright red blood as it bubbles out of my body. And I think about a movie I once saw where the main character falls ill and her doctor orders to have her bled. Mama said, "This is what they used to do," and Daddy said, "It was truly barbaric."

The actress did a good job at looking sick. She was distraught, with sweat on her brow, lying in a gigantic bed with four big posts, the thick velvet curtains pulled back. The doctor used a scalpel to make the incisions; the cuts were always horizontal. Red ribbons like a ladder climbing her pale arm. The nurse kept the woman's arm over a white enamel basin. And there it rested as she bled. The container caught the blood and prevented any mess from ever being made.

I hear Gran tell Daddy that Mama is disintegrating. And I remember when Mama once said Gran was nothing more than a bitter gossip, all alone except for God.

One day, Mama leaves the burners on and the copper tea kettle explodes. I ask her questions—easy ones, like where the bath towels are, but she won't answer me. The psychiatrist comes once a week, and Mama's therapist comes every day, except on weekends.

I'm to play outside or in my room whenever they are here.

"You're going to have to make a sacrifice," Daddy says, and then he tries to explain. "The psychiatrist and the therapist both think Turtle is too much of a trigger. They've asked me to ask you to let go of her."

Daddy acts like this is the worst thing in the world he could ever ask of me. "Do you think you can?" he asks, and then he says, "If you can, I promise to buy you anything in the world—that is, anything but another baby doll."

I already know what "sacrifice" means, but I prefer the definitions that dictionaries provide. They're more clinical, like a diagnosis from a doctor.

You have a severe case of sacrifice.

I can't find the big dictionary—it's not behind the glass door on the shelf and hasn't been for a long time, so I use Mama's pocket dictionary instead. There is no check next to "sacrifice," which means she has never looked it up before—but there are other words on the page that she has marked. Words like "sacred," "sacrilege," "sacrum," and "sad." Check.

Words that feel connected, like they are trying to tell me a story.

For "sacrifice," there are three major definitions, and some of them have addendums: *A sacrifice can be an offering to a deity. The forfeiture of something highly valued for the sake of one considered to have a greater value or claim. The giving away of something in exchange for loss.*

I use a pencil to make a check next to the word. I check off "sacrifice." I make the check look like the checks that Mama makes. By checking off "sacrifice," I am adding my story to her story.

I think Daddy is finally right. If I make enough sacrifices, Mama will get better.

But here's the problem: Letting go of Turtle is *not* a sacrifice. The sacrifice must be worthy. And one sacrifice is not going to be enough. It needs to be a sequence of sacrifices—like fasting, or everything a woman does to become a nun. Despite what Daddy thinks, Turtle

———

was never really mine. She's always belonged to Mama, even before Mama got confused and thought she was real.

Giving up the cradle is closer to a sacrifice because it was made by Daddy, even though he still credits the craftsmanship to Santa's elves. He refuses to believe that I don't believe. "Believing in all that stuff," he says, "is what makes being a child so wonderful." And I hate how sad he looks. I feel like I just told Peter Pan I don't believe in fairies—as if, somewhere, a fairy has just died and fallen from the sky. This is why I pretend to believe; otherwise he will think he failed me as a parent.

Both the cradle and the crazy quilt have to go if Mama is going to stay. If I can't make these sacrifices, then she will have to go back to the hospital. Daddy doesn't actually say this, but he does insist on explaining everything I already understand.

He says, "Anything that might remind her of Turtle must be removed."

And he is careful.

He gathers up the cradle, the crazy quilt, all the doll clothes and cloth diapers, the unopened package of baby bottles, and Turtle herself. Last of all, he takes away the flannel blanket that once helped this world receive me. He donates everything to the Salvation Army in Topeka where Mama never shops—not that she's allowed to drive these days. Daddy did something to the Volvo so it won't start, but this is just another detail I'm not supposed to know, another bit of information collected by listening to the walls.

Uncle Billy came back from Colorado a Buddhist. After the skiing season ended, he spent the early spring fly fishing, and somehow ended up in a place called Boulder, where he met a Zen monk and started meditating. Searching for books on Tai Chi, he takes me to the public library in downtown Lawrence. While he stands in the aisle practicing different positions, I wander away. I act like I'm only wandering, but I know exactly where I am going. I wander into the quiet reference room, where I look up "sacrifice" in one of the gigantic dictionaries with the gilded lettering.

Different dictionaries have different definitions. And this definition says "sacrifice" way better. This dictionary defines "sacrifice" the way I think when I think about a sacrifice. Now I can put my thoughts into words.

sacrifice: the act of offering the life of a person or animal in propitiation of or homage to a deity.

Sacrifice: the offering over of my life for Mama's needs.

CHAPTER SEVEN

THE CALENDAR OF
ORDEALS

chronology: n., pl. *-gies 1. The arrangement of events in time.*

October 1985

I begin by sacrificing my beloved rabbit foot.

"I sacrifice my own good luck to bring Mama all the good fortune she might ever need."

This is what I say as I stand at the top of the waterfall before I throw the blue charm into the rushing white water of the Silver River. There are two directions it can go. The rabbit foot will either resurface in the pool along our side or follow the river as it rushes on—through the town of Eudora, out of Kansas, and eventually out to sea. The water folds over my sacrifice, and then I see it one last time, carried over the rocks and tossed into the deep black chamber below, and this is when I say, "Please make my mother better." And when I do, I feel as if I am talking to a god.

When Mama does come downstairs, her eyes remain empty. Full of medicine, she is still focused on somewhere far away from here. Marmalade follows her, stretching and rubbing against her ankles. The cat does not give up, and finally Mama stoops down to pick

---

her up. She stands in the middle of the living room, holding the cat against her chest and stroking Marmalade's neck. Mama continues to stare at a world I can't see. The world is somewhere inside the north wall, or perhaps she can see through the house entirely.

Mostly Mama stays in her room with the door closed. When her therapist comes, I listen through the heating vent to the murmur of the strange woman's voice, and I am reminded of how adults sound in the Charlie Brown cartoon Uncle Billy loves. Sometimes when I come home from school, I catch Mama leaning out her window smoking. She is a Rapunzel, only she doesn't let down her hair; there is no way for me to climb up to her. Instead, Mama blows gray clouds into the sky as if to summon the coming winter. I hide behind the catalpa so she won't see me, because I like her best when she thinks she is alone. Somehow she doesn't seem as crazy as she does in the company of others.

But even so, I know my sacrifice was not enough, and this is why I must try again.

This time, I begin the procession to the river with intent, in a solemn march. I walk with great purpose; this time, I begin the ritual as soon I set out, much earlier than before. One foot in front of the other, I walk tall and look straight ahead. I keep my eyes steady and focused on my mark.

In my hand, I hold the sacrificial object; I suffocate the solid wood with my sweaty palm as I march forward. I walk the maze of apple trees, and then I stretch out my arms for balance as I cross the board that spans the lazy ditch as a makeshift bridge. I resume my soldier stature once I reach the other side, pushing my way through the woods. I quicken my stride when I come to the expanse of the autumn-tinted pasture where the goldenrod is on fire.

—

In my mind, I can see myself: a bird's-eye view, a girl determined. She walks toward the river, and when she reaches the bank she turns to follow the direction of the running water. She walks until she comes to the top of the waterfall, and there she stands forever, watching the water break over the slick rocks to tumble away. The sound drowns out all her other thoughts, and she can focus on her one true desire.

"Today," I say, "I make this sacrifice for my mother."

I watch the tiny Matryoshka doll as she bobs in the water. And just before she's swallowed by the white foam, she turns as if to look at me. Her delicate rosebud lips curl into a final smile, and she does not take a gulp of air before she goes under.

"This baby is me," I say. "By sacrificing all my childish needs, I give my mother all the time and space she might need so she may recover." This is what I say, and when I speak I echo the tone of the priest at the Sacred Heart of Mary. And then I kneel in the grass as if to pray, although I am only listening to the song the river likes to sing.

When I go home, I find Mama in the kitchen, smashing dishes. I stand on the porch holding my breath and crossing my fingers. I am hoping the sacrifice I just made has not yet gone into effect. Daddy leans against the back door watching my mother, and despite the wavy glass I can see his grave expression and I can hear his silence. Neither one of them knows I'm here. I stand outside the front door, watching through the window as if it was a television.

My mother hurls another plate at the black and white tile before she folds over to curl into a ball. On the floor, she rocks back and forth and begins to wail. Daddy crouches down beside her. As he rubs her back, she begins to quiet and to still. He pulls her long hair away from her face, and Mama responds by sitting up. She rearranges

—

herself into what she calls the lotus position, or what my kindergarten teacher referred to as "sitting like an Indian," which Uncle Billy says is offensive.

Like this, Mama begins to braid her hair. Daddy stands, and as my mother separates her hair into three long plaits he takes the broom from the pantry and begins to sweep. Mama continues braiding. When one braid is done, she unravels it and starts again. As her fingers work through her pale hair my father cleans. He sweeps up all the shards of the broken Blue Willow and empties the dustpan in the trash. And I don't enter the house until he has Mama seated at the table, drinking tea.

I wait a week, but my mother still shows no signs of improving. She swallows the blue pills, one after another, and this is how I come to know the carved-out hearts are really letter Vs for Valium.

I return to the river, but this time I do not go to the waterfall. I go to a place more suitable for meditation even if Uncle Billy says a good Buddhist is a Buddhist who can sit quietly in any spot or condition. I sidestep the set of stones until I reach the grass below the waterfall, and I go to sit inside the heart of the weeping willow where the water is calm, encircled by the stone walls made by a grandfather I never knew. The feathery willow boughs sweep the shallow pool, which seems to open up around me like a mirror. My face wavers in the water as I watch myself watching me. And then I vanish from the surface, replaced by a vision of my mother.

The water is playing tricks on me, but it doesn't tell me anything I don't already know. It shows me once again how much I look like her. And then it reveals how I will someday age. The yellow leaves tremble, dropping into the water, and before Mama's image disappears she shakes her head at me. I lean forward to clear away the debris, and that's when I find her, only I don't recognize her—that is, not right away.

The river has washed her clean. Has washed away her bright colors, her costume, and all her features, but when I lift her from the pool I come to remember. I know her by the familiar weight and shape of her once-painted body and by the way she fits inside my palm. Faceless now, the figure reminds me of a question my uncle asked me just the other day.

"What did your face look like before you were born?"

The question bothered me, and when I told him so he laughed. He laughed, then winked at me and said, "It's a koan," and he acted as if this explanation was enough. A few days later, I pressed him to say more even though I knew he didn't want me to. Finally, he sighed and said, "Sometimes the point of a question is not to find the answer but to find more questions."

Cradled in my hand, the smallest nesting doll stares back at me even though she is now faceless; her eyelessness bores into me from her place amid my palm lines of life, love, and fortune. I know why she has returned. She is the answer I was seeking; or, rather, she is a question I didn't know I had to ask. She looks at me and says, *How do you get a mother back?*

My mind begins to race. I realize I've been taking the easy route by only forfeiting material items. Their sentiment was not enough. I must find a way to truly give myself away—to sacrifice myself for Mama—to return as the doll returned to me. I must strip away the face I was not meant to wear and wear the face I had before I was born. Only then can Mama heal. I must sacrifice all my needs for the needs of Mama, but then I cry. I still don't know what to do.

—

"Don't worry," the doll says. "When you are ready, I will send a sign, and this sign will tell you what you need to do."

Just when I'd forgotten about *The Headless Cupid* by Zilpha Keatley Snyder, Mama gives it to me for my tenth birthday. She gives it to me just when I thought she'd forgotten my birthday was even coming. In fact, Mama orders several of Zilpha's books from a catalog, and UPS delivers them right to our front door. This is way better than Santa ever was. I finally get to read *The Headless Cupid*.

Mama was right. It was worth the wait.

I hold my breath and cross my fingers, and then I ask Mama if she will read the book with me. I'm scared she will say no, but she doesn't. She smiles at me and pats the empty bit of bed beside her body. It takes us three nights to read, tucked under the covers in her room. We're supposed to take turns every other chapter, but Mama falls asleep every few pages. I know she can't help it, so I read on—anything to be close to her again.

The story begins the day the Stanley family is joined by their new stepsister. Twelve-year-old Amanda steps out of her mother's car wearing a large, colorful shawl, her snakelike braids coiled into a looping crown atop her head. Drawing emphasis to her third eye, Amanda's forehead is adorned by a mirrorlike triangle, and to complete her costume she carries a crow in a giant cage.

Amanda announces herself as a witch and says the bird is her Familiar, and I am drawn to her. She reminds me of Mama. This is what my mother must have been like when she was twelve—that is, minus the dark hair and upside-down smile and the wild animal held in hostage. Nonetheless, this recognition lets me know I'm about to receive the sign I've been waiting for.

—

The only chapter Mama doesn't sleep through is chapter six, and this is the second sign that I'm about to receive my instruction. Chapter six gives me the idea to make the calendar. The idea comes when Mama interrupts my reading to say, "I think the initiation is interesting." Because she's the one to speak, I pay attention. The sign is revealed. I know what to do. The initiation into the occult involves what Amanda calls an "ordeal." The ordeal is an entire day where the Stanley children cannot touch any kind of metal with their skin. The ordeal is a way to perform a sacrifice, or at least this is how I come to understand it. I even hear the voice I sometimes hear—the one inside my head—and I know exactly what I need to do. But *The Headless Cupid* is just a children's book, and a single day and one ordeal will never be enough to accomplish what I must accomplish. I will need to perform an ordeal every day for a very long time if I'm ever going to cure my mother.

I design the Calendar of Ordeals to begin tomorrow. What remains of 1985 will be my warm-up round. But then the handmade calendar will continue into the year to come. It envelops 1986, and 1986 will be the real test. If I can sacrifice myself every day, everything will be okay.

As I work on the calendar, the smallest nesting doll watches me from her perch upon the shelf above my desk. I like her more without the paint. Featureless, her face resembles my face before I was born. For the template, I use two calendars. For 1985, I use the one on my bedroom wall—the one I got for Christmas last year. This one features illustrations of different fairies, and all the different trees or flowers with which they are associated. I also use Daddy's new calendar. I use my fingernail to slice open the cellophane; already printed, this calendar is for 1986. Every year, he gets these calendars for free from the feed and seed on Route 72. These calendars always have season-appropriate color photographs of life on the farm.

Taking Daddy's yardstick from its outlined spot on the wall, I go back to my room and begin by making careful grids. I am using big sheets of Mama's watercolor paper because they're the closest thing I can find to papyrus scrolls. Day by day, and month by month, I create squares and columns to represent what still remains of 1985. And I do the same for 1986—beginning with January and ending with the close of December. I pencil everything in before retracing it with permanent black ink. In my best handwriting, I write the names of the months, the days of the week, and all the numbers, too.

I mimic calligraphy, making all the capital letters pretty the way they are in fancy children's books. I drape the letters with tiny flowers and curling leaves, filling the insides of Os with night skies: crescent moons, twinkling stars, and wispy clouds.

I go over the pencil with the fine felt tip of a Sharpie pen. The black ink is elegant. The thick paper seems to drink it up. I don't include holidays, because I need the room for the actual ordeals.

ordeal: a difficult or painful experience.

The Calendar of Ordeals is my own special sequence of sacrifice—one after the other, they will take time, but they will accumulate. And grow into something sacred and profound.

I start out easy, beginning with tomorrow, November 1, 1985.

Inside the square, I write: *Do not touch the color purple.* For the second I write: *Do not touch snow.* And the days go on: *Do not eat bananas. Do not smile. Do not drink milk. Do not touch any animals.*

The ordeals get more difficult and painful as I go: days where I

———

cannot drink water or eat, days when I cannot talk, and days when touching Mama is forbidden.

Sunday is the only Sabbath from the practice of ordeals. But Sundays aren't about resting. They are days reserved for redoing any failed ordeals. Sunday is for erasing any mistakes I might make.

Sometimes it's not about what I cannot do, but what I must. One day, I will have to count every step I take, and if I lose track, I must backtrack and start over. There are penalties. And lots of rules. Like Gran, and her need for routine, these rules are important; they create an ongoing ritual.

I can never tell anyone what I am doing. This means I cannot explain myself—even if it means being rude or having to lie or appearing to have gone absolutely crazy. The Calendar of Ordeals must be challenging or it will not work.

Every day, a sacrifice.

Six Signs the Calendar Is Working
Sign Nº 1: November 9, 1985
Mama decides to quit smoking.

It's a bitter cold Saturday, and because I don't have school the ordeal is more difficult. Today I am not allowed to be around fire of any kind. In part, by practicing this particular ordeal, I am honoring my maternal grandparents.

I can't go into the living room or the kitchen for risk of Daddy building a fire or someone striking a strike-anywhere match to light a burner on the stove. This means I have to stay in my room all day. Daddy doesn't miss me at breakfast because I often sleep in on the weekends. And he doesn't miss me at lunch because he's fixing one of the many fences on the farm. But dinner becomes a problem.

———

Even if we ate in the dining room like normal families, the dining room opens into the living room, where the fireplace is, and on a November night there is always a fire burning.

First he calls for me, but when I don't answer he comes to look for me. I have to hide in the linen closet, surrounded by the smell of lint and lavender. Last week, I got to go to the library in Lawrence, and I borrowed the book on floriography Sissy Baxter was reading on Mother's Day. According to this book, lavender means distrust, which doesn't seem fair to the nature of this flower. I listen to the sound of Daddy checking my room and then knocking on the bathroom door. He says my name like a question. And each time he has to ask for me, he sounds more and more irritated. He doesn't look that long, nor does he seem worried about the fact I'm missing. He just sighs a lot.

I hear him knock on Mama's door. Mama hides in her room all the time, especially around dinnertime. He knocks lightly before he opens it. He asks if she'd like him to bring her a plate, but she says, "No." And then he goes back down the stairs and I picture him eating all alone in the kitchen. I can see it clear as day on the television screen of my closed eyes.

And now I'm in my room again, and Daddy is knocking on my door.

I keep expecting him to open the door since I'm not answering, but he doesn't. This time, he knocks and then he waits in the hall. My clock reads 7:59. I wait to open the door. I am waiting for the grandfather clock to begin chiming the hour, and then I wait for all eight chimes to finish chiming eight o'clock. I am practicing patience, and this is not strictly about the Calendar; like silence, it is something I've been practicing forever. After eight chimes, I open the door.

———

"You need to eat," he says, "And the dishes are piling up."

I can tell by the way his jaw works against his cheek that he is clenching his teeth. This is what Daddy does when he is focused, concerned, impatient, or angry. He tells me my dinner is in the oven, and this means I will not be eating, because the oven is gas and the pilot light is an eternal blue flame always visible whenever the oven door is open.

Hard work, however, is always rewarded, and I still intend to do my chores. By now the fire will be dying out in the living room, and it's possible to veer toward the kitchen from the stairs without looking in that direction. Still, I'm worried Daddy will come into the kitchen and make a pot of tea for Mama or check to see if I have eaten, and I'm trying to find a way to ask him not to go in there at all when my mother opens her bedroom door.

She peers out at us. She's wearing one of her long white night-gowns, and I'm relieved to see she isn't wrapped inside Daddy's awful bathrobe, which no one ever seems to wash anymore.

"I know you're both aware of my smoking," she says, and she is wringing her hands the way she does when she is anxious. "I've failed miserably at keeping it a secret," she admits, "but I'd like you both to know I am quitting." She tries to look at us, but her eyes are bloodshot—tired. "I am quitting once and for all," she says, stepping back into her dark room, closing the door as she does.

I can tell my father is surprised. It was only yesterday he insisted on having a discussion with me about her smoking. "It's a nasty habit," he said, "but incredibly common with schizophrenics." I remember his words exactly because it was the first time my body didn't shudder to hear any form of the *s* word spoken out loud.

I no longer deny my mother's disease, but I do deny the idea that

—

143

there is no cure. Sometimes science is not enough. Uncle Billy has a friend named Chuck who lives in Boulder and is a Buddhist too. Chuck was in a fire, and his burns were so severe, he spent months in the hospital and then a year in full-body bandages. The doctors said he'd be scarred for life, but Chuck didn't want to be, so he meditated for hours and hours every day. He visualized the thick white tissue melting away until his body was the same glowing pink of a newborn baby.

And when the time came to remove the bandaging forever, there was not a single scar on his body. Even the scars he had from before the fire had all healed, his body once again a blank slate. His face the face he had before he was birthed into this world. The Calendar of Ordeals is my meditation, a practice in sacrifice and a different way to be reborn.

Sign Nº 2: November 15, 1985
Mama starts coming downstairs for dinner.

Daddy made meatloaf, and I made the mashed potatoes and the green-bean casserole. While Daddy is aware of my choice to abstain from meat, it doesn't stop him from preparing it. "After all," Daddy says, "I do raise pigs solely for the purpose of eating and selling the meat." And at every meal, he is sure to offer me a serving of whatever flesh is being served; he does this even though I always politely say no.

Today's ordeal dictated never being still. If there was room to run, I had to run. If I was doing something where I would ordinarily stand, I had to jog in place or perform some other exercise. This meant doing leg lifts and ankle rolls while sitting at my desk as Mr. Denmar taught long division. And during language arts, I pointed and flexed my toes instead.

———

Principal White issued me a warning when he caught me running in the halls. And he did not appreciate all the motions I was making while he lectured me. But I lied and told him I was under strict instruction to keep my heart rate elevated at all times. "My heart has a murmur," I explained, and this is true. I was born this way. "It's in my file," I said, but I was running out of breath.

I was careful to use fancy words like "cardiologist" and "echo-cardiogram" as I began to jog in place instead. It helps sometimes to have a high IQ. Adults like Principal White worry I am smarter than they are. I continued to slowly run nowhere as Principal White wrinkled his forehead and stammered. "Go back to class," he finally said, and then he yelled after me, "But slowly!"

So I turned into a speed walker like the women Mama and I used to see when we would go to Mirror Lake to feed the ducks or paddle around in the paddle boats. I speed walked to class, my motions exaggerated. I didn't dare look back.

Sign Nº3: November 17, 1985
The big dictionary returns to the cabinet with the glass door in the living room.

The brown cover is completely covered in tape, as is the spine; the silver duct tape works to hold the book together, completely bound. The dictionary is bandaged like a mummy now.

Today certain actions had to be performed three times in a row. This included actions such as turning a light on or off, tying my shoelaces, or brushing my teeth. Each ritual was to be done thrice—three times in a row and as quickly as possible. The point was to make the repetition of three as smooth as the action of one.

This is easier said than done.

After dinner, I teach Mama a new word: "sesquipedalian." It's the first time I've ever known a word she didn't know. I spell it out loud, only I have to do so three times in a row, but she doesn't seem to notice. She looks "sesquipedalian" up and reads the definition out loud once I'm done spelling it the third time.

sesquipedalian: noun, a long word. 1. *Given to the use of long words.* 2. *Polysyllabic.*

"That's a good one," Mama says, and smiles at me.

She checks it off with a pencil and puts the dictionary back. She does not acknowledge that it's been missing or that it's been repaired. I hold my breath three times in a row, crossing my fingers each time. I decide it really doesn't matter where it was or why it seems to be a secret. I focus on what matters instead.

The dictionary is back and the ordeals are working. Mama is still coming down for dinner every night, and even helping to prepare it. She no longer smells of breath mints and amber and myrrh oil, which means she is no longer smoking. And Daddy is starting to smile more and more—he is turning back into the father I used to know.

Before I go to bed, I kiss both my parents on the cheek—first Daddy and then Mama. I have to make a total of six kisses because each gesture must be done three times. And when they return my kiss, they too perform the act in a series of three without understanding why. One after the other after the other. Three times three is nine. Nine kisses. I am ten years old. Nine plus ten equals nineteen. And I think everything is working out.

Everything is going to be okay.

* * * *

Sign Nº 4: December 1, 1985

Mama starts waking up earlier, usually around ten in the morning.

And she doesn't spend all her time locked away inside her room. Instead, she sits at the dining room table drinking coffee and working on a new project. I like this mother—the one who grows quiet and focused.

She calls them Victorian paper cuts, and I can't help but remember the Flower Lady, Sissy Baxter, and the secret language of flowers.

Mama uses her light table to cut the black paper after she draws on it with a special drawing pencil. The X-acto knife strips the paper away, and what is taken works to reveal the images. "I'm going to do portraits of all the saints," she says.

"Well," Daddy says, "that certainly is ambitious." He kisses the top of her head. I have to hold my breath and cross my fingers to make the look on Mama's face go away. And it works. She shakes her shoulders like she is shaking out the condescending tone of my father's voice, which he probably didn't even mean to make.

Daddy goes to check on the animals. This time of year, he is forever checking their drinking water for ice and making sure the stables are clean. During the winter, they get sick from the ammonia from their urine because they can't go out to pasture all the time.

"And when they get sick," Daddy says, "so do we."

I stay to watch Mama work. Today is a Sunday and there is no ordeal to be done. Sundays are turning out to be a break after all because I perform the ordeals perfectly and haven't had to redo a single one. Everything really is getting better. The cure might take time, but this is it.

———

As she slides the X-acto knife along the silver pencil lines, Mama begins to talk to me.

"All religions parallel one another" is what she says. "Catholicism and Hinduism are strikingly similar when you think about it. They are both polytheistic and monotheistic all at once." She pauses and lifts the piece of black paper she is turning into Saint Rita. The cutout is still hanging on by a few uncut fibers, and to free the saint, Mama gently pokes the paper with the triangular blade.

"You see," Mama says, "all the saints and deities can be seen as the many aspects of one God." Saint Rita comes loose and flutters in the air before landing on the light table. Mama says that all different kinds of mythology systems suggest God has a million different faces, and I think about Uncle Billy, who says he can see his maker in the trees or in the river or in the clouds. Uncle Billy who always says, "Figaroo, we are nothing more than hairy bags full of water."

Mama smiles to herself as she leans forward to work on all the little details to create Saint Rita's face, and just when I think she has nothing else to say she leans back and looks at me.

"The saints and deities all work as a distraction," Mama says, "because to look upon the face of God will drive a person mad."

And this is the first time we have ever talked about mental illness. Mama is no longer looking at me. She is looking at Saint Rita. The brightness from the light table underneath shines through all the cut-out places, which create the different features of the face. But I am most drawn to the sacred wound at the center of Rita's brow. Mama cut the wound so it appears to be a shining star instead of the festering sore the saint received from Christ. The sore that refused to heal, and because it festered as it did the other nuns couldn't bear to be around poor Rita—but according to the legend, after Rita died the sacred wound only omitted the sweet fragrance of fresh roses.

Sign Nº 5: December 7, 1985
Mama begins to lose weight.

She spends a lot of time in the shower or soaking in the bath. She says the hot water helps her relax. She uses so much Epsom salt she turns the well water into one of the seven seas, which I will probably never get to see in person. The hot water and the salts seem to melt away her bloat, and as the bloat dissolves her smile comes back and her eyes aren't hidden anymore.

When evening arrives, she goes with Daddy on his walks—just the two of them. They hold hands as I watch from the day porch. I watch their bodies turn into silhouettes. Dark and outlined, they stand out against the backdrop of watercolor sunsets and the whiteness of another winter. They turn into the paper cuts Mama is forever cutting.

It's as if everything was on pause; and there is a sense of waiting.

I fill time with ordeals. There are days where I cannot say verbs out loud. Days where I can't touch anything the color brown. Days where I blink three times every time someone says an adjective. Days where I clear my throat when a person tries to look me in the eye. And there are days where I have to walk backward and days where I must laugh at everything anyone says.

I fill time with ordeals.

I fill and fill and fill. And I do not fail.

*   *   *   *

Sign Nº 6: December 20, 1985

I stop picking.

I spend the last day of school before the winter holiday speaking entirely in whispers. No one seems to notice—that is, except for Candace Sherman. She keeps trying to get me to talk, and to talk loudly. She tells Mr. Denmar she's worried I'm sick. "I think Fig has laryngitis," she says, "Or maybe strep—she's probably contagious." Candace Sherman is obsessed with germs.

Mr. Denmar asks me to talk. I shrug because I don't know what to say, and I'm surprised when he understands. "Tell me your mother's name and where she's from," he says, and when I answer I answer all in whispers, and then he wants to have a look at my throat. This time he's the one who shrugs. "Looks fine to me," he says, but Candace Sherman isn't satisfied. "I really think you should send her to the nurse," she says.

Later, on the bus, Candace Sherman pinches me really hard. She has no idea how accustomed to pain I have become. She pinches me again and leans forward from the seat behind me. "Freak," she says, only she whispers. She tries again. "Freak!" Candace Sherman says, and this time her voice is even fainter than the time before, and as Candace Sherman tries to speak louder I swear Sissy Baxter cracks a smile, but as soon as Sissy sees me see her smile she turns the other way.

Candace Sherman grabs her throat and glares at me. I think she thinks I stole her voice. As she struggles to talk, I wonder if I did.

That night as I lie in bed thinking about the Calendar and all the Ordeals I've accomplished, I realize I haven't picked at all, nor have I even had the urge.

Last summer, I spent a lot of time peeling off the scabs that

—

formed again and again on my elbow. It took forever to heal because of this, but I did not get an infection. I only picked in the bathroom, and when I was done I drowned the open sore in the relentless sting of foaming white hydrogen peroxide. And once, I used rubbing alcohol just to see how much it could hurt. But now I keep my fingernails cut shorter than I should. And I don't wake up in the morning anymore to find dried blood on the sheets. I no longer find sores on my body I opened while I was dreaming.

This is the first time I've even thought of picking, but this is different from before. This is not like the thoughts I used to have that weren't really thoughts but irresistible urges. I might be thinking about picking, but I'm not thinking about how much I'd like to do it again. In fact, the idea makes me feel sick to my stomach—the way I feel when I think about eating meat.

For Christmas, Mama gives me another calendar. This one is full of Hindu deities. They have extra arms and eyes—and they make me nervous, even though they're still wrapped in cellophane. I feel like I am cheating on the Calendar of Ordeals; I worry about being jinxed, and this is why I have to hide the new calendar from my mother.

Instead of hanging it on the wall above my desk where the other calendars used to hang, I hide the new calendar inside my Dorothy suitcase. I keep Dorothy at the very back of my closet, which means I can almost hide the calendar from myself. I will remain fully committed to the one true calendar, The Calendar of Ordeals. Then I sit on my bed. The faceless nesting doll stares at me and I have no choice but to hold my breath and cross my fingers.

I consider throwing the Hindu calendar away, or feeding it to the fire, but I worry Mama will ask where it is even though I can't remember the last time she came into my room. From the space between my mattress and my box spring, I slide out the water paper scroll and spread the twelve pages across my floor like the tarot cards Mama used to read. Each ordeal punctuates a day to come the way Mama's checks signify all the words she's looked up. I've been successful. I made it through every single ordeal dictated by the last few months of 1985. I closed out the days by turning the appropriate squares into squares of black-out, so why am I suddenly so worried?

I use the same marker every time. The black one that smells like licorice. And I will do the same as I embark upon 1986, the year when I will turn eleven. I've grown more confident with every passing day, and I must remain this way. I will continue to blacken squares.

I will mark the time I fill, the time I sacrifice for her—every future turned into a yesterday. Every day and every ordeal will end as a perfect square of perfect black. And each morning, I will repeat the ritual: I will speak the new ordeal out loud. One vow after another, sacrifice after sacrifice, I will continue to work toward saving Mama.

The twelve pages curl and I smooth them out again. I hold my breath and I cross my fingers: I will turn these months into twelve black squares—set in ink, not stone, I will conquer time.

And I will cure my mother.

Today, the calendar dictates making physical contact with people whenever possible. I have to touch other humans if and when opportunities present themselves.

Today is indeed a challenge.

Douglas Elementary has borrowed televisions for the big day, and Mr. Denmar's fifth-grade class gets one of the color sets. He puts the TV on his desk, and the tinfoil-wrapped antennas make the appliance look like a cross between a rabbit and an alien from outer space. The class sits in a semicircle on the floor, and with the special ed. kids from the blue trailer, it is crowded. I point outward with my elbows, and my arms turn into wings. And I jab each one of my neighbors.

Alex Turner elbows me back, but Trent Wallace does not. Trent Wallace glares at me, and then he says "ow!" so loud, everyone turns around to stare at me. The popular girls all giggle, even Sissy Baxter, which hurts my feelings even more. And everyone continues to stare at me—they stare until Mr. Denmar hits the television with his fist, and then they turn back to look at the teacher. Mr. Denmar hits the TV again—really hard; he is trying to stop the screen from going in and out, and it works. The picture comes, upside down at first, then corrects itself and fills the frame.

Candace, Sissy, and Tanya are in front of me. They are triplets in their Guess jeans with the little triangles on the butt and the zippered ankles tucked into their puffy white Reeboks. They take turns touching one another. One girl lies still while the others run their fingers along the insides of her arms and make her smile and shiver all at once. I stretch out my left leg and my foot touches Sissy Baxter's back, but she doesn't even notice. I swear she smells like lilacs.

The broadcast begins—first an image of the shuttle; pointed at the sky, it reminds me of a shark. In white letters, JANUARY 28, 1986, CHALLENGER, KENNEDY SPACE CENTER runs across the bottom of the screen. The camera zooms in on the crowd of people watching but favors the schoolteacher's family, although we do get to see the kids from all around the country who were invited to come as well.

—

A woman newscaster in a Windbreaker smiles at us as she explains the Teacher in Space program. This is the first time a citizen passenger has been aboard a space shuttle mission. "Someday it will be normal for everyday people to go to space," the woman says. And I swear she is looking right at me. She even smiles a different smile—a secret one to let me know I am not imagining this.

I wonder if she is telling me that I will be one of those people. Or maybe she knows about my tendency already to float away. I want to touch her face. "Today," she says, "will be the ultimate field trip, not just for Christa McAuliffe but for the entire nation."

Now it's Candace Sherman's turn to be caressed. Tanya and Sissy gently touch her arms. Candace has her sleeves rolled up, and even in the middle of winter her skin is a golden brown.

The final countdown begins.

"We have main engine start," a man without a body announces as the shuttle lifts into the blue television sky.

The heat from the shuttle turns the blue pink, and then the pink turns to lavender. A long, thin cloud of exhaust follows. Science is Mr. Denmar's favorite subject. "That's called a contrail," he explains, and just as he taps his finger on the screen to make sure we know what he's describing, the contrail splits and the new one slopes away to become the gentle curve of a swan's neck.

The reporter's microphone picks up the muffled sound of wind. And then the sound of people screaming, muffled by the muffled wind. The camera doesn't know where to look. For too long, we are left staring at the schoolteacher's mother.

It feels wrong to be watching her. This is voyeurism. I note her fur collar and how she won't look down. She won't look away from the sky where her daughter is, and she keeps shaking her head. Finally, the camera follows her eyes back into the sky, and we see what she sees: The television frames a square sky, now dark blue and criss-crossed with chaotic lines of white—contrails propelling everywhere like the smoke from fireworks out of control. The disembodied voice again: "Obviously a major malfunction."

Mr. Denmar is still standing. He never had a chance to sit down. He stands there looking as if he wants to turn it off, but he doesn't. His hand is frozen in the air, reaching for the knob. As the television repeats the explosion, Principal White comes over the intercom—yet another voice without a body trying to talk to me. He says, "Today is a tragic day."

He'd like to lead us in a moment of silent prayer. "To honor the fine men and women who sacrificed their lives for our country, and for the sake of science."

And there's that word again: "sacrifice."

At home, I watch the footage, and this time the seventy-three seconds last forever.

The shuttle will never explode.

I remind myself there were people on board, that they are there, somewhere—a part of the repeating imagery. This is not a movie.

Daddy sits in his chair, and Mama's on the sofa with her knees pulled to her chest. I'm on the floor, kneeling. This is the first time in a long time I want to pick. There is a scab on my right knee, and when I press this knee against the floor the pressure radiates; the wound shoots pain into my nervous system, where it detours into unexpected journeys, traveling the atlas of my body like the contrails on the TV. I am trying to resist the urge to pick.

I'm too close to the television set, and I can see all the tiny dots.

———

They get inside my head and make a fuzzy noise. I wait for Mama to make me move back. To say, "That will ruin your eyes," but she doesn't say anything at all. She is quiet. She is watching the shuttle explode. Again and again.

Christa McAuliffe submitted her application on the last day, just before the deadline. "Deadline" is a word I never thought about until right now. *Deadline*. Deadline is like a finish line, only different. The dead teacher was thirty-seven years old. The same age as Mama is now. As the newscaster tells us how old Christa McAuliffe was I turn to see how Mama will react. I think I catch the end of a flinch, but with the medication it's hard to know anymore. Some of the pills make Mama's face twitch, twist, and contort. *Side effects may include*. And she must be taking more of these particular pills because her face has been twitching, twisting, and contorting all the time.

The newscaster explains how no one there expected NASA to go through with the launch because of how cold it was. "It was thirty-eight degrees outside," he says, "thirteen degrees colder than the coldest liftoff in history." Then he offers his microphone to one eyewitness. The stranger looks at me. He looks at America, and he says, "It felt like limbo waiting for the shuttle to leave the ground."

In theological terms, limbo is the abode of souls excluded from heaven but not condemned to further punishment such as hell. According to Gran, limbo is where I will go because I wasn't baptized. Limbo was derived from the Latin word *limbus*, which means "border," and limbo is a region or condition of oblivion, neglect, or prolonged uncertainty.

A place of nowhere. "Nowhere," a compound, as in "no where," or "now here."

Daddy suggests turning off the television, but Mama says, "No."

—

She says it too fast—almost as if she anticipated his asking. "No," she says, and she spits a little without meaning to.

I know Daddy is worried. I can feel him watching me. "Hey, Figaroo," he says. "I sure could use your help making banana splits." As I follow him into the kitchen, I make it a point to bump into his body three times. "Walk much?" Daddy asks, and I know he is trying to make a joke, but it doesn't work because he is looking at me in a way that isn't even close to funny.

Today, I didn't do nearly as much touching as I should have. The scab on my knee wants to be touched. It's practically screaming. I cut the bananas down the middle with a paring knife. I cut them with their skin still on and then I peel it off. I peel off the thick yellow skin instead of peeling off the red-brown scab on my knee as Daddy scoops out ice cream. He drizzles chocolate syrup on the bananas and vanilla-bean ice cream. And then he adds a generous plop of homemade whipped cream, finishing off all three desserts with a handful of salty chopped peanuts.

We don't get maraschino cherries anymore because the red dye might make Mama worse, according to something Daddy read. He is always reading books about schizophrenia and how to make Mama better. He keeps the books under his bed in the guest bedroom that is also his office. This is where I go when I have questions I need answered. Like with a koan, I often find more questions, though.

I don't miss the cherries so much as I miss how Mama could tie the stems into knots using her tongue. She can't do it with the regular cherry stems—we've tried. The flexibility has something to do with the sweet red marinade. I pause to look at Mama before I bring her a banana split. With her knees still pulled to her chest,

Mama is hugging herself. And she is rocking back and forth, her eyes fixed on the television. Her lips move, but I can't tell what she is saying.

Daddy asks Mama if she'd like to join him for a walk, but she barely answers. She mutters something about how cold it is outside.

"Fig?" Daddy asks, and now he is looking at me. He has only ever asked me along one time, and I declined then, just as I decline now. It makes me feel sick to my stomach because of the thought my action brings to mind: *If I had to, I'd choose Mama over Daddy.*

I try to erase the thought by holding my breath and crossing my fingers, and I blame the nausea on the banana split. Mama is still sitting on the sofa, holding the remote in her hand, but her knees are no longer pulled to her chin. Her feet are on the floor and she is staring at the television. The volume has been muted. Without sound, the explosion is all the more frightening.

I sit beside her and I lean my head into the hollow of her shoulder. Just me touching her makes her relax. She falls back, supported by the red velvet couch. Mama's body is hot to touch like she has a fever, and compared with this old house, which never gets warm, she feels good. Her sleeves are bunched at her elbows, her long arms exposed, revealing she has skin the color of milk, soft as silk, and splattered with pink star freckles.

I am touching her. I am practicing the ordeal for today. The word "limbo" is also related to the word "limb." Like a border, limbo has to do with where things or places attach, like arms or legs—like how, once upon a time, I was physically attached to my mother's body. I was a part of her.

I take my fingers and lightly touch my mother.

I run my fingertips along her inner arm the way the girls at school touch one another. This is the ordeal, and this is everything. Mama doesn't say anything as she continues staring at the television, but her body begins to respond: tiny little tremors like she is shivering. And now she's smiling and I sense her body relaxing even more. The sensation is contagious. Touch is the conduit.

This is when I pull my own sleeve up and offer my arm over to Mama.

It extends over her lap like a bridge, and she responds. She touches my arm the way I touched her. Fingers barely touching skin. Unexpected loops that turn and spiral. Mama turns my body into a crazy quilt.

I close my eyes and relax into Mama, waiting for the same shivers to erupt from me. Today's ordeal is not only to touch but to be touched. And Mama tries.

She runs her fingers along my arm forever, but the shiver never comes. Is something wrong with me? And in the end, I have to pull away before she has the chance to give up on me. I pull away and I hold my breath and cross my fingers: Don't let this ruin the ordeal. *Please, please, please.* When I finally open my eyes, the *Challenger* is lifting off.

This time, I see all seven passengers as they eject into the sky. They are wearing silver space suits with big round shiny helmets as they burst forth from the splitting contrails.

They somersault in the air like kids jumping on a trampoline. One turns his body into an X to mark the spot. And there is no gravity until there is. Mama gasps when they hit the surface of the Atlantic, swallowed by the deep cold water. Then the newscaster tells us that all the passengers were found inside the capsule, and

—

I blink my eyes. I do this to see the reality, and all I see is Mama. She switches from station to station, chasing the *Challenger*. Stuck inside the loop, she searches for this scene. She needs to watch it again and again and again.

She isn't seeking the actual explosion; she is searching for the second when the fragments of the shuttle scatter across the sea like seeds. She is looking for the trajectory of bodies, the trajectory that never was.

February 3, 1986
What seems like a good sign, a sign that the Calendar of Ordeals is working, comes at a time when it's clearly not. A time when Mama seems only to be disintegrating.

Mama is sitting beside me on the sofa when the evening news comes on, and *Breaking News from Australia* writes itself across the bottom of the screen. I glance at Mama, and her face has a blank expression, as if she has no memory of Baby Azaria.

"English tourist David Brett was climbing Ayers Rock when he fell to his death over a week ago." The female newscaster has big hair and white teeth and is wearing a blue silk blouse with enormous shoulder pads. Mama thinks shoulder pads are silly. "They have no place outside of football," she has said, so I decide the shoulder pads are the reason my mother isn't paying attention to the woman talking.

"Brett's untimely and unfortunate death led to the immediate release of Lindy Chamberlain, the Australian mother who now appears to have been wrongly convicted of killing her nine-week-old daughter."

Mama still doesn't react. Her glassy eyes stare at the wall, at a point in space somewhere above the television set.

"During the eight-day search for Brett's body, police discovered Azaria Chamberlain's missing matinee jacket in an area riddled with dingo lairs."

The camera cuts to an Australian newsfeed dated yesterday and shows Lindy Chamberlain being escorted through a crowd of people by her lawyers. The dead baby's mother is wearing large black sunglasses and keeps her head down as a disembodied voice finally explains the meaning of Azaria's name.

"Azaria," the Australian voice begins, "means 'helped by God,' and it's both ridiculous and tragic that anyone ever said anything different." And then they show us the one photograph of Baby Azaria where she's dressed in white, cradled by her mother's arms. They do not show the picture of the black dress trimmed in red. Just before Lindy and Azaria Chamberlain's image dissolves into the next report, Mama reaches for my hand. Without looking at me, my mother says, "I always knew she was innocent. I never had a doubt." And I know exactly what she means.

I hear Mama at night, downstairs in the kitchen or the dining room. Sometimes I stand at the top of the stairs where she can't see me, and I watch her pace. She wears Daddy's terry-cloth bathrobe, and some-times her nightgown shows, but mostly she's still dressed—baggy jeans or frumpy sweatpants.

I prefer the nightgown.

I feel sorry for all the vintage dresses hanging in her closet. They look lonely whenever I dare to look at them. They remind me of the abandoned houses that always worry me, and I wish I knew which ones belonged to my mother's mother, but I don't.

And Mama's gone without washing or brushing her hair again,

which she wears in a messy bun atop her head. I understand why Gran calls it a rat's nest.

And her lips never stop moving. She whispers and paces and I still have no idea what she is saying. I do my best to listen, but she's too far away and when I creep closer she falls quiet, eyeing me suspiciously. The Calendar of Ordeals is testing me. It is becoming more and more real, forever pushing me. I talk to the faceless nesting doll. I seek advice. The time has come to beat my personal best. And I will do this for her. For Mama, I would do anything.

March 3, 1986

Tonight, I go to sleep only to wake to the usual sounds of my mother's insomnia. Tonight, I find her sitting at the kitchen table, no more pacing. All the lights in the kitchen are turned on. Not just the overhead but the porch light, the pantry, and the small bulb above the stove.

The lights burn hot and yellow.

I sit across from Mama, and she looks at me. Her eyes have been swallowed by dark circles. She's wearing Daddy's robe, and the black sleeves are crusty with something white. She doesn't say anything. She returns her focus to a mechanical pencil.

Using her thumb, she pushes the graphite out—the graphite everyone calls lead. The pushing makes a clicking noise, and when she goes to write, the graphite is too long and it snaps. She pushes again and more graphite slides out. People who call graphite lead must not understand how poisonous lead is. It has many of the same ill effects as mercury if ingested. I know because Mama worries about the heavy metals in the environment. She worries I've been exposed.

"You're so vulnerable," she will say, and then she'll shake her head and ask the impossible—"Fig," she'll say, "How do I save you from the world?"

There is a pad of graph paper on the table next to the same feed-store calendar I used as a template for this year. She is drinking a cup of black coffee, and on the counter the pot is still on and I can smell the burning coffee and the red light is a warning.

It's after midnight, which means yesterday's ordeal is over. Yesterday, I had to skip every third word I would normally use when speaking or when writing. For example: *It was ____ hard to ____ these words ____ thinking.* Translation: *It was too hard to skip these words while thinking.* But I did my best; I kept my thoughts slow and still the way my grandmother seems to always do. I will probably fail the reading test I had to take. Especially the five-paragraph essay on *Where the Red Fern Grows.* Mr. Denmar is forever assigning sad books for us to read. *Bridge to Terabithia* was my favorite, although *Tuck Everlasting* was a close contender.

This won't be the first time the Calendar has affected my grade-point average. And poor Daddy—he keeps asking, "Is there something wrong?" "Is something bothering you?" "Is something going on at school?" He of all people should understand. He does everything for Gran. Even Mama sees. She is forever calling him "Mama's boy." She is jealous, and she has every right to be. I am jealous too.

Technically, I'm between ordeals right now. In a state of limbo. The ordeal begins once I've woken up for the day and announced the particular constraint out loud to myself and the powers that be. Like Azaria, I too need help from God, even if I don't really believe in him. I still plan on sleeping more tonight. For now, I excuse myself from the calendar. For now, I am between time. And I do not have to worry about the color red. Not yet. Which is good because I swear the light on the coffeemaker is burning brighter and brighter despite the ferocious brightness of all the other lights turned on in here.

Mama looks at me the way she does when she doesn't seem to remember who I am, but when I smile she smiles back and I can see the flash of recognition.

"Triskaidekaphobia," she says, leaning forward and locking eyes with me. "That's the key."

And now she's looking around, worried someone might be listening. With all the lights blazing, we are indeed surrounded. The lights have turned all the windows into mirrors. From at least three different perspectives, I can see my mother searching for spies. And in the window glass, I see myself times three. The reflections multiply Mama and me, and I'm claustrophobic in the crowd of duplicates. Now I understand what people mean when they say, "The walls are closing in."

Mama knocks on the table thirteen times. She looks at me as she does. And she counts each knock out loud: "One. Two. Three. Four. Five. Six. Seven. Eight. Nine. Ten. Eleven. Twelve. Thirteen." Thirteen knocks on the table, and I think about the boys at school who play bloody knuckles and the girls who play Bloody Mary in the bathroom.

"See?" Mama says. "It's all coming together. I *will* break the code. Thirteen degrees. *Thirteen*. The *Challenger*. I always did appreciate a *challenge*." Mama is talking in sound bites. She is speaking newspaper headlines. "Don't worry, Fig," she says. "The ever important Friday is coming—it's just around the corner, come June." And now she taps her finger on the open calendar. The image for June is a shimmering lake reflecting a clear blue Kansas sky. She has her finger inside a square. "See," she says. "The next Friday the thirteenth is in June, and I am the Judas at their table."

———

Mama smiles and I smile back. I nod my head to mean *Yes, I understand*, even though I don't. I make her think I do, and she is relieved, and this brings me more relief than it should. Mama nods at me. She nods at me as if I am the only person in the world she can trust.

Then she pushes her chair back and stands. She walks to the counter and turns the radio on, twisting the dial from clear to unclear. Another red light burns in warning of tomorrow.

Through the static, I hear the disembodied voice of another man: "Art Bell. Coast to Coast AM." Art Bell takes his first caller, and the caller sounds nervous. He is talking too fast, the way Mama does when she's excited. "The *Challenger* was a test run," he says, "for sending nuclear waste into outer space, but the aliens caught wind of what we were doing and shot it down."

"Imagine, folks," Art Bell responds. "What if the shuttle had actually been full of nuclear waste?" I think of everyone out there who is listening too. I turn them into bodies I can see, and then I watch them all react.

Their eyes open wide. And they shake their heads in disbelief the way Mama is shaking her head right now. Some tremble while others shake. One is squeezing her eyes shut to keep from crying, and another woman throws her radio out the window, where it smashes against the street and that red light burns out. A man who looks like Uncle Billy if Uncle Billy was an old man takes a drink of whiskey straight from the bottle, wincing. He closes his eyes as if in prayer.

Mama stands there, but now she's nodding her head and not shaking it anymore. She's hunched over the radio the way some people worship at a shrine. I wish I still had the rabbit foot, or the scab that was on my knee. Mama nods and hugs herself, and I see her jeans poking out from below her robe. Her socks don't match. The static thickens, but Mama does not adjust the dial.

She shuffles across the kitchen to stand by the back door. Still turned away from me, she looks out the window in the door, and she is face to face with a portrait of herself. And I can kind of see her face as she leans into the glass. Her forehead touches her other forehead, the one reflected in the pseudomirror. She feels around for the light switch on the wall and turns the porch light off by flipping the switch. I expect her to repeat this action thirteen times, but she doesn't.

The radio antenna reaches into the radio waves, feeling around, and now an oldies station is trying to compete with the conspiracies. Through the static: "*Mr. Sandman, bring me a dream.*" And Mama just stands there. "*Sandman, I'm so alone.*" Mama will not move again—that is, not for another thirty-four minutes. I know because I stay to keep track—to keep watch, I keep count.

March 24, 1986
At school, the kids are all talking about the movie *Poltergeist*, which just became available on video at Wilma's. Most had to sneak seeing it because their parents would never have allowed it. Ever since that boy killed himself in Nevada after listening to heavy-metal music, devil worship has been all over the news. And the good people of Douglas County are concerned about the spiritual welfare of their children.

On the bus, the kids who have seen *Poltergeist* talk about it all the time. Trent Wallace, who is the strongest boy in my grade, says, "Dude, now I'm afraid of clowns."

—

I think about the Calendar of Ordeals. I keep messing up. At least once a week, if not more. And the blank Sundays are quickly filling up with ordeals to be redone. I am losing stamina. I can't seem to ever catch up. Mama is relapsing back to bad. Daddy is taking her to Kansas City today to get another brain scan and to participate in some kind of drug trial. They'll be gone for three days.

Instead of sticking me with Gran, they ask Uncle Billy to look after me. They do this because he can also take care of the animals. They do this because my grandmother doesn't like to have me.

Uncle Billy has been renting a room above Wilma's, where he has a bed that unfolds from the wall the way our ironing board does. Wilma's is how everyone knows what road to take to get to Mirror Lake, because someone stole the street sign eight years ago and it hasn't yet been replaced. On the highway between Eudora and Lawrence, Wilma's operates as a gas station, a breakfast diner, a bait shop, and now the video store where *Poltergeist* can be rented out.

Uncle Billy called yesterday to ask what movie I wanted him to bring. I told him, but he didn't say yes. He said, "Well, Figaroo, let's see what my big brother has to say."

Daddy must have consented, because Uncle Billy brings *Poltergeist*. I'm surprised it's even available, but there it is on the coffee table, inside the plastic case. He also brings a VCR, which he hooks up to our television set, and then he makes popcorn and we sit on the sofa to watch the movie. Yesterday I would not have been able to eat popcorn because the ordeal was no touching anything that is white. All my panties are white cotton, so I had to go without—and going without made me feel weird, especially whenever I looked at a boy or a boy looked at me.

—

Yesterday was no white, and today I can't say proper nouns out loud.

For example, I can't say, *Hey, Uncle Billy, thanks for renting* Poltergeist. Instead I'd have to say, *Thanks for renting this movie,* but I still feel guilty when I think in proper nouns.

One of the reasons *The Headless Cupid* was banned from the school library by the PTA is that the Stanley children believe their new house is haunted by a poltergeist. Because of Zilpha, I've read a lot about ghosts and hauntings.

According to my research, the little girl in the movie is too young to be an agent for a poltergeist. That's what they call them—agents, as if I could hire one to work for me. I'd hire it to go after all the popular kids at school, to haunt and torment them as they do me. Generally, the girls who attract poltergeists are in their teens instead of little like the girl in the movie, and the clown part isn't scary because it's just a toy. Only real clowns *are* scary. I can't tell whether or not they're actually smiling.

Nonetheless, I am captivated. Especially when the house swallows the little girl and her mother goes in to rescue her. I'm convinced they will never return, stuck forever. In the walls, the space between, stuck in limbo for infinity—but they do return—mother and daughter. They return from the ceiling like a tornado, only backward because it gives instead of takes. With a rope, they are pulled back into this world, and the mother and daughter hold on to each other like they will never let go. And my body remembers being held like that. My body remembers everything.

It's not until after the movie is over that I realize what I did. It must have started just by scratching. Sometimes the skin around the scar from the cellulitis gets dry—and sometimes the dryness gets

———

168

irritated, itchy. I did not mean to do what I did. This is forbidden. But the body does remember, and so did my fingernail. It found a way in without me even noticing, and now the skin is reopened and I am bleeding.

I not only hid the picking from my uncle, I hid it from myself. I picked inside the shelter of the quilt, which I now use to wipe my ankle clean of blood. Made from pieces of my paternal grandfather's suits, the quilt squares are dark wool, navy blues and brown tweeds, so no one will ever notice. Hidden still by the covers, I pull my sock up over the open sore. I do this before I stand to go about getting ready for bed. Uncle Billy watches me in a way no one else does. He's noticed other scabs before when no one else ever did. And when he did, he asked a lot of questions.

Questions like "What happened to your arm?" or "Haven't you had *that* an awfully long time?" Like his koan, his questions only invite more questions, and all these questions are questions I don't want to answer.

When my parents return early Thursday morning, I have already failed the ordeal for that day. I failed the second I went to read from the sacred scroll of sacrifices. Holding the sheet of watercolor paper designated for the month of March, I took a deep breath, located the appropriate day, and read out loud, "Today I will not touch a single tree." And then I read the addendum even though I already knew it was too late. I read, "Because I cannot touch a tree today, I cannot touch paper or wood of any kind." Today is just one more white square, and white is the great void of failure.

*   *   *   *

April 22, 1986

Today I barely made it through the Ordeal: *no water*. No drinking—not just water, but juice, milk, tea—all beverages banned. I fast from liquids. And of course, no bathing and no washing dishes.

I saved this ordeal as the day where I get to fake being sick. I'm excused from having to go to school, and I stay in my room all day, but Daddy doesn't even bother to take my temperature.

He checks on me three times, and each time he lectures me about not drinking the water or the tea he brought the times before. He comes into my room, and he says, "Fig, I think you're dehydrated. I think this is why you aren't feeling well." And then he stands there forever waiting for me to take a drink, but I just lie in bed, curled into myself, a faceless nesting doll inside my fist.

I knew the ordeal would be difficult. The sound of melting snow grates against my ears, and I am forever tense. I stay inside surrounded by the sound of dripping. *Drip, drip, drip*. It reminds me of ticking, and I remember reading about clocks in China that told time via dripping water. There are too many ways to tell time. And by telling it, there is no way to escape.

After I eat ten crackers, I hope evaporation is on my side. I need these Saltines to be dry enough. Everything else not wet is too moist. I stay in my room, afraid to run into anyone else. Uncle Billy's right. People are approximately 70 percent water. Maybe this is why our blood is blue inside our skin? We truly are nothing more than hairy bags full of water, which means I can't touch anyone. Not today.

Today, I try not to even touch myself.

I keep my fingers away from the rest of me. When I do walk, I walk with my arms spread out like wings and my legs do not touch. I worry about going to the bathroom. There is water in my urine and in the toilet. And I pee a lot despite not drinking any fluids since yesterday. In bed, I turn myself into the letter *X*. I am the Roman numeral for how old I am. I mark the spot for where I am in time. But no matter what I do, I still touch myself. So I tell myself my own body doesn't count.

I don't count.

But still I won't allow myself to cross my fingers, not today. And I regret holding the nesting doll as well—all my digits gathered together, knuckles folded and touching, fingernails cold against the inside of my hand, and I am left muttering an incantation: *"I can't count. I can't count. I cannot count."*

Mama is bathing again. She seems to wash herself all the time—long, hot baths, or showers like right now. I hear the water through the walls as the pipes shudder, and then it starts to rain. The pitter-patter on the roof announces the arrival of spring, and even though I'm inside I don't feel safe.

I am surrounded by the threat of water, and the only comfort I have is that the day is almost over. Outside, the rain falls; inside, condensation collects on the cold glass and watches me through tear-shaped eyes. I go to bed. I go to bed hours earlier than I normally do.

Outside, the lightning turns the farm bright white, and from the boom of thunder more rain releases, and the sky is weeping. It is hysterical. I worry about Mama, who once told me I could get struck by lightning when taking a shower or a bath. Water is a conduit, but I can't hold my breath because I can't cross my fingers, so I change my incantation: *"She will survive. She will survive. She will survive."*

I uncap the magical licorice-scented marker. I am careful not to touch the tip of the marker, because the tip should be wet. I begin to color away today, only no ink will come. There is no black to make

— 177 —

today obsolete, to make it *over*. I shake and press, but all I get are streaks of pathetic gray until there is no gray at all. Despite the water-logged world all around, my sacred black marker has run dry. It is as dry as a sun-bleached bone. Even when I succeed, I seem to fail.

The calendar is becoming impossible. Today is the first day of May, a Thursday, and today is the day I cannot touch metal. No steel, no lead, no brass, no iron, no silver, no tin, no gold, no copper. I cannot touch any metal of any kind. This was the same ordeal the Stanley children had to do in Zilpha's book—only they were allowed to cheat. They wore gloves and used their clothes as a buffer.

I'm allowed no such assistance. I am allowed no crutches.

This is the most important ordeal for me to master because it is the ordeal from the book, the instruction I'd been waiting for. I hold my breath and cross my fingers: If I can only get through today, life *will* improve. Everything will stop spiraling out of control.

Today, I cannot touch metal. And the ordeal begins the second I awake.

My door is shut, the keyhole watching me. The brass doorknob tarnished green from a century of handling. Getting out of bed, I am aware of the headboard and the footboard. The wrought iron reaches for me, fingers made from twisted antique tendrils. Despite a coat of white paint, the metal latch on the windowsill still winks at me. And the heating vents all yawn as if to swallow me.

I can tell someone's in the bathroom by the way the old pipes cough. They cough to let me know what they are made of—they cough-talk the way Phillip Booth does whenever he is making fun of me. The pipes talk to me. They say one word, again and again: *copper*.

It must be Daddy in the bathroom, because Mama has been

staying up all night again. Her insomnia is so contagious: I lie in bed at night, unable to fall asleep. I listen to her take long showers or pace the house. I watch her from my window as she walks the yard, her nightgown white and trailing. My mother is a ghost.

I knock on my own door.

I knock as loud as I can. I have no other choice, or else I'm trapped.

"What is it?" Daddy yells.

I just keep knocking.

Ever since the calendar began, Daddy's grown more and more impatient. He looks at me the way he looks at Mama when she's not well. I wish I could tell him what I'm doing, but I cannot break the rules. So I keep knocking. I knock until my door swings open and my father's standing there—white T-shirt, striped boxers, freshly shaved. He looks annoyed.

"Is there something wrong with your door?" he asks, but I push through the open space without answering. He is already testing the door. Swinging it back and forth to study the motion of the hinges. Using the eyes on the back of my head, I can see my father as he looks up to watch me disappear into the bathroom, the door of which is miraculously still open.

I'm careful not to close this door all the way. Keeping my hands clear of doorknobs and hinges, I tiptoe around the grate, the radiator, and the claw-footed bathtub. I can't flush the toilet or wash my hands, and I have to brush my teeth without rinsing.

I hold on to the walls to keep from falling. My room and the bathroom are only tiny tests. An entire day awaits me. I am so consumed with all the potential metal ahead, I forgot to say my vows.

I forget the point of what I am trying to do.

—

*   *   *   *

Coming down the stairs, I'm mindful of the tiny nails masterfully hidden in the Victorian woodwork. With arms stretched out, I descend—a tightrope walker once more, like when I used to walk the plank that bridges the ditch.

I don't use the banister or rely on this wall where the molding divides the rosebud wallpaper from the rosewood paneling. I'm grateful for the Oriental runner, but I am also aware of the brass-plated borders that keep it tacked down.

"Good morning," Daddy says when I come into the kitchen.

I absorb the fact of certain objects in the room: step stool, toaster, and the chrome edging along the counters. Daddy looks at me. "There's something off about today," he says, and he shakes his head the way he does. And what he really means is there is something off about *me*.

When he opens the door to go feed the chickens, I grab my backpack and push through before he has the chance to exit. I am aware of zippers, buttons, and the snaps. I avoid the metal bucket that holds the feed.

Tin.

I know Daddy is watching me. I don't need to turn around to see. He is watching me the way he watches her.

Our driveway is over a mile. And the long walk gives me time to prepare.

My days used to blend together, but now each one is marked unique by its ordeal even when I fail. Today, I see metal everywhere when yesterday I did not. The fence nails gleam, and the parallel lines of wire stretch forward into the future—both to follow and avoid.

———

I think of Sleeping Beauty. Despite the banishment of spindles from the kingdom, she still managed to prick herself on one.

Waiting for the bus, my brain extracts the soda pop and beer cans from the new grass in the ditch. It extracts the painted crushed aluminum from the other litter tossed from cars. I am a robot now with robot vision. I see the world through a computer screen that targets metal. The red X marks the spot and tugs at my nervous system.

The bus, of course, is one gigantic metal box.

As it approaches, I hear the gears grinding—the downshifting that comes with slowing down and with stopping. Having read the reports Daddy keeps in his desk, I know I have an IQ of 187. It is recommended I attend another school. A school for children who are gifted and talented. But the tuition is twelve thousand dollars a year, and I'd have to move far away from home.

When the bus stops, it vibrates because the engine is still on. The engine is mostly made from metal. The driver manually opens the door for me. The lever is metal too—coated in black rubber. While this is something he has always done for me, I have never noticed until today. And I remember the need for ritual. I bow to him and he bows back. "My lady," he says, and winks at me as I climb aboard.

I am surrounded.

Exposed metal everywhere—the ceiling, the sides, and even the bars for holding on are all made from metal. I see the places where the rubber matting has worn away and the metal is waiting there. My robot brain turns these areas red and the word "warning" blinks urgently as I follow the careful grid. I sit where I have never sat before: in the front. I plant my feet in the aisle where the black mat looks brand new, and I use my backpack as a buffer from the metal floor under the seat in front of me. This is not the same as cheating.

———

It is a precaution. I brace myself by holding on to the seat. I can feel the metal springs through the plastic green upholstery and *this* feels like cheating.

I hold my breath and cross my fingers.

In Daddy's desk, I've also read Alicia Bernstein's diagnosis—not only do I have obsessive-compulsive disorder, I am hypervigilant. Neither dictionary at home included "hypervigilance," so I cut the compound in half and looked up "hyper" and "vigilant" separately.

"Vigilant" means *on the alert, watchful*, and comes from vigil.

There was a candlelight vigil at my school for the boy in Nevada who committed suicide because the lyrics in a Judas Priest song told him to. This is how I learned the word "subliminal." Gran wanted to take me to the vigil, but Mama said, "No way, Fiona."

She said she had to draw the line somewhere. Somewhere over the rainbow.

"Hyper" has two definitions: 1. *Over; above; beyond.* 2. *Excessive; excessively.*

I already knew what it meant, but the dictionary always says it better. In the case of "hyperthyroidism," "hyper" alludes to the abnormal and excessive. The word "hyperventilate" is where "hyper-vigilance" would have been had this been the *DSM IV*, where I first read about schizophrenia before Mama fed that book to the fire. I'm not the only one who knows about Daddy's library beneath his bed. When a person hyperventilates, she's breathing so hard that she can't get any oxygen into her brain, which seems ironic.

I am abnormally alert and excessively watchful.

I am hypervigilant.

* * * *

There is metal everywhere, not just the lead hidden in the paint on all the walls at the farm. There are doorknobs, handles, pencil sharpeners—there is metal everywhere. There is metal on my pencils, and there is graphite inside the wood. I look up "graphite" during recess. I use the encyclopedia. I learn it is a semimetal, and semi counts. I am semi-Mama. And graphite has the same f-sounding *ph* as "phobia" and "schizophrenia."

There are metal rings on my shoes to feed the laces through, and all those hooks in the coatroom. There are zippers, clasps, and spiral-bound notebooks, and there is jewelry hanging off all the bodies around me. The silver and gold chains reach for me, and the earrings flash like lightning.

And then there is my desk: a combination of wood and steel, it is bolted to the floor. Once I find a way to safely sit, I cannot move. For geometry, Mr. Denmar asks us to draw the perfect circle, which I know can only be done with a compass. The teacher says it's sweet I tried to do otherwise, an important thing to attempt as an artist, "But this is math," he says. "Do you understand?"

At home, I am confronted by silverware and wire hangers, spatulas and cast-iron skillets, pots and pans, the stove itself, the kitchen sink, and there is no end.

I fail.

And Mama doesn't come down for dinner. She's been in the bathroom all afternoon, once again. She was in there forever, both with and without the water running. But now she's in her room, and I can hear her crying. At the table, I ask if she's okay, and Daddy looks up as if he can see her through the ceiling.

"Today was just a bad day," he says, standing up.

He starts clearing the table even though we just sat down to eat.

—

He takes away my fork, spoon, and butter knife—the utensils I wasn't going to use—and puts everything in the sink. He scrapes the meat I never eat into the trash, and then he goes outside to check on all the animals.

June 13, 1986
The failures have been accumulating, and it's all my fault.

Mama has been experiencing tactile hallucinations. I find her getting ready to take a bath dyed blue with window cleaner, and I make the mistake of going to get my father. She was naked and just stepping into the tub when she looked at me. She looked at me like she knew she was doing something wrong. She recognized it in my eyes.

Mama looked at me and she said, "I'm just trying to get rid of the bed bugs."

I didn't even know she was in the bathroom. I'd been waiting for this day—for Friday the thirteenth—but Mama doesn't seem to care anymore. She only cares about the bugs. "But there are no bugs," Daddy says. He says this again and again and again; he is stuck on repeat.

He teaches me the word "formication," as if vocabulary is the only way I can understand the world. "Formication" is one letter away from "fornication." And it's the medical term for a sensation that resembles insects crawling on or under the skin.

This time Mama was not triggered by anything related to birth or babies, but it was still my fault. I've been punished for reversing the roles of mother and daughter. For tucking her in at night. And whispering the bedtime charm she used to say to me. My father's black hair begins to turn to white like the squares for all the failed ordeals. And the failed ordeals add up. I ran out of Sundays a long time ago, and 1986 is no longer long enough. I'd have to create four more calendars just to redo what I failed to do before. I wave my white flag instead; I surrender.

August 22, 1986

Everyone is asleep and summer is almost over. I take the Calendar and the faceless nesting doll outside. I must absolve myself.

I strike the wooden matches against the rocks lining Mama's herb garden—the garden with the sinkhole I was meant to fill. The hole is no longer as deep as it once was; once upon another time, this is where Mama was going to bury my placenta and plant a rosebush in remembrance. "But the hospital stole it from me," she has told me more than once. And she never filled it in, nor did she plant the rose amid the silver-green sage and feathery-soft chamomile. I strike one match after the other, and the sulfur is pungent; it pollutes the sweet humidity of late August.

The Calendar and its effigy must be banished.

I am not alone. The statue of Mother Mary watches me. Once, she belonged to Gran, but when she moved she left the deity behind. Made from plaster, Mary's flesh is pocked by time and by weather—her blue robes washed white from many years of rain and snow; like geography she is eroding. I'm beginning to understand that Mama might not get better, but I might be able to keep her from getting worse. If she gets worse, Alicia Bernstein from Social Services will surely return. And this time, I'll be taken away.

From now on, I will protect my mother. If I find her doing something she shouldn't do, I will deal with it by myself. I will take care of her. I will not go to Daddy, not ever. The time has come to grow up instead of trying to start over.

———

The moonflowers open as the calendar agrees to burn, the twelve pages fanning. The matches turn paper into fire as I cremate the corpse of time. I add the doll to the fire and wait for wood and paper to make ash, for the phoenix to rise above. The paper burns: the months that were, and the months that never got to be. The watercolor paper curls—first orange, then blue-violet, and I imagine Mama's parents watching over me as the smoke rises toward the sky.

The ordeals absolve. Becoming nothing more than soft gray ash. Dust to dust. The faceless nesting doll does not burn but she does turn black; she is impossible to lose.

Mother Mary stands as my only witness. Her arms outstretched— a gesture forever unfulfilled. She beckons. I want to curl up in her arms. To nest inside her flesh. She looks like she could save a soul, but she can't.

Her dead son is my proof.

CHAPTER EIGHT
TRANSITION

alarm: n. 1. *A sudden feeling of fear* 2. *A warning of danger;*
signal for attention 3. *A device that signals a warning*
4. *The sounding mechanism of an alarm clock.*

September 2, 1986

I'm late to the first day of school. The sixth grade—the last grade
before I go to junior high. The sixth grade with Mrs. Landry, who all
the kids call Mrs. Laundry, and sometimes Dirty Laundry.

I am late because the pigs got out. They got out even though the
gates were latched.

I help Daddy corral the pigs back to where they need to be instead
of where they were in the road that is really just a long driveway. The
sheep stand in the north paddock where the motherwort grows wild,
and they watch as we scour the fencing for a break, but there is no
break. Daddy spent the entire summer upgrading this fence. Wood
and wire: My father fortified the farm.

"Maybe it's the wind?" Daddy asks, but he isn't asking me. He
seems to be asking the latch itself. He stares at it as if it will come
undone of its own accord. Provide the answer he needs. The latch
remains shut. It keeps silent. We get in the Dodge, and Daddy
drives me to school. Before I climb down from the cab, he writes a

—

short note on the back of an old grocery list. Daddy always writes in tidy block letters and in only capitals. Addressed TO WHOM IT MAY CONCERN, the note is for the secretary. My excuse for being late.

I'm handing the note to the secretary when I see her. It's been five years, but she looks the same. Same black leather briefcase. Same dull brown hair. And there's even a run in her panty hose, only in a different place this time. I hold my breath and cross my fingers: Alicia Bernstein from Social Services has not come for me. I will not allow it.

The secretary takes the note, reads it, crumples it with a tiny fist, and tosses it into the wastebasket bin even though the cardboard recycling bin is right beside it. The social worker is talking to Principal White. Two walls of his office are made from thick glass, and the blinds are up. His office reminds me of the refrigerated room at The Flower Lady, only it's not filled with beauty.

Divided by glass and one closed door, their conversation is on mute. Alicia Bernstein is opening her briefcase, and I can almost hear the click of the hardware as it echoes from past to present while she reaches in for a manila folder. The secretary cracks her gum to get my attention. She holds the tardy note for my new teacher, and I almost rip the paper when I grab it.

I walk so fast, I run out of breath, and when I stop to get it back I read the note. The secretary forgot to mark the time of my arrival, which means I have all the time in the world. I duck into the girls' bathroom, where I sit inside the last beige stall trying to catch my breath.

I am hyperventilating. I cannot catch my breath. This morning when I was helping Daddy herd the pigs back into captivity, I rolled my jeans up to keep from getting muddy and a mosquito got the front of my calf. Sitting on the back of the toilet, I roll my jeans up to compare the injured leg against the uninjured. The difference is so small.

The mosquito bite is a tiny mound of swollen pink flesh peaked by a scab so new, the brown is still translucent. And the itch is still there. It talks to me. I scratch myself open—I scratch past the point of itching, and I can breathe again. My blood intermingles with the oxygen in the air, and my lungs inflate. I feel my body rising. I float until I empty myself of air again. Deflating, I bleed. And then I inflate again, and still bleeding, I deflate. I fill and deplete, I rise and fall. Sometimes floating away is the only way I can get myself back to reality; if I go away, I can then return.

Alicia Bernstein doesn't come and pull me out of class, nor does she drive out to the farm. The social worker does not come to take me away. I don't see her again that day, or the days after.

Time passes, and the leaves on the trees turn yellow, orange, and red; autumn sets the world on fire, and yet the weather turns crisp and cold. I try not to count the days without any further sign of the social worker, but I'm also trying not to count the days until I turn eleven, because then I'll have to count the years before I turn nineteen.

Mama pulls it together as she usually does and makes the annual carrot cake for my birthday, and Gran and Uncle Billy come over for the celebratory dinner, only Gran still calls it supper.

Mama puts all the candles on the top of the cake—eleven plus one to equal twelve candles altogether. "One to grow on," Mama says. "Either that or this one counts for all the time you spent inside me." She can't decide. She never can. She is repeating what she says every year. "Did you know women aren't really pregnant for nine months?"

she says. "I don't know where that myth came from, but it's not true. Human gestation takes ten months instead."

Mama made the usual cream cheese frosting and used the icing tube to make the white roses. She planted them all around the circular edge. Last year she made candied violets and this year she uses carob chips to make spirals all around the top. Gran wants to know what carob is, and Daddy shrugs and says, "It tastes like chocolate."

My grandmother scowls, and I can see the coffee stains on her teeth. Turning to Uncle Billy, she says, "Then why bother? Why not just use chocolate chips?" And Uncle Billy nudges her softly and whispers, "Ma, let it be."

I wish I had a soft grandmother. The kind of grandmother who bakes chocolate chip cookies and knits pink-and-brown-striped leg warmers like the ones Sissy Baxter wore to school yesterday. I want the kind of grandmother you call Grandma or Nana. My soft grandmother died before I could even meet her.

Like a clock, my body is wound. It keeps going. I am eleven years old today, and this makes me think of something Mama does. Whenever a digital clock reads 11:11, Mama says, "Make a wish!" I do make wishes, only I make the same wish every time. I will wish this wish until it comes true, and then I will never make another wish again because I will have everything I could ever want or need; because it would be selfish to ask for anything more.

Daddy lights the candles and everyone sings "Happy Birthday," and before I blow all the candles out I make this wish, my one and only. And as the ritual requires I do not speak it out loud or else it won't come true.

*　*　*　*

—

Five days after I turn eleven, the time to fall back arrives. I help Daddy reset all the clocks in the house, in the barn, and in the truck. He winds his wristwatch, and we all gain an hour just like that.

I take the slop out to the pigs, and that's when I see her.

The sky is a lavender dome of dusk and the trees are skeletons again and the straw man is a silhouette of himself. Like my grandmother's Jesus, his head lulls forward, and because it does the scarecrow appears to be headless. She, too, is a shadow—a cutout of herself as she prances along the edges of the pasture where the sheep are no longer grazing. She is alone this time, but then I realize she might be one of the pups from before, only grown. Her ears reach for sound, and she stops to listen. She is listening to me. She listens to the pigs that have come to greet me, sniffing the table scraps with their sensitive snouts and snorting with pleasure.

She postures the same as the wolf in the pop-up book I made with Mama. She is trying to camouflage—to dissolve into the sharp fringe of Johnsongrass harvested black by the coming night. Her feral fur is tense, electric with life and nerves, and something tells me she knows I'm watching.

She doesn't move—a statue of herself, but in the stillness of her shape I can feel her breathing. I can even picture her lungs; they are two wings flapping. They work to keep her heart beating, and just as I begin to see the red inside her chest she runs away. She disappears into the foliage along the ditch, and swallowed by the shapes of trees and bramble, she is devoured by the night.

January 19, 1987
The nurse wears a stiff white coat and orange lipstick. Her lipstick makes the situation ironic.

—

irony: 1. The use of words to convey the opposite of their literal meaning. 2. Incongruity between what might be expected and what actually occurs.

"Ironic" is one of Mama's favorite things to say. To her, everything is ironic.

I don't know why I didn't expect it to be the same nurse. Of course it is. This is her job. She is the school nurse. She not only remembers who I am, she makes it clear she does not like me. It's been four years since I last went to her.

"Girls your age don't have periods," she says, as if I've made a mistake.

The nurse rummages around in the supplies closet until she finds something like nothing I have ever seen before. She appears just as mystified, holding it in the air for further examination.

"Now this is a relic from the 1950s," she says, and shakes her head the way grown-ups do whenever they are overcome by nostalgia. Lately, I've been overcome by this word: "Nostalgia." And I am absolutely in love with the idea. Aster and Zinnia indicate nostalgia according to *Floriography.*

nostalgia: 1. A bittersweet longing for the past.
2. Homesickness. The Greek root, Nostos, means
"return home."

My quest: *to bring Mama back.*

The pad looks nothing like the ones Mama uses. This is a large white butterfly. And there are a lot of strings. It is not designed to stick to your underpants. The nurse looks at me. "It's all I have," she says, "other than the tampon dispenser in the ladies' room. As

—

I said before, you are much too young for all of this."

As I try to put on the white butterfly, the nurse stands on the other side of the bathroom door. She has X-ray vision, sighing every single time I fail. The strings are confusing: Cat's Cradle. Cup and Saucer. Jacob's Ladder. They get tangled, and I have no idea where they go or what I'm supposed to tie them to. In the end, the pad is no better than the bed of paper towels I used to line my panties with during morning recess.

I drape the used paper towels over the edge of the trash can as my proof.

I leave them in case I'm about to bleed to death. I leave them for the nurse to see because if I'm actually dying, she will have to save my life—no matter how much she hates me, she is a nurse. And she must be bound to a code of ethics that dictates saving lives when they need saving.

It's no secret Daddy is struggling to make ends meet.

Gran calls the farm "high maintenance," and she's right. Everything needs to be repaired. The roof is leaking. The house needs to be painted. The John Deere has trouble starting.

Daddy decides to lease out a little bit of the land. This bit runs along County Road 42. He chooses this plot because we can't see it from the house. My father draws up all the paperwork, and Larry Byrd signs. This man plans on using the patch of earth to grow animal-grade grain sorghum.

No one talks about what this means because we don't have to. Everyone knows—even Gran, who probably doesn't care. Larry Byrd will use pesticides and herbicides, and because he will, Daddy will never get certified organic, and this is yet another dying dream.

———

187

* * * *

Mama abandons the meticulous Victorian paper cuts and all the detail-oriented art she normally does. She gets large and messy instead. And the only color she uses now is red.

Mama works on the floor—sprawled out across gigantic sheets of newsprint that come on big rolls like toilet paper. When she runs out, she goes and gets the butcher paper from the barn, which Uncle Billy uses to package all the meat. She smears the red oil pastels, making red tornados that spin into sizes bigger than me. She spins a web of utility string from one room to another and hangs the red work on it using the wooden clothespins, which look like little people—which look like the smallest nesting doll before she turned black.

"Prayer flags," my mother says as she steps back to admire the artwork suspended throughout the house. She is always out of breath because she has taken to smoking again. She smokes ten cigarettes a day. I'm told this is nothing compared with what other smokers smoke. Especially the schizophrenics. But Mama is also growing larger and larger.

Mama sits down amid the sloppy red spirals, the intense red circles, the bursting poppies, the smashed tomatoes, and she smiles. There are entire rectangles of paper so red, they are bleeding.

"This is a breakthrough," she explains, but I'm pretty sure she's not talking to me. She is talking to herself. Mama's smile grows until her mouth takes over; it swallows her face, another gaping redness, and now she looks at me, and when she says "I can breathe again" I know exactly what she means. I, too, paint red breakthroughs, only I use my fingernails instead of brushes. I use blood instead of watercolors or acrylics, and skin in place of paper.

—

Like Mama, I paint my breakthroughs because it is the only way I can breathe.

Winter turns to spring, and I see the feral dog walking the borders of our land. Crepuscular, she only comes at dawn or dusk, and I have no evidence to prove she is female, or to know she is dog and not wolf or coyote or dingo, and yet I *do* know.

She always emerges from the woods along the ditch before she dares the open horizon of Kansas flatness. And because it's just before the sun has risen or set all the way, she is nothing more than a shadow against the canvas onto which she chooses to paint herself.

She takes her time. She wants to make sure I see her. I watch from windows, or from the porch, and sometimes I watch from the heart of the orchard from my perch in the apple tree in the row farthest from the house. She appears and disappears at the same gate of wild raspberry that curtains the ditch. And she always walks a full circle around the house. She tells time. Like the hands of a clock, she begins where she ends and ends where she began.

The sixth graders are herded into the gymnasium, where we're told to sit on the old wooden floor.

I sit inside the faded orange curve of a line that has something to do with basketball.

Mrs. Landry leans against the wall, looking at us like a mother might, like she's about to cry. I heard her tell Mrs. Jefferson she wasn't sure how much longer she could teach the sixth grade. "I can't stand sending them away," she said.

I look at Mrs. Landry, and there is a handkerchief in her fist, the white cotton contrasting sharply with her long red fingernails.

—

Principal White is standing on a makeshift stage, in front of a microphone, waiting for us to settle. Mrs. Landry gets our attention and whisper-screams, "Crisscross applesauce," and puts her finger to her lips and hisses a long "shh!" But I'm the only one watching her. Everyone else is too excited. Our time at elementary school is nearly over.

Principal White taps on the microphone, and the large room fills with the amplified sound of his tapping. I look up, drawn to the lights swinging idly inside their metal cages. Basketball hoops stand at both ends, and both are missing their white nets. Last night, Mama went after the prayer flags. She ripped all the red sheets off the string and burned them in the fireplace. I don't know why.

"The adviser from Keller is here to talk to you about junior high," Principal White says, and everyone is quiet now. I'm not the only one wide-eyed and scared. Principal White steps aside as a woman takes the stage. I look down. Through the pale fringe of my eyelashes, I watch the woman gathering herself to speak to us.

"I am here to talk to you about the transition," the woman says.

I scrape notches into my skin. I count the minutes as they pass, or maybe I'm counting seconds instead.

Mrs. Landry sniffles, and now she is hiccupping against her tears. When she blows her nose, she sounds like a foghorn, and the adviser says, "You will all succeed at Keller Junior High!" And Mrs. Landry begins to clap. Her clapping is muffled by the white handkerchief, and yet it sparks a wave of clapping, and now everyone around me is clapping—everyone but me.

CHAPTER NINE
NEGATIVE SPACE

*continue: 1. To persist 2. To endure; last 3. To remain in a state,
capacity, or place 4. To go on after an interruption; resume
5. To extend 6. To retain 7. To postpone or adjourn.*

September 11, 1987
Seventh grade is where sex education changes from an anatomy
lesson to something different, and in health class the boys and girls
are no longer separated. The kids talk about sex all the time—in the
halls, in the cafeteria, and especially on the bus. But during sex ed,
when they're supposed to talk about it, they are suddenly quiet.

Some of the girls will talk about pregnancy. They talk about it like
they know everything there is to know. They've had mothers pregnant
with younger siblings, or aunts round with cousins. And they love
to read about pregnant celebrities in the magazines Mama calls trash.

They talk about babies, too. How cute they are, or how ugly. And
they all describe childbirth as "painful" and "excruciating." They talk
about it like they know firsthand.

They're obsessed with the idea, while the boys fidget—their faces
hot and red. Come Monday, Mrs. Gallagher begins passing out the
bags of Gold Medal flour. Even I've heard about this assignment.
Everyone talked about it back in the sixth grade. This assignment is a
true rite of passage into junior high, and we each receive a bag.

—

"I used to use eggs," Mrs. Gallagher explains. "There was the special challenge of not breaking them, but parents complained about them breaking—they claimed they broke all the time, so I switched to flour, and really, these bags are closer in size to an actual newborn." She jiggles a bag to test the weight while watching the girls who always sit in a cluster.

Mrs. Gallagher continues to look at them and says, "Rather, they're the weight of a premature or low-birth-weight baby." She looks at the girls like they've done something wrong. "Teen mothers are more likely to give birth to premature or low-birth-weight babies," Mrs. Gallagher says, and one girl turns to another girl and says, "Preemies are so precious! I hope I have one." Mrs. Gallagher asks her to speak up. "Mary, it isn't fair when the rest of the class can't hear, and it must be important, since you had to share right this moment. So, Mary, do share."

Mary stands up. I've seen her in the halls. Another new face from Sacred Heart. Mary clears her throat. "I said, preemies are precious. I have a Cabbage Patch preemie. Mother said she was very hard to find." The popular girls giggle. They giggle because Mary still plays with dolls. Charity Murphy smirks. I've heard the boys talk about her on the bus. They use words like "slut" and "whore" and "loose" and "easy." Charity also went to Sacred Heart, and from the way she's glaring at Mary right now, I think they've known each other for very a long time.

"It's not like I play with her," Mary says, looking around. "Dolls are for little girls," she says. She says the word "little" like it's a disease. "Mother said she'll be worth a lot of money someday. All the Cabbage Patch kids will be collectible, but especially the preemies."

Mrs. Gallagher doesn't say anything. She shakes her head and looks out the window. The teacher looks at the tree where all the crows are perching. The cafeteria Dumpsters are below the cotton-wood. Uncle Billy says scavengers are the trash collectors of the animal kingdom; he says, "We could not survive without them."

Finally, Mrs. Gallagher turns around, smoothing her skirt with her hands. "I almost forgot," she says, her glasses slipping down her nose, "I need your permission slips before I can continue."

I sit at my desk, ready. Daddy signed my permission slip last night without looking. He's been distracted.

The slip is pink and rectangular, one third of an $8\frac{1}{2} \times 11$ sheet of paper. I watch the boys fumble for theirs—reaching into their jeans and pulling out crumpled wads of pink. They can't even look at Mrs. Gallagher when she comes to collect their permission slips. When Mrs. Gallagher takes mine, I know everyone is staring, and I wish I was invisible. I try to blend in to my desk, to turn into wood and steel and plastic.

Mary and Charity don't have permission to participate, and I can tell this upsets the teacher. "I'm afraid you'll have to spend the next two classes in study hall," she says. "Stay after and I'll go over the alternative assignment, but for now, wait in the hall and read chapter seven."

Mary goes to the door, stopping as if to wait for Charity. Chewing on the end of her pencil, Charity stares at Mrs. Gallagher and doesn't move—not right away. Her eyes are so brown, they are black. She takes her time sliding out of her seat and grabbing her leather jacket. And she makes a point to leave her textbook on the desk next to her orphaned flour sack. As Charity makes her way to the door, Phillip Booth coughs: "Slut."

Mrs. Gallagher distributes our homework. We are given a

handout on infant care and a calendar for keeping track of feedings and diaper changes, only the teacher calls it a log. "You are to go everywhere with your babies," Mrs. Gallagher says. "This is your life for the next forty-eight hours. Welcome to teen parenthood!"

"Technically," I want to say, "we are either twelve or about to be." But I don't. I don't say anything at all.

On Wednesday, the completed log, a five-paragraph essay, and the flour are all due for us to receive credit. The flour is not to be damaged. "Not only do you need to prove to me that you can keep a tiny human alive," Mrs. Gallagher says, "we donate the flour to a charity that helps unwed mothers." And then the bell rings and it is time to go to my next class.

In the hall, the boys throw their flour babies in the air and catch them. They punch one another and say, "Dude," and call one another "Mr. Mom." The girls giggle, forming into small groups, holding their flour like they're actual newborns. The girls are making fun of the assignment, yet there's something serious about the way they're overacting motherhood. The girls compare babies and make-believe what each one looks like.

"Mine has curly blond hair," Candace Sherman says. Sissy Baxter says her baby looks just like the Gerber baby. They name the babies: Barbara, Jack, Melody, Connor—and talk-whisper who the fathers are. This makes them really giggle. They pick off the popular seventh-grade boys. Trent Wallace is picked again and again, until one girl claims her baby was fathered by a ninth grader. But she's outdone by Tanya Jenkins, who confesses: "I have no idea who my baby daddy is." Laughing, Tanya loosens her hair from a ponytail, and the burst of blondness turns her into a movie star, or model.

I am not like them. I don't want to have a baby. I've already decided. I will not have kids. I will stop the bloodline. I will stop the schizophrenia.

"What is that?" Mama asks when I come in through the kitchen door. She is looking at the flour.

The table is littered with shredded magazines, and there are mannequin heads all over the room—on the table, the counters, the step stool, and the floor. This is what happens when Mama runs out of space.

I'm carrying the flour sack. It is sweating a fine white dust. I've checked the bag for tears, but the packaging is intact and the top folded over, still sealed. I have no idea where the flour is coming from, but my shirt is white from carrying it and my arms are tired. I'd put it down but there isn't a bare surface left, so I shift the bag to my other arm.

"It's supposed to be a baby," I tell her. "It's for health class." I wonder if Daddy would have signed the permission slip if he'd bothered to read it.

Mama is plastering a mannequin head with human eyes torn from *National Geographic*. Last night, Mama tried to tell Daddy about the evil eye, but he wasn't listening. He does that a lot these days. And sometimes he does it to me. He forgets who I am, and who I am not. He'll be ignoring me and then all of a sudden he will realize it's me, and he'll snap out of it and start asking questions. He will ask one question after the other—too many to ever answer. He doesn't listen like I do. I listen to everything.

Surrounded by all these eyes, I feel like I am being watched. Mama has a paper eye stuck to her cheek, upside down and starting to curl. She holds her hands in the air the way surgeons do after they've scrubbed in for surgery. Sticky with clear glue, they look webbed, and her long hair is coming undone—strand by strand, it escapes the spiral bun held in place with only a pair of chopsticks.

"You mean *your* baby," Mama says, and she has that look, the serious one. And I wish I'd come in through the front door instead. It's getting harder to know which door to use.

I look at the flour sack. "Okay," I say. "*My* baby."

"You know, Fig, it's true I wasn't feeling well when it was time for orientation, but your father still filled me in. Junior high is a big deal. *You're* a big deal. This project is for sex ed, right? Your father wasn't sure, but I think it's absolutely brilliant—especially with all those damn pro-life billboards popping up across Kansas like burning crosses. No wonder teen pregnancy is skyrocketing. I say pass out condoms with the milk, but this at least is a good start."

Her cheeks are flushed and her pupils big and black, two holes to fall into.

"Okay, Mama."

"You have a schedule for the baby, right?" she asks.

I nod my head.

"Well?" Mama says, looking at me. She wants to see the log book. The last time she even looked at my homework was in the third grade. The pop-up book. *Little Red Riding Hood.*

"It's just . . ." I look around. "It's in my backpack, and there's no place to set *it* down." I jiggle the flour so she understands. I jiggle it like I would a real baby.

Mama frowns at me. "It?" she asks, but then she's distracted. She looks around like she's just now noticed the state of the kitchen. She looks irritated. I can't tell if she's irritated with me, herself, or all of it. She goes to the sink and turns the faucet on with the side of her wrist. Considering the chaos everywhere else, it's a strange precaution. She squirts dish soap on her hands and uses the vegetable scrubber to scour her fingers.

"I wouldn't want to get the baby sick," she says. She isn't looking at what she's doing. The glue is washed off by now. Her hands are red—raw and inflamed. And I wish she'd stop. I wish she were joking too. I see how other mothers might tease their daughters—the mothers on TV, or the mothers who give birth to Candace Sherman. But my mother is dead serious. This is a dead end. There is no way out.

She holds the flour with her red hands while I take off my backpack and get the handout. She continues to hold it as she reads the instruction sheet Mrs. Gallagher had also given us. Mama holds the flour like the girls at school held theirs, and I can't watch her anymore. There are magazine pages scattered all over the floor. The large faces look at me, except they have no eyes. Their eyes have all been torn away. The eyelessness acts like strange blindfolds on these paper faces, which is not the same as the eyelessness of the faceless nesting doll. This eyelessness is like negative space instead.

When I was younger, Mama taught me about negative space. She looked at all my drawings, tracing the negative space with her fingers—the space between or around the matter. She taught me to see not only the value of nothing but the value of what is missing. I don't draw anymore.

"This makes it sound much simpler than it really is," Mama says, shaking her head and blowing her bangs out of her eyes. "It doesn't take into account all the emergencies that happen."

Emergency C-section, twelve years ago, come next month.

"It's only forty-eight hours, Mama." And when I tell her this, she seems satisfied. She hands me the flour, instruction sheet, and the log, and then she returns to her work. To all those eyes. And it's like I'm not standing here anymore. Like I never even came home.

Daddy comes in for dinner, and Mama explains the high chair. Daddy smiles at me as he sits down, but I see the way he eyes the flour. He shakes his head, and I know what he is thinking. But it's too late. The flour baby is already here.

The bag of Gold Medal flour is sitting in the high chair because Mama insisted. "You have to treat it like a real baby," she said before my father came inside. And somehow in the time it took for me to do my pre-algebra upstairs, she got the kitchen to look like a real kitchen again—no sign of shredded eyes or mannequin heads. They've all vanished like a magic trick, and Mama, too, has been transformed. She is a TV mother, a TV wife. She not only cleaned, she also cooked.

I play along with Mama. And the flour-sack baby turns into a real baby. We name her Daisy, and Daisy likes to play with her food. Daisy gurgles when she laughs, and her laugh makes us all laugh—even Daddy. We all love Daisy. And now we're the family we are supposed to be. A family on the television.

We laugh and talk and eat together. Our conversation has absolutely nothing to do with anything. And Daddy isn't dressed like Daddy anymore. Instead of jeans and a T-shirt, he grows a necktie, which he's loosens because he's at home now, and his suit is navy blue with gray pinstripes. For dessert, he makes chocolate milkshakes. I drink mine too fast and get an ice cream headache, and the way I pinch my nose with my fingers makes us all laugh even harder. Behind our laughter is a laugh track laughing with us.

—

The person in control brings up the volume of it whenever we are threatened by an awkward silence. The person in control brings up the volume of strangers' laughter whenever Mama messes up and says something strange or wrong. The laugh track cues the studio audience, and they start laughing too. I try not to look at them—just like looking at the camera is considered bad acting, it would be unprofessional. Instead, I catch them in my peripheral vision; they look like mannequins. That is, they look like mannequins before my mother gets hold of them, before she paints their hard skin or glues magazine clippings to their faces. They look like mannequins before she decapitates them.

They look like mannequins, only real—flesh and blood; they are animate, perfect people. Laughing, they rock back and forth and slap their knees. I laugh until I almost pee my pants. I laugh so much, my cheeks begin to hurt from smiling, working all the muscles in my face that never move.

But then someone turns the TV off. The screen goes black—goes black in an inward way, where the last thing left is a white dot in the center of the screen. And when the white dot burns out, it makes a soft electrical pop that makes me think, *God has gone to bed.*

Mama wakes me at midnight to feed the baby. She sits with me in the kitchen as I make believe heating up water, mixing formula, and warming milk. She tells me to nurture the baby. I rock the flour-sack baby on my no-hip hip as Mama rants about breast-feeding being better than formula.

Daddy opens the door to his office, which is also the guest bedroom, which is also where he sleeps and keeps all his clothes. I still don't know what to call this room. He's wearing long underwear, and he stands in the frame of the open door, watching us. I smile as much as I can and thank Mama again and again for helping me until he seems satisfied. He finally turns to go back into the room. He shuts the door, and the ribbon of light underneath goes black.

Mama drinks her tea, watching me with tired, bloodshot eyes. When I'm ready to go back to bed, her eyes flash with anger—but it was just a flash, and now it's gone. "Daisy is not my baby," Mama says. "You're going to have to wake up on your own from here on out." She reminds me of everything I already know. I'm supposed to wake up every three hours, which really means one more time. On schooldays, I always wake at 6:00 to eat breakfast and get dressed in time to catch the bus.

I set the alarm for 3:00 a.m. but I'm too tired to get up when it goes off. I barely manage to reset it for 6:00. As I fall back to sleep I think about the assignment. How it's designed for us to cheat. That's the beauty of it, and Mrs. Gallagher knows it. The reason it works is that we have to also write the essay about what it feels like to be responsible for another life. Imagining alone is enough to scare us. The assignment works even if a student leaves her flour in her locker instead of taking it home. As long as the log is filled in, even if the entries are all false, the assignment works.

When I wake up to the alarm, I don't have to get out of bed to know. I see before I even sit or have a chance to turn off the clock. There has been a snowstorm.

My bedroom is covered by a blanket of quiet white flour. It is everywhere, like someone took the bag, ripped it open, and spun around and around. My desk, my window seat, my dresser, my floor—there is flour on my bed and in my hair. There is flour everywhere.

———

I hear Daddy's steps coming down the hall and I jump out of bed. Slipping on the flour, I throw myself against the door just as he knocks. "Fig? You up?" he asks, and the knob turns and I can feel him pushing on the door. I push back. I tell him I'm awake. That I'm getting dressed. I tell him I'll be right down. Then I get dressed as fast as I can.

I find the empty bag buried in the flour. I exhume it, shake it off, and then bury it once again—deep in my trash can. I bury the empty flour sack under wads of crumpled-up notebook paper, a week's worth of messed-up homework—essay answers that couldn't find the right words. I am running out of time. Daddy cannot see. He cannot know what she just did.

I brush the flour off my body, and then I sneak out of my room. I am quiet as I pass Mama's door, but then I rush down the stairs. Daddy is frying bacon in the kitchen and doesn't see me snatch the broom and dustpan from the pantry. Mama is nowhere to be seen, and I am quiet when I pass her room again. I worry she's in there, listening for me. That she's not really still asleep, because there is no snoring. I grab the bathroom trash can and take it to my room because it has a trash bag and mine does not. I sweep the flour as fast as I can, but fast is a mistake. Fast makes it spread.

The flour takes flight, and my room becomes the inside chamber of a terrible snow globe. Spinning around, I see the mannequin heads. They are blindfolded and laughing. They laugh because they cannot cry, and they cannot cry because they have no eyes. As the room spins I catch glimpses of my mother. She won't look at me. She is too busy caring for a baby.

Mother and baby become white dust. I am holding the broom, waiting for the flour to settle—for the vision to fully dissipate. And

—

then I sweep again, slow but deliberate. I sweep the flour, I sweep the mother and her child, emptying dustpan after dustpan into the black trash bag. I sweep the rest of it under my bed to deal with later. I wipe the flour off my desk and shake out my quilt. I brush the walls and use my hands to beat the cushions from the window seat, and I do the same with all the pillows on my bed. And then I sweep again.

I erase anything Daddy might notice if he was to come in here while I'm at school. I stash the trash bag in my closet and put the now-bagless trash can back into the bathroom. I hold my breath and cross my fingers, trying to erase my worries about the bagless-ness. And then I head back downstairs. I act like this is the first time I've come down today. Daddy is scrubbing the cast iron with coarse salt and steel wool and doesn't see me put the broom and dustpan away.

We eat scrambled eggs on toast with bacon, only I don't eat the meat. Daddy drinks black coffee, and I drink a small glass of orange juice. When he goes to the bathroom, I check the cabinets for flour but find what I expected to find. Our flour is whole wheat. Bought in bulk from the health food store, it's kept in large Mason jars with cloth lids. When Daddy returns, I pretend to be looking for the granola bars.

"You're a hungry girl," he says, and before he sits down he gestures to the plate of bacon on the table. "There's still some breakfast left," he says, arching an eyebrow. Then he sits down again and opens the newspaper from yesterday. On weekdays, he is always a day behind because I bring the mail to the house after school. Otherwise, the mailbox is just too far to go.

I grab my backpack and give him a kiss good-bye. I kiss his third eye and I say a quick prayer in my head. I hold my breath and cross my fingers that he will not look in my room.

As I open the door he puts the paper down and looks at me. "Fig?" he says. "Aren't you forgetting something?" His words are like a spell. They turn me into ice. And I freeze. He could mean anything. The studio audience returns, only they are frozen too. Mouths gaping, they are waiting to see what will happen next, and the drums roll. "Honey," he says, "aren't you forgetting your baby?" and his tone is sarcastic. The laugh track rumbles—low, waiting for a chance to crescendo.

I tell him I haven't forgotten—the flour is in my backpack, I say. I tell him I put it there because I want to hide it. And I try not to check the stairs for Mama, or worry about the vents and the way this house can carry voices.

I smile like I'm shy about the subject. The way the daughters on TV smile at their fathers when they're embarrassed. I explain how no one else actually carries their babies around, and I'm sure to end with a sweetly saturated "Daddy." And this alone breaks my heart. The audience is divided. Half of them are with me, and the other half with Daddy. Either way, they are captivated.

Daddy nods his head and smiles at me. He says, "I won't tell if you won't," and then he looks at the ceiling the way he always does, because my mother is on the other side. My father thinks he understands, and this hurts even more. The guilt pain radiates from every broken shard of heart, spreading into my fingertips, into my toes. The guilt hurts. But he cannot know.

I leave Daddy to his day, and the theme song and credits begin to roll.

On the screen, I walk away from the house. Down the long driveway I slowly disappear, and the audience gets ready to leave the

———

studio. Standing, they stretch first, and then they begin to gather their belongings, their jackets and purses, and they chat about what they think they just saw.

I walk fast and faster still. Lungs wide open: I inflate.

I fill myself with the crisp morning air, inhaling the possibilities of a new day. I baptize myself in oxygen. I swallow the sky. Clouds and starlings drift across my lungs. I fill myself with the endless blue until there is no more room for all the pain.

I ditch health class.

I decide to lie when I get home—tell Daddy there was an accident with the flour. I consider the accident. Maybe I tripped and it broke open, but that doesn't explain why I wouldn't go to class.

It has to be someone else's fault.

I think of blaming Phillip Booth, but I know better. I don't need to make him mad—he's already terrible enough. Instead, it was a ninth-grade boy. He was teasing me. He grabbed the flour and held it in the air so I couldn't get it. He held it out the window on the third floor, but then he dropped it. I'll tell Daddy I don't think he meant for this to happen. And I will have no idea what his name is. The incident happens right before class, and because I'm so upset I hide in the bathroom and I miss health.

But I don't know how to tell Daddy without Mama being around. Even if I find a way, it will be impossible for us to replace the flour without her asking questions, or knowing what we are doing. The story of the ruined flour will prompt a trip to town to go to the grocery store, and a trip to town will get her attention. And then what? What would she say? Or do?

I need another plan.

———

I forge the letter to Mrs. Gallagher using one of the electric type-writers in the little rooms connected to the library. I fake Daddy's signature—a squiggly line, like he lost control of the pen. Tobias Johnson. The fake signature looks a lot like his real one. His signature is nothing like his regular penmanship, something I've never considered until today.

The letter I write is written by a father who adamantly opposes sex education. "Adamant" comes right after "Adam" in the pocket-book dictionary at home—as in the biblical Adam, the first man. From Adam's rib, God carved Eve. "Adamant" is defined as being "impervious to pleas or reason; unyielding."

This unyielding father explains to Mrs. Gallagher how I forged his signature on my permission slip. Now I understand what people mean when they say there is a truth in every lie. This unyielding father tells Mrs. Gallagher she had better find a way to ensure this never happens again. As this father writes, his character grows stronger. This father would never let his wife go crazy.

This unyielding father is offended that something as banal as a sack of flour is being used to represent something so precious as a human life. He had no choice but to take it away, and now he's forbidding me from returning to class—not until this dreadful assignment has been completed. He writes, *Seventh graders are far too young to be exposed to such adult subject matter.* This father concludes by asking Mrs. Gallagher a question: *Have you ever considered the role you play in introducing sexuality to the youth of today before they are mentally and spiritually ready?* And then he blames her for teen pregnancy in Douglas County.

His daughter will be a virgin forever and ever and ever. And there is a truth in every lie.

"Thanks for meeting with me," Mrs. Gallagher says, taking off her reading glasses and setting them on her desk. She smiles at me. I don't say anything, and I don't dare look at her, because she's an eye-contact person. Eye-contact people freak me out.

"I got the letter you wrote," she says. And she pulls it from a folder, holding it for me to see.

I look out the window. This second-story window frames the sky and the tree where the crows perch. Daddy always says a gray and empty sky like this means the first snow of the year is on its way. I hold my breath and cross my fingers: Maybe this is a bad dream. Maybe I'm still in bed waiting for the 6:00 alarm to ring.

"You're not in trouble," Mrs. Gallagher says, leaning forward the way people do when they are trying to get me to look at them. She wants me to feel safe. I think about the third grade. How everything changed when Mrs. Jefferson found out about my mother. I don't want that to happen again. I wait for Mrs. Gallagher to say, *I've spoken to your father*, but then I cross my fingers and hold my breath again: *Please, please, please, let it be him and not my mother.*

I was hoping junior high would be different. I knew the kids wouldn't forget, but I hoped I could at least transition into a world where my teachers didn't know, and wouldn't have to. I can feel Mrs. Gallagher studying me.

"I haven't spoken to anyone about this matter," she says. "I wouldn't dream of embarrassing you like that. Everyone develops at a different rate, some girls slower than others. Honestly, I'm always relieved by the girls like you. It's extremely hard work to stay a little girl in today's world." She sets the letter down, and I think, *There are girls like me?*

"I admire your conviction—your resistance to growing up," she says. "But in the future, Fig, this is not the appropriate way to handle this kind of situation." And she taps her finger on the letter as if I've already forgotten. She explains how she caught me. She doesn't know Daddy well, but she does know him well enough to know he's not a Christian. "In a place like Kansas," she says, "I have to keep track of my enemies and my allies."

She says the letter was otherwise too convincing. Had she not met my father at orientation, she would have been forced to show it to the principal. And she shakes her head the way Mama does when she is sad. This is when Mrs. Gallagher gets up. She comes around to stand in front of me. She is so close, I have to look at her. I hold my breath again and recross my fingers, hoping this will be enough to make her go away.

"Fig, I'm not your enemy," she says. "I wish you would have come to me."

Mrs. Gallagher looks at me like this is an easy thing to do when I have never asked for anything from anyone in my whole, entire life. She blinks, and then she tells me seventh grade is not only the worst grade to be in but the worst one to teach. "Worse than kindergarten," she says. "Some kids are having sex already," she announces, pausing long enough to gauge my reaction. So I make sure to give her the reaction she needs from me. And in doing so, I confirm her theory: I am the epitome of immature. Too shy to carry a sack of flour and pretend it's a baby, because by doing so I am implying that I've had sex, even if it's only make-believe.

She is wrong after all; there are no girls like me.

—

And I'm not yet off the hook. Mrs. Gallagher assigns a standard five-paragraph essay.

The topic: teen pregnancy. "Take an angle," she says, "and support your thesis with plenty of evidence and valid research."

When she finally releases me, lunch is nearly over. She never once inquires about my missing flour baby. Instead she signs a permission slip that allows me to spend tomorrow in the library instead of in her class. I will return to health only after the assignment is complete, and all the other flour babies have been donated to the real young mothers and their children.

I write the paper Mrs. Gallagher wants me to write. My thesis statement: *How sex education helps prevent teen pregnancy.* It is a cliché.

Preaching abstinence is not enough. I advocate for informing students about birth control and abortion. I steal from Mama. I propose that public schools should distribute prophylactics. I conclude that abortion should be legal in every single state and made available to minors without parental consent.

I'm getting better at providing people with what they want and acting like the girl they think me to be. And most important, I am learning how to help Mama when she needs my help. I am her protector.

Daddy is counting sheep when I get home from school. I see him when I decide to cut through the pasture, toward the orchard, instead of walking the long driveway home. My father always jokes about this particular job. "There are things," he says, "like counting sheep, I never imagined myself really doing." And then he'll pretend to yawn and fall asleep.

—

I wave, and he waves back. Then I head for the orchard. It was snowing in town, but not here—not yet. The sky is gray and empty, and it won't be long before the storm comes. Before the giant dome above shatters into a million snowflake shards of winter.

Mama doesn't see me, but I see her. I hide behind one of the thick cottonwoods that encircle the house and protect the structure from the midwestern tornados.

I watch her dig a hole. She stabs the backyard with a shovel. I haven't seen her use a shovel since she gave up on gardening. The mannequin heads are on top of the wood pile, and the carelessness of how they were dropped reminds me of a photograph I once saw of a mass grave at Auschwitz. A picture that made me sick to my stomach.

Mama uses the wooden yardstick to measure the distance from one hole to the next. The yardstick has warped since I last used it to construct the Calendar of Ordeals. And she seems rushed as she attacks the cold earth with the sharp steel. I count twelve piles of dirt, which means she has already dug twelve of these holes.

She keeps looking at the driveway, where I would normally appear. And then she appears to be done with the digging.

One by one, she takes a mannequin head and places each one into a hole of its very own. When there are no more heads, she fills the thirteen holes with dirt and uses her feet to stamp the earth back to flat again. She even gets on her knees, smoothing out the dirt and pressing down with her palms. She keeps looking up, like she's afraid to be caught.

I turn into the cottonwood when she looks my way, and I can't be seen. I am a tree nymph. Finally, Mama stands, and as she brushes the dirt from her hands she examines each grave that is no longer a hole, and then she goes inside. She leaves the shovel leaning against the side of the house.

I count to sixty. Then I count to sixty three more times. When I'm done, it still doesn't seem like long enough, so I do it one more time. After six minutes, I reemerge. Three hundred and eighty seconds. I walk toward the house. I open the door, and I go inside just like I would any other day. That night, it snows one foot, and the white layer of cold makes the world appear pure again.

The snow continues to fall.

As predicted by the *Farmers' Almanac*, winter comes early. The farmers in Douglas County scramble to harvest their crops but suffer plenty of losses. The price of hay skyrockets. While the pigs are smart enough to dig through the snow and find the clover, the sheep just stand there looking dumb, bleating to be fed. We buy more feed for winter than we have ever done before.

I keep expecting the snow to stop—to melt—to reveal one more time the red, orange, and yellow colors of the autumn, but this fire continues to be extinguished by the silent snow. And the snow is steady; it keeps falling and falling and falling. It comes, but it never actually blizzards. Not even wind. Just a white sky and the steady white of falling snow. The white blanket grows thicker, and the quilt squares of Douglas County disappear for now. Like the thirteen heads buried in the yard, the snow buries us; and it makes no plan to uncover what it hides.

I hold my breath and cross my fingers to keep my father in a permanent state of ignorance. And it works. He doesn't find out about the flour, and by the time I turn twelve I can breathe again. Like skin growing over a wound, the hurt is hidden. Maybe even healed. And the snow falls. The world is a clean slate, and even Mama doesn't seem to remember, which is for the best.

She sets aside her art for books and for sleep. And she isn't the only one swallowed by the need to hibernate. Everyone in Douglas County goes through the motions of life, but after the hurried harvest we are all slow—lethargic, almost drugged. We do as we have always done, and yet we are so far away. We dream the collective dream that is also the longest winter I have ever seen.

CHAPTER TEN
TO ESTABLISH INTIMACY

meridian: 1. An imaginary great circle on the Earth's surface, passing through geographic poles. 2. Either half of such a great circle, all points of which have the same longitude. 3. (Astronomy) A great circle passing through poles of the celestial sphere and the zenith for a particular observer. 4. (Mathematics) A similar line on any general surface of revolution. 5. (Alternative medicine) Any of the pathways on the body along which the vital energy (Qi) is thought to flow and, therefore, the acupoints are distributed. 6. The highest point or state of consciousness and enlightenment achievable by a human.

March 19, 1988

It's more than just the engine or the rain that wakes me. It's a bad feeling. I've been dreaming, but the dream runs away fast.

From my window, I watch Daddy in the dark rain throwing stuff into the back of the truck. I grab my robe and go downstairs. Gran is in the kitchen. She looks at me, surprised. "Why are you here?" I ask. She tells me Daddy called and asked her to come stay the night with me. "All the pigs got out," she says, stirring her instant coffee. "And he needs to clear them out of the road and get them back into the sty."

"I'm twelve years old," I say. "I don't need a babysitter." *Besides*, I think, *Mama's here.*

I slip on my galoshes, and then my rain slicker. Ignoring Gran's protests, I rush outside into the wet night. After the long winter, spring is still a shock to me. The farm is no longer asleep, smothered by a blanket of quiet white; the coma is over and the rain has washed away the frozen dreamscape.

Daddy doesn't see me slide into the truck, not until he gets in too. For a second, he stops and looks at me. His eyelids droop the way they do when he is tired, and his eyes are sad. He nods, then shifts the truck into gear. He has the brights turned on, and they highlight long strips of rain and road.

The headlights pick up the pigs where they stand in the road snorting at the sky, awkward and miserable in the storm. It isn't until Daddy pulls over that I see Mama. She's wearing one of her white-linen nightgowns, and she glows against the black night. She's soaked through, and even from inside the truck I can see her body through the wet fabric.

She's standing on the side of the road with her arms raised, orchestrating both the rain and the escaped pigs. She is smiling like she's an actor on a stage, in the spotlight—she pays us no attention. Daddy doesn't say anything.

He gets out of the truck and pulls the hood of his jacket over his head. He starts leading the pigs back through the gate, and he doesn't tend to Mama—not until he's finished with the livestock.

And this is how I know everything has changed.

At school, Alicia Bernstein takes me to a room I never knew existed.

The room is across the hall from the principal's office and through the classroom used for special education. At first, I think she's only getting something from a closet, but when she opens the door I see it really is a room. And we both go in. There are no windows in this room.

A desk is pushed against one wall, and there are three plastic chairs. Two are yellow and one is blue. I choose the blue chair when the social worker tells me to have a seat. I don't move the chair. I sit where it is—in the middle of the room, slanted sideways. Awkward. The fluorescent lights are particularly fierce because the room is so small. Every time they flicker, I see floaties.

Alicia Bernstein moves her yellow chair so she can sit facing me. She sits and looks at me for a long time. She tries to smile, but it's something she still can't do. She looks inside her manila folder instead, and once again she finds solace there. In my file. Written on the tab with a blue ballpoint, I see my name and birthdate: FIONA JOHNSON, 10.21.75. She used periods to separate the numbers in the date where I employ dashes.

The social worker finally speaks. "Fiona, my name is Alicia Bernstein, and I'm from Social Services. We've met before. Do you remember me?" As if I could forget. I nod my head.

I think about Mama and what Daddy politely calls "her episodes." Sometimes during an episode, Mama will panic about Social Services. She insists they are coming. She confirms my anxiety. "They will take my baby away," she will say. But Uncle Billy always tells me not to worry so much. "Worry is like praying for something bad to happen," he will say, and I guess he's right. Together, Mama and I have managed to manifest our worst fear: She is currently staring at me.

If you were to abbreviate Social Services, you'd get SS—the same abbreviation for the Nazi paramilitary organization the *Schutzstaffel*. And the SS soldiers, with their lightning-bolt double-*S* insignias, were connected to the Gestapo, and it was the Gestapo who tore all those people from their homes and from their families—throwing them into cattle cars, taking them far away, some of them forever. But I think I'd rather die. To survive the Holocaust would be even harder. Alicia Bernstein tilts her head, watching me the way people do when they are waiting for me to speak. To say anything.

She can't stand to wait. Her mother probably didn't teach her the value of silence or negative space. Instead she seeks refuge within the paperwork again, the file she holds on me, and she deliberately holds it so I can't see what she can see. And I think of Emily Dickinson, and my favorite poem about death, and the line that reads "I could not see to see."

This is the line Ms. Sylvia copied onto the board in her beautiful cursive, which spirals away like bindweed tendrils, and then she asked the class what it might mean. I didn't even have to think about it. I just knew. To see to see, which is not exactly what Dickinson wrote, means knowing how to look. How to look to understand. How to look without your eyes. And to die, is not to see at all. Of course, I didn't actually say this out loud. I never raise my hand, but Phillip Booth did, which is weird because he never volunteers to answer; he doesn't ever willingly participate in classroom discussion, but this time he did. And he seemed excited. He raised his hand, and when Ms. Sylvia called on him he asked: "Is it a typo?" And I couldn't help but feel sorry for him. I really think he thought he was right. He didn't understand the repetition of the word "see."

I pretend not to care about the social worker's stupid folder and what it may or may not contain. I stare at the surface of the desk instead. There is nothing on the desk, and the gray plastic is cracked down the middle like someone heavy sat on it. Mama is fat, but no one talks about it. It's another secret. Another unspoken. We try to keep her safe through silence. I can't help but sneak my hand into my sleeve to find the scab on my arm, the one below my elbow.

Once I get started, it's impossible to stop scratching. Scratching turns to picking, and I convert itchiness into pain and turn pain into pleasure. This is alchemy. Trying not to draw attention to what I'm doing, I touch the scab with careful fingers. And once again, I am reading my body like I am reading Braille.

The scab is perfect.

Not just the toughness, or the way it rises from the healthy skin, but because it's a circle. A perfect circle created without a compass. I don't have to look to know. It's dark brown, but reddish too—the color of crispy bacon, which is how my uncle likes it. I rub the scab with the soft pad of my forefinger. And then I press on it. I press harder. And harder. And harder yet.

I glance at Alicia Bernstein to see if she is looking at me, but she's not. She is busy reading her top-secret file on me, so I bend my forefinger and position my nail at the edge of the scab. I tuck the crescent moon of fingernail into the crescent curve where the scab begins to rise. I allow myself a few practice picks. I go through the motion without actually doing it. I practice-pick in the air, and after each swing I realign my nail with the scab, and finally, in one quick but satisfying pick, I scrape it off. The process is surgical—a part of me has been removed forever.

I watch the social worker through the fringe of my eyelashes as I find the loose scab in my sleeve. I pinch it between my finger and my thumb, and then I slowly slide my hand out. I drop the scab onto the floor without Alicia Bernstein ever noticing. And this is when the blood begins to surface. It is hot. The increasing throb connects back to my heart, and my body tingles.

I am alive.

"It seems there was an incident at home the other night," the social worker says. She says, "incident" instead of "episode," and she also says "home" without a pronoun—like it's her home too. And what she says is both a statement and a question, and this is when I begin to truly hate her.

She leans forward the way people do when they are pretending to help. I read about this technique in one of the books Daddy has underneath the bed where he sleeps at night. It was a manual for other therapists, written by a therapist who specialized in schizophrenia. The author listed strategy after strategy to be applied in one's private practice. This is how I know what Alicia Bernstein is trying to do: She is trying to establish intimacy.

I look at her for a second but only to try to figure out whether or not she really knows what happened at *my* home the other night. I'm quick. And then I look away. I guarantee that intimacy is not established.

"It seems your mother wasn't feeling very well," she says. "The pigs were talking to her. It seems they told her they needed to be freed." The word "freed" startles me, and I move my right hand to the spot where the scab was. I touch the open rawness through my sleeve. The fabric sticks to the wound because blood can act like glue. After all, it is just one of the substances that binds me to my mother. And the social worker keeps saying "It seems," and I think about that word. Actually, I think about "seam," which is not a homonym with "seem" because the two words are not spelled the same, although they share the same exact sound.

———

Rather, they are homophones, and I meditate on the latter: a seam as in clothing, where the different cuts of cloth are stitched together—joined. The scar on Mama's belly is also a seam. Her skin was sectioned. Her organs all removed, arranged on the stainless-steel table next to her. After I came out, she was put back together and stitched shut again. This seam was supposed to keep her from spilling out. But I no longer can blame it on the doctors. Mama is falling apart now because of me; I'm the one at fault—I created the Calendar of Ordeals, only to fail.

The social worker asks a lot of questions. Does Mama let the animals out often? Does she do other unusual things? Does she talk to people who aren't there? I think about dear, sweet Emily and the poem in which she wrote *And Kindred as responsive / As Porcelain*. This line resonates because it's the perfect way to describe my mother when she's the opposite of manic. But right now it could be used to describe me and how I have to be: as responsive as porcelain.

But then Alicia Bernstein from Social Services asks if Mama has ever hurt me. And I have to speak up. I say, "No." And my voice comes out louder than it should. I try to lower it. I tell her my mother is an artist. "That's all," I say. I make sure my words don't come out too fast. "That's why she's not like other people." And then I cross my fingers and hold my breath, but the ritual doesn't work. The situation doesn't end. In fact, the social worker makes me undress.

"It's procedure," she says. And she takes up her legal pad for now, flipping through her notes to find a new sheet of the yellow paper with pale green lines. She clicks her ballpoint pen into place and poises herself. She is ready to turn my nakedness into a permanent record.

I'm allowed to keep my underwear on, and for the first time ever I'm relieved to be wearing the training bra Gran insisted I had to wear every day. But I still feel naked. Actually, it's worse than being naked, and naked is already terrible. When I take off my shirt, I do my best to wipe the blood away. I use my sleeve, but it ends up smearing all the way to my wrist. It looks like Indian war paint.

Alicia Bernstein points at my elbow with her pen and asks, "What happened?"

I shrug. I shrug in a way that tells her whatever happened is no big deal. Unimportant. I shrug as if to say I had no idea I was bleeding or even hurt. My body is the one to tell the lie.

Daddy put up electric fencing where Mama tried to free the pigs. He says it's to keep the pigs from getting out, as if I wasn't there that night and didn't see, or understand.

I can tell he doesn't want to talk about the new fence, but he has to. I'm the one who will pass it the most. Five days a week, back and forth from house to highway to ride the bus to school and back again. And sometimes on Saturdays to fetch the mail or on Sunday to collect the newspaper. He says the fence won't hurt the pigs. "It just stuns them," he says, but the words come out sloppy—a tongue twister, even though it's not. "They learn not to touch it after that," he says. The fence is designed to keep predators out as well. "It's a win-win," he says, and I wonder what he said to Mama. I wonder if there's a part of him that hopes she will touch the fence.

During lunch, I look up electric fences using the encyclopedia in the school library. This encyclopedia is like the one we have at home. One volume, only bigger, it is kept on a podium by the checkout desk. It has a lot more information about electric fences than

I expected. I had no idea there were so many different kinds, or so many histories. I use the magnifying glass to read the tiny font. This magnifying glass has no black velvet case. Instead, it's kept tied to the podium by a length of utility string, and someone labeled the handle with a piece of masking tape that reads PROPERTY OF LIBRARY.

The topic of electric fences takes up almost three pages. The paper is tissue thin, and I worry about tearing it by accident whenever I turn the page. We have an agricultural electric fence—nonlethal. I read about the lethal ones next. The ones used for high-security reasons; for example, the ones that surround prisons to keep the inmates from escaping, or what the Nazis used to contain their concentration camps. The prisoners often used these fences as a means to commit suicide. And I think of Anne Frank, and how she was so full of life the way people always like to say.

I think about all the things she did that I have never done—like kissing Peter in the attic, or fighting with her mother. I've never even yelled at Mama. If I did, she might come undone forever.

I decide if I'm ever put into a concentration camp, I will touch the fence. The choice is easy.

I still haven't told anyone at home about Alicia Bernstein coming to visit me at school. That was Monday and now it's Wednesday, but nonetheless I'm convinced Social Services is going to take me away. This must be my punishment for ruining the calendar.

When I get home today, I'm going to make Mama a pot of chamomile tea. Maybe it will make her feel better, but when I get home the social worker is there and Mama is not.

Alicia Bernstein is here to help Daddy and Gran tell me Mama has gone to the hospital. I see the way Daddy glares at the social worker when she says, "This is the kind of hospital where people go to live." And then she uses the word "permanent" and even tries to explain what it means. The dictionary definition for "permanent" has been filed away in my brain for a very long time. I can see it now: typed on thin white paper in black ink. When I committed it to memory, I recorded it using Courier New because it was the most matter-of-fact-looking font I knew of.

Permanent, as in lasting, or fixed. As in *We fixed this.* As in *The game was fixed.*

I think about Mama and the episode she had the other day. Before the incident with the pigs. She was mad, but not at me. She was yelling at my father.

"I wanted something more," she said. "I wanted more babies, remember? I thought you did as well, then you went and fixed that, didn't you?" Daddy didn't engage her. He just looked sad. He studied the world on the other side of the window.

And because he wouldn't look at her, Mama turned and looked at me. "Do you know where your father was that night?" she asked, and she didn't have to tell me what night she was referring to. I knew she was talking about the night in the orchard: the night when everything changed. "He had Billy take him to the hospital in Kansas City," Mama said, and her eyes were red and swollen.

She looked at me, but I knew her words were directed at my father. "He went and got a vasectomy, and it was supposed to be a secret," she went on. "I wasn't supposed to know. But your grandmother! She just couldn't help herself. She spread the news like it was gospel, and the gossip came around like it always does, and that's how I got to find out about something my husband did."

"Permanent" is derived from the Latin word *permanere*, which means "to endure."

I have endured, and I will continue to do so. I will endure. This is not like the time before when Mama only went away for the summer. This is different. And I think I know everything the social worker is about to say, until she explains how Mama made the choice herself.

This is called voluntary commitment. I thought I knew everything there was to know about the word "commitment." This word defines my relationship to my mother, and like a palindrome, I thought she was as committed to me as I am to her, backward and forward, both of us the same—that's what I thought until today. And now I wonder if Mama knew about the Calendar. Is she leaving me because I couldn't get it right?

It hasn't rained in over two weeks, and the dirt road leading home is sunbaked and hard.

I see the impressions left from Daddy's truck—from the tires, a rolling pattern of diamonds—two fixed rows, each wide enough to walk in. My peripheral vision expands as soon as I step off the bus. The Kansas landscape surrounds me, flat and gently sloping. Pasture, field, and prairie interrupted by the occasional house, windmill, barn, or tractor, and of course all the sad-eyed cows standing on the other side of the highway.

The bush honeysuckle swallows the ditch, creeping thicker with every passing day it threatens to overtake the road/driveway. The only way to get rid of this noxious weed is with fire. Soon, Daddy and Uncle Billy will do the first controlled burn of the year. I remember the honeysuckle in the tussie-mussie I never really got to give to Mama; with accelerant and a match, my father will set fire to the bonds of love; in a holocaust, he will wipe the honeysuckle out.

———

* * * *

I stop and stand in front of the electric fence.

I think I hear it humming.

While some of the pigs root around, most of them lie on their sides. Fat and lazy under the spring sun. I wonder what it'd be like if they started talking to me the way they did to Mama. What do they have to say? And what did Mama say in return?

I think about all the books Mama and I used to read together. Not just the Peter Rabbit stories, but *The Wind in the Willows*, *Dandelion*, and *The Story of Ferdinand*. I can't remember if Ferdinand talked, but I know the others did. I think about *Charlotte's Web*.

The old wooden fence has been dismantled and is leaning against the back of the pen in pieces. Even taken apart, it looks far more substantial than does the electric fence—far more capable of keeping. This means the electric fence must be on, otherwise the pigs would have snuck through the suspended wires a long time ago. Pigs are very smart. Back in the third grade when Phillip Booth called Sissy Baxter a pig, she turned around and said, "P.I.G. stands for 'pretty intelligent girl.'"

I know Sissy Baxter is the one who left the white hyacinth in our mailbox after Mama went to Saint Joseph's. Wrapped in white lace, the tag on the nosegay read *To Fig* and nothing more, but I recognized the smell immediately. Like lilacs, only so much stronger: Now I know that Sissy Baxter smells like hyacinth. Without saying anything at all, Sissy said, "I am praying for you."

I look at the wire and wonder if Mama will have to do electric-shock therapy.

After the social worker pulled me out of class, the kids started talking about Mama again. How crazy she is. It doesn't help that

—

223

Tanya Jenkins's mother finally did become a nurse—a nurse at Saint Joseph's, where Mama now lives.

Everyone knows, and they all keep asking about electric-shock therapy. "That's just what they do in the loony bin," Phillip Booth said earlier today. "Either that or a lobotomy," and Ryan Hart started to head-bang with his shaggy hair in his face. Using his fist as a microphone, he scream-sang, "*Lobotomy.*" And something about a teenage lobotomy, having no cerebellum, but getting a PhD.

As usual, Sissy Baxter remained quiet. She pretended to read the textbook as Phillip Booth and Candace Sherman got into an argument about how the electric chair is different from electric-shock therapy. Phillip swore to God and crossed his heart that mental hospitals use electric chairs to administer shock therapy, "But with way less voltage," he said, and then Candace called him a retard.

"Everyone knows there's a difference," she said. "Didn't you watch the special news report about how they're getting ready to fry Ted Bundy?"

They agreed on one thing only: Mama would not be lobotomized. "Because she didn't kill anyone," Phillip said, but then Candace yelled across the classroom, as if I couldn't hear otherwise. "Hey, Fig!" she said. "Has your mother killed anyone?"

All this took place while we waited for Mr. Arnold to come back from the bathroom. It didn't matter that I didn't say a word or react—not reacting *is* a reaction. Nothing stops them. I buried my head in my arms and focused on how the cold desk felt against my hot face.

When I think of Saint Joseph's, I think of the movie *Return to Oz.* How much it scared me. Not just the lady with the different heads in the glass cabinets, or the Wheelers—but the beginning of the film, when Auntie Em takes Dorothy to the hospital to be cured. To get fixed. Because she won't stop talking about a place where all the animals can talk. But it's not a hospital. It was an insane asylum with medieval-looking contraptions and evil devices—images I can't get out of my head. I see Mama captured. She's locked inside an iron maiden, and no one can hear her screaming.

Her doctors still won't allow visitors—not even Daddy.

First, they need to establish a therapeutic relationship with my mother. That's what they say. They are trying to establish intimacy, and I wonder if Mama will let them.

I decide to touch the fence. I don't know why. Maybe I want to check to see if it's really on, or maybe it's because I'm mad at Daddy for keeping it up. Is he worried I will free the pigs as well? Or maybe I do it to punish myself for not talking to the social worker like a normal kid would have. And I definitely do so to punish myself for everything else I've done wrong.

I have to step onto the dirt mound that separates the road from the pasture—what must have been knee-deep mud when Mama freed the pigs. I keep one foot in the ditch for balance, and I reach until my hand is above the top wire, on the other side. The pigs come. Sniffing the air, they keep their distance; they know this fence and what it does. When they find I have no food, they go back to ignoring me.

I let my hand hover over the wire the way a magician does before he reaches into his hat and pulls out a white rabbit by its long ears. I feel the electricity before I make contact.

The fence does and doesn't want me to touch it.

I don't feel anything the first time, either because it knocks the wind out of me or because it knocks me out. I don't know, because I've never passed out before. I find myself sitting in the middle of the road with a terrible ringing in my ears. Shrill, the sound lingers. The ringing doesn't stop, and my tailbone hurts so much, I think it's broken. But I manage to pull myself up. After that, I remain fully conscious. The second, third, and fourth time, I touch the fence.

And all the times after.

I build immunity. The fence has an incredible force. It feels like getting kicked by a horse—not that I've ever been kicked by one, but my uncle has. It feels like this, only it doesn't hurt, not exactly. The charge is instant, felt in every part of me: flesh and bone—all at once. I try to hold on to the wire, but the electricity pushes me away. The shock outlines my nervous system as my body becomes an anatomy lesson. When the world goes dark, I can see my nerves—bright and white and ragged, they look like tree roots and they tremble.

I am surrounded by white light. It is blinding. And I feel warm all over and I hear myself cry out. I make noises I've never made before. And this is the part that feels good even though it feels like I'm peeing my pants when I didn't have to go.

When I was younger, Uncle Billy tried to teach me martial arts, but I was too little, and got bored too fast. All the beginning lessons were about learning how to safely fall. I didn't understand what he was doing at the time. I just wanted to kick and punch and knock people out.

One day, he took me for a walk along the Silver River. We went farther than the waterfall and the pool my grandfather built once upon a time. My uncle wanted to show me one of the century-old cottonwoods that had fallen during a recent snowstorm. He described the tree as having shattered because of the way it broke. Then he showed me the younger trees—and the way they bent instead, and how they still continued to bend under the weight of the new snow.

"It's like they are bowing to the storm," my uncle said. "Like the storm is their master and they are showing their respect." Because they were young and flexible, those trees could not shatter. They went along with the massive blows of wind and snow instead. While he was impressed by the saplings, I was more affected by the impact of the ancient cottonwood and its total demise.

He also made me watch Marmalade. The way she jumped from the rafters in the barn, always landing on her feet. He said, "There's a time for landing on your feet and a time for falling like a drunk man would, or a baby." He was serious, and I made him mad by giggling. "You take all that force against you," he said, "and, Fig, you turn it into a power you can use."

When I touch the fence, I use a combination of all the falling methods my uncle taught me. Where I drop and roll. Where the last thing I do is try to land on my feet. The fence can't knock me unconscious anymore, but it still throws me every time. But if I just take it—that is, absorb the power—I can make it my own. And each time I touch the fence, I fall.

Each time, I fall more safely than the time before.

I've perfected the art of falling safely by the time Daddy turns off the electric fence, dismantles it, and takes the copper to be scrapped. He rebuilds the old fence, and the pigs continue to be contained. I turn my focus elsewhere.

The calendar is titled *The Work of Salvador Dali*, and even though the melting clocks are appropriate, I'm not interested in the images. Daddy gives me the calendar, telling me how Dali is one of Mama's favorite artists—only he said "was." He often talks about her like she's gone, as in gone forever.

I keep busy keeping track. I am counting. I record each day without my mother. And I can't help but wonder if this is the sacrifice I'm supposed to make. Is this the only way she might get better? Perhaps when I see her again, she will be back to normal.

I use the Dalí calendar to keep track of her absence. I don't blacken the squares, nor do I use the crossroads method of making an X. Instead, I make the same careful checks Mama makes in dictionaries. They are the same, only smaller. I make them as small as I can, despite all the room the insides of the squares provide.

I make each check before I go to bed. I make the check next to whatever number represents today. The checks are camouflaged by the numeral for the days—so tiny, they can't be noticed by anyone who might be snooping around my room, checking to see how I am holding up.

I check off the entire summer, and I check off the first day of the eighth grade. I make a special note for September fifteenth, the day both Lindy and Michael Chamberlain's murder conviction is unanimously overturned by the Northern Territory Court of Criminal Appeals. The day Azaria finally gets to rest in peace, I write R.I.P. and not an X. I am meticulous. Especially when it comes to the twenty-first of October. The tiny black check is perfect; the best I've made so far.

I check off October 21, 1988, and I am thirteen years old.

And this is my first birthday without my mother. I think about the number thirteen, and that night in the kitchen with Mama. Her thirteen knocks echo from past to present. *Knock, knock—who's there?* I can hear her knocking, and I understand why people develop a phobia of this number. This phobia is about betrayal. That which is gone.

As I record the days without Mama, I can't help but fall back or spring forward. I think more and more about the days to come. I think about the days remaining before I turn nineteen. I was six years old that evening in the orchard, and the math is simple. I work the equation on the chalkboard of my mind: $6 + 13 = 19$. My brain is dark matter, and the math problem is white—easy to see to see.

CHAPTER ELEVEN
EMPTINESS

*determinism: the philosophical view that past events
and the laws of nature fix or set future events;
given these conditions, nothing else could happen.*

September 1, 1989

Without Mama, the house sounds different; even now, after all this time I still notice the sound of her absence. At night, I try to keep from picking at my scabs. I'm embarrassed because I'll be fourteen soon but I just can't seem to stop. I fall asleep, and in the morning I've reopened my skin and the white bedsheets are constellated with the brown bursts of dried blood.

Laundry is one of my many chores now that Mama is no longer here. I bleach the bedding back to white. This is erasure, but I am not done with my mourning.

We visit Mama whenever we can. The visiting room is noisy and full of stale smoke. This mother trembles. Her hands and her face. The shake inside this mother is another kind of echo. It is the echo of electrical currents charging through her soul. Daddy promises it doesn't hurt. And no one here calls it electric-shock therapy. They all call it ECT. Acronyms and initials are employed like camouflage or buffers; they are the sugar coating on a bitter pill, or the mittens worn by the Stanley children when they practiced the ordeal of no touching metal.

Mama won't look at me, and she won't look at Daddy. Instead, she counts each drag she takes, lighting one Salem off another. Her complexion blends in with the hospital walls, and through the window in the one door I glimpse the corridor leading to another world: the world where my mother chooses to live instead of with me. Voluntary commitment. I wish I could see to see; I want to see where she sleeps at night and what pieces of home she brought along. More than anything, I wish I could see the view from her window.

Instead, we sit in silence like we always do.

Daddy goes to get a cup of coffee from the vending machine by the bathrooms. He leaves me and Mama alone. There is a television mounted to the wall, and it is always on. People talk, and one group plays a board game, but no one laughs in here.

Mama finally looks at me. Her eyes are no longer hazel; they are now the same empty gray as the sky before the first snow of the year arrives. "You're not mine, you know?" she says. She says this as she lights another cigarette. And then she smiles. Amid the twisting smoke, she smiles at me, and then she says, "But don't worry, dear. It's not your fault."

On the drive home, Daddy takes a detour.

He hasn't been talking much since Mama went to Saint Joseph's, and he doesn't say anything about where we're going, and I don't ask. We pass a sign that reads KICKAPOO INDIAN RESERVATION OF KANSAS. The name makes me wonder if there are Kickapoo reservations in other places.

Daddy pulls off the road and into the dirt parking lot of a gas station/convenience store. There is one pump, but evidently he's not here for gas. He puts the truck in park and leaves me to watch a group of Indian kids as they sit around a dilapidated picnic table sucking on Popsicles striped red, white, and blue like the American flag. When he returns, he's carrying a plastic grocery bag. He gets in the truck and tosses the bag onto the floor by my feet. He pretends to be adjusting the rearview mirror, but really he is watching me from the corner of his eye as I examine the contents of the bag.

I am trying to see to see.

Through the thin white plastic, I see green packaging, which I recognize by now. I begin counting. I count ten cartons of Salem Lights 100s. The packaging design is more suitable for mint gum than it is for cigarettes. "No tax on the reservation," Daddy says, putting the truck in reverse. As we drive away, we pass another sign, and this one reads NOW LEAVING KICKAPOO INDIAN RESERVATION. It does not specify which reservation or what state.

In school, we studied the Kickapoo Indians, and Phillip Booth couldn't get over the name.

He said, "I thought Kick the Can was a dumb game, but kicking turds is even dumber."

He didn't pay attention to what the teacher was saying, and I doubt he read the book we were assigned. Otherwise, he would have known what I and the rest of the class knew. Kickapoo comes from *kiwikapawa*, which means "stands here and there." It refers to the migratory patterns of the tribe and means "wanderer."

I might not actually go anywhere, but I do know how to stand here *and* there.

* * * *

The next time we go to visit Mama, Daddy brings all those cigarettes and I give her a bouquet of flowers.

I picked the last blooms of Johnny-jump-up from our yard, and I bought the orange daylilies from The Flower Lady because Sissy Baxter, who is now officially employed there, said, "Daylilies are the Chinese emblem for Mother," and the Flower Lady explained, "Probably because it's easy to make an exact clone of the parent." In *Hamlet*, Ophelia says, "There's pansies, that's for thoughts," and this is what I mean to say to Mama with the Johnny-jump-ups: *You are not only in my heart, but forever in my head.*

Mama doesn't even say thank you. Ignoring the vase I've set on the table, she takes the bag of cigarettes from Daddy and pulls a carton out. She isn't rushed, but she is methodical.

She uses her thumbnail to cut a slit in the cellophane. She slides the cellophane off and uses the same nail to open the cardboard flap at one end, before she shakes a pack out. I think about fingernails, and I think of my nesting dolls while Mama repeats her actions—only this time she's removing the cellophane from the individual pack, and now she's shaking out a long, white cigarette.

Filter down, she taps the cigarette on the table, and I almost expect her to do this thirteen times—but she doesn't. I count three taps before she sticks the Salem 100 between her chapped lips, lighting it with a lighter that reads COUNTRY GIRL. The lighter is decorated with a picture of a lipstick tube and a pair of spurs. I excuse myself.

I say I have to use the bathroom, but I don't. I do this all the time. I excuse myself to go ride the elevator up and down. There are six floors if you count the parking garage down below. People get on and off the elevator, and I don't know anyone.

From the main level, a boy wearing plaid pajamas gets on the

—

elevator with a woman who must be his mother. The boy is my age. Our eyes meet for a second before he looks down, focused on the carpeted elevator floor. There's a name-tag sticker on his chest, only it's upside down, but the word *Satan* is not. I can't help but smile, and I do everything I can to force my lips in the opposite direction. I end up holding my breath and crossing my fingers to make it stop.

Satan is wearing a pair of brown fleece slippers, and I can see his toes and what's remaining of the black nail polish he applied before he came here. His hair is dyed black, but his roots have grown long—at least three inches of painful-looking strawberry blond. His natural color is the same as Mama's.

His mother clutches one of his arms with her hand. Her grip looks tight, and her fingernails are long and red. She holds on to her son, waiting for the elevator to take them to the third floor. They both smell like cigarette smoke, and they share the same scowl, only hers is made more severe by age and all the facial lines around her mouth. The elevator dings and the doors open. She pushes Satan into the corridor, but this is when he breaks free. He turns around and uses his foot to keep the doors from closing. And then he pushes up the sleeves of his hooded sweatshirt.

He wants me to see. And I do.

I see every single sliver of thin white scar. And I can almost see what they looked like before—slender strands of fresh vibrant red. He is covered in these scars. And the scars remind me of the shading technique Mama calls crosshatching. I look at his arms, and then I look at him. His eyes are blue—blue like a summer sky, and he looks at me. And when his mother grabs his arm and yanks him back, he yells at me. "Pay attention!" he says, before he turns around to let his mother steer him away from me, to the left.

—

The elevator doors close, and I'm left staring at a dull reflection of myself in the shiny steel.

I ride the elevator to the fifth floor and then back to the garage. I do this three times. And only three people and one baby ride the elevator during this time. After three rounds, I ride the elevator from the garage, but this time I stop at the third floor, and I'm the only who gets off. This hall looks like the hall on the fourth floor where my mother is committed. According to the directory on the wall, if I turn right, I will go to Cognitive Therapy, but if I turn left, I'd be headed to the Juvenile Psychiatric Ward.

Because the hallway bends, I can't actually see the ward. This hallway bends like the hallway on Mama's floor, and there's the same set of vending machines by the drinking fountain and the public restrooms with the blue wheelchairs stenciled on the doors, but the fluorescent lights work better. They still buzz, but they don't buzz quite as loudly as they do on Mama's floor. I should get back to the fourth floor but I can't move. I'm thinking about those scars. And I'm wondering what it'd be like to turn left—to commit myself. Head tilted, I stand here staring at a place I can't see.

October 21, 1989
Uncle Billy gives me a set of the *Encyclopedia Britannica* for my fourteenth birthday. The volumes are stacked up in the back of his truck bed. The books are white with red lettering and remind me of Daddy's varsity jacket—the way the red is tinged with gold.

Gran and Daddy should be here soon. They went to pick Mama up from the hospital. The doctors call this "a temporary release." They say Mama wanted to spend the weekend at home because it's my birthday. The doctors also use the term "trial." They say, "If she

—

can handle being home, she can visit more." That's what they say. They say this more than once, yet they never notice the contradiction or acknowledge the oxymoron, and I want to ask, *How, exactly, does a person visit home?*

"Well, they're not going to sprout wings and fly up to your room," Uncle Billy says, and I realize I've been standing here, on the porch, staring at his truck. I've been standing both here and there, but I return. I come back.

Together, we carry the encyclopedias up to my bedroom. I kneel on the floor, lining the volumes up in alphabetical order. I don't have a shelf big enough, so we make one using some of the old wooden crates left over from when the apple orchard was still in operation.

"I'm sorry they're used," Uncle Billy says. He's just inside my room, leaning against the wall. He is wearing a pair of black cowboy boots.

I insert the last volume into the place where it belongs—between the L and the O—and then I look up at him and smile. My smile tells him I love them just the way they are.

"I wanted to buy you a brand-new set," he says, "But they were too expensive."

I tell him I've always wanted a set, and how once upon a time I even asked Gran for one. But she refused. "Encyclopedias are too much clutter for a young girl's bedroom" is what she said, and what she really meant was *All that information is too much clutter for a young girl's brain.*

Uncle Billy smiles back at me, and then he begins to wander around my room. He stops by my desk and picks up the Matryoshka doll, and my heart begins to pound. The burnt-black faceless one is hiding within the core of all four mothers, so I hold my breath and cross my fingers that he doesn't open the matriarch, and it works. He sets her down and strolls over to the window seat.

—

He stands there looking out the window with his legs spread and his hands on his hips, and he reminds me of Peter Pan—the Peter Pan who's just about to fly away: out the open nursery window. "You know," Uncle Billy says, "this used to be my room."

I look around as he looks around. And I try to imagine a little boy in here. I see the miniature Uncle Billy from all the old pictures lining the hall at Gran's. This little boy sits in my window seat. Captured on black-and-white film, he looks at the orchard and the sky and he fidgets.

"Yup," Uncle Billy says, shaking his head, and there's something strange about his smile. He is smiling the way Mama sometimes does—where the smile means the opposite of happiness.

"I hated this room," he says. "All I ever did in here was imagine the day I'd finally get to leave. I'd think: I'm going to go far away and I will never, *ever* come back."

Uncle Billy is just beginning to go gray at the temples. Daddy's black hair is all salt and pepper now. As he looks out the window, I wonder why he broke his childhood promise. I let him read my mind. And he looks at me again.

"I did go, you know?" he says, "And I stayed away until your daddy went and had you."

Uncle Billy is smiling for real now, "After you came along," he says, "there was nothing in the world that could keep me away. You, little lady, officially turned this old house into a home."

Gran makes two pots of split-pea soup for dinner. One has ham hock and the other doesn't. Mama has decided to be a vegetarian. And I wonder if this is something she has always wanted to be.

I've read about vegetarianism. How people don't eat meat because

—

237

they don't want to harm animals. As much as I do love animals, this is not the reason I don't eat meat myself. I actually have no idea why I don't want to. I just don't.

Mama's new therapist told Daddy how it's important to honor Mama's choices—that is, the choices that are logical, like this one. And I wonder why he doesn't honor my choice not to eat meat. He still serves it almost every night, and he always offers me a piece.

Daddy prepared everyone this morning. When he explained to Gran what the therapist instructed, Gran said, "I don't see any logic in Annie's choice. She's just seeking special treatment." But Daddy ignored her. "Whenever possible," he said, "Annie should feel that she is in control." And that's when my grandmother rolled her eyes. "Did the animals tell her not to eat them?" and that's when Uncle Billy said, "Ma, stop it!"

I take a bowl of the vegetarian soup, and Gran lets me know I chose wrong. "This is the real soup," she says, pointing at the other pot. I shrug to let her know that I don't care. And then I think, *How is it she's never noticed me not eating meat until today?*

I take my bowl of unreal soup and sit down. Everyone is busy watching Mama, who barely touches her soup even though it was made vegetarian just for her. She brings spoonful after spoonful to her lips, and then she blows on the soup like it's still hot. She blows until she thinks no one is watching and she dumps the spoonful back into her bowl. She does, however, eat four thick slices of my birthday cake.

Everyone but Mama and I sing "Happy Birthday." And when the song is done, Mama leans forward and blows out the wax 14 my grandmother bought from Kmart. My mother blows away my chance to make my one and only wish.

Gran baked the cake to look like a wedding cake, white on white.

"This is how we used to celebrate birthdays when I was in charm school," my grandmother says. I've never seen Mama eat so much. If I took a picture of her right now, the dictionary publishers could use the image to accompany the definition for "gluttony."

gluttony: one of the seven deadly sins.

A glutton takes from those in need. I need my mother to come back.

I miss the carrot cakes Mama used to make and the cream cheese frosting that isn't so sweet. And I miss the candied violets she used to handcraft herself. Violets mean affection, and I wonder if she knew this when she used to decorate my cakes with those tiny purple flowers, hardened by sugar and egg white.

Mama drinks coffee with her cake. She uses cream like she always has, but now she takes six sugars per cup. She drinks so much coffee, Gran has to make another pot.

Even though Mama has been fat for a while now, the weight still looks wrong on her, like she isn't meant to be this way. The way she doesn't look like a smoker even though she smokes all the time. Gran calls this chain smoking. And Mama doesn't try to quit, nor does she apologize the way she used to. She just smokes and smokes and smokes some more.

Daddy spent the entire afternoon reminding her not to smoke inside until he finally gave up. He gave her permission to smoke in the day porch and called it "a compromise." And this is where Mama always is. It was even hard to get her to come eat dinner with us, but Uncle Billy did something magic, and she finally agreed to join us in the dining room.

—

In the kitchen, I help clean but I'm also watching Mama. Through the French doors, I can see her in the day porch, smoking. "She's smoking menthols," Uncle Billy says. "You know, those things are twice as likely to kill you." And Gran shoots him a look to remind him not to talk that way when I'm around. *Little pitchers have big ears.*

Daddy is drying the cake platter. He's been rubbing the dish towel in circles for over ten minutes now. He is watching Mama too. He looks almost catatonic, and it's not the first time I've wondered what it'd be like if both my parents were insane.

I know what Daddy's doing because it's what I am doing. We are waiting for my mother to step out of this strange woman. She'd shed her fat like a snake sheds skin. She'd step out of herself like the weight was just a jumpsuit and she'd be slender once again. She'd come into the kitchen and complain about the cigarette smoke in the house and scold Gran for the cake she made.

This mother doesn't do this. This mother just sits in my old mother's rocking chair. And she lights one cigarette off another, and the Mason jar ashtray is already half-full.

"Well," Gran says, "I can always mix the two pots together come Monday." She sighs, looking at the soup on the stove, and I realize everyone is planning to stay the weekend. I assumed we'd eat together—celebrate my birthday—but then Gran and Uncle Billy would leave. And the three of us could be alone again. The way it's supposed to be. With Gran here, Mama will never reemerge.

I go join Mama in the day porch, and I can feel three sets of eyes watching me. The air is silver with cigarette smoke, and I refuse to look toward the kitchen at my audience. The smoke tickles my throat, and I can hear an old echo from my other mother—the one who would warn me of all the risks associated with exposure to secondhand smoke. That mother says, "Fig, it's far worse for you than smoking is."

"Hi, Mama," I say.

I'm sitting across from her, but she doesn't look at me. I look out the window instead. I look for the feral dog, but she is nowhere to be seen. She's been hiding. I haven't seen her forever, and I wonder if I will ever see her again. I study the orchard. The apples have fallen from the trees by now, left to rot. I can almost smell the fermentation. The trees have become infected with a blight called apple scab. My uncle showed me the black velvet lesions bruising all the fruit. He said, "The orchard can still be saved," but he didn't tell me how.

According to the book at the library, the one Sissy Baxter was reading the first time I went to The Flower Lady, apple blossoms mean better things to come.

A flock of birds startle. They flutter into a careless splatter of black against the sunset sky, and then they settle back, ready to slumber away another night. The average person spends one third of her life asleep. These calculations are based on a person who sleeps eight hours a night. My mother doesn't sleep at all or else she falls into a coma and sleeps for days.

Mama doesn't look out the window, even though she's facing the orchard. She isn't interested in beauty anymore. She stares at the wood paneling instead, and I wonder what she actually sees. I see the ash on her cigarette. It has grown long and gray. Suddenly, Mama clears her throat and drops the cigarette in the jar, where it smolders. And she does not light another.

She is looking at me now like she wants to say something.

"You know," Mama says, and she sounds excited. I smile at her, leaning forward—I am trying to establish intimacy, and now she seems embarrassed, but just when I think I've lost her she clears her throat to try again. She smiles at me the way Candace Sherman, Tanya Jenkins, and Sissy Baxter smile at one another whenever they are discussing boys. "I'm with child," she says.

"Look!" she almost shouts, and Mama lifts her breasts with both hands. "See?" she says. "They are so much bigger now, and I'll tell you something else. I do *not* miss getting my period." And this mother giggles; she does not laugh. I've never heard my mother giggle; the sound is enough to awaken the scab that's on my wrist.

"The doctors tell me, 'Any day now,'" she says, and she drops her breasts and leans back in her rocking chair—the one my father made for her when she got pregnant with me. She touches her belly now the way pregnant women always do. And she has that same look of wonder. Like she can't believe a life is really taking form inside her.

"It's my first, you know?" she says. While her breasts are indeed swollen, her belly is not round or hard the way it was when she was pregnant with me. I've seen the pictures. *This* belly is flabby and soft, a worn-out feather pillow. She is a Mother Goose. I want to lift her dirty purple sweatshirt and pull back all the rolls of fat and show her the scar she got from having me. This is why she's forgotten. The weight of this mother conceals the mother she was before.

She's not the only one who forgets. I forget too. I forget all the rules I make about not picking—and then I forget all the rules I make to try and control the picking. And I forget where I got the wounds I perpetuate. The first rule: *Don't pick.* But I end up making compromises with myself. The second rule: *Only pick one sore at a time.* Third rule: *Only pick for a week. Then I have to heal.* But I break all my rules. I am currently attending two sores.

———

I open one while the other has the chance to scab back over. I prefer the sanctuary of the bathtub, but that doesn't keep me from picking whenever and wherever I might need to pick. *As long as no one sees.* This is my other rule, and the only one I never ever seem to break.

The sore on my ankle is new; it's been a part of me for fifteen days, but I'm most committed to the one on my wrist, even though it's the hardest one to hide. It is my jewel.

I switch the letters around in "sore" until I arrive at "rose." And then I bloom. They open, red and unfurling. I hide the rose on my wrist: long sleeves, bracelets, gloves, and even the occasional bandage. I tell Daddy, "I hurt myself," and then I pretend to heal, but he doesn't pay attention. He doesn't even ask about it later. He just assumes the wounds will go away. He doesn't see how I've been growing this particular rose now for over three months. Almost always, roses mean love.

The seed was planted when my sleeve snagged on the wall in the barn and the splintered wood stabbed me. While I remember how I got this one, I can't keep track of all of them. I get hurt all the time. So I forget. But I never forget to pick. I pick on myself: *pick, pick, pick.* And I will pick until there is nothing left to pick.

———

CHAPTER TWELVE
DIVINE
INTERVENTION

synaxarion: a short version of the lives of the saints, arranged by date.

November 9, 1989

Today the Berlin Wall comes down and Miss Pratt and Miss Avery come all the way from Kansas City. Part of a volunteer program aiming to bring charm to rural Kansas, Gran calls it social education—a term she lifted from the brochure. The motto of the program is "Teaching the Art of Sense and Civility."

Each time Gran drops me at the Sacred Heart of Mary Church, she reminds me of all the strings she pulled to get me in. And I imagine Miss Pratt and Miss Avery as marionette dolls. Gran holds them above a stage and makes Miss Pratt curtsy and Miss Avery twirl—but, really, I'm the one dangling at the bottom of my grandmother's manipulation.

Gran tells me how she met her best friends for life in charm school. She is quite concerned about my lack of friends—especially now that I'm in high school. "What do you do by yourself?" she is forever asking. And this isn't the first time I've wondered if Sissy Baxter is my friend or not.

There are twenty-seven girls enrolled in the school, and Sissy is not one of them. Miss Pratt instructs us in proper etiquette, and Miss Avery teaches dance. I'm told it will be a long time before I work with Miss Avery. I'm placed into the class called Introduction to Social Skills. This means I'm at the table where the eight- and nine-year-old girls all sit. At fifteen, I tower above them—an awkward, clumsy giant. And I wonder if this is how my father always feels.

Miss Pratt has a conductor's wand and walks circles around each table, only she seems to favor ours. When she isn't pointing out a misbehaved child or piece of misplaced silverware, she taps the wand against her palm, and her constant circling reminds me of kindergarten. I keep expecting her to say, *Duck, duck, goose!* And I am ready to run.

We role-play how to meet someone. We meet one another again and again. I meet all six of the little girls at my table. I meet each one at least ten times, but according to Miss Pratt I never properly introduce myself. Or show appropriate interest in others. She tells me this while tapping the wand against her palm for emphasis. She wears the same white gloves we all have to wear, and her lips are red and sharply outlined with darker red. While she smiles at all the other girls, she never smiles at me.

The girls my age sit at the table designated for the advanced version of my class. It's called The Power of Good Social Skills. They've been in the program for seven years, since the third grade—the age a girl typically begins charm school and cotillion—with the exception of Candace Sherman. Candy, as Miss Pratt and Miss Avery call her, has been studying since kindergarten. And I wonder if they'd even bother to come all this way if it wasn't for her.

They use Candace Sherman as an example all the time. "See how

Candy stands?" Miss Pratt will ask, and Candy will stand for all of us to see. Miss Pratt's smile softens as she assures us that someday we'll all be that poised. "Candy's been working at this longer than the rest of you," she says, scanning the girls and making eye contact with everyone but me. Who will never learn to stand or flutter my pinkie when I sip tea.

"You girls mustn't compare yourselves with Candy too much," Miss Avery interjects. "Candy plans on being a model. In fact, she's already had a job."

I wonder if Candace has done anything besides the pictures in their brochure, and that's when Miss Avery looks at me. She frowns like she knows what I am thinking. Then she looks away and continues, "But remember, my future debutantes of America, techniques for proper sitting, standing, walking, and pivoting aren't just for models! They're for all young ladies who wish to be sophisticated and graceful."

I tell Mama about the class when I visit her. I hope she'll understand the severity of the situation. And come to her senses. Get discharged, withdraw me from the program, move back home and take charge. But Mama doesn't always hear me. On the one good day this month, Mama looked at me and said, "Good sense can't be taught." She said it like she didn't understand why she'd have to tell me something so simple. Then she lit another Salem, to hide in the blue cloud of smoke where she knows I can't get to her.

The girls at my table make faces whenever Miss Pratt is busy at the two other tables. The second table is Developing Social Intelligence, which I'll take next, before I can finally move on to the appropriate age bracket.

Having met the girls at my table so many times, I know all their names by heart. Katie, Wilma, Mary, Lizzie, Tatiana, and Sara. But I do not like them. They stick their tongues out and sneer at me, pushing their noses into pig snouts using white-gloved fingers. When Miss Pratt comes floating back, so do their smiles. They flash wet pearly teeth and bat their eyelashes like frantic butterflies. Tucking their hands into their laps, they are little praying angels.

Miss Pratt looks at them as would any adoring mother and says: "So much of charm school is learning one's place." And then she looks at me—long and hard.

November 30, 1989

"Today, we have a surprise!" Miss Pratt exclaims. Her cheeks are round, made rosy with a generous application of pink blush.

She has us stand in rows. One on each side of the large basement room so we are facing one another. Miss Pratt and Miss Avery pace the wide-open space between. They look like china dolls, made from rigid porcelain—yet, they don't seem to touch the ground, especially Miss Avery, who glides across the coffee-stained beige carpet. This is where everyone gathers after church services to eat and spill.

"You future debutantes of America have been working so hard," Miss Avery says, and her blond hair curls around her face like a frame. It bounces ever so slightly as her head bobs up and down with enthusiasm. "We thought you deserved a little treat!" And as she talks she walks back and forth the way the Miss America contestants walk across the television screen back home. The catwalk. The runway. She looks like my fake Barbie. And this is when I crucify Miss Avery: I nail her to the wall amid the collection of donor plaques. Her tiny high-heeled feet wriggle about as she tries to be graceful without any footing. I watch her slowly bleed to death.

———

"We are going to give one another manicures!" Miss Pratt says, gesturing her arms into a curl that arches around her head like Vanna White on *Wheel of Fortune*. She brings attention to her hair, her face, and her smile just as she has taught us all to do. She's already confessed to having her teeth professionally bleached, and when she did Miss Avery said a true sign of friendship is when one gal shares a beauty secret with another. And I wonder if secret conversations using flowers count?

Miss Avery and Miss Pratt's teeth are so white, they glow in the dark. At night in bed, I see them smiling, like the Cheshire cat from *Alice in Wonderland*. I see nothing but the girls' white teeth floating in the ether above.

Miss Pratt and Miss Avery each claim a line of girls. Miss Pratt takes my row. I stand somewhere in the middle and forget to breathe. I'm not sure whether we are practicing how to stand again or being paired off for the manicures. I have a tendency to daydream. I get lost. I am planning on getting sick. This way, I can get out of doing the actual manicure. I do my best to turn green.

It isn't until Miss Pratt reaches Sara that I realize the instructors are asking all the girls to take off their gloves. Miss Pratt nods her head, and Sara takes her cue. She removes her white gloves, pulling at each one like she's presenting a special treat—unwrapping a gift. Her hands are diamonds or white chocolate. Mama once told me how some Chinese women seduced their husbands by unwinding their bound feet. Ten feet of binding cloth took a long time to unravel, and the exposure was all about the anticipation. They unwound until their dainty and deformed feet were at last revealed. Cloven and putrid smelling, their feet were coveted by their lovers.

I watch Sara and Miss Pratt from my peripheral vision. My

hands are beginning to swell within the confines of velvety white cotton. They bloat the way Mama did from antipsychotics: *Thorazine*, *Prolixin*, *Compazine*, and *Haldol*. And when my turn comes, my hands will be too large to come loose from my grandmother's gloves. Either that or the seams will have busted.

Burning hot, my fingers and palms are tingling—too fat for blood to circulate. I wait for my heart to fail.

Miss Pratt takes Sara's hands into her own and caresses them. Sara is a china doll as well. They hold each other with cold carved porcelain fingers. Then Miss Pratt lifts Sara's little hands, to take a closer look. Sara's nails are not cut too short or left too long, but lurking inside my gloves are callused fingers, shredded cuticles, and nail beds caked with dirt and blood from picking scabs.

And on my wrist—

"Exquisite half moons of smoothly finished and sparkling clean fingernail," Miss Pratt says. Now she's a food critic describing the high-class French cuisine we are all preparing for: the grand-finale dinner that will either mark our transition from one level to the next or serve as our graduation. After graduation, someone like Candace Sherman will go to finishing school—"finishing" is supposed to imply the act of perfecting. "The final touches to a masterpiece," as Miss Pratt has explained, again and again. But I think it sounds like the girl is finished. Done for, as in "That's all she wrote," which Uncle Billy likes to say.

I told Mama my theory. I thought she'd laugh, be proud of my dark sense of humor and my feminist inclinations, but she didn't seem to hear me. Aside from the involuntary twitching, which is called dystonia, her face was blank. So I repeated myself. And the second time, the words sounded overrehearsed and too heavy. I even raised my voice, but she still didn't hear me.

Sara's skin is almost as white as the instructor's gloves holding them. So white, they turn powder blue like she's more dead than alive. I think about my name. Not Fig, but Fiona, which means "fair and white." Sara means "princess." I know because I've read everything written by Frances Hodgson Burnett, including *The Little Princess*, which is about a girl named Sara. Miss Pratt's holding her breath the way people do when they're impressed. And when she finally lets it out, there is a little puff of air accented by delight, and under her blush her cheeks burn a true pink.

"Perfection," she announces, but she doesn't move on. She knows I'm next. Everyone is aware of this. After an eternity, because she has no other choice, she takes her position in front of me. She clears her throat, and this indicates that it is now my turn to remove my white gloves.

The first class I attended, Miss Pratt tried to be nice. She gave me the booklet that serves as the textbook and promised to go over it with me after class. But then there was the incident regarding my name, and everything changed.

Gran introduced me to the teachers as Fiona. After a conversation in the car on how it'd be best if no one learned about my nickname. And this is why Miss Pratt introduced me to all the girls as Fiona—girls who already know me as Fig. From school or from the Sacred Heart of Mary. Candace Sherman was the one who pointed out that no one ever calls me Fiona.

She said, "I think it's sweet you tried," and smiled the smile she's praised for.

———

"I'm not sure I agree, Candace," Miss Pratt said, making the hard C harder and the soft *c* at the end hiss longer than it should. She was emphasizing how Candy is a nickname too. "Remember, dear," she'd said, "some nicknames are meant as terms of endearment."

Then Miss Avery listed off a variety of becoming nicknames—beginning with Trixie and ending with Candy, to prove she and Miss Pratt still adored her. When she had finished, she asked what my nickname was, but as soon as I told them their cheerful demeanor changed. "Like night and day," which is one of Gran's favorite things to say.

Those three letters told them all they needed to know.

Miss Pratt took the most offense. She didn't ask how I'd come to get the nickname, like most people do. Instead she said, "Well, that's not very attractive, is it? It reminds me of a prune, and we all know what prunes are for." This sent a case of giggles around the room. When there are no adults around, the girls still call out, "Hey, Prune!" and shout "Diarrhea, diarrhea!"

Their shouting has a singsong quality, and the words reverberate. At night in bed, I still hear their taunting, and the only way I can escape is by picking. And when I do, it has to be the sore on my wrist. But the worst is still Miss Pratt. I think she thinks I tricked her into thinking I was someone else. I couldn't crucify her if I tried.

Miss Pratt clears her throat again. And I know I can't just stand here like I don't know what I'm supposed to do. She is tall in her heels—shoes that make her look like she hasn't any toes.

As I tug on the first white glove, I see the rows of girls in front of me and to my sides. They bend at the edges like we're stuck inside a crystal ball or the world is collapsing at the sides. Their faces and bodies warp into fun-house-mirror reflections, and I can hear every

—

breath and whisper—each girl has been magnified by some invisible microphone, feedback included. The glove slips off my left hand faster than I expected and it falls.

Even the hush of the glove hitting the carpet is audible.

My naked hand acts of its own accord by trying to take cover. It hides behind my back, instead of being seen or starting in on the other glove. "Both gloves," Miss Pratt instructs. Her voice is so clear and cold, it hurts.

The fluorescent lights hang low beneath the drop ceiling. The plastic covers are cracked or broken, and the yellow light quivers from harsh to harsher. My other glove comes off, and this time I let it drop because I don't know what else to do. I think about the booklet from Miss Pratt. I'd taken it home and read it cover to cover, including the section on hand care: "A hostess's hands are what guests see most as they are served food and drink." I should've known they'd check, but I honestly wasn't sure we were allowed to take off our gloves, the way some women have to wear scarves around their heads or get their feet bound. The yellow light turns my skin into something grotesque.

On my wrist, the open sore awaits. For me, it is as permanent as a tattoo because no matter what I do I cannot leave it be. I become two different girls, and one of them is in control. I peel the scabs away as soon as they have formed. I've had this wound for six months. Like the checks I make in my calendar, this sore also tracks the absence of my mother; but the picking follows another chronology—one less linear. In the car to church today, I picked it open, so the blood has coagulated by now. My pulse increases, and my veins are bulging—big and blue, and every pore on my body opens like a sinkhole.

Miss Pratt tells me to lift my hands. "Higher," she says. Again and again. "Higher." And my hands are now close to her chin, and her eyes cross to look at them. She does not touch them like she did with Sara. Across the room, Miss Avery stops her own inspection. Everyone is watching. "And turn," Miss Pratt says, and she shakes her head the way Mama does when she sees the commercials about the starving children in Ethiopia—all those hungry eyes and distended abdomens.

As I turn my palms upward my hands and arms balloon. The more people stare, the larger they will grow. I am worried about explosion, but I'm also concerned about imploding. I want to hide my hands, to hide the open sore. I'd take amputation. Like a scab, my hand would fall off of me and I'd run away. I'd leave it behind: bloody and infected on the stained carpet with my white gloves. Instead, I stand.

I stand like this forever, rotating my hands—palm up, palm down.

I stand like this and rotate my hands for each girl in the class to see, and I am so glad Sissy Baxter doesn't go to charm school, and yet, I know she'll hear all about my rose, my awful sore. Miss Pratt forms a line where the girls all stand waiting for their turn to look. Palm up, palm down—they shuffle past and observe. I am a sideshow freak. I stand on a stage of my very own. I keep company with the Three-Legged Man, the Lobster Boy, and the Camel Girl.

As the girls parade past, Miss Pratt taps her wand against her palm as if it's all she can do to keep from striking me. "This is what neglect looks like," Miss Pratt announces. And then Miss Avery chimes in. "My future debutantes of America, what does neglect say about a girl?"

The girls all answer in unison. It means I have no self-confidence.

—

"And what happens to a girl without her confidence?" Miss Avery asks. "Nothing," the chorus answers. "Nothing," they say. "Nothing." And the collective "ing" rings from all their lips.

I'm sent to the vestibule to wait for Gran while the other girls divide into pairs to trim, file, buff, and polish one another. As they sit cross-legged amid cotton balls and nail polish fumes, I sit on a wooden bench alone. The oak is hard and the tiny room is freezing. My breath comes out like the endless clouds of smoke Mama is forever exhaling. Through the clear glass below the stained-glass angel, I can see the street.

The angel is fragmented—different shapes and colors, she is broken like a Picasso.

I am the dead squirrel in the road surrounded by a murder of crows.

The crows abandon the dead squirrel whenever a car comes along. And I wonder why it's a murder when the birds are crows and a flock when they are any other kind of bird. My hands are cold. I shove them back into my white gloves. I put aside the folded note I've been told to give to Gran—the one from Miss Pratt.

The note goes into great detail about my hands. *Ragged, filthy nails that are screaming for a professional manicure.* Miss Pratt tells my grandmother she is a fine lady. She and Miss Avery pray to age as gracefully as she has. *Because of this, we know you'll understand the importance of this request.* Miss Pratt does not wish to offend my grandmother. *We understand the situation, and we simply applaud you, Mrs. Johnson, for all your efforts to better that poor neglected child.*

Gran is St. Jude, Patron Saint of Lost Causes.

Miss Pratt writes, *For the time being, we simply aren't equipped to handle a girl like Fiona.* The open sore is never mentioned. Undoubtedly, Miss Pratt found it too terrible to acknowledge. And compared with my other flaws, it's just a gaping wound—given the proper time and care, if left alone, it will surely heal and go away forever.

Gran puts her reading glasses on to get a better look. I lean over the front seat from the back seat where I have to sit even if it's just the two of us. She is stiff, and I can tell it hurts for her to turn and look. She holds each hand long enough to see the flaws. What disgusts her the most she looks at the least, and I'm not entirely sure she even registers the open sore.

"Put your gloves back on," she says. "This instant."

I understand her need for my hands to be hidden. I want this more than she could know. I pull the white gloves back on, snapping the buttons shut where they close just above the wrist as if they were specifically designed to cover my rose. I sit back and pull the safety belt over me before she can tell me to do this as well. Gran takes her glasses off and stares at the world through her windshield. She looks at Main Street like there's something she must confront.

All I can see is the tiny town of Eudora.

The stop and go lights turn from green to yellow to red, and soon they will switch to flashing yellows and reds for the nearly non-existent night traffic. There is a bank of plowed snow—cold and gray with soot—and the streets are clear. No ice, just worn-out asphalt. And the water tower stands where it has always stood lookout. This is the heart of Bleeding Kansas; a tense division line between the South and the North before the Civil War.

Uncle Billy says, "Every place has something to be famous for."

—

My grandmother sighs and puts the car in drive, and we lurch forward. We listen to the radio long enough to hear a repeat of the weather report I heard this morning. Snow is likely, but the Cold War is finally over. Gran takes me home and tries to drop me off without getting out of the car or seeing my father, but he appears just as I'm shutting the car door. He comes from nowhere with an axe over his shoulder. He's been chopping firewood with the red blade. He's smiling because he's been outside doing something physical. He waves for Gran to roll her window down. I hold my breath and cross my fingers.

"And how are my two young *ladies*?" he inquires. He exaggerates the word "ladies," and he winks at me. He will never be able to wink like Uncle Billy does. Gran nods her head the way she does when everything is in perfect order, but she won't look my father in the eye. Her hands remain on the steering wheel, her rosary wrapped around her fingers. I stand there with my white gloves still on and I tug at my jacket sleeves to make them longer. I keep outgrowing all my clothes, even the new outfits Gran bought for me last month.

I wait for Gran to tell Daddy how I have failed her. I can hear her, clear as day: *What a disgrace! Such a disappointment* and *I am absolutely ashamed.*

I stand there in the cold waiting for the world to end.

"Same time next week?" Daddy asks.

Gran looks him in the eye and smiles her pinched-lip smile. "Yes," she says. "But, Tobias, please be sure Fiona's ready. She often isn't."

"Yes, ma'am," Daddy says, saluting her like a soldier would his sergeant. He uses the hand not holding the axe, and I know he's thinking what I am thinking: I am always on time. In fact, I'm often early. Then he puts his free arm around my shoulders and we stand like this as we watch my grandmother drive away. She drives too fast on the gravel and I don't have to look to know my father is grimacing. Driving fast like this puts extra wear on the driveway and costs Daddy money he doesn't have. Her tires spit out gravel, and in her wake Gran leaves behind a small dust storm.

When Gran picks me up the following Thursday, I'm not sure what to expect. Maybe she convinced Miss Pratt and Miss Avery to take me back. Or maybe she intends to take me for a manicure.

I've done my best to leave the sore alone, but last night my fingers betrayed me in my sleep. In the morning, I woke to find the sheets stained with the telltale rust, and the sore itself was an open rose—the reddest a rose can ever bloom. Washing was not enough to make it go away.

"Put your seat belt on," Gran says, already pulling away from the house, and the Buick slips on a patch of black ice. My grandmother has never been in an automobile accident, and my uncle says, "This is a matter of divine intervention." Daddy agrees. He says, "It's got to be some miracle that Gran was born in Kansas—a world both flat and straightforward." And I think, *Some of us are never meant to leave this state.*

Gran uses her turn signal although no one is behind us. She does this despite that she's simply turning off one driveway onto another. She slips onto the driveway that is like a road. Daddy plans on naming it someday—getting a green-and-white street sign and everything—but when I asked what he was waiting for Daddy said, "The right name, of course." Sometimes I feel so stupid.

The sun is already setting even though it's only four fifteen. I look for the dog. I've seen tracks in the snow. I think about following

---

them through the dormant bramble of wild raspberry—toward the river, to hide awhile in the comforts of her den. The days have been short and dark, so I use my eyes to drink the orange-and-pink horizon. This color is only temporary in a landscape otherwise woven from shades of constant gray, filthy white, and relentless black.

When Gran gets to the highway, she turns left when right leads to charm school. She is following the direction of the sore on my wrist. Left. As in *Mama left*. After she drives another ten miles, I figure we are headed toward Lawrence. And this is confirmed when we enter the city limits. I wonder what we are doing. Gran is quiet, and I know better than to ask. Mama isn't the only one who prefers silence.

Again, Gran follows the compass rose of my wrist, steering the long Buick into the left-turn lane and cutting off the car behind us. They slam their brakes and honk three times, but Gran doesn't seem to even notice.

She uses a gloved finger to crank the heat, and the hot air comes blasting out and the turn signal clicks as we wait for red to change to green. As the Buick purrs I look out the window and find myself face to face with the hospital where I was born fifteen years ago. Where Mama lived that summer when I was six. Is this where my grandmother is taking me? I hold my breath and cross my fingers. And the turn signal continues to click, and "clicking" rhymes with "ticking" for a reason. In the tinted glass, my reflection is ephemeral. Double exposed, my expression is not just constructed from soft pink flesh but built from white bricks, square windows, and plastic blinds.

The arrow turns green and the car moves forward, turning left. The clicking stops. Gran drives another two blocks, and everywhere there are signs for hospital parking.

At each intersection, Gran breaks the law by not coming to a complete stop, and finally she eases the long car into a parking spot on the street. And I see where we are: We are parked in front of her doctor's office. But when we go inside, I find I'm the one with the appointment.

"Your grandmother tells me you were once hospitalized for cellulitis?" the doctor says. He keeps asking the same questions: "How did you get the sore?" "How long have you had it?" and "Does it ever scab over?"

He wears latex gloves the same powder blue as Sara's hands. After having to wear white gloves for charm school and to hide my wrist, I feel claustrophobic when I look at his gloved hands. I wonder if he wants to crawl out of his skin the way I do.

He is rough with the sore.

He presses down on the flesh all around it, asking if it hurts. He palpates, and then he presses down into the center of my rose. "What about this?" he asks. "Does it hurt when I do this?"

Each time, I shake my head. I shake my head to say no.

I know better than to tell him the truth. I do my best not to talk at all. He sits on a stainless-steel stool that has wheels.

He peels his gloves off and tosses them into a trash can that is also made from stainless steel. The can is overflowing with other discarded powder blue latex gloves. The exam room needs to be cleaned. There is blood splattered on the ceiling. DR. HENRY BURNS has been embroidered onto the left breast of his white jacket.

"That's what I thought," he says. But he doesn't actually say what he thinks. Instead, he pulls a prescription pad from his pocket, and this is what the other doctors are always doing when they talk to my mother. His pen makes a scratching noise as he writes. He has gray-blue eyes and white bushy eyebrows, while the rest of his hair is black and cut short.

He holds the prescription in the air, and when I reach for it he draws back the way a bully would. "That sore," he says, "is infected." Then he pauses, looking at me the way people like him do—everyone is always trying to figure me out, even when they don't like me.

Finally, he hands me the prescription.

"This is an antibiotic ointment," he says. "You can only get this strength from a doctor, so once this sore has healed, the ointment is not to be used again. In fact, you should throw it away." I have always hated the word "ointment."

"Wash the wound with soap and water, then apply the ointment and a bandage," he says. "Once in the morning and again at night before you go to bed."

He narrows his eyes, trying to stare into my soul, and then he says, "The rest of time, the sore must be left alone." And everything in my life is an echo.

The ointment makes the sore vanish—almost overnight. Like magic, half a year of picking is gone, and there is no scar in its wake. Like it never even was.

I touch the spot where there is no scar. I use the pads of my fingers. When I rub, I think of Gran, who doesn't tell anyone about my expulsion from charm school, the sore, the ointment, or the doctor. I've seen my grandmother rub the ground where my grand-father is buried. When she touched the grave, it reminded me of how I now touch the skin where once I was hurt. First she pats the grass, but soon she forgets herself. Her hand begins to circle like she's going to conjure his spirit from the dirt. She rubs the earth this way because she misses him, and I touch my wrist because I miss the girl who arrives whenever I am picking.

Gran comes for me at 4:15 every Thursday. We don't return to the doctor. I sit in the back of the long Buick and she drives. For three hours, my grandmother drives. Never too close to the farm. Gran follows other desolate back roads, and I memorize the Douglas County countryside—all the houses, and all the different routes. She pulls over whenever a car comes from the other direction. She is trying to keep the Buick clean. More often than not, we still get splattered by the exhaust-stained slush. And I watch the sun dip into the white horizon of winter.

The falling sun turns the snow into a wash of pastels and the initial pink and orange fade into lavender and lavender into gray, and gray into night. As soon as the numbers on the dashboard clock turn to 7:00, Gran makes an abrupt turn and heads back to the farm. We fishtail on black ice, but she never once loses control. Uncle Billy's right. It is a miracle. A matter of divine intervention.

The digital numbers of the car clock glow blue and so does Gran. She looks like a ghost. Like she's barely even there. She hunches so far forward, it is hard to see her head from the backseat, and this is from the osteoporosis. We never talk, and when Gran drops me back at home we don't say good-bye. I just climb out and watch her drive away. I watch the trail of exhaust follow her—alchemized by the winter air, the hot turns to cold.

Gran comes even after 1989 turns into 1990, and winter turns into spring and spring into summer and summer into fall. She comes for me and we drive. The routine is soothing, and I leave my sores alone. I am alchemized by the ointment; I think I'm healed.

———

Gran continues to pick me up every single Thursday even though charm school officially ended back in April, and then my freshmen year in June. Forever punctual—she is never late. We loop through country roads, driving around and around, and everything loops, including me.

Gran gives me the pearl rosary, which I wear around my neck. And I am another link on a chain of Fionas. When Daddy sees the rosary, Gran explains. "Fiona is a woman now." Her words echo, and later I have to look at myself in the mirror. I am trying to see what she sees, but all I see is the little girl I've always seen staring back at me.

CHAPTER THIRTEEN

EMERGENCE

loop: n. ⅃. *A length of line, ribbon, or other thin material doubled over and joined at the ends* 2. *Something having a shape, order, or path of motion that is circular or curved over on itself*
3. (Comp. Sci.) *A sequence of instructions that repeats either a specified number of times or until a particular condition prevails.*

loophole: n. ⅃. *A means of evasion.*

loopy: adj. ⅃. *Offbeat; crazy.*

October ⅃8, ⅃99⅃

Gran and I are in the Buick, circling around the lake, when she doubles over and vomits everywhere.

I break free of my safety belt, scramble over the seat, and grab the wheel. Even though I don't know how to drive—even though both Daddy and Uncle Billy are always pressuring me to learn—I manage to steer the long car around the curve of Mirror Lake before I can get my foot on the brake, and I stop the vehicle.

I shift the Buick into park. My grandmother is drooping. She leans against the window—her eyes half-closed and fluttering. Her face twists and I read the language of her body. She's in pain. I switch the ignition off and take the keys.

Wearing the inside of my grandmother, I run and walk a

---

quarter-mile to Wilma's, where Uncle Billy hasn't lived forever, and I use the pay phone bolted to the cinder-block wall to call 911. I tell a woman's voice where the paramedics will find us. And then I rush back to the Buick, where my grandmother is sound asleep in a bad way. I wrap the rosary around her hand and my hand, and I wait for help.

The paramedics ask me to climb into the ambulance, and I can't move. I stand in the dust kicked up by the speed of the emergency vehicle. Everything is fast. Too fast. And Gran is already strapped to a gurney, and I am scared. She mumbles, falling in and out of consciousness, and when I hear her say, "I need my granddaughter," I end up running. I run for the woods, where I hide.

My heart tries to break me open. It is a bomb inside my chest exploding as I watch the paramedics trying to figure out what to do. They keep looking at the woods, at the place where I disappeared and the shadows I let swallow me. I think of Snow White and the woodsman hired to cut out her heart, but no one comes after me. The paramedics practice triage; as always, the matriarch is the priority. They are not the seven dwarves. They are medical professionals, and they do not care about me.

Clutching the crucifix, I watch the red and blue lights circle on the cold surface of the lake until they vanish. The ambulance goes racing away toward the finish line, and the sirens scream, *Emergency! Emergency! Emergency!* and I can't believe I just abandoned my grandmother. There is nothing left to do but run.

I run through the maze of trees until they give way to a field of cut corn. I zigzag through the toppled blond stalks as the sun heads for retreat in the world beyond the western horizon. I jog along the

McAlister side of the Silver River and up onto the highway. I run across the steel bridge through a wave of vertigo as the gray sky pulls back and the wide ribbon of water below rushes on, and the world reels and I keep running.

I run until the railing ends and I'm on the other side. I stop long enough to vomit. I turn inside out like my grandmother just did, and then I run again. I run along the Silver River once more, but this time I run after the running water. The bank is littered with wet pebbles, and they reflect the fire of the setting sun. The air stuck inside my body slices into my lungs and organs; it tries to dissect me, and when the river begins to crash over rocks and into the falls, I cut away and run north again.

My shadow chases me as I cross the ditch; she stalks me as I tunnel through the twisted corridor of trees in the orchard. And I am running the same path now I ran with Mama all those years ago, but this time I don't trip once or fall. The miasma of the putrid apples in the grass is intoxicating, and I am drunk by the time I pass through the ring of cottonwoods, and the house is there to welcome me. Daddy's truck is nowhere to be seen, which means he's not here. I cross the threshold called home, and my shadow is close behind.

I find the X-acto knife in Mama's art supplies, and the razor blades are in the bathroom cabinet where they've been waiting—waiting behind the looking glass just for me, always and forever. And all I had to do was open this small door above the sink.

I'm all alone with my shadow. Everyone else is in one hospital or another, and when I climb into the claw-foot, I am trying to be seven years old again.

I'm wearing one of Mama's old nightgowns and there is no water.

—

Just the cold white enamel and the same plug and chain that can't be lost—and yet everything has changed. Nearly sixteen, I fill the tub, and around my neck a virgin now hangs. Three more years to go until nineteen, and the daddy longlegs who lived in the drain died years ago and left behind a legless corpse long since turned to dust. And there is no mother at the end of the hall, resting in her room—there is nothing but an empty chamber full of echoes.

I pull up my sleeves and tuck the long white nightgown around my privates like a diaper. And I take all the scars from the boy at Saint Joseph's and transfer them to myself. *Pay attention*, he says. And I do. I pay attention. I pay one toll after another. I rub my fingers across my skin and I can feel the tiny ridges—the texture of his flesh on me—and the texture provides a grip, something to hold on to, something to keep me from slipping all the way away.

I have my own scars, but they are different. My open sores bloom into rotting roses and leave scars like shooting stars: dreams that never do come true. These scars are not the perfect lines that made the body of the boy at the hospital. Mine are messy, and I want what he has: I want self-control. I take the safety cap off the X-acto blade and compare this sharp edge with the razor blade. One is a triangle and the other is rectangular. Basic geometry: perfect shapes, straight lines, angles, and precise points—this is something even Miss Pratt and Miss Avery could appreciate.

Clean and sharp, these blades will be tidy when they open me. Clean and sharp, they will work as God did when he carved Eve from Adam. I, too, will give birth to a girl who will fall for me, and she will handle everything I cannot. The shine of the blade is dangerous. And I think, maybe this is what it feels like when people try drugs for the first time—a certain dread, and a lovely anticipation.

—

I try each blade to compare the danger. I turn their potential into a race. This is biology, basic anatomy—science. And in science, the setting must be controlled, and my hand doesn't once waver. The X-acto knife is exact. Easy to control, the handle is also crosshatched to provide the grip I am seeking. I draw a long red line across the white canvas of my thigh. In the gallery of the tub, my shadow does the same. She draws a shadow line across her shadow thigh.

While the X-acto knife is exact, the razor blade is more than just an instrument for cutting; it is a tiny mirror, another reflection in which to find myself. I see everything I'm about to do, and then I see what I just did, and I am learning. It doesn't take long to turn right now into gone.

Both blades help me breathe again. They open so much faster than fingernails ever did or could; like magic, they part my skin, and in the blood the red sea divides and I am warm and tingling—from pain. I am overwhelmed by the pleasure of another girl. Just as the doctors once cut me from Mama, I cut this girl from myself and she steps out of me to run her blade along the inside of my arms just as Sissy and Tanya did to Candace with their fingertips.

She waits for me to shiver, and smiles to see me smiling.

She switches back and forth—from one blade to the other, from one limb to another. She opens me. She builds a bridge between our bodies, and we are symbiotic; the blade serves as a prosthetic in which to bind and connect. I belong to her just as much as she belongs to me. The blood is hot and leaves me cold as I turn blue into red.

The blades part the skin, and the red sea rises. I chase the purple in the split second between blue and red, and in this borderland my chest can expand; my lungs open and close like the wings of a butterfly, and I am ventilated—I am cutting away the cocoon, and I am opening. I am changing.

But blood mimics skin. It reacts to air, turning colors. The chemistry continues: The blood begins to die, and the thin ribbons of liquid all turn hard. Each cut seals itself. It turns into a crust of rust: a call and response, my blood answering my body by not being blood anymore. It changes just like that. No attachments to what it was. It turns into a scab, and this scab saves my life—a life I am not trying to take, but to prove. I think of Alexis Romanov, whose blood refused to coagulate.

Heir to the Russian throne, he inherited an X chromosome from his mother, and this X carried a copy of the mutant gene for hemophilia. If Alexis did as I do now, or even as I have done before, his crimson tide would have washed away the world.

I'm not afraid of growing old, but I am afraid of growing up. I think of the song forever looping on the radio. The song the popular girls listen to as they sprawl across the lawn during lunch or after school. Serenaded by their ghetto blasters, the lyrics to this song also loop as the singer sings: *"You will remain forever young."* But I don't want to be forever young. I just don't want to turn nineteen. Like Alexis, I, too, have a copy of my mother in my genes. Three more years to go. And the blue turns red and the blood is hot and it leaves me cold.

Uncle Billy's eyes are full of tears, and when I look at him he blinks, and the tears spill down his face. Salt and water, they are the substance of the sea, and they are meant for me.

The bathroom window frames a night sky, and this perfect square of sky frames a full moon surrounded by an aura of silver rainbows.

———

268

I want to go outside—to lie in the cold grass covered only by the vast dome of stars above—of universe; I want to feel small like that instead of the kind of small I feel right now. I don't believe in God, but I do believe in heaven.

And I am also crying. My tears are hot, but they don't leave me cold—they leave me warm—and Uncle Billy is surrounding me with mother arms, and mother arms are always warm and they are always strong. He helps me stand, and then he guides me to the toilet, where I sit. I watch everything he does. Every cut he cleans. My uncle washes me. He washes away the hurt and the smallness I am feeling. He baptizes me with hydrogen peroxide, and when he's done I glisten: Made from love and a generous application of Neosporin, I've been dressed with a new skin.

My uncle turns away so I can undress. And I will not be bleaching red and brown back to white this time, because Uncle Billy doesn't hesitate to throw away my mother's nightgown; he stuffs it into an empty carton of Epsom salts that he tosses back into the trash, and I come to understand that he won't be telling anyone about tonight, not even Daddy. Billy is still turned the other way as I step into a pair of clean pajama bottoms and button up the flannel top.

"You can't pick on yourself like this," he says. "Not anymore." And this is how I come to know what he knows. What he sees. And what he understands. Someone has been paying attention. "And you certainly can't do this," he says, turning now to look at me. With my finger, I draw an X across my heart. I promise him.

Bandaged, I go to bed, and Billy stays the entire night in my window seat. He doesn't want to talk about Gran. "Tonight is about you," he says, although he does assure me that she will be okay. He sits in the window with a quilt wrapped around his shoulders, and with the lights turned off the moon turns his silhouette into a soft grandmother wearing a shawl.

Billy stays like this all night, and in the morning, when I awake, he is still there.

Billy and I drive to the hospital in Lawrence, and Daddy explains what happened to Gran.

"She's all hollowed out inside," he says, and then he lists off all the operations she's undergone, and every organ removed from her body: minus one uterus, one gall bladder, and one spleen, my grandmother is a lesson in subtraction. With all that extra room inside, her intestines tied themselves into a knot. In my head, I see them trying to form the loop for infinity.

"She's under observation for now," Daddy says—which is exactly what Uncle Billy said to me this morning before we left the house. Only I'm the one under *his* observation.

While the doctors decide what to do with Gran, my uncle is also working on a treatment plan just for me. I look at Gran asleep in her hospital bed full of needles, tubes, and morphine, and I hold my breath and cross my fingers: I want her to feel as safe as I do now.

All I ever needed was for someone—anyone—not just to notice but to see, and to ask me to stop, and Billy is the one who stepped up. It's a relief to be held accountable. Knowing that my uncle knows— knowing that he will be keeping tabs on me—feels like picking felt, only better; because he knows, and because he will not stand for it, everything has opened and it is easier to breathe again.

Gran has to have another operation. They cut out the section of knotted intestine. This time the surgery is laparoscopic and she only has to stay in the hospital for a few days. Daddy and I come to take her home while Billy stays at the farm, where there is always work to be done.

As the oldest son, my father has the power of attorney. He doesn't just control Mama and me. Daddy signs paperwork and then he goes to get the Buick, to bring it around to the front.

"The pain medication is making your grandma act strange," the nurse says, and I nod like I understand. We are waiting for a wheelchair, and when it comes I'm allowed to push Gran by myself. "Just leave the chair in the vestibule," the nurse tells me, and then she leans over to say good-bye to my matriarch. "Fiona," she says, "I hope we never see you again," and then the nurse winks at me.

I push the wheelchair through the hospital, down the elevator, through the large white lobby, and into the vestibule, where we wait for my father. Every thirty seconds, we are blasted by hot air, but it's too cold to wait outside. "Dearie," Gran says, and I can't help but think of the grandmother in *Little Red Riding Hood*—the one who is really the wolf. "Come around so I can see you."

I do as she says. My grandmother never calls me "Dearie" or "Honey" or "Darling"—only Fiona, and usually my name is no more than an angry whisper. This grandmother sounds like a soft grandmother. "Oh, Alma," Gran says when she looks at me. "It's so good to see you," and this grandmother reaches for me—something else she's never done. But I am not the subject of her endearment. She is reaching for her little sister: When I was six, I died from scarlet fever.

Gran takes my hands, kissing each one—she won't let go. "Not this time," she says, and this is when Daddy pulls up, forever the doting son. A better son than he is a husband or a father. He is always promising to take care of Gran no matter what. He makes this vow again and again. "I will never put you in a nursing home," he will say, and when he does, my grandmother smiles at him and says she's proud to be the mother of such a good boy.

Daddy pulls up to the yellow curb, and I have to let go of Gran to push her wheelchair through the sliding automatic glass doors, and it is colder outside than I expected.

I think about Mama's nurse and what she explained to Daddy and me last month. She said Mama would be deinstitutionalized soon, but she didn't know when. "It's the new policy," she said. "This is why the streets are suddenly full of homeless people talking to themselves, eating out of the trash, and freezing to death come winter."

She also said we could always put Mama into a nursing home. "They aren't just for the elderly or the dying," she explained. "They're for anyone who can't take care of themselves." And even though she was talking to both of us, I don't think Daddy was listening, because he didn't once interrupt to say, "I will never put my wife in a home." He just nodded his head, thanked her for the information, and shook her hand to say good-bye.

He is always shaking hands with the staff at Saint Joseph's, and thanking them. "Thank you," he says. *Thank you for taking my daughter's mother away from her.*

Daddy gets out of the car and tries to get Gran to stand—but she's confused. She doesn't know who he is. "Stop calling me that," she says. "I am nobody's mother." But he doesn't listen. He just continues to call her "Ma." He says "Ma" like he thinks saying it again and again is enough to prove his point, and in the end Alma is the only one who can get Gran into the car.

Daddy stands on the sidewalk, glaring at the sky. Yesterday, he said he understood why I ran away like I did, but I know he's a liar. He will never forgive me for leaving his mother all alone like that. I know this because I will never forgive him for letting Mama commit herself. I'd like to ask my father, *How many times have you abandoned my mother?* but I don't.

Instead, I ask Gran if she is comfortable. I sit in the backseat with her, and as Daddy drives away I realize what my future is. It is time to be strong. I drew an X on my heart for Uncle Billy, and this X is the crossroads where I've been stuck. I take my first major step away from the center toward another tomorrow. Tomorrow I will care for Mama, and all the tomorrows to follow. I will be there when Daddy can't—when he gives up.

And I finally understand the reason I was born.

Gran lets go of my hand, and by the time we've pulled into her garage she is an old woman, a mother, and a hard grandmother again. And I am no longer Alma. I am the granddaughter who abandoned her grandmother in her time of need.

Gran ignores my efforts to help, only letting Daddy assist her; she acts like I'm not even here. My father takes her back to the bedroom while I stand in the kitchen feeling useless. I put the bouquet I bought for Gran in a vase with water and stand the flowers on the dining room table. Purple hyacinth for *please forgive me* and maidenhair fern for our secret bond.

My cuts are hidden inside my clothes—beginning to heal already, and Daddy has no idea. He closes the door to Gran's room like she is a sleeping baby, and when he comes into the kitchen he looks at me like he wants to talk—but in the end, he doesn't say anything.

He takes a can of condensed Campbell's tomato soup from

the cabinet and uses the electric can opener mounted to the wall above the sink to open it. He fills the silence with the hum of the appliance and the sound of metal being cut. And while the soup warms on the stove, he makes two grilled cheese sandwiches. The only time I ever eat Campbell's anything is when I'm here. We boy-cotted Campbell's for years; when they finally agreed to treat their farmworkers better, we continued to not buy their products because of the pesticides they use. Gran has Wonder Bread, when we only eat whole wheat at home. I bake the bread myself. Every Sunday, between the loads of laundry, I mix flour, water, and yeast, and then I knead. I wait for the dough to rise, and then I bake while I sort and fold the clothing and the linen.

The more I think about it, the more I know I can care for Mama. I know with absolute certainty that I am capable. But if this is truly to be my fate, I will have to keep my promise to my uncle. I cannot pick or cut myself, not anymore. Not if I'm going to be my mother's caregiver.

We sit at the kitchen table to eat. The house is quiet. The refriger-ator hums and Daddy chews, and underneath these sounds I can hear the ticking—faint, but consistent. It is there.

After dinner, I wash the dishes while Daddy unfolds the couch and makes the bed. I wash the dishes by hand because I don't know how to use the dishwasher. I wear Gran's rubber gloves to hide my sliced-up skin. When my father finishes with the bed, he sits on the edge of the mattress with his elbows on his knees and his head held by his hands. I spray the sink clean, remove the long hot-pink gloves, pull down my sleeves, and go to sit beside him.

We sit like this for ten minutes, still not talking. We sit so still, I can't breathe. I've sat like this with Mama, Uncle Billy, and even

Gran—but never with my father. The headlights from the passing cars cast shadows across the walls, but I've grown accustomed to their puppetry.

Daddy breaks the stillness by standing, and then the silence when he says, "You should get some sleep." At his side, his hands turn into fists. "I need to get some air," he says, and his jaw is clenched. Like Alice in Wonderland, Daddy doesn't always fit the insides of houses or other structures. His head and arms go crashing through the walls, ceilings, and even the floors. I am Alice too—only I am shrinking: picking away at myself, and if I don't stop, I will definitely disappear.

Gran gave me a shelf in the bathroom years ago. Here I find a nightgown, toothbrush, tub of Noxzema, and comb, and a box of superabsorbent maxi pads. I pull the nightgown over my head. Instead of Mama's white cotton, the gown is made from red flannel, and both the sleeves and the skirt are long, as if specifically designed to keep my secret. Then I watch myself in the mirror as I brush my teeth. With the three panels of glass positioned just so, I am reflected into infinity.

I wonder where Daddy will go. No one walks in suburbia at night. Porch lights send warnings, and each house is wired with an alarm system. I brush my teeth so hard, I spit blood. The bathroom is pink and black with gold seahorses everywhere. I fill my hands with water from the tap, rinse, and then I drink.

I stand by the door to my grandmother's room. I comb the long fibers of the carpet with my bare toes. I put my ear to the hollow-core door and listen to the other side. The quiet is thick with static, and listening to her room and to the air inside the wood is like listening to the ocean trapped inside a seashell.

—

When I get into bed, the furnace ticks and a blast of hot air answers; blowing through the vents, the forced heat fills the small house. The other ticking grows so loud, I feel like I'm inside a cuckoo clock. I'm careful to stay close to the edge of the bed so there's enough room for Daddy. It's been years since we slept together. When I was little, his body next to Mama made a tent of blankets for me to sleep inside—safe and sound. I pretend I'm asleep when he does return, and the second he steps into the house the ticking grows faint again, absorbed by his large body.

I listen to him use the bathroom. I hear him urinate, and the muffled sound makes my belly butterfly. I remember being little, when he and Mama still undressed in front of me. I remember splashing in the farmer's ditch or under the boughs of the weeping willow in the wading pool along the Silver River. We were naked then—still brand-new. The toilet flushes, and the water from the sink turns on and runs forever. I'd get in trouble if I let water run like that at home, and then the water stops and I hear the sound of the bathroom door opening.

I anticipate the mattress giving when first he sits, and then again as he lies down. But my father doesn't come into the living room. I open my eyes, and there is Christ on the wall watching me. I listen to the shushing sound of Gran's bedroom door brushing against the dense carpet.

Hush, Jesus says. *Hush*.

I hear the hardware click as the door closes behind my father, and then there is nothing more than the river sound of the interstate three blocks east of here. The ticking grows loud again. Coming from all four directions, the ticking also comes from the space within, from above and below. The ticking ticks inside me too. *Tick. Tick. Tick.*

—

I can hear the grandfather clock back home at the farm as it chimes twelve times. Twelve chimes for midnight and tomorrow has arrived. Yesterday is gone and I am now officially sixteen years old.

Sweet sixteen.

Today is my birthday, and all I want is to crawl into a bed and sleep beside a mother—and if I could, I would give anything to sleep once again inside her perfect skin.

CHAPTER FOURTEEN
AS NEEDED

prescribe: v. 1. To set down as a rule or guide.

January 10, 1992

"Reintegration" is the medical term for Mama's transition from hospital to home. The reintegration trials are the first major step in the official process called deinstitutionalization.

Daddy is exhausted. He's been fighting every release date proposed by Saint Joseph's. For months, he's campaigned for one postponement after another. He will do anything to delay my mother's return. He writes letters, attends meetings, and even spoke at a conference titled "The Hard Truth: Society and Deinstitutionalization." Last night, I heard him on the telephone. "I just need one more year," he kept saying. "Please, can you just wait until *after* my daughter graduates?"

The support team provides Daddy with the final date: Mama will be deinstitutionalized on September 1, 1992, at nine o'clock in the morning. She is to be discharged one year earlier than the date my father was requesting. When Daddy tries to make another compromise, asking for a release date anytime during the summer of 1993, we learn Saint Joseph's is being shut down by the state.

This is happening everywhere—as part of deinstitutionalization, hospitals are closing despite a grave lack of alternative resources like outpatient treatment centers or halfway homes. But Mama does not require such facilities—she has us, and more specifically she has me, always and forever. The president of Saint Joseph's looks just as tired as my father does. He looks Daddy in the eye and tries to explain how far he has already gone for our family.

He says, "September first is the very last release date. Unlike the other patients being let go that day, your wife is not only incredibly high-functioning, she is the only one who actually has a place to go, let alone a supportive family." I bite my lip to keep from smiling. "Integration" means "to make whole," so "reintegration" means "to make whole again." To reintegrate is to return—to return home, to return to how it was supposed to be.

"In the meantime," Dr. Stein says, redirecting the conversation, the way he always does, "reintegration will give you all the time you need to learn to live together." And I want to tell him, "We lived together just fine for thirteen years," but I don't. I don't say anything.

He tells us not to expect home life to return to how it was before Mama had herself committed. He says this to both my father and me, yet he only looks at me, and he is nothing more than a psychiatrist trying to shrink me. He is disappearing everything I've ever known.

I hold my breath and cross my fingers and focus on being here the way Uncle Billy is always telling me to do. Today we are bringing Mama back to the farm for her first two-week trial at home. The big dictionary in the living room lists six definitions for the word "trial," but I prefer the fourth one because it complements the definition of "permanent" still filed away in my memory.

—

trial: a test of patience or endurance.

While I have proven my ability to endure, I still need to practice patience.

Uncle Billy is concerned about reintegration. He is full of warnings.

"You might be triggered," he explains. "You must try to remain in the present."

The cuts on my body turned into red lines, which turned into brown lines and then purple lines, and now they are white. Healed. The scars are even beginning to fade. Uncle Billy prescribed Vitamin E oil, which I'm supposed to apply twice a day. I end up applying it more; I apply the golden oil whenever I am tempted to hurt myself. Billy says this is good, but he also wants me to find something else to do with myself—something else for my hands to worry; something else to connect me to my heart. Billy says, "Fig, I just want you to find something that you love to do." And he made me think of Gran, who always says, "Idle hands are the devil's workshop."

Daddy is doing paperwork with the administrator while the nurses explain Mama's schedule to me. Like Gran, they believe in routine, and Mama's routine revolves around her medicine. The nurses get excited as they discuss my mother's medication.

"They aren't different kinds," they say, "but they've come out in a different form."

Instead of pills, the antipsychotics and the tranquilizers now come in wafers that dissolve on the patient's tongue. This will make it difficult for Mama to hide and spit out later. The new wafers work nearly as fast as injections, and this means Daddy and I can now manage episodes of extreme psychosis all by ourselves. We will no longer require the assistance of doctors, nurses, or their orderlies. And this is one more sign that I am meant to take care of my mother.

Daddy and I give Mama the wafers three times a day, with every meal—not that Mama consumes anything but sugar, caffeine, and cigarettes.

There are other wafers to be administered as needed. AS NEEDED, as typed on the box, below Mama's name, ANNIE JOHNSON. As needed. I need Mama to come home. I need to be the best caregiver in the world. I kneel before Mama, and she opens her mouth and sticks out her tongue for the medicine. She calls it communion. She wants wine. "You can't eat the flesh without the blood," she says. What began as a joke is no longer funny; it's just another monotonous routine.

Mama keeps her mouth open, and I watch the wafer dissolve. It turns to a lavender paste on her pink-brown tongue and then she closes her mouth. She scrunches her face against the bitterness, and this is the only time I can get her to drink water instead of coffee or flat Mountain Dew.

Daddy is not good at administering the as-needed medication, especially when Mama doesn't think she needs it. The as-needed wafers come with a special prescription: AS NEEDED TO TREAT ANXIETY, AGITATION, OR AGGRESSION. On the ward, the nurses say, "It's time to call Triple-A."

I bribe Mama with lollipops. At the bank, I fill my pockets with Dum Dums, and I hoard them for her. My bribes might increase her blood sugar, but they keep the monsters away. Mama has developed type 2 diabetes. This is common with schizophrenics. The disease is a long-term side effect from the antipsychotics.

Daddy doesn't approve of the bribes, but he doesn't tell me to stop and he doesn't lecture me. He teaches me to check her blood sugar levels instead and how to inject her with insulin.

I'm good at doing what I'm told.

Everyone wants to talk about my future. College applications, SAT scores, and the forever-repeated question *What do you want to be when you grow up?*

I don't tell anyone what I really want. What I am actually planning. If Daddy knew, he'd put Mama in a nursing home tomorrow and send me to boarding school even though he'd have to sell the farm to pay for it.

Uncle Billy says, "It's normal not to know exactly what you want to do, but it's time to start exploring all your options." Gran shakes her head and clicks her tongue. She says, "Let's not explore the arts," and that's when Daddy firmly says, "Fig can do *anything* she wants."

But all I want to do is take care of Mama.

I will care for her around the clock. And the routine will imprint itself on everyone, even Daddy. Secretly, he'll be relieved. He will see how much my mother needs me. He will need me. He won't be able to maintain the farm without my help. Over time, he will forget what he wanted for me. Next year, I will finish high school and then I'll turn eighteen, and since I'll be an adult he won't be able to make me do anything I don't want to do.

I hold my breath and cross my fingers: Daddy *will* come to see how happy I am caring for the woman who gave me life. He will come to understand. We are both better suited for life on this farm than anywhere else, and with me around Daddy can continue to do as he does. Surrounded by open sky and the seemingly endless expanse of earth, he can remain where he belongs—outside, and outside he is still my hero.

I roll the tiny vial back and forth between my palms until the insulin clouds over. I fill the syringe like my father demonstrated. I use rubbing alcohol to sterilize the site for injection, and then I stab my mother.

I push the orange plunger down, and the needle disappears into the soft white fat of her belly. I do exactly as I was taught and yet I leave her riddled with black bruises. I don't mean to. The bruises multiply; they swarm and form black storms, and these tornados punctuate the silver lightning strike of her Cesarean scar.

Daddy leases land to Mr. Fergeson, and with the help of two yapping blue heelers the old man herds his Jersey cows across the highway. The procession is slow. Mama sleeps in her rocking chair as I stand beside her in the day porch looking out the window, keeping watch.

Even though I administered a tranquilizer for the occasion, I find myself holding my breath and crossing my fingers to keep the dogs from barking. When the dogs do bark, I hold my breath and cross my fingers that the barking doesn't wake her, and if the barking does, I will repeat the ritual to keep the dogs from scaring her. And I will give her more of the medicine.

But Mama only sleeps. She doesn't even stir, so I step closer to the window. I lean my forehead against the glass and study the outside world. Mr. Fergeson and his dogs walk away. They leave the cows behind. The large black-and-white animals stand in the snow looking around their new home with sad eyes as I reach for my pearl rosary.

And this is another prescription from my uncle, when I feel tempted to pick, or nervous, or sad, or even angry. "If you feel unsettled," is what he said, "take the rosary and begin your counting." I run the rosary through my fingers, counting pearl after pearl. *One, two, three, breathe.* Once upon a time, Gran told me how every prayer sequence on a rosary is called a decade. I run the rosary around and around, and my fingers swallow time. *One, two, three, breathe.* Made from sand, the pearls are the same substance as the time-keeping method inside an hourglass. I run the pearls through my fingers. *One, two, three, breathe.* With my thumb, I collect each pearl. I get lost in the waves of reaching and pushing the pearls. I keep time and time keeps me.

"Every day is a near-death experience," Mama says, exhaling a cloud of blue smoke. She isn't talking to us, but that doesn't keep me from listening. She hasn't spoken in three days, and every time she stops talking I worry she might never talk again. So I always pay attention to what could be her final words.

Daddy grips the steering wheel like the blacktop isn't smooth—like this highway is not a highway he's traveled a million times over the duration of his life. He grips the steering wheel like this isn't Kansas; like it's a difficult road to drive instead of one so straightforward.

He's headed for the interstate, and I hate the interstate: the rush, and the passing—the complicated loops of highways all coming together like a complex nervous system. I push the pearls through my fingers. *One, two, three, breathe.* I watch the oil rigs alongside the road dip back and forth like grasshoppers, and the rhythm of the rigs is in time with the rhythm of the beads.

One, two, three, breathe. Today is Sunday. Today we take Mama back to the hospital, and the next two week trial isn't scheduled until March. All this back-and-forth is dumb. I am ready.

—

Daddy merges, squinting ahead, his eyes bloodshot from my mother's cigarettes. He lets Mama smoke in here because driving makes her nervous. And now we're on the interstate: the freeway, only there is nothing free about it. Trapped between exits, there is no escape, and this is the stretch where all the catastrophes happen: ENTIRE FAMILY KILLED. SEMI FULL OF HAZARDOUS CHEMICALS OVERTURNED. Mama's right. Every day *is* a near-death experience.

My fingers push pearls, and I pause to hold Mary between my thumb and knuckle. I stamp her black heart into my skin, and then I start counting again, passing beads. *One, two, three, breathe.* And I'm not the only one counting. Mama is tracking every exhale exhaled, and I'm recollecting a statistic from seventh-grade health with Mrs. Gallagher: *The average smoker forfeits eleven minutes of her life for every single cigarette she smokes.* One pack alone equals almost four hours subtracted from my mother's life, and I realize that Mama is literally killing time.

A silver station wagon drives beside us, and I don't feel as anxious as I would if it were a semi. The car is full: father driving, the mother beside him with a map folded in her lap. Three stair-step kids are strapped into the backseat, and I can tell they are singing, by the way their mouths move and their heads sway. In the far back I see a red-and-white cooler, pillows, stuffed animals, and suitcases. As they pass us, I see the Colorado license plate—the white outline of mountains against the green, and there's a bumper sticker too. It reads: WHAT IF THE HOKEY POKEY REALLY IS WHAT IT'S ALL ABOUT?

I go into Mama's old room and try on her clothes—the clothes that no longer fit her. Attached to the inside of the closet door hangs a

---

full-length mirror, and I look at myself standing here. The vintage dresses fit my reflection perfectly, including the white one that used to belong to the grandmother I never got to know.

Gran decided to remedy my bowl cut and took me to her new hairdresser at Curl Up & Dye. She turned her arthritic fingers into a pair of scissors to show the woman how and where to cut my hair. And now I have something called a pixie cut. I love my new hair, but I don't say so. I don't say anything. If I did, Gran might change her mind and not like my new haircut anymore.

I go downstairs and lie on the red velvet sofa. Like the bathtub, the sofa has clawed feet—only they are made from wood instead of iron and white enamel. When I was little, I used to pretend the sofa was a mythological beast and I was riding bareback, but I can't recall where I was going.

I only know that I was going somewhere.

I lie on the sofa and look at *Christina's World* where it hangs above the fireplace. I search the dark prairie grass for wildflowers and find only what might be the empty pods of milk thistle; while I don't know the message of this specific botanical, I do know that regular thistle is used to communicate vengeance or grief.

When I look at Christina, I no longer feel like I need to crawl out of my skin, I just feel restless. I read an article about Andrew Wyeth, but despite my photographic memory, I can't remember if Christina was paralyzed or blind. I look at her now, and I can see her internal struggle: She is trying to get to the house painted far away. Christina is trying to go home.

Uncle Billy gives me a guidebook to North American wildflowers. Pocket-size, it is color coded and water resistant. "I'd like you to find a way to integrate the outside world with the inside one," he says, and he reminds me how walking can be a form of meditation. And like the rosary beads, walking will give me something else to do when I feel like picking.

I'm worried he's going to ask about the lucky rabbit foot. I worry he will say, "You can always rub the charm with your fingers," so I break down and confess. Only I don't tell the whole truth. I tell him I lost the rabbit foot. And I don't say anything about the charred nesting doll hidden inside the iron maiden of wooden mothers.

He gives me the field guide the same day I unearth all of Mama's old books about Tasha Tudor and her lovely loping gardens. I realize this is the woman who illustrated some of my favorite children's books—the ones by Frances Hodgson Burnett. Like I'm discovering a secret garden, I find the books at the back of my mother's closet, and like a series of strange gifts they are wrapped in brown paper. When I handle it, the masking tape is so old and brittle, it turns to dust.

As I look at the pictures of Tasha in her gardens or wandering her estate, I come to have a deeper understanding of the word "affinity." Affinity is a natural attraction or feeling of kinship. And I feel akin to this old woman. I feel that she is me and I am her.

She is content in her own private wilderness.

Tasha Tudor gazes back at me before she wanders away. She is barefoot, and her long skirts trail behind her as she parts a field of flowers. She cuts pussy willow and cradles the bundle in her arms to carry home and arrange. I don't need to buy a copy of *Floriography*, because I've checked it out so many times that I've memorized the meanings of all the flowers it has listed. And this is how I know pussy willow means either motherhood or a recovery from illness.

I stand at the window, looking out, and the farm appears anew; it opens and invites—it calls to me. I see everything I have never seen before, yet I also feel a sense of déjà vu.

Today, I open Mama's closet, and I close my eyes as I run my fingers across the dresses. My hands select by touch: Today, I will wear blue velvet. I like to imagine this dress once belonged to my soft grandmother, but I don't know for sure. Mama can't remember anymore, or else she doesn't want to think about the answers.

Today, I will wear the blue velvet dress, a pair of gray tights, and Mama's old boots. I remember the day she bought the boots from the army surplus store in Lawrence, and even then the black leather toes were scuffed.

I slip the dress over my head and pull the rosary out. I take Mama's black peacoat from the hanger and put it on, and I button all the buttons except for the one at the very top. When I'm done, I look at myself in the mirror, and in the glass I see a young woman.

And she smiles back at me.

Uncle Billy stays at home with Mama. Today is the third day of the third reintegration trial, and my father needs my help running errands.

Daddy parks on Main Street and sends me into Eudora Drug to pick up my mother's Thorazine. The bells ring when I open the door, and the clerk at the register is already watching me. Pregnant, she can't be older than twenty; she holds her swollen belly like she's afraid it will fall off her body. Her brown hair is permed and frosted, and she's chewing gum.

She blows a big pink bubble, which pops as I make my way

through the greeting cards. In the round mirrors used to catch shop-lifters, the clerk watches me as I head for the pharmacy at the back of the small storefront. I see my reflection in the curved glass, where I, too, appear pregnant wearing Mama's white Gunne Sax dress. But when I look down, I'm just as skinny as I ever was.

I love this dress. The neckline trimmed in lace, the bodice hugs my chest—secured by a long cream-colored sash of silk tied tight around my lower ribs, it fits like me like a second skin. From there, the fabric falls—as soft as gauze, the dress is like a bandage to dress a wound. The dress flows as I walk toward the pickup window, and the movement of the material is soothing. It is hard to hurt yourself when you feel pretty.

I hold my breath and cross my fingers to summon the courage to ring the bell. I hate the pharmacist. I hate the way Mr. Edwards looks at me—and the way he looks at my family. Everyone in town might know about my mother, but Mr. Edwards knows even more. He not only understands what each pill does, he understands the reasons a prescription is prescribed.

I ring the bell, and Mr. Edwards sticks his head out from behind the white laminate shelving. Squinting at me through his square-frame glasses, he says "Ah!" and wrinkles his fat red nose. "Your mother's prescription isn't ready yet. Give me another fifteen minutes."

I try sitting on one of the chairs and reading the out-of-date maga-zines on the table, but they stink of perfume. It bewilders me how these synthetic scents are often named after flowers, and yet they smell nothing like their namesakes. A Norman Rockwell painting of another small-town pharmacist watches me, and I can't sit still. I begin to wander around the store—that is, I make it look like I am aimlessly meandering, but really I know exactly where I am going. I'm headed for the unattended cosmetics counter. Mrs. Sherman must have the day off, or else I'd never dare.

Displayed like candy, there is a row of lipstick next to another mirror that magnifies every pore in my face. In a vast array of reds, the unopened lipstick tubes stand erect—missiles ready to be launched—and I try to ignore Mama's voice inside my head. She is ranting about the patriarchy and the cruelty of animal testing. She doesn't bother to tell me I don't need makeup; she doesn't say, "You are pretty the way you are." She just assumes I already know this. She forgets I never really got to have a mother. I want eyeliner, black as kohl; I want to outline my eyes—catlike or Egyptian.

Mr. Edwards rings me up. I buy Thorazine and the Cover Girl–brand Midnight Black eyeliner pencil. The pregnant clerk blows another bubble as I exit, and the bells ring again. I'm blinded by the sun and the glare of the sun on the white pavement, and I stand there blinking until I can see again. I look down the street, and Daddy's truck is still there. Glinting in the sun, the Ram hood ornament stares forever forward as my father talks to Mrs. Sherman.

Daddy is leaning against the side of the truck, and Mrs. Sherman is on the sidewalk teetering in her heels, listening to him talk. I had no idea he had so much to say.

As she listens, Mrs. Sherman chews on her straw when she isn't taking long drinks from the perspiring wax cup, and I can almost see how they used to be—two teenagers in love. Daddy keeps talking and she is nodding her head, and never once does she look away. Then she touches him. She reaches for him with her manicured fingers, and I can see her long red claws as she squeezes his shoulder.

Daddy looks at her hand, and then he looks at her, and they don't say anything.

They just look at each other forever before Mrs. Sherman steps forward and closes in on my father. She kisses him on the cheek and lingers there until finally she pulls back and walks away. She looks sad, and Daddy is staring at his feet. I see the way his fingers flutter to his face, touching where she just was, and I wonder when the last time was a woman kissed him.

Mrs. Sherman comes clicking toward me on the sidewalk, and when she sees me she looks down. Like most people, she pretends I don't exist. She passes me, and I hear the drugstore bells on the door ring again and I feel the breeze of the door swinging shut. Across the street, I see Sissy Baxter pretending not to be watching as she waters the potted geraniums in front of The Flower Lady.

When I climb into the truck, Daddy is behind the wheel, pretending to read the newspaper.

"All set?" he asks, and when he looks at me I see the red stamp of lipstick on his cheek left by Mrs. Sherman, and the cab stinks of her perfume, but I say nothing.

Daddy turns the key, shifts into first, and pulls the truck onto the street. Shifting gears again, my father heads for home as if he's done no wrong.

Mama is watching me.

I feel her eyes follow me as I set her breakfast tray down on the little wooden table in front of her—and she continues to watch as I empty the ashtray and prepare to administer her morning medication. The wafers sit behind small plastic windows like an Advent calendar, and I have to use my fingernail to peel away the

—

foil backing, and this motion alone is enough to trigger picking.

Today is the last day of the final reintegration trial. Next time my mother comes home, she comes home for good.

Mama opens her mouth and sticks out her tongue, but her eyes still wander. They wander all over me. After the wafer dissolves, she takes a long drink of water. She hands the glass back to me, letting her fingers trail—they trail down my arm, reaching to touch my long crimson skirt.

Mama touches the skirt like she remembers, and she should; this skirt belongs to her, to my former mother, and when she searches my face her eyes fill with recognition. They fill with recognition the way I've seen them fill with tears, and I hold my breath and cross my fingers to keep her from wiping this away like she wipes away her tears every time she cries.

CHAPTER FIFTEEN
ARRANGEMENTS

commencement: n. 1. A beginning; a start 2. A graduation ceremony.

September 1, 1992

Everything is a test.

I am tested again and again, and yet I haven't picked or cut myself in forever. Billy's treatment plan is working, although he insists I'm the one doing all the work.

"Kiddo," he says, "you need to give yourself a lot more credit."

But how can I give myself credit when Daddy increasingly treats me like a little girl? The older I get, the more patronizing he becomes. I've been waiting and waiting for today to come, and now that it is finally here my father is refusing to let me come along. He wants to pick Mama up from the hospital by himself, even though he knows I thought we'd do this together as we should.

"Don't you have homework?" he asks when I protest. "Or the SAT to study for?" And then he leaves, all fast; he acts like I'm going to stop him or hijack the truck—like I'm going to do something crazy. So I call Billy to calm down.

"Fig," he says, "you've got to remember, Annie is his wife."

This is what he says because he has to. After all, Billy is my father's brother, and his younger one at that. But I know what Billy

—

really thinks; he doesn't always agree with Daddy, especially when it comes to me. Billy understands and appreciates the bond between Mama and me. He sees how I help her to remember who she is and all the good she has ever done. Billy tells me all the time how good I am with her, whereas Daddy never does. This is because my father secretly blames me for every single time my mother has come undone.

Daddy is a contradiction. He doesn't want me around Mama, yet he expects me to help out. For example, we spent the entire summer getting the house ready for Mama's final return. Gran called it "babyproofing," and everyone ignored her. Dr. Stein, my mother's psychiatrist, advised us to buy a large steel lockbox, and this is where the medication is now kept to prevent Mama from ever helping herself to it again.

While I was taking a walk with my uncle, Daddy programmed the four-digit code that opens the lock on the lockbox. And now he is the only one who can open Pandora's Box. "Just in case," he says, but he doesn't finish. "In case of what?" When I make it a point to ask him, he acts like there is no answer, and when I ask again he suddenly cannot hear me.

During the last reintegration trial, Daddy doled out enough pills every morning for me to administer to Mama throughout the day: breakfast, lunch, dinner, bedtime, and as needed. He is paranoid. He hides the daily dose in a new place every time. So every morning before he goes to work, he has to stop and show me where he hid the medication for that particular day. This ritual seems like overkill; aside from Mama's overdose over ten years ago, she hasn't exhibited any signs of being suicidal.

Mama still refuses to sleep upstairs, so we found her a recliner at the same garage sale where I bought a narrow pair of black leather Mary Janes, an Edwardian nightgown with a crocheted neckline, and a leopard-print pillbox hat that looks amazing with my new hair. Unlike the clothes, the recliner is hideous—something my former mother would have detested. But the recliner is more comfortable than the rocking chair that Daddy made for her once upon another time.

Outside, in the driveway, Daddy sprayed the recliner with fire-retardant. He soaked the ugly blue upholstery. "Just in case," he said, and I didn't need an explanation, yet this time he insisted on providing one. I kept telling him I understood, but he would not stop talking. If Mama fell asleep with a lit cigarette, she could die. This is what I tried to tell him, but he just looked at me grimly and said, "Fig, we could all die if that happened." Then he shook his head.

Once the upholstery was dry, we carried the chair into the day porch, and I covered it with a crocheted wool afghan I'd found in the attic. The outline is black, but each square contains a different-colored flower. I found it when I was going through my paternal great-grandmother's steamer trunk looking for more vintage clothes. The uglier something is, the harder I work to make it beautiful—the afghan will not only hide the terrible chair, it will create a barrier between the fire retardant and my mother's precious skin. And this is what I do for myself: I wear only beautiful clothing now, and each garment works to keep my fingernails away from my flesh.

Maybe because of Mama's parents, Daddy is prepared for fire. His precautions make me think about *Jane Eyre* and the madwoman in the attic who liked to play with matches. And I wonder if he's ever read the book. He screwed a smoke detector to the ceiling in the day porch and mounted a red fire extinguisher to the wall above the

—

washing machine. The extinguisher is the same stop-sign red as the blinking light on the detector. I inspected the devices while Daddy watched. And once again, he said, "Just in case."

He says "just in case" so much, he is beginning to sound like a paranoid schizophrenic. "Just in case," I said back, and I didn't say it nice. I sounded a lot like Mama when she has an episode.

Later when I tried to explain to Billy why Daddy and I are fighting all the time, he smiled a sad smile. "Fig," he said, "you do realize what you guys have in common?" And when I shrugged and looked out the window, he said, "You two worry more than anyone I have ever known."

The red light on the smoke detector winks at me from the ceiling and brings me back into the present moment. I clear my head. I'm working on a bouquet to welcome Mama home for good. Rather than worrying about the secret meanings of the flowers, I am trying to be like Tasha Tudor.

I do as she would do.

The boughs of Japanese maple I cut are waiting in a pail of water on the floor with the fern, chicory, marigolds, puncture vine, gray goldenrod, and Indian mustard, all of which I gathered this morning at dawn after a night of insomnia. I harvested the materials from the pasture south of the orchard, and from along the banks of the Silver River.

As I walked beside the river I saw the feral dog again. Walking along the other side, she didn't feel as feral as she did before, nor does she look as old. I watched her from the corner of my eye, and I watched her in the mirror that was made by the water running between us. She looks a lot like a blue heeler, the kind of dog the Fergesons use to herd their cows.

Every time I stopped, so did she.

I stopped to identify the wildflowers by flipping through my field guide and comparing the pictures against the reality. The dog traipsed through my peripheral vision, but when it was time to go home I looked for her and she was gone. Aside from the Japanese maple, the chicory, and the dark green fern, I only picked yellow flowers. I am not only bringing inside the gardens and the land she used to love, I am bringing her the light and warmth she must be missing. When Mama comes home today, she will find a benign sun waiting for her.

Money has been tight for everyone, and Billy finally took the job at Wallace Dairy they've been begging him to take for years. As their vet, he's at their beck and call. In return, he receives a solid salary plus room and board. When I called this morning, Billy told me he couldn't come.

"The cows have pinkeye," he explained. "They need to be treated with antibiotics, and then I have to figure out what to do about the flies." He sounded worried, but not about the animals; he was worried about me. That was when I realized I'd be okay. That I already was.

The wildflowers had filled, and would continue to fill, the void of waiting. They took the place of old habits; instead of tracking time by carving notches in my skin, I can arrange the plant material.

I found the floral frog when I was looking for the ashtray back in May. Gran swore to Christ there was an ashtray somewhere in the kitchen cabinets. "It's crystal," she insisted. "Your grandfather smoked cigars on occasion—besides, we used to entertain, and back then everyone smoked. It was considered fashionable, but I've always found the habit to be repulsive." Gran continues to be an expert at making remarks about my mother without doing so directly.

—

I used a step stool to search the high cabinets built along the ceiling in the kitchen, and just before I found the ashtray, I found the frog—only I didn't know what it was until Gran explained. "You put it at the bottom of a vase," she said, "And then you stick flowers into it." She was sitting at the kitchen table as she held the small bed of pins in her palm; it was the first time I'd ever seen her look nostalgic.

"Flower arranging was yet another skill I learned in charm school," she said, but when I asked why the metal object was called a frog, she didn't know. "Maybe because it's green?" she offered, and then I wondered why the Flower Lady didn't sell them in her store.

I cut the maple at an angle so the branches better stick into the frog just as Gran showed me to do, and then I trim the marigold and add the spicy-smelling flowers to the arrangement. I use the kitchen scissors for the flowers, but for the branches I'm using a pair of pruners I found in the potting shed by the orchard and the remains of Mama's flower beds.

It's as if the potting shed had disappeared for years and years and the structure had suddenly reappeared. I swear I hadn't seen it there until I needed something to cut the branches from the trees, and as I remembered the potting shed the stones materialized as did the actual structure. The window was curtained with cobwebs, and the terra-cotta pots were beginning to crumble. Mama's straw hat was still hanging on the back of the door, and on the worktable, I saw her gardening gloves, the leather fingers stiff and brittle after so many damp summers and frozen winters—after so many years of not being worn.

I've decided to turn this building into my sanctuary.

I want to grow flowers of my own. I can make arrangements, both fresh and dried. And I can press the flowers too, and even sell them. Last spring, I began cutting branches of apple blossom from our orchard and gathering moss to sell to the Flower Lady. I can learn to make sachets and potpourri, and maybe even extract the essential oils of rose and lavender.

I'd like to live a life surrounded by flowers, but I could never work in a flower shop or deal with people all the time like Sissy does. I'd like to live in a home full of flowers, and I think Mama will like this too. It will be good for the both of us.

As I imagine my own gardens and how they will wander away from the immediate yard to blend into the wild beyond as do the gardens of Tasha Tudor, I add more flowers to the bouquet for Mama, and I'm just finishing the arrangement when Daddy's Dodge comes rattling down the driveway, followed by a long trail of brown dust.

There's been a terrible drought this summer, and when I went to church with Gran last Sunday, everyone prayed for rain. I held my breath and crossed my fingers instead, and Gran didn't scold me when she saw. She just pursed her lips, nodded as if to approve, and went back to praying.

I watch the truck approach and the dust storm chasing after and my heart begins to race. It beats so hard, I can feel it in my throat. I begin to choke. I slip the rosary off my neck and use the pearls to breathe again, and then I return my focus to the flowers. I step back to examine what I have created, and the deep pulse in my neck begins to slow. I sit where Mama sits to see what she will see, and I find I built a fire and not a sun and I wonder if my father will try to extinguish it.

The maple leaves burn like red-hot stars and the yellow flowers blaze up from below. The feathery tips of the goldenrod resemble candle flames, while the delicate puncture vine and sprinkled mustard

—

seem to spark and scatter, further spreading fire. Cut the shortest, the sprigs of chicory work to ignite the yellow, orange, and red; they rise from the water to act as the true-blue heart of this accidental inferno.

I hear the sound of the truck doors slamming, and I rush out to the porch to greet Mama. I find her standing in the driveway lighting a long white Salem. The dust has not yet settled. Mama looks at the house like she's never seen it before, while Daddy struggles to pull her suitcase from the truck bed. Mama holds another bag of reservation cigarettes, and as she smokes I remember something she once said to me about chicory when I was four or five years old.

We were walking through the meadow by the train tracks when she picked the wildflower and handed it to me. From a single stem, the chicory forked into other stems and formed a natural bouquet of eight blossoms total. I remember because I'd just learned how to count, so I went about counting everything I could find to count.

After I counted the last flower, she said, "Now look up," and I did. I looked up, and then she told me to look back at the chicory, and when I did she said, "Do you see how the petals look like broken shards of summer sky?"

She was right. The blue was the same, and the petals resembled glass fragments from something shattered. With my face tilted up to heaven, I stood there forever and studied the sun-saturated blue dome of July. I wondered if the sky could break, and I'd wonder this again years later when my mother read *The Snow Queen* out loud to me, during the scene when the little boy looks up and his eye is penetrated by a shard of ice. This icy dagger, which worked to distort the way he saw the world, also turned him cold and hard from the inside out.

—

But that day, I was thinking about Chicken Little. He was running around inside my brain, screaming "The sky is falling! The sky is falling!"

I sit with Mama after dinner in the day porch even though Daddy doesn't want me around the secondhand smoke. Mama sits in her recliner, smoking, and the silver smoke twists around the flowers and contributes to the overall effect of fire. Just before her eyes glaze over and Mama falls into another tranquilized trance, she smiles at me and she says, "The flowers are gorgeous, Fig."

After school and on the weekends, I resurrect my mother.

The wildflowers help bring her into the moment—into the season—but she also needs my help remembering who she really is.

I make the alterations when Daddy is not inside the house. I make the rearranging look like Mama's doing, not mine. I bring apple crates in from the barn and line them up along the walls. I'm careful to put them under the windows, where the sun can't damage the books, and then I line the crates with texts written by all my mother's favorite authors: Sylvia Plath, Virginia Woolf, Angela Carter, Tanith Lee, Walt Whitman; I align their spines to create a library of memories—a collective body of books.

I take both dictionaries and flip through all the pages to show her all the words she has ever looked up and checked.

"Is there a word you'd like to look up today?" I ask, and she looks at me forever before she answers. "Not right now," she says, and she is whispering the way she does when she doesn't want the other voices in her head to hear. And this is a good sign. I can tell she is thinking hard. She is searching for herself in the inner chambers of her mind where she's been hiding from her disease.

Daddy makes me put *Christina's World* back above the fireplace, which works to divide the living room area from the dining room, so I special order a calendar of Andrew Wyeth's work from the bookstore in Lawrence, and when it arrives Mama helps me tear out all the paintings. I run a length of twine like I'm about to hang a curtain over the middle wall of windows—the ones across from Mama's recliner—and I clothespin the portraits and strange landscapes to the line, where they flutter like prayer flags, and when the sun rises behind them they are luminescent like stained glass.

To keep Mama company while I'm away, I give her back the button-eyed teddy bear. When I can't be there, he sits in the wicker love seat to her left and recounts how once he was put together.

Annie, he says. *Do you remember? Do you remember how your mother cut the pattern and stitched my stitching and stuffed my stuffing?* And she does remember. Mama nods her head, and then she says, "I do." Next to the flowers I pick and arrange for her, I keep the picture of her parents. I imagine her tracing the figure of her mother with her finger, and then her father, and again she remembers—"I do," she says. "I really, really do."

The last object I transplant is the mirror.

I wait until a Sunday when Billy is here to help Daddy deworm all the sheep, and while Mama is showering I take the mirror and carry it down the stairs and position it dead center on the apple crate in front of Mama's throne. Then I sit where she sits and I practice being her. Holding a pencil like a cigarette, I smoke. I exhale a cloud of blue-gray, and when it clears the oval mirror offers itself to me— to be scried, and as I look I imagine Mama looking too.

I see her there: my face in her face and her face in mine.

We float in this pool of reflective glass; we drift across the mirror sky, and on either side the two brass birds remain ready to fly away. As I look, I fill the frame with memories. I project them from my heart into the glass, and later they will play back to her—again and again, and I know she will remember. She will re-become.

The seniors are herded into different classrooms depending on our last names, and we are supervised by strangers from the school district. I'm directed into a classroom with the J–O students, and I sit where I am told to sit. I sit next to Tanya Jenkins, and when she sees me she pinches her big nose and makes a face like I smell bad, but I don't. I smell good.

I smell like jasmine now. I buy it from the health food store in Lawrence where my father sometimes shops. Unlike the synthetic perfume sold in drugstores, this is an essential oil made from the actual flower, and scent is just another way to transform ugly into beautiful. Fragrance and vintage clothes are nothing more than masks, but like bandages, they are something worn for protection.

I sit at a desk with a pile of freshly sharpened number two pencils, scratch paper, and what is now the second booklet for the practice SAT testing. Everything is like it was yesterday, only we're in a different classroom. The same woman from the school district supervises us, and once again we will sit here and darken the multiple-choice circles on the sheets of paper before us. The woman drinks coffee from a homemade mug, and she reminds me of Alicia Bernstein. The mug is white with red lettering and it reads BEST MOM IN THE WORLD!

This woman keeps time—she tells us when to begin and when to end.

———

I finish early again, and again she eyes me suspiciously. But I don't care. I'm only practicing for the real test. I practice connecting all the dots. I connect them into lines to draw pictures to illustrate the stories in my head instead of answering the questions I'm being asked. Sometimes I just fill the circles in accordance with the phases of the moon—they cycle across the page, waxing and waning, and sometimes I just fill the entire page with graphite until I can see myself in the shiny gray; the reflection is dull and double exposed by the blackness of my shadow looking over my shoulder to see what I am doing.

The prayers from the Sacred Heart of Mary are finally answered. Rain falls on Douglas County like it is spring instead of fall, but this rain is cold and will only serve to deliver yet another winter and I am dreading the absence of the wildflowers on the farm.

At night, the waxing moon rises and the Silver River swells and the dry earth can't absorb the rainfall, and our cellar floods. I pull the doors open to look. The benches are buried by water, and I see dead leaves floating on the surface with one of Mama's pill bottles. She must have left it here the last time there was a tornado or a warning—that is, the last time she was here for one.

The white childproof lid remains screwed on, and despite the water damage a tiny island of the label still remains. I can clearly read my mother's name: ANNIE JOHNSON. She is there, typed across the wrinkled paper still clinging to the orange-brown plastic.

Wearing his waders, Uncle Billy climbs down into the cellar like it's not even flooded. He reaches down to clear muck from the drain, and then he climbs back up and squats down beside me. Together we watch the dirty water whirlpool away. The water swirls and pulls the pill bottle under where it disappears, until the cellar has completely emptied.

Mama's psychiatrist recommends having a family night once a week. The adults decide on Sunday. Family night is nothing more than dinner, only Gran of course still calls it supper like it's the olden days and not 1992.

Family night is the only time Mama actually comes and sits at the table for a meal. She pretends to eat, and sometimes she even talks. Dr. Stein is pleased with her progress, but when he says as much Daddy looks at him like the psychiatrist is the crazy one.

Daddy doesn't seem to notice Mama's increasing moments of clarity—moments I choose to savor rather than ignore. I even keep a log. I record the date and time and the nature of the event: what she said, or didn't say, if she smiled or frowned, and how long it lasted. In the two weeks since Mama was officially deinstitutionalized, she has exhibited clarity twenty-three times. For statistics I keep a chart, and from the graph I discover a trend: Mama is most clear when she and I are alone. We are most often alone after dinner, in the hours before I go to bed.

Billy helps me make the macaroni and cheese, and when I serve the meal Gran doesn't make a fuss about the meal being vegetarian. She and Daddy have a more important issue to address. "Fig," Daddy says, "the adviser from Carter High called today." He doesn't look at me, because I am looking at him. I am staring at him in the way I know will make him uncomfortable.

"She wanted to talk about the results of your practice SATs," he says, passing the casserole to Gran. Taking the hot dish, my grandmother says, "The results were not what we expected."

—

I hold my breath and cross my fingers as they go back and forth—a relay team; Daddy and his mother pound into me while everyone else remains silent. Mama watches her food while Billy eats. He never participates in the lectures. "I try to remain neutral," I once heard him tell my father—Daddy was complaining that he needed backup, and Billy said, "Toby, I'm her uncle. I'm not her parent." And while I didn't understand, I know my father did by the way he said, "Okay."

Later, of course, Billy will take me aside to check in with me. This is what he always does. As my uncle. He will sit with me as I count pearls and breathe. And he will show me different mudras and teach me how to breathe in through one nostril and out the other. When I am calm again I will show him all the flowers I've recently discovered on the property. Like Mama and the dictionary, I check off the botanicals listed in my guidebook—I check off the ones I now know. I show him the pictures of what I've identified, and what I've cut and brought home: Jerusalem artichoke, blazing star or gay feather, kiss-me-quick, switchgrass, azure aster, false dragon-head, Western ironweed, and my new favorite—self-heal.

When I despair that winter is coming, he will remind me how the autumn palette of yellow, gold, and purple is blooming now to sow its seeds to be reborn in the spring. "Everything happens for a reason," Billy will say, and then he will sit with me until I fall asleep, and in the morning I'll be cross-examined by my father. "What do you two talk about?" he will ask, and then he will want to know, "What exactly do you guys do up there?"

"The school is quite concerned," Daddy says. Now that I am looking away, my father watches me. I'm looking out the window and thinking about how much I miss eating in the kitchen, where it feels warm and comfortable. Upon my grandmother's request, family night must be proper; we are to always dine in the dining room with real silver and a tablecloth, and whatever bouquet I choose to arrange.

"After all," Gran said, "Fiona needs to practice everything she learned in charm school or else she will surely lose it for good."

I can feel Mother Mary on my skin, hanging between my small breasts. Whenever I notice her there, she is always cold. I'm having trouble staying present, but I know better than to take the rosary off and work on my breathing in front of Gran, especially with her gift to me. So I uncross my fingers and I run a string of phantom pearls between my fingers. *One, two, three, breathe.* This is not the first heated conversation about my future. They seem to happen all the time now. Sometimes, Billy will try to change the subject—but not tonight. Tonight he works on eating.

"What happened?" Daddy asks, and now he wants to know about my college applications. "Have you been working on them at all?" he asks, and keeps asking even after Gran has given up.

My grandmother doesn't eat; she drinks instead. She is working on her second tall gin and tonic. Her rings clank against the crystal. Every now and then she leans forward and fusses with the center-piece I made of Lady's thumb and Queen Anne's lace.

Daddy tries a new angle.

"Fig," he says, "we only want you to succeed," and I can tell he wants someone to chime in; he needs support. He says this, and then he pauses. He wants the silence to be interrupted. He needs Gran or Billy to agree—a ringing chorus to echo him and to say, *Fig, we only want you to be happy.* But instead the silence burns, it is a static— absolutely overwhelming—and just when I think it will swallow all of us someone speaks.

"Your father's right," she says. "He really is."

And when I look at her, I see *my* mother. She is sitting next to me, and I have no idea what happened to the fat chain-smoking schizophrenic who was just there seconds ago. Mama's hair is clean and shiny under the light, spiraled into a bun and held in place by a pair of ivory chopsticks. She smiles at me, and her smile is a gentle smile—a mother smile. Her lips no longer chapped but soft for kissing. "Fig," she says, "we only want what is best for you."

I am worried that I am hallucinating. Is this the onset of my schizophrenia? Seventeen instead of nineteen? Or perhaps I've been the crazy one all this time? The room is spinning, and everyone seems to be holding their breath—that is, everyone except for Mama.

The precision of her words cuts into me, and my eyes answer by filling up with tears, and the tears warp my vision—they further distort the delusion. I blink and the salt water falls, but it doesn't matter; the image of my mother is already wavering. Everyone is staring at her and I'm not the only one who is crying. I see Daddy, and Mama sees it too. I see her see it, and I watch her pupils dilate; they expand into two black pools for drowning, and now she is wringing her hands again, and I sit there watching as her fingers twist themselves into a nest of hissing serpents.

Daddy and I get into another fight while Gran and Uncle Billy sit in the living room and Mama sleeps in the day porch. Daddy claims Mama fell asleep after dinner with a lit cigarette in her hand. "I can prove it to you," he says. "Fig, her finger *is* burnt. Why can't you see how bad she is?"

He doesn't believe what happened at the table was a moment of clarity.

"You need to realize that your mother is never going to get better," he says. "Never, Fig. Not ever."

According to the pocket dictionary, the second definition for the word "never" is "not at all; in no way," followed by the word "nevermore," which means "never again." The word "never" kisses the word "neurosis," and "neurosis" is on the same page as "nettle" and "neuter." Stinging nettles grow along the farmer's ditch as if to guard the water, and my father fixed himself when I was six years old.

He didn't want another me.

I blame my father for everything. I finally say it out loud. And this alone makes it seem truer than it ever seemed before. My father turns away, and I know he is crying because I see the way his shoulders shake. This is when Uncle Billy clears his throat. I had no idea he was even there. I can feel him behind me, standing in the doorway.

"Fig," he says, "that's enough. It is time for you to go to bed."

But I don't. I don't go to bed. I deliberately disobey everyone.

I sit in the day porch instead. I sit in the wicker love seat and I don't look out the windows. I look only at my mother, who is asleep.

I can hear the hushed whispers of Daddy, Gran, and Billy holding conference in the kitchen. I was wrong. Billy will not be coming upstairs to check in with me—not tonight, and quite possibly never again. Not ever. In fact, he might never ask about the latest flowers or wild grasses I've discovered on the farm or along the highway. He might not even care if I was to hurt myself again.

I press my fingernails into the pads of my thumbs to remember what it was like to pick. I do this to quiet the other pain I feel, because I hurt everywhere. But there is no need to deliberately harm myself any more than I already have by hurting everyone else around me.

—

I listen to the sound of Billy and Gran saying good-bye to my father—the front door opening and closing, and then the sound of Billy's truck driving away. The headlights flash through the room, bouncing off all the glass the way light travels through a prism trying to escape, and then the truck is gone and there is only the dim light from the bulb above the barn door that is yards away.

Daddy goes to bed. I watch the ribbon of light under his door go black, and I am left alone in the dark with my mother. The light from the barn turns the latest bouquet I've made of bluestem, switchgrass, and azure aster into a silhouette of itself. And like all silhouettes, this black shape can shift. From atop the makeshift shelf, it shape-shifts into a head of hair—like a wig on a mannequin, and I remember the cemetery of heads buried in the backyard. I realize my father doesn't know about this strange graveyard, even though it was planted on his property by his wife.

"Fig?" Mama says, and her voice is groggy from sleep and medication. She is asking if it is me sitting across from her in the dark. I lean forward. I lean into the light from the barn, and I reach out to take her hands.

"I don't want you to throw your life away," she says, and her voice is clear again. "You have given me the greatest possible happiness," my mother says, "And because you have, I need you to be happy. You need to live your life and you need to forgive your father. You both have been so incredibly good. So patient. You have been in every way all that anyone could ever be."

Now she is sitting beside me. But this time, I am not hallucinating. She is not a memory, even though I feel as if I've heard her words before; when she speaks, it feels like something remembered, and yet this has never happened.

Mama is no longer the specter of her former self like the person I saw earlier at the table. Her body barely fits into the seat beside me, and I can smell her breath and her skin—cigarette smoke and body odor—she needs to bathe and to brush her teeth, and yet her voice is so very clear, as are her eyes, which are looking right into me.

My real mother uses the body of this other mother to talk to me like a ghost employs a medium. As she speaks to me she continues to hold my hands. I study this place where our bodies join—this bridge to cross the vast between, and I realize we have always been connected. And this connection cannot be broken. Despite the dim light, I can see the burn on her finger from the cigarette. The raw wound weeps, and this fluid is called ichor.

Ichor is the watery discharge from an ulcer, but it is also the ethereal fluid that flows through the veins of a god instead of blood.

There is a fable both Mama and Daddy used to tell me when I was younger. About a scorpion and a frog. The scorpion wants to cross the river, but he can't swim, so he asks the frog if he can catch a ride across. The frog is insulted. "Do you think I'm stupid?" he asks. "You'll surely sting me."

"Do you think *I'm* stupid?" the scorpion replies. "If I sting you, I'll never get across—either you wouldn't take me or we'd both drown."

And so the frog eventually agrees to take the scorpion to the other side, but this is the point where Mama and Daddy always tell the story differently.

In Daddy's version, the frog swims all the way across the river with the scorpion on his back. As soon as they reach the other side the scorpion stings the frog, and the frog dies.

—

In Mama's version, the scorpion stings the frog while he's still swimming—somewhere in the middle of the wide river, and the two creatures die by drowning. In both versions, the dying frog asks, "Why?" to which the scorpion always replies, "I can't help myself. It's my nature."

The flowers should last longer than they do. The day porch is much colder than the main part of the house, and it should work as the refrigerated room in The Flower Lady does, and yet the flowers seem to wilt within mere hours. Maybe there is too much light? Maybe the flowers die because of Mama's space heater? Maybe they choke to death on her endless cigarette smoke?

Or maybe the flowers die inside because they are only meant to be wild.

Come spring, I will plant my own garden beds of flowers— daisies, peonies, sunflowers, tulips, passionflower, and lots and lots of roses. I want roses everywhere, and I want more moonflowers than the ones we have already. I want to plant gardens that open and glow in the night as well as during the day. For now, I'm using my window seat to grow Christmas cactus, rose geranium, night-blooming cereus, mother of thousands, jade, and wandering Jew, but none of these plants will flower for quite some time. When I'm ready, I will give Sissy Baxter bluebell to express my gratitude. I will give her chrysanthemum to let her know she's been a wonderful friend even if it's just a secret.

Mama asks for Daddy a lot these days. He sits with her, and I'm not invited. I'm not allowed. She wants to talk to him alone. She cries and he holds her. I see them when I happen to walk by—both inside the house and outside. I see them through the French doors or through the windows from the yard as I scour the earth for the last of the autumn dandelions. I pick the dandelions that have gone to seed, to blow on them: I make wish after wish as I watch the starlike seeds scatter. I make the same wish every single time, and this wish is the wish I have always wished.

My one and only.

Through the heating vents, I hear my father call my mother Annie.

"Annie," he says, "I swear to you—everything is going to be okay."

He makes this promise a lot these days, and the more he says it, the more he sounds like he believes in it. I don't try to convince him about Mama anymore; I see him beginning to see, and I even overhear him talking to Billy one afternoon when they don't know I'm there.

"Maybe Annie just needed to come home," he says, "Maybe coming home really is all she ever needed?"

Later, when I come to replace more dead flowers with ones I've recently gathered, Mama watches me. "I got that dress in Ithaca," she says. "I bought it at a yard sale for ten cents." The dress is a pink housedress from the 1950s; it has white scalloped trim and a built-in apron with deep pockets. I insert Devil's claw into a spray of false mint and Spanish needles, and when I step back to show her, Mama says, "That sure is pretty, Fig. I think you've found your calling."

She doesn't seem to notice or mind how quick the wildflowers keep dying. Instead, she wants me to make a promise. "Don't ever stop doing this," she says, and she sweeps her hand across the air, gesturing to all the flowers in this room, in the house, and growing wild upon the farm. She is also indicating all the flowers I will

—

someday grow, and the flowers I've hung to dry—the ones I get to keep forevermore. And because I love to see her smile, I do. I promise her. "I cross my heart and hope to die and stick a needle in my eye," I say, but this upsets her, and she makes me start over.

"All I want is your word," she says, and in the end my word is all it takes to make her smile. Mama smiles at me, and then it begins to rain again.

I sit in the wicker love seat with the teddy bear. Mama watches the rain run down the window glass and whispers a line from a nursery rhyme: "It's raining, it's pouring. The old man is snoring." She smiles at me and doesn't finish; instead, she leans back, kicks up the foot rest, and falls asleep.

Lulled by the rain, I, too, drift away. Curled into the fetal ball of the unborn, I sleep most of the afternoon and wake later to the mighty crash of thunder. As the lightning streaks the violet sky I pull myself together to go clean the kitchen and cook dinner, but even these banal chores feel unearthly, like a dream.

I go fetch Daddy from the barn, and hanging from the rafters three dead pigs sway from the motion of me pushing the big door open. Upside down, their feet are bound, sharp hooves pointing toward heaven. Skinned and gutted, their meat is the same pink-white as my skin, and I'm confused. We sold our pigs years ago. Have I gone back in time?

But then Daddy looks at me, and he says, "I got them in a real good trade."

"I might be gone all night," Daddy says when I come into the kitchen to get a glass of water to take to bed. "Did you give your mother a flashlight?" he asks, and I nod.

She was asleep, so I left it on in case she wakes up and can't figure out why the lights won't work. This is what my father said to do; he swore the batteries would last all night. The storm knocked the power out and Daddy and I are each holding emergency candles. The yellow light exaggerates the dark circles beneath his eyes, and he looks even more tired than he usually does.

I hate him for never having more energy. It makes me feel like I don't do enough.

"Here," he says, and he's whispering even though Mama's been asleep in the other room for hours now. And he slides the silverware drawer open to show me where he's stashed Mama's medicine this time—"Just in case," he says, and his whisper is like a hush. The pills and wafers are hiding beneath the butter knives in the narrow slot beside the forks.

Stepping into his insulated coveralls, my father grabs the thermos he just filled with hot coffee made cowboy style on the gas range. "The phone lines are still working," he says, "so if you need me, you can call." Then he opens the door, and before he walks into the night he turns to look at me. "If I can't get that generator to run," he says, "I'll likely be gone till daybreak helping Old Man Fergie hand milk all those cows."

October 3, 1992
The relentless rain drowns out my dreams and will not let me sleep. It beats against the roof and trickles down the window glass like tears on a human face. All I hear is rain: *rain, rain, rain.*

It drowns out every other sound.

It's after midnight when I give up trying to fall asleep; I feel as if I might never sleep again. Not ever. When I go downstairs to make a cup of tea, I find the front door blown open by the wind. Flung outward, it reminds me of a wing, slightly fluttering but never shutting.

The electricity is still out, and the light from my candle leaps around, unreliable; I can only see my immediate surroundings. The rest of the world falls away, swallowed by the darkness and silenced by the sound of rain. Rainwater pools on the hardwood just inside the door where a welcome mat should be and reflects the candlelight in my hands. The orange light leaps across the glassy surface, repeating and dancing there. Fire on water: It is a mirage.

I stand barefoot in the open door, looking out at the night. Somewhere on the other side of the slanting black rain is the moon, and I know it's full, even though I can't see it. The space beside Mama's old Volvo where Daddy parks his truck is empty, which means he's still helping Old Man Fergeson. I close the door, and the motion blows my candle out and everything darkens.

The darkness sharpens the beam of flashlight still shining in the day porch where I left it for my mother. The squares of window pane in the French doors dissect and fragment the light; these frames throw the artificial light around like a Cubist painting. I walk toward the broken light, remembering my way around the furniture, and through the living room. I open the doors and step into the day porch, where the rain is loud against all the glass.

The flashlight has fallen over and no longer points at the ceiling like a makeshift lamp. Instead, the light pierces the window, turning the glass into a mirror and magnifying the light. I don't need Mama's lighter to relight my candle, because I can see in here without it.

Stretched along the arm of the recliner, Marmalade is sleeping; old and arthritic, the cat doesn't stir. The rest of the chair is empty. Mama is not here.

———

I look through the darkness of the living room to where I remember the front door to be. And I remember standing there. How I looked at the night before I closed the door on the storm. I even locked the door against the wind so it might not blow open anymore, but I should know better by now: Nothing on this farm ever opens on its own, especially when Mama is here.

Before I go to grab my coat and boots, I look to the flashlight again; this time, I follow the beam as it tunnels through the cold glass to penetrate the black orchard like a searchlight searching.

The lightning cracks the sky like an egg; the white veins of electricity reach across the black expanse, and in these short flashes of brilliant light I think I see my mother up ahead and running. She is running through the pasture, toward the orchard. I call out to her, but the thunder follows and I can't even hear myself, and the night goes back to black and I can't see again, so I run.

I run until the next bolt of lightning illuminates the farm, turning my mother into a silhouette running through the rows of silhouetted apple trees. I watch her disappear into the woods along the ditch, and I keep running.

Crossing the ditch, I slip and fall into the water. I grab the bridge just in time. Fed by weeks' worth of rain, the water is deep, cold, and fast. I can feel the pull, and I almost let go, but then I remember Mama. I cling to the board instead, and use it to pull myself to the other side. Grabbing tree roots and rocks, I scramble onto the bank, where I lie in the mud, trying to catch my breath. The lightning stops and in the absence of the thunder I hear the call of the rushing river. And then I hear whimpering.

I sit up, looking around and trying to place the sound. The

darkness seeps into my eyes, and just when I think I've gone blind my eyes adjust and I can see the wild dog. First, I see her yellow eyes, but when she whimpers again the sound helps me to distinguish her outline from the surrounding shadows, which tingle against my eyes like static, only black. The dog keeps whimpering, and when she turns to look toward the river her eyes disappear. I retie my boot-laces and pull myself up. I straighten my wool overcoat, which is soaked and even heavier than it was before.

I follow the dog into the shadows and through the thick bramble and tangled branches. In the dark, it's hard to see and the foliage reaches out for me; it snags the long skirt of my nightgown, and the thorns scratch my face and draw blood. The dog runs ahead, only to stop—looking back as if to confirm I'm coming. And when I step forward, she proceeds again, and I hope I'm headed in the right direction. The rain has stopped and once I'm out of the woods, the sky opens again and I see the first signs of the moon above; the blue light edges the black clouds, which are thinning as they begin to disperse. The dog runs ahead, stopping to check on me as she did before.

I follow her toward the Silver River, but the tall prairie grass is slick, and I need to be more careful; I've already wasted so much time by rushing. I head for the property line dividing our farm from the McAlisters, and as I do a song my mother used to sing begins to loop inside my head.

"Take me down in the river to pray."

By the time I make it to the river's edge, the dog has disappeared. I find Mama's worn-out tennis shoes on the shore by the top of the waterfall. Side by side, they are an inch apart and pointed toward the water.

—

The scuffed toes point forward to give way to the five footprints set deep into the mud. And in each impression, I see the shape of my mother's long naked toes: right, left, right, left, right into the cattails.

Right into the river.

As the storm rolls away the clouds drift apart. Sifting into long, thin wisps, the opal moon emerges and her light turns the river into a river of mercury as it hurries toward the falls. On the other side, the McAlisters have piled sandbags along the bank, where they stand like castle walls fortified against the wrath of the raging river. But despite the swell of rain, our side of the river flows as it always has— from the short falls, the water follows the channel of stone walls to collect in the shallow pool circling out from around the weeping willow, its surface as calm as a mirror.

The scene below is like a scene from a Japanese woodblock: The still and silver water works to contrast the inky black tree, but as I look I begin to see something unfamiliar—something that complicates the design. Through the sweep of willow, I see my mother lying in the water.

I want to run, but I can't. The steep path requires patience, and I have to sidestep the small slick stones embedded into the hill. And even though I take my time, I slip twice before I reach the shore below. When I brace my last fall, I scrape my wrist on a rock and the blood blooms red. I suck it clean and pull myself back up and walk toward the tree. I part the curtain of willow and step inside its shelter, where I am now close enough to touch her.

Mama's face is the one smooth stone along the wall of rock, and her pale hair spreads across the water like a halo, the blond streaked black with blood. I see bits and pieces of my nightgown reflected in the water, tangled amid the rotting hyacinth and floating around her body like white flowers. My mother stares upward, through a veil of river, and her head appears to be on backward. Where her chest should be I see instead the shape of her shoulder blades.

I want to pull her out, but I can't—the river, the falls, and the rocks have broken her, and I can't bear to break her even more.

But I must touch her face. This is not a painting or a story. This is Mama. I once lived inside her body. And this is her face before she was born.

I step into the water and kneel beside her; first, I touch her cheeks, then her lips. I can't stand to see her eyes open, her pupils fixed and dilated, but when I try to close them they just reopen. She is looking ahead. She is still looking at a place I can't see, only this time I know her eyes are fixed on a place where she will be happy. I am shaking. Her skin is colder than the water, and I know I must get dry again, and warm, and soon. It's almost like she is the one who is telling me this.

On the horizon, I see the violet line of morning, but before I can go and get my father, I must first build a dome around my mother as she used to build for me. I build it from memory. I build the dome to keep away the monsters. I build the dome so I will never forget, not ever. I build a dome around my mother to protect the world she sought—a place like heaven.

The willow branches already form a wall to protect my mother, but there are gaps in the places where there are no boughs. Like a conductor conducting an orchestra, I use my hands like wands. I stand at the edge of the pool, inside the shelter of the tree, spinning air into patches. I stitch the negative space to the water and the willow. I tuck the invisible edges under rocks, and I make the dome from love, and love is hard and so is the dome; nothing will get through in the time it takes to find my father.

When I am done, the sun has risen and the horizon is on fire and I feel warmer, although I'm trembling and my hands are now the same blue-white as my mother's skin. I stand inside the willow and I do the weeping. My tears are hot and the salt water turns the morning light into a constellation of rainbow stars refracted by the see-through surface of the dome. Just like the domes she used to build for me, this one will keep her safe until my father comes to carry her home.

Only he will know the ways to lift a broken body without further breaking it, and this he will need to do alone.

And it is time for me to go. I step out of the willow to find I'm not alone. In the morning light, her eyes are no longer yellow; one is periwinkle, and the other full of clouds. Sitting by the steps at the bottom of the hill, my feral friend appears to be waiting. When I approach, she does not shy away, nor does she leap ahead to run and stop and look back, or to run away and disappear again. This time, she follows me. She follows me up the hill, and she stays close while we venture through the woods and over the water. She walks inside my shadow and never strays.

She follows me through the paddock and the maze of apple trees, and all the way into the house, and just like that, she is tame.

October 7, 1992
Sissy Baxter sends a bouquet of twenty-four dark crimson roses and a generous gift certificate to The Flower Lady. This time Sissy does not leave it to me to decipher her message; this time she uses words and she signs her name.

I chose the color of the rose to symbolize your mourning, Sissy wrote.

—

And the number twenty-four is to let you know that you are in my thoughts every hour of the day. According to the postscript, the gift certificate is from the Flower Lady herself.

Mama is cremated and given back to us in a small white gift bag, like she's a present we just bought. Daddy writes the mortician a check, leaning over so I can't see the cost. He continues to treat me like I'm a little girl.

Inside the white gift bag, the ashes are inside a plastic bag, which is inside a black box with a white label on the top where the weight of my mother's remains is recorded next to her name. Daddy sees this equation and begins to cry, which I haven't seen him do since Mama's accident.

"That's what she weighed at birth," he says, and then he explains how I, too, weighed this amount—nine pounds and three ounces— and I remember my mother telling me, "There is no such thing as an accident." The mortician said my mother must have had strong bones for this to be the weight of her remains.

As we drive home snowflakes flutter from the gray October sky, but they are few and far between, and the first real snow won't come until after I've turned seventeen; like grief, the winter to come will be cold and all encompassing.

April 3, 1993
We wait for spring to bury Mama's ashes, and I wonder what it was like for my mother when she had nothing left of her parents to memorialize. I wonder if she chose cremation to be closer to them in death. When we bury her cremains, we don't invite Gran or Uncle Billy; it is enough for them to come to my graduation next month, it is enough for me to graduate at all.

—

The Flower Lady has expanded, and attached to the back of the shop is a small nursery; the Flower Lady has merged with Baxter Lumber. Daddy takes me there, and I use the gift certificate to buy the rosebush I want to plant over Mama. The eglantine rose, also known as sweetbriar, blooms pink; each flower has five heart-shaped petals, and in the center burns a yellow stamen heart. According to the language of flowers, this flowers means a wound to heal.

I am still healing, and it hasn't always been easy to leave my skin alone. Especially right after I lost Mama forever and I was all scratched up from the thorns and bramble—nature's fingernails—and I proved that I'm not perfect. I perpetuated all these marks on my arms and on my face; I slipped into a relapse of self-harm, and Billy had to tell Daddy, and Daddy had to send me to a therapist, and just as my rosary and flowers help, so does hypnosis. Like schizophrenia, there is no definitive cure; like a garden, I will have to tend to this habit, forever weeding out the urges.

Around the sweetbriar I planted Little Red Riding Hood tulips to represent my undying love, and forget-me-nots and rosemary for remembrance, and last of all a carpet of snowdrops to give me hope. The location of this grave and garden was chosen long ago by my mother, even though she intended it for something else. Daddy redigs the hole as I clear away the debris and plant the other flowers. Where once I tried to burn the smallest nesting doll, we scatter what remains of my mother. The ash and bone turn the black soil white, and then we cover Mama.

We tuck her in.

When I do show Gran, I can feel her looking at the statue of the Mother Mary, and I wonder if it's blasphemous the way she's been left to the elements. Her long white skirts continue to turn into soil and she is sinking farther into the garden, to someday be entirely swallowed by the dirt.

Gran crosses herself, and then she reaches for my hand like this is something she has always done, like we are always intimate. Her rings press into my fingers: The sharp diamond is for engagement, while the soft gold is for marriage—solid, but also malleable.

Green tendrils of new life shoot off the rosebush like strange stars. This comes from pruning. Come fall, I will cut the branches back. It will feel unnatural to interfere with nature, but after another winter I will see what comes from cutting. This wound will heal; it will become a bouquet of pink hearts amid the yellow stars inside the blue aura of forget-me-nots.

CHAPTER SIXTEEN

ALCHEMY

hereafter: adv. 1. *After this; from here or now on*
2. *In a future time or state.*

hereafter: n. 1. *The afterlife.*

April 10, 1993

Daddy needs my help with the lambing. Uncle Billy is available only on call. He's still working for the Wallaces, but now he's saving money to go to Idaho and Montana to fight forest fires.

I stand around holding a light so my father can see. He pulls the babies out of the ewes, and they are long and skinny like wet greyhounds. The lambs are all legs. There is no meat or wool.

My other job is to keep the stables clean. Blue sticks close. This is what I've come to call her, my new dog; according to Uncle Billy, I was right—she is a blue heeler. It is her nature to be good with animals, and through the lambing we've grown even closer. She sleeps on the rug beside my bed, and sometimes she curls up beside me, her body next to mine. Blue is indeed my healer.

Betty is the last pregnant ewe to go. She is the youngest, and she's never lambed before. We know she's ready. Her belly dropped yesterday, and through the static of the baby monitor Daddy woke to the sound of her bleating growing lower. Betty has been restless for hours now, pawing at the ground, trying to dig herself a nest, but as soon as she lies down she gets back up and starts the process all over again.

We talk even less than we did before Mama died. He doesn't ask about my future anymore, or my plans. Asking me to help with the lambing is the most he's talked to me in months, and I know he must be desperate to do so. When he took me to the different nurseries, he didn't talk, and he didn't say anything when we buried Mama's ashes. It's like he lost his voice.

The days are getting warmer, but the nights are still cold. The snowdrops are blooming for the first time, and the three white petals droop from each flower like lambs' ears. With midnight behind us, today is Easter and later we are going to my grandmother's house so everyone else can eat ham.

Daddy works on Betty for an hour, but her lamb won't come. Daddy has me call Uncle Billy from the telephone in the barn. Billy doesn't have a phone, and I know my father hates to call there, especially late at night, because it means waking up the Wallaces.

I repeat everything Daddy tells me to say.

I ask Mrs. Wallace to tell Billy to come right away. "Ask her to tell him to come prepared," my father says. And I do. I say all of this, and then I apologize for waking her. There is something wrong with the connection, and every time I talk my voice echoes back and I flinch to hear myself.

"That's all right," Mrs. Wallace says in her shaky voice. "We farm girls know the drill, don't we, dear?" Rumor is, Mrs. Wallace always wanted a little girl but there were complications with Trent's birth. After he came along, the doctors told Mrs. Wallace she was done having babies. Once upon another time, Mama said Mrs. Wallace's shaky voice came from drinking all the time. Trent and I were cut out of our mothers by the same surgeon.

Daddy sends me to the house to make coffee and fetch a bag of frozen colostrum from the deep freeze. Blue chooses to stay with Betty. Outside, the cusp of sky and earth to the east burns a fire orange, and I think of Emily Dickinson, who favored this direction in her poetry because it was thought to point toward eternity. The sun is ready to rise as my legs scissor across the pasture, and I am tired; my body moves of its own accord.

I come upon the cottonwoods, and through the circle of trees I can see the yellow glow of the kitchen. As I step forward a screech owl comes tearing out of the treetops and dips so low, I can feel the wind it makes from having wings, and flying. The bird screams at me as it ascends into the sky for one last hunt before the day.

Neither Daddy nor Uncle Billy drinks the coffee I made for them. They are too busy, preoccupied. Daddy holds the lamp now because the job is suddenly important. I pour myself a cup of the coffee and it is black and hot and unsweetened. I've never had coffee before without milk and sugar, and the bitterness is jolting as it shivers through my bloodstream. I am waking up. As the caffeine electrifies my nervous system Uncle Billy gives Betty a shot that puts her to sleep.

I should have known what they had to do. What the directions meant: *Come prepared*. But I didn't, and it isn't until my uncle makes the long incision that I really do begin to understand. And this is not the neat and tidy procedure I've always told myself it was. This is not God carving Eve from a rib. It is not simple or easy like Daddy pulling out the lambs and life beginning as life continues. I keep telling myself, this is a sheep, in a barn with a vet. This is not Mama

———

in a hospital, with a surgeon, where everything is clean and in perfect order.

Daddy shines the light on the hole Uncle Billy made, and the cut is big and wet. The hole yawns, filling with blood and other liquids that look like blood. The wet shines, and it sparkles like something precious in the harshness of the light. When Uncle Billy reaches into Betty, the gesture is not at all tender. He reaches into her the way he does to gut and clean a dead chicken. He goes deep, and the hole gapes wider to allow room for his big hands and his thick wrists. And I can hear the wetness. It must be hot and slippery inside, difficult to grip the lamb.

"There's only one," Uncle Billy says, and not only are his hands amputated by the wet red hole, but his forearms disappear as well. Her womb is an underworld, and it seems like he will never find the lamb, let alone get a hold on her, but then he does. He brings her head to the surface, and I can see her. Her eyes are closed and she is peaceful. She is still dreaming. I think of Mama and all the reasons she used to list why natural childbirth is better. The drugs administered to the mothers pass into the bodies of the babies; I don't remember being born, but I do remember being drugged, just before I was pulled into this life by the hands of a stranger.

Uncle Billy has the head, and then he doesn't. She slips back in, under, and this is when my soul vacates my body. It feels like rubber bands—really big and really long—my spirit is being pulled out of me, and from the tugging the rubber bands are growing longer and longer. I don't know what is pulling them or where the other end might end, but now I know where the soul attaches to a body. It attaches to the spot below my ribs where the meat of me is soft and unprotected. Where there are no ribs or other bone. Leashed by the invisible rubber heaviness, I rise into the rafters. The sky is a milky blue, with the incredible brightness of early morning, and I realize it is the body that can hear and feel and taste and smell—all a soul can do is see.

I can't hear the birdsong that always accompanies the dawn, or the rooster who must be crowing. I can't hear the insistent bleating of the sheep all around or the suckling of the anxious offspring who didn't have to be cut out. The world is mute. It mouths the words to me—a silent film, there is no narrator, no subtitles to tell the story. I have no mouth to taste the aftertaste of coffee, or nose to smell the ripe ammonia of the barn. I am senseless, except I can still see, but if I was to continue to rise any higher? To flap my arms into wings and let the rubber bands stretch until they broke? There would be nothing left to see but the nothing shade of blue above waiting for us all.

Uncle Billy takes the head again, and this time he does not let go. I study the expression on my face as he tries to find a way to handle all four of the long lamb legs. Some are tangled, others stuck inside impossible caverns. The spindly legs point in nonsensical directions like the straw man in *The Wizard of Oz* pointing all the ways at once Dorothy could choose to go. The expression on my face is no expression. My face is blank. Eyes wide and open, I can see myself: I'm wearing pinstriped Oshkosh overalls over my nightgown, and my feet are stuffed into a pair of black galoshes. I've got Daddy's large Cornell sweatshirt zipped up, and the gray hood hides my big ears and short hair.

I am nothing but a face without an expression stuck inside a lot of clothing. I don't like looking at myself like this; it is worse than any mirror. I look at Daddy instead. He looks tired the way he always does, his jaw set hard and in need of a shave, and he holds the lamp the way he does everything in life: with determination.

Uncle Billy tosses the lamb into the straw the way he'd cast off a jacket because he got too warm. He focuses on the empty hole that is the body of the mother. The crater is impossible—a sinkhole, and I know he can't make her live again. This was why I was ordered to get the Ziploc bag of frozen sheep colostrum and set it under the heat lamp to defrost. And the heat lamp is not only here to melt colostrum, it is here to mimic the warmth of a missing mother.

Daddy yells for me to hold the lamp, and I do, but only my body reacts. The rest of me still hovers somewhere above, watching: My body has two arms, and these arms hold the light on the lamb while my father buries her with straw. He buries her with straw, and then he rubs the straw all over her with his cold hands. He rubs hard, and his touch is heavy. He has to move her body to teach her to move it on her own. He brushes away the straw to see if she is moving.

Daddy covers her with straw again and rubs even harder than before. As he forces life into the lamb I see how he is creating her just as much, if not more, than her mother ever did. When my father lifts his hands from her body once more to look, I snap back into my body like a whip recoiling.

I am drenched in sound. I am drowning in the sound of crying sheep and impatient hooves; and life is deafening. Uncle Billy curses the dead mother while Daddy coos to the baby in her bed of straw. There is the nagging sound of everyone, and every animal around: breathing, and my own breath, nagging. Inside, there is the sound of my heart: It is no longer ticking but it is beating. It beats hard like someone knocking on a door.

The blood smells like copper. Then it smells like cold steak on

—

the hot surface of a cast-iron skillet. There is also the sweetness of the straw—the sugary scent of early rot—and the sourness of the coffee on my breath, the need to brush my teeth. I'm shaking, but I don't feel cold. The sense of touch is the last to return. When it comes, I find myself uncomfortable: My clothes are scratchy, I need to pee, and the muscles in my neck are burning ropes.

The lamb pulls herself up, front legs followed by hind legs. She is wobbly, and then she is steady, just like that. She goes right for Daddy to nuzzle him. She wants his body heat, his milk, and his love, and I know what this is called.

This is called imprinting.

———

CHAPTER SEVENTEEN
THE LAST SUPPER

epilogue: n. 1. A short poem or speech spoken directly to the audience at the end of a play 2. A short section at the end of a literary or dramatic work, often discussing the future of its characters; an afterword.

April 11, Easter Sunday, 1993

There are all kinds of tricks to get a ewe to take on an orphaned lamb, and Billy has tried them all in the course of his career. If a ewe has a stillborn, you can skin it and wrap the skin around the orphan to make the mother think the living lamb is hers. The orphaned lamb can also be rubbed in the afterbirth of another lamb and presented to the ewe, and again, she will think it's her own, that she had twins, or triplets, depending.

In extreme cases, you can make the ewe think she's giving birth when she's not. If the orphan lamb is presented right away, the ewe will believe it belongs to her. Sometimes a ewe will take an orphan without any tricks; more often, she will not, and sometimes rejection is violent.

We don't try any of these methods. Instead, Daddy gives the motherless lamb to me and Blue to nurse and care for. I name her Esther because today is Easter. I give her a baby bottle full of colostrum we take from other mothers and save for situations like this,

—

and then I give her milk. As Daddy watches he tells me I was once wet nursed too.

"We needed the money," he says, "so we decided to sell the land where your grandparent's house had been—we just didn't expect it to sell so fast. You were just a newborn, and it seemed easiest for you to stay with me while Annie went to take care of the loose ends in Connecticut. It was only for a day or two, but you refused to take a bottle, so I called one of the women from the home-birth group and she came and stayed with us until your mama came home."

I feel weird knowing I had such an intimate exchange with someone I wouldn't recognize today. I wonder how it made Mama feel.

Daddy makes a nest in the kitchen where Blue and I can sleep with the lamb. It's either here or in the barn. Esther sleeps a lot, but when she's awake she is nothing but energy and spindly legs slipping across the kitchen tile.

We can't leave Esther alone, so Gran comes to the farm for Easter supper. She comes early to clean before she cooks the feast. She doesn't like Esther or Blue in the kitchen, and I don't help matters by falling asleep and not always minding the lamb when I should. Esther slips out of my arms to nibble on Gran's skirt while Blue tries to pull her away. I startle awake to the barking and bleating and Gran looking angry. Billy comes inside and tells me to go take a nap. He promises to watch Esther, assuring Gran he will do this outside and out of her way.

Half-asleep, I stumble up to my room, and Blue follows close behind.

While I'm sleeping, Gran transforms the dining room, and coming downstairs is like walking into someone else's house. She instructed Uncle Billy to stretch the table out as long as it will go; after the four

—

of us sit down, there will still be room for eight more people. The table trespasses into the living room area.

Gran draped the table with hundreds of crocheted stars, and Daddy tells me she made the tablecloth herself. "It was for her hope chest," Daddy says. I touch the hem, surprised. I didn't know my grandmother was capable of such beauty. Looking like crowns and scepters both, my arrangements of dried poppies stand at either end of the table; each contained in its own narrow vase, they will flank our meal.

Gran insists that we sit while she brings in the food; she wants to serve us. Every time Gran either comes in or returns to the kitchen, I peek through the door to check on Esther, who is sound asleep next to Blue, the two of them wrapped in old wool blankets.

"She's all tuckered out," Uncle Billy says. "She did nothing but eat and play while you two were sleeping." He winks at me. "She won't be waking up anytime soon," he says.

Daddy sits at the head of the table, and Gran will sit opposite. Uncle Billy and I sit across from each other. It is strange to have so much table spreading out on either side of me—as if there are still people coming or there's company I can't see.

We might be a million miles away from one another, but there is magic in the presentation: The way the candles warm the otherwise dark room—their light makes everything else fall away, and we are left with only our faces, the crocheted stars, the green poppy pods, and the food.

Usually the old candelabras sit on the mantel over in the living room collecting dust as Christina crawls back home in the painting above, but tonight they are centered on the table and Christina has disappeared, either swallowed by shadows or somehow safe inside

—

her house at last. The warm candlelight wavers and turns the silverware into gold, and this is alchemy. As Gran sits down, it's not just the rest of the room that floats away, but the entire world.

Gran puts her napkin in her lap and looks around, and she is smiling a smile I've never seen her smile before, except in the photographs taken back when she was still young. She is the statue of Mother Mary. She watches over a garden of roses, ashes, thyme, and memories. *Mary, Mary, quite contrary, how does your garden grow?* This is the smile of a mother, but it soon disappears.

"I almost asked your father to lead us in a prayer," she explains, looking down at her plate. I'm worried she might cry, which I have never seen her do.

Daddy pretends he misunderstood. "I'd be happy to," he says, even though we all know who she really meant when she said "your father." Gran looks up, and her eyes sparkle despite her cataracts, and the mother smile resurfaces. Uncle Billy winks at me as Daddy begins.

My father says the prayer like it's something he says every day: *"Dear Lord."* Only he doesn't say "Lord" again. I close my eyes like Gran and Billy do, but I steal glances at my father as he continues. I can't tell if his eyes are open or closed; he might just be looking down. It is strange to hear him talk this much after such a long silence.

"Spring has always been my favorite season," he says, "when everything is so full of potential, and bursting with new life."

I think about Betty and the last time I saw her. With her face covered by a gunnysack, she was nothing more than a large hole. She died before my uncle even had a chance to stitch her shut. I feel sad. Like Mama, I will never see her again.

When the prayer closes, we all open our eyes. Billy joins Gran in "Amen" while Daddy and I refrain. I look at the platters of

---

food spread before us. Steamed asparagus with butter, lemon juice, and ground pepper. Scalloped potatoes. Creamed pearl onions. A tossed salad: baby greens, chopped walnuts, currants, and poppy-seed dressing. And in the center—right in front of me, I see the roasted lamb, and the meat takes my breath away. Like everything else tonight, the wide-open hole has been transformed by my grandmother's touch. It is no longer something wounded. It glistens in the candlelight. Seasoned with sprigs of fresh rosemary from the garden where my mother sleeps, the lamb is brown and tender, and it gives itself to the carving knife.

As Daddy cuts, I become aware of him watching me. I am in his peripheral vision. He imagines me saying no, and this is what everyone expects. They all hold their breath and cross their fingers.

"Fig?" Daddy says, turning me into a question. He has finished slicing the lamb and hasn't served anyone. He stands there, holding the serving fork midair. The same fork that helped the knife cut the lamb now holds a piece of meat, ready to be consumed.

I become more and more aware. I, too, am holding my breath, but I haven't crossed my fingers, and I don't feel the need to reach for my rosary. Instead, I let the air out, and I feel like I am melting. I look at Daddy and I smile a smile I have never smiled before. I feel the unfamiliar stretch of muscles in my face, and the way these muscles lift my shoulders, and how my lifted shoulders work to straighten my spine, and I grow taller.

Smiling, I look at my father and I nod. I nod, and then I speak. "Yes," I say. "Yes."

*　*　*

*　*　*　*

———

ACKNOWLEDGMENTS

First of all, I'd like to thank my parents, Tom and Enid Schantz. Thank you for raising me in a bookstore, for teaching me to read, and for always supporting my dream to write. While my father helped me with the novel, my mother (who was not a schizophrenic), edited the original short story, "The Sound of Crying Sheep," from which the book was born; while she didn't live to see me finish the book or to see it published, she did see the story win first place for a contest hosted by *Third Coast* magazine. This contest brings me to Brad Watson, the writer who judged the competition, and everyone at *Third Coast,* who I'd also like to thank: they not only hosted the award, they published me, and went on to nominate the story for *The Pushcart Prize: Best of the Small Presses* and for *New Stories from the Midwest.* I'd like to thank the editor of the latter, Jason Lee Brown, who accepted my story for inclusion in his anthology. When Jason invited me to be a panelist at the First Annual Midwest Small Press Festival, I finally got to *feel* like a real writer. Everyone I've listed so far helped give me the courage to turn "The Sound of Crying Sheep" into my first novel.

I'd like to extend my gratitude to the following writing teachers I've had over the years. Molly LeClair and Suzanne Hudson, thank you for believing in me back when I was fresh off the streets and college still seemed utterly impossible; because of you two, I continued to write, and I now have a MFA despite having never graduated from high school or gotten my GED. Meg Gallagher, thank you for teaching me the art of public speaking; I think of you every time I give a reading. Bobbie Louise Hawkins, you taught me almost everything I know about good writing, but most of all, thank you for believing in Fig's story from the beginning (before she even had a name). Joanna Ruocco, thank you for reading my manuscript, providing extensive feedback, introducing me to Gaston Bachelard's *The Poetics of Space*, and for truly going above and beyond the call of duty. Selah Saterstrom, you gave me the permission I needed to write a young girl from the point-of-view of first person in the present tense. Bhanu Kapil, you helped create the space for writing and for the writing to come. Keith Abbott, thank you for always checking in with me. Junior Burke, thank you for saying, "Sarah, I think it's time for you to write a book." Thank you to Indira Ganesan for magical realism, to Elizabeth Robinson for Leonora Carrington and Joseph Cornell, and finally, to Sara Veglahn, who reminded me to look outside the frame to find the real story. As a collection of teachers and mentors, you all compose the antithesis of my sixth-grade teacher who accused me of plagiarism and actually sent me to the principal's office. So once more, thank you!

Other writers have also served as my teachers: They demonstrated all the ways to craft a story or form a sentence, and they provided imaginary worlds and the sanctuaries I was seeking. While many different texts influenced the writing of this book, I'd like to reserve this branch of acknowledgment for one writer and one writer alone: Zilpha Keatley Snyder. You were my absolute favorite author as a child, and like Fig, I read *The Headless Cupid* and got the idea to create my own Calendar of Ordeals. While I wasn't trying to cure mental illness, my magical thinking still had everything to do with trying to survive my own painful adolescence, and in a way, it worked.

I'd like to thank all the writer-friends who helped midwife the birth of this book; I am forever in your debt. Thank you Elisabeth Sowecke, Sherri Pauli, Catlyn Keenan, Ellen Orleans, and April Joseph; your close readings, line edits, long discussions, and love for Fig truly inspired me to keep going. I am just as grateful to all those who ever workshopped an excerpt of this book, whether at JKS or elsewhere, thank you. And thank you, Julie Kazimer, for providing priceless advice about the world of agents and publication and for supporting me when I most needed it; please know I appreciated every *single* word.

Several excerpts from the book (as well as the original short story) either won awards or were shortlisted by the following competitions, and I'd like to tip my hat to each one: Winner of the Jaimy Gordon Prize in Fiction hosted by *Third Coast* (2011), Finalist for the Alexander Cappon Prize for Fiction hosted by *New Letters* (2011), Finalist for the Howard Frank Mosher Short Fiction Prize hosted by *Hunger Mountain* (2011 and 2012), Finalist for the Fiction Contest hosted by *Cream City Review* (2011 and 2012), Honorable Mention for the *Zoetrope: All-Story* Short Fiction Contest (2011 and 2012), Honorable Mention for the New Millennium Prize for Fiction (2012), Semifinalist for the Katherine Anne Porter Prize for Fiction hosted by *Nimrod* (2012), Honorable Mention in the *WOW!* Summer 2012 Flash Fiction Contest, Honorable Mention for *Glimmer Train*'s Very Short Fiction Award (2012), Honorable Mention for the Reynolds Price Fiction Award hosted by Salem College (2012), Winner of the Fourth Annual Flash Fiction Contest hosted by Monkey Puzzle Press (2012), Honorable Mention for the Katherine Paterson Prize for Young Adult and Children's Writing hosted by *Hunger Mountain* (2012), Finalist for the National Writing Contest in Fiction hosted by *Alligator Juniper* (2012 and 2013), Finalist for the H. E. Francis Short Story Competition (2013), and Winner of the Saturday's Child Press Fiction Contest (2013). I'd also like to thank Jeff Pfaller and Robert James Russell at *Midwestern Gothic* for publishing three excerpts, interviewing me, and for generally making me feel like a rock star.

When *Hunger Mountain* published "The Breaking Wheel" in 2012, editor Miciah Bay Gault, who'd been following the progress of this novel, wrote to say she hoped to get me the attention of a literary agent. I thought Miciah was sweet, but I didn't actually think anything would come of it. I definitely never expected the amazing Heather Schroder to call me up and ask to represent my first book. Miciah, I will never be able to thank you enough; you truly are the fairy godmother of my particular fairy tale.

Obviously, I am eternally grateful to Heather Schroder and her extraordinary assistant, Julia Johnson; you both worked hard, and because you did, I got to beat my personal best. Thank you! Thank you! Thank you! I'd also like to thank my editor, Rūta Rimas, and the McElderry team at Simon & Schuster. Without Rūta's Excel spreadsheets and everyone's keen eye, *Fig* would not be the book it is today. I will never be able to thank you all enough.

Last, but not least, I'd like to thank my friends and family: Rozie Vajda, I honestly don't know where I'd be without you—you are a best friend, a sister, and a soul mate. Thank you, Lesley Evans; you always read my work, and you always have my back. Thank you, Raven Tekwe, for truly believing in me and my work, and for the two celebratory sushi dinners you bought for me. And thanks to Leona Sweat and all the letters we've exchanged; you were there for me during some of my darkest hours of self-doubt, and like Raven, you always had faith the book would make it into the world. Now, I'd like to thank my cousins, Claire and Karin; you either promoted me or came to my readings or gave me financial advice. I'd also like to thank my aunt Sallie for being there. And most of all, I'd like to thank my husband, Fish, and our two daughters, Kaya and Story: You three are my everything. I know it's not easy to share your wife-stepmother-mother with all the characters in my head, but please know this: Without your love, devotion and support, this book would not exist. It's not just my blood, sweat, and tears on these precious pages, but yours as well.

AUTHOR'S NOTE

For me, being a writer is like being a medium. I channel the stories as they come to me. A character forms for me when she or he begins to whisper in my ear. I write what these characters tell me to write. I write their stories.

Fig showed up after I moved into an old farmhouse on the outskirts of Boulder, Colorado. As long as I don't look toward the west, I can't see the mountains, and I might as well be living in Kansas. This house summoned her story. I knew Fig was lonely, intelligent, and devoted to her mother, and I also knew her mother was mentally ill, but I wasn't sure about the specifics. I began to do some research, and through my findings, I realized Mama was schizophrenic. However, Mama is far more than her disease (just as anyone is with this diagnosis); Mama is an artist, a feminist, an activist, a mother, a wife, an orphan, and a good person.

At the time I first began to flesh out the story, my daughter was still a little girl, and many of my friends were busy having babies. As someone who is still considering becoming a certified doula, I believe women are entitled to certain rights when they give birth. First and foremost, I believe a woman should be able to give birth wherever she is most comfortable doing so, whether that's at home, a hospital, or a birthing center. While birth is not a medical emergency, I also understand that sometimes birth doesn't go the way we'd like it to go; "Meconium happens" (old midwife joke).

I was fortunate to have had an ecstatic homebirth with my daughter Story. I gave birth to her in a shotgun shack with no running water on top of a mountain in Tennessee in the winter with the assistance of my midwife; my husband; my bonus daughter, Kaya; two close friends; a cat named Snowball, and the dog, No Name. While my labor lasted a very long twenty-one hours, there were no complications, and from the experience, I learned I was a superhero. The experience was empowering, and afterward, I found I was capable of anything. Unfortunately, this isn't always the case. Sometimes medical emergencies do arise and women must be transported from home to hospital or from delivery room to the operating table. Sometimes women don't have the option to give birth at home, and sometimes doctors don't respect a woman's birth plan. Sometimes women don't even know they have the right to write a birth plan in the first place, and so they don't. Sometimes women are forced to give birth in traumatic situations, and instead of feeling empowered, they are belittled. Sometimes C-sections are absolutely necessary, and sometimes they are not. Sometimes C-sections are performed for insurance purposes only, or because a doctor wants to go home, or because there was too much intervention in the early stages of labor.

In Greek mythology, Zeus is the male god who gives birth through his forehead to his daughter, Athena, and the act represents a shift from a matriarchal society into a patriarchal one as Zeus literally steals pregnancy and birth from the female. Sometimes women feel their doctors are stealing their pregnancies and birth when their babies are cut out of them. I knew that Mama's mental illness was complex, conditioned by both nature and nurture, and I also knew I

—

343

was rewriting the fairy tale "Little Red Riding Hood." Therefore, the emergency C-section echoes the woodsmen and his axe.

Personally, I have never known anyone with schizophrenia, and I wanted to make sure that I got the disease right. I relied heavily on the following texts for my research: *Surviving Schizophrenia: A Manual for Families, Patients, and Providers*, fifth edition, by E. Fuller Torrey, MD, and *Schizophrenia for Dummies* by Jerome Levine, MD and Irene S. Levine, PhD. (The particular copy I own of the latter was ordered used from the Internet and bears the mark of a lighter; I like to imagine someone like Mama trying to set it on fire.) In order to get a more personal understanding of the disease, and specifically, what it would be like to grow up around it, I read the following memoirs: *The Glass Castle* by Jeannette Walls, *The Memory Palace* by Mira Bartók, and finally, but perhaps most helpful of all, *My Mother's Keeper: A Daughter's Memoir of Growing Up in the Shadow of Schizophrenia* by Tara Elgin Holley with Joe Holley. I also talked to friends who know schizophrenia firsthand and I took a writing workshop on "madness" from the author Brian Evenson.

As for creating Fig, I read the book *Forever Marked: A Dermatillomania Diary* by Angela Hartlin, and I perused the website skinpick.com, reading the articles posted as well as the forums. Obsessive-compulsive disorder manifests in so many different ways, and dermatillomania (also known as compulsive skin picking) is just one of them. As I was developing the character of Fig, I learned the term for something I did as a child, and continue to do: magical thinking. Magical thinking is considered a disorder after the age of seven, and when and if it presents in an adult, it can be considered a possible symptom of schizophrenia (with the exception of religious experiences).

———

I truly believe there is a fine line between sanity and insanity. What I often joke about as being traits of my own OCD are not really OCD, because rather than causing me harm, the habits serve me. However, while the rituals of a habit can be supportive (like meditating for fifteen minutes every day), they can get out of hand and become destructive (perhaps the meditation practice morphs into agoraphobia and you never leave your house). What I refer to as my magical thinking is really the practice of visualization: I see myself succeed at whatever I am trying to accomplish. I also know when I'm being superstitious; for example, I know that knocking on wood won't really keep something bad from happening, but it doesn't hurt to do it as long as I know there are some things in life I cannot control.

I suppose I planted the seed for Mama's death when I had her reading stacks of books by Virginia Woolf toward the beginning of the story. I like themes to come full circle whenever possible, and to return to Woolf, I had Mama weave lines from Virginia Woolf's suicide letter to her husband, Leonard, into her own speech when she talks to Fig on page 340. While Woolf's letter is widely available online, I specifically used the copy as provided by The Virginia Woolf Blog. While I used the following lines from her note: "You have given me the greatest possible happiness" and "You have been in every way all that anyone could ever be," I created a variation of: "You have been entirely patient with me and incredibly good" for Mama to say. I believe Mama would have identified with both Woolf, and her last letter, and like Mama I wanted to honor this important literary figure. By quoting Virginia Woolf, Mama's words take on an agenda, becoming her official farewell.

Fig's OCD manifests in both healthy and unhealthy ways, and

—

part of her journey is learning how to tell the difference. Fig's skin picking gets out of control and is a form of self-harm, yet her obsession with looking words up in the dictionary helps her to better understand the world. The dictionary Fig uses in this book was created by me, but to inform the definitions I wrote for Fig, I referenced actual dictionaries and dictionary/etymology websites such as *American Heritage Dictionary*, third ed.; dictionary.com; etymonline.com; and merriam-webster.com. As for the flower meanings, I employed the following websites: victorianbazaar.com/meanings.html and send-great-flowers.com/meaning-of-flowers.html. And then I had to go and read the exquisite novel *The Language of Flowers* by Vanessa Diffenbaugh.

One of my old writing teachers, Junior Burke, talks about the emotional truths that come up in our writing, the little bits of yourself that end up in works of even the purest fiction, and in the end, I think both Fig and Mama are woven from numerous strands of my own DNA. At the same time, they are also one hundred percent who *they* are and who they were born to be when I first birthed them from my mind. When a writer gets a character right, it's because that character holds up to the Jungian theory of the collective unconscious, and I hope you, dear reader, find Fig, Mama, Daddy, Gran, Uncle Billy, Sissy Baxter, the Flower Lady, and even Candace Sherman to be as real as both you and me.